Big Mouth

ALSO BY DEBORAH HALVERSON

Honk If You Hate Me

DEBORAH HALVERSON

Delacorte Press

Published by Delacorte Press
an imprint of Random House Children's Books
a division of Random House, Inc.
New York

www.randomhouse.com/kids

Educators and librarians, for a variety of teaching tools,
visit us at www.randomhouse.com/teachers

Library of Congress Cataloging-in-Publication Data
Halverson, Deborah.
Big mouth / Deborah Halverson.—1st ed.
p.   cm.
Summary: Fourteen-year-old Sherman Thuff, a student at the tomato-obsessed Del Heiny Junior High, has his hopes set on being a competitive eater, but when his training regimen begins to seriously interfere with his enjoyment of life and he even starts losing his friends, he decides he should rearrange his priorities.
ISBN 978-0-385-73394-6 (hardcover)—
ISBN 978-0-385-90408-7 (Gibraltar lib. bdg.)
[1. Food habits—Fiction.   2. Weight control—Fiction.   3. Friendship—Fiction.
4. Junior high schools—Fiction.   5. Schools—Fiction.   6. Bullies—Fiction.
7. Humorous stories.]   I. Title.
PZ7.H1678Bi 2008
[Fic]—dc22   2007034718

The text of this book is set in 11-point Sabon.

Printed in the United States of America

10 9 8 7 6 5 4 3 2 1

First Edition

For my sweet men
Bus Driver, Tom the Trash Truck Driver, and Tractor Man,
whose amazing napping skills made writing this book possible

because sometimes you feel like a nut

CHAPTER 1

My eyeballs bulged. Tears blasted like water rockets. Blood flooded every cell in my face—a good thing, because the blood-bloated sockets were the only things holding in my eyeballs.

Aaaagggh!

Another brutal barf. This time, puke spewed through my mouth *and* nose. My guts blasted into my head.

Panting, I slumped to the floor and rested my throbbing head against the toilet seat. One more heave like that and my skull would explode, I just knew it. My throat and nostrils burned from the acidy vomit, my ribs ached as each sour breath filled the room with the nasty, unmistakable smell of—

Aaaagggh!

Aw, man, what is that? My spleen? I sagged to the floor again. This wasn't right. Food was supposed to go down your throat, not up. I should know, I'd just wolfed down ten hot dogs and buns in twelve minutes flat.

Aaaagggh!

Now those dogs were coming *up* in twelve *seconds* flat.

I stayed on my knees, hugging the bowl. My puffy, leaky head drooped forward. The view was disgusting. Yellow corn from last night's dinner dotted the beefy muck, and bits of ketchup-pinked bun bobbed on the tide. My toilet looked like a salsa bowl.

I lurched forward, nearly losing it again.

I swear, from now on, I fast the day before I gorge. The key to effective training was strategy, and I had to learn from my mistakes—

Aaaa . . . Aaaa . . .

Nothing.

Wait, Shermie, wait. . . .

Still nothing. *Oh, thank you, dear God of Regurgitation: my first dry heave.* The worst was over. A few more dry heaves, then I stood, wobbly but upright, and flushed.

Next time, *eleven* hot dogs in twelve minutes, I just knew it.

* * *

Puking made me late for my shift at Grampy's shop. Located at the edge of the food court on level seven, Scoops-a-Million was the only ice cream shop in the whole mall. There were three Mexican restaurants, two smoothie counters, and five different pizza joints, but only one of us. Grampy scored this sweet deal because he was the last holdout from the crumbling strip mall they demolished to build Mid-Cal County Fair Mall. The mall management even threw in a giant neon sign with exhaust ports in the middle of each *o*. So from ten to ten each day, the Scoops-a-Million *o*'s burped out mouthwatering wisps of sugared cream, rich clouds of chocolate, and the sweet vanilla of waffle cones baked to a golden brown. The aroma worked on shoppers like a watch swinging on a chain. I swear, my Grampy could talk a goldfish out of his bowl.

2

Wheezing and sweaty from pedaling through the park like a crazed psycho, I finally stumbled through the Scoops doorway and found Arthur pacing behind the sherbet counter. His rheumy eyes zeroed in on me. Hissing like a cornered cat, the old guy started hucking things my way. I ducked the fudge-dipped waffle cone, but a juicy maraschino cherry plunked me in the left eyelid.

Great, the shrunken geezer had seventy years to my fourteen, but even he could throw better than I could. Not that I was a small target.

"It's three-twenty-two," Arthur crabbed. He was standing in front of the huge smiling sun mural on the back wall. He wasn't smiling, though, and he certainly wasn't sunny. "Goldanged kids. No respect for anybody but yourselves. I got me a life, too, Sherman Thuff. You think being fourteen makes you the big enchilada? I got things to do, too. Places to go, people to see. If I had my way, every crummy one of you . . ."

I tuned him out. There weren't any customers in the ice cream shop to be offended by his cranking, and I'd stopped paying attention to him months ago. Arthur was a nasty old prune. I knew that anything I said would only rile him up more. If only he'd quit. Why he was slaving in an ice cream shop when he could be hucking bingo chips at attendants in a cozy nursing home was beyond me.

I wiped red syrup out of my eyebrow with my Windbreaker sleeve, then reached out to lift the hatch in the metal countertop—

ZAP!

I yanked my hand back and shook it. That was the third time I'd been shocked today. Stupid dry wind. This weird weather front was supposed to last through Halloween, maybe longer, but I didn't know if I'd survive that long. I had more charge in my fingertips than Darth Vader had stormtroopers.

Ever . . . so . . . carefully . . . I reached out a second time and—

"Ow!" A cherry had thumped my right earlobe. "Dang it, Arthur!"

I wiped my other sleeve across my ear then checked my reflection in the raised hatch to see if any red gloop had splooged into my hair. Nope, no gloop. But, man, those were some electrified blond needles. I was Woodstock from Peanuts.

I spit into my palms and patted down the frizz. Globby spit hair was better than frizzy static hair. People would just think I moussed.

Sucking in my stomach, I squeezed through the opening, pulled my bike through to stash behind the counter, then *gennntly* lowered the metal slab back down. Arthur liked to let it slam down. He knew the tinny sound it made worked on me like a rake dragged across concrete. I'd rather chew aluminum foil than hear either one of those noises.

Next to me, Arthur was still mouthing off. ". . . shoulda been off twenty-two minutes ago. Twenty-two! Where have you been? It's like Grand Central Station around here. Kid after kid after kid. It's a Friday, don't you slackers go to school?"

He didn't know that today was a half day for all the schools. Some special school board meeting or something. Not that I'd waste my breath telling him about it. I just flipped him the finger when he turned to shove his pink smock under the counter.

"Now, don't go eating all the gummy bears." He ducked

4

through the hatch. "We only got one box left." Then he rushed out of Scoops like the world would end if he wasn't sitting on his peeling barstool at the Broken Yolk Diner in the next thirty seconds.

"Oh, hey, Arthur, thanks, you have a good day yourself," I said to the air. "Jerk."

The rest of my shift didn't get any better. Right off, I discovered that Arthur had taken or hidden the only XL-sized smock. His idea of getting even with me for being late, probably. Funny guy, that Arthur. I would've just "borrowed" his smock if I could, but it was an S. I couldn't borrow Grampy's either. It was an L, which was close, but it had THERMAN THUFF, OWNER & PROPRIETOR stitched on it. Having no choice, I squeezed myself into an old M. I had to cinch it too tight around my waist just to tie it closed. My still-queasy gut wasn't thrilled about that. And then the stupid pink smock kept pulling open when I stretched, so each time I stepped on the footstool and leaned into the display case to hack a scoop of ice cream out of a frozen tub, my fly got slathered with the flavor of the moment. The poo-brown Rocky Road smudge was downright embarrassing.

It didn't take long to see that Arthur wasn't just blowing smoke. Except for a few lulls, Scoops really was hopping. I guess Grampy didn't know today was a half day, either. I was on my own as every elementary, junior, and high school student in the Mid-Cal area came in for ice cream. Scoops was always their first stop in the mall, especially now, with our California October being as warm and sunny as any June. As customers stepped into my hallowed realm, they took deep, sugary breaths, they dipped their fingers into the leaky water fountain to slick down their own frizzed hair, and then they turned to me for salvation. Wide-eyed and reverent, they pressed their noses against the glass display case and invoked the sacred words: *Bing Cherry* . . . *Cookie Dough* . . . *Fudge Ripple* . . . Picking out flavors to sample before committing to a scoop was a very serious ritual. Once they made their selections, they lifted their faces up to me, where I stood in front of the smiling sun mural with my scooper at the ready, sunrays shooting outward behind me. It was a total power trip. I could live with being worshipped.

My right forearm ached from gouging, gouging, gouging the hard-packed ice cream. But being busy kept my mind off the afternoon I'd just spent praying to the porcelain god, so it wasn't until Grampy finally arrived to break me that I noticed my stomach felt fine. Empty and normal. Hungry, even. I hadn't eaten since breakfast, after all, if you took into account that I puked up lunch.

The instant Grampy plodded through the doorway, he froze in his tracks and gawked at all the kids in the shop. Then he crunkled up his nose and squinted his black-olive eyes nearly closed, making his face look all cheeks.

"Oh, jeez," I muttered. *I'm on to you, Grampy.* That same expression washed over all us Thuffs when we were plotting something. I braced myself even before he flashed his fake grin and let fly with the family motto.

"Sherman T. Thuff," he declared, now striding across the shop, "this crowd looks tough, and you know what that means." He waved a knuckly fist in the air. "When the going gets tough, the Thuffs get Thuffer! C'mon, young Thuff, man your post. Make your family proud. All for one and one for all!"

I would have acted like I didn't hear him, but he knew darn well I could hear a gnat sneeze in the next county. "Can't, Grampy. It's five-twenty-seven. I'll be late."

"Late? For what? Wait . . . no . . . Shermie . . . "

Wrestling his arm from behind his back, I pried open his stubborn fingers and forced the scoop and my latest work permit into his palm. Not only had Mr. Smooth Talker convinced my folks that child labor was character building, he'd also charmed my counselor at Del Heiny Junior High #13 into making it legal. Now she got her ice cream here for free.

Grampy eyed the kids who were jockeying for position around the display case. "Shermie, wait, listen to me . . ."

I paused, vaguely curious which compliment he'd try this time.

He saw the hesitation and pounced. "You can't go, Sherminator, your fans *need* you. Just look at them, you're their star. Scoops is nothing without you. *Nothing.* You're the backbone of this entire operation."

Ah, the backbone . . . I made a move toward the counter hatch, but he blocked me.

"Wait! Wait. You're the muscle, too, haven't I told you that? Look at that gun of yours—" He tried to squeeze my biceps but I dodged around him. "C'mon, Shermie, give your old Grampy a break."

"Can't, Grampy. Lucy's waiting." I ditched the ice cream–smudged size M under the counter.

"But Shermie—"

"You're the one who says never make a girl wait." I lifted the counter and squeezed through quickly.

"But . . . but . . . oh, fine!" His pouty voice chased me as I stepped into the busy promenade. "But don't be late coming back!"

"I won't!"

It took more fancy footwork to dodge the shopping masses, but I managed to reach the center table of the food

7

court right on time. Part of the deal in "agreeing" to slave for Grampy was that I could time my breaks to match Lucy's. She worked one level down for her own slave-driving relative at the Chocolat du Monde cart, where she sold gourmet chocolate to stuck-up ladies at several bucks a chunk.

When I dropped into the seat across from Lucy, she flipped open a brand-new yellow binder. It had to be an inch thick with graph paper, all tabbed and labeled in cotton candy colors.

She poised her pen over the paper. "How many did you eat?"

"What, no hi?"

"Hi. Now how many did you eat?"

I held up ten fingers. "I ate ten—count 'em, *ten*—whole hot dogs *and buns* in twelve minutes flat." *Hey, she didn't ask if they stayed down.*

"Ten, huh? Not bad . . ." She gnawed the tip of her pen. "You know, your horoscope did say that betting on a long shot today would change your life. Hot dogs are long. And ten is the number of rebirth." She gnawed the pen a little more, then nodded her head. "Yep. I'm sure of it. Ten is a sign."

Whipping the pen from her mouth, she attacked the graph paper. "Okay, our base number is ten. Now that we know where we're starting and where we're going, we just need to strategize the best way to close the gap. Let's see, that's 0.83 dogs per minute . . . and you've got forty-seven months to match Tsunami's record of fifty-three and three-quarters dogs in twelve minutes, which means increasing your intake by .08 wieners per month . . ."

And we're off! I leaned back in my chair and relaxed. It

was a stroke of brilliance to recruit my oldest friend as my eating coach. She'd lead me to victory on the competitive eating circuit for sure.

I'd called Lucy with my plan to become an eater two nights ago, right after watching an old TV special called *The Glutton Bowl*. What I saw on the screen amazed and inspired me: men and women eating hamburger after hamburger (bun and all!), oyster after oyster, sushi roll after sushi roll, egg after egg. They were incredible! Racing the clock and each other, they chowed down *insane* amounts of food . . . and got paid for it! There was one guy named Gaseous Maximus who wore a gladiator suit and ate gobs of mayo. And this other guy, Big Rig, ate a mondo pile of butter sticks. The coolest guy, though, had to be this skinny little Japanese dude they called Tsunami, who wolfed down thirty-two hot dogs in twelve minutes flat. I'd never seen anything like it. As it turned out, that record was only the beginning. Tsunami's most recent record was fifty-three and three-quarters hot dogs in twelve minutes. Fifty-three and three-quarters! And as for prize money—wow. For the Glutton Bowl win alone he scored twenty-five thousand bucks. Now, I loved to eat—and, frankly, I was good at it—but who would've guessed *that* could make you rich? By the time the Glutton Bowl was over, I knew exactly what I wanted to do with my life: I was going to be the fastest, richest, most famous competitive eater in the world.

"You're a natural," Lucy had said when I announced my new purpose in life. "Leos are born showmen, and your sun is in the tenth house. Plus you ate four hamburgers at lunch today, so I know you've got the appetite."

Actually it was only three hamburgers. But we weren't keeping track then, so it didn't matter.

Lucy had done some research and found out that I couldn't compete until I turn eighteen. But when I could, I'd hit the scene with a bang. The entire world would tremble when Sherman Thuff bellied up to the table. All I had to do was follow Lucy's master plan exactly as she'd laid it out in her graphs. "Just leave the details to me," she'd told me. "I may be a Cancer, but I've got Virgo rising hard." Whatever that meant. I wasn't going to argue with her; I certainly didn't want to handle the details. Besides, she once told me that as a Leo, I wasn't allowed to argue with her, and it had worked for us so far.

So, according to Lucy's grand plan, establishing the base number this afternoon was step one, graph one. I could eat ten hot dogs and buns in twelve minutes. Make that ten HDBs. That's what we eaters called them, HDBs. By Lucy's calculations, I'd be eating fifty-four HDBs by the time I turned eighteen. Piece of cake!

As Lucy neatly plotted her numbers into a line graph, my eyes wandered across the rows of restaurant counters that lined the cavernous food court: China Town, Roberto's Taco Cabana, Pie in Your Eye Desserts . . . You name the restaurant, it was here. And man, were they busy with customers. All around us, people scurried and weaved through the maze of tables, their red trays piled with food and drinks. A fine mist of deep fryer grease flavored the air, and the vapors of countless grills and ovens danced about our heads. The low grumble of a squad of industrial-sized air conditioners soothed me, like a waterfall in the forest.

I drummed my fingers as Lucy dipped into her apron pocket for her calculator. *Man, that apron.* Milk-chocolate-brown and shin-length, it had CHOCOLAT DU MONDE stamped on it sideways in huge, silver-foiled letters. She was a walking Hershey's bar. No joke. The rest of her clothing just added to that image: Her long-sleeved shirt and creased pants were almond-colored, her clunky work shoes were a dark chocolate of the Milky Way Midnight variety, and even her hair was cocoa-colored. She was turning into the very candy she sold. Even from across the table, I could smell the lush cocoa scent she got after an hour or two of work. But even as bad as that apron was, a job that made you smell like a chocolate bar sounded like heaven to me.

"Hey, Lucy. Do I smell like ice cream?"

"*Shhh.*" She held her hand up like a stop sign. "Busy minds at work."

"Sorry." I rested my chin on my hand. *How long does it take to calculate a few HDBs, anyway?*

A few more minutes passed. Over Lucy's shoulder I caught sight of a guy creeping low behind a short lady with tall hair. His head kept peeking out quickly, then darting back behind the hair tower again. Gardo. And he was up to something, as always.

When he was right behind Lucy, my buddy winked at me, then leaned his mouth down near Lucy's ear. "Take off your shoes," he hissed. "You can count higher that way." He playfully poked her in the side with the corner of a pizza box.

"Gardo! You made me lose count."

"I made you jump, too." He laughed and high-fived me, then sat down next to me on the plastic bench.

I wagged a finger at him. "I expect a little more maturity from you, sonny."

"How about a little maturity from you both?" Lucy muttered, straightening her Hershey's wrapper, er, apron. She was kind of smiling as she said it, though.

11

Good ol' Lucy. Always a sport.

She went back to marking the graph.

I took the pizza box from Gardo and set it on the table. "I was starting to think you wouldn't show."

"Hey, it's crowded. I had to push my way to the counters and talk fast. I barely had time to get off a wink. You should be thankful I made it at all."

"Oh, we're thankful," Lucy said without looking up.

"We *are*," I stressed. Unlike Lucy, I meant it. Gardo's supreme flirting skills scored us the best free food in the mall. Not even the high school girls could resist him. We couldn't risk him holding back because we were ungrateful. "Hey, hey. I see more donations there, Romeo. C'mon, fork 'em over."

"What, these?" He held up a cardboard carrying tray with three shakes, then grinned. "You should be extra thankful I can work the magic at high speeds." He jiggled the tray. "I scored a bull's-eye every time, baby. Girls might as well have targets on their foreheads."

Lucy whipped her head up. "Excuse me?"

"What?" He lowered the shakes and looked to me for a clue. "What?"

I shrugged.

Lucy narrowed her eyes. "What do you mean, *what?*"

Uh-oh. Better batten down the hatches, Gardo. Tropical storm Lucy is starting to swirl.

"What you just said about girls," she continued. "It was insulting."

"What's insulting? I'm not insulting. Shermie, am I insulting?" Gardo looked at me again.

This time, I didn't even flinch. Shermie Thuff was no dummy.

Lucy started to say something but then just sighed

instead. "Why waste my breath?" She went back to writing again. "It's not like you can help it; you *are* a *Libra.*" She said it like the guy had infantigo or something heinous like that.

Gardo mouthed *"PMS"* my way, then spit his gum into the trash can by our table.

I eyeballed the Slimmy Jim's pizza box he'd put on the table. There were about a million smells swirling around the food court, but I could clearly pick out the salty aroma of pepperoni wafting from the square box, along with the smoky perfume of crisp, browned crust and the subtle undercurrent of woodfire-smoked tomatoes and the . . . the . . . *hmmm, I can't quite place that smell . . . It's kind of sweet . . . kind of . . . citrusy!* "Ew! Is there pineapple on that pizza?"

"I swear, Shermie, you could be a bloodhound with that nose." Gardo flipped open the box. I nearly shielded my eyes at the sickening sight of charred fruit infecting innocent pepperoni slices. "Beggars can't be choosers."

"Maybe not, but that pineapple is out of here." I started flicking off the greasy chunks. Warm, seared pineapple baked into cheese and tomato sauce was a terrible combination. No one cooked strawberries or plums into a pizza, why would they try pineapple?

My first pineapple flick went wild, though, pegging Gardo's red *Go, Plum Wrestling!* T-shirt. "Sorry, man."

Gardo retaliated by snicking a golden chunk back my way and cheering when I dodged it. Then he tilted his head back and lowered a shiny circle of pepperoni into his gawping mouth, letting the grease trickle down his chin. *"Umm-umm!"*

He might've loved pepperoni more than I did.

I folded two slices into a sandwich and bit big. In the

Sherman T. Thuff Book of Good and Tasty Things, Slimmy Jim's woodfired pizza ranked five stars out of five.

Across from me and Gardo, Lucy carefully capped her pen and tucked it into her binder pouch. When she clapped the binder shut, she looked pleased as pie. Another graph up and running. "Follow me, Sherman Thuff, and you will be a star."

As if to celebrate, she reached into the front pocket of her Chocolat du Monde apron and fished out two truffles. "Ta-da!" She set the truffles next to the pizza box.

"Score!" I shouted. Add those beauties to the slightly green banana and the cup of Cookie Dough ice cream that I'd contributed, and we had a break feast.

Gardo motioned his head toward the notebook. "I see you've got Shermie's road to glory all plotted out." A half-circle of pepperoni fell from his slice. I snagged it before he did. "Hey!"

I grinned and chewed real big.

"Strategy is everything." Lucy picked up the banana and started peeling. "Competitive eating is the up-and-coming sport of this century. It'll be in the Olympics soon. If Shermie wants to be a champion eater, he has to do it right." She swirled the banana in the soupy part of the ice cream. "Olympic gymnasts and swimmers start training when they're babies. Shermie's way behind. He's got fourteen years of goal-less eating to make up for."

Gardo slugged my shoulder. It smarted, but I didn't let on. "You're gonna kick butt, Shermie. But you do know that color-coded graphs will only get you so far, don't you? You guys are forgetting something."

Lucy set her banana in the ice cream cup, then leaned back in her seat and crossed her arms. "And just what are we forgetting?"

"An image."

"An image?" I said, a fleck of pizza flying out of my mouth. Lucy frowned as I wiped it up with a napkin. "Sorry."

"Yeah, an image." Gardo continued. "All famous competitors have images. Just watch ESPN and you'll see." Gardo knew about ESPN. He watched it every night, studying the sportscasters for the day when he anchors the highlight reels. He's going to be rich and famous, too. "Fame is all about sponsors and advertising, and to them image is everything. We have to make Shermie bigger than life. We have to sell him to the fans."

"We can make signs." I swallowed before talking that time, so no pizza spray. "There's some green paint in our garage from when Grampy moved in and made my dad paint his room. We can hang the signs around campus. We can even put my picture on them. People will notice that." I smiled my cheesiest all-cheek Thuff smile.

"That's not what he's talking about," Lucy said. "He wants you to dress up in some stupid costume, like that Gaseous Maximus guy. He'll probably have you in a giant hot dog suit, dancing around like that old drive-in snack bar cartoon."

"A dancing hot dog?" *Over my dead body.* "No way!"

"It's not stupid," Gardo protested. "And you won't have to wear a giant hot dog suit. Quick, Shermie, who's the most famous wrestler ever?"

"Easy. Hulk Hogan." Of course I knew that. Gardo made me watch his WWE videos whenever we were at his house. I hated wrestling, but I didn't complain because that's what friends do for each other, they like the other's stuff. At my house, he had to watch Galactic Warriors. The only ones running around in spandex shorts clotheslining each other on that show were the female aliens. "Hulk is the most famous ever."

"You got it, Shermie. The Hulkster." Gardo sat back and crossed his arms, a mirror image of Lucy. "Now that's what I'm talking about."

"*Ahhh.*" I nodded slowly, like I knew what the heck his point was.

Lucy didn't nod. "*What's* what you're talking about?"

Gardo leaned forward and talked slowly. "Hulk Hogan has been retired for years, but even people who don't like wrestling know him." He shot me a quick look when he said that last part.

Yikes. I didn't know he could tell I hated wrestling. "Gardo's got a point, Lucy." I nodded real hard. "Hogan didn't wear weird stuff, and he is famous."

"Well, he did wear feather boas sometimes," Gardo admitted. "But what I'm saying is, it's not about the costume. All the wrestlers have costumes of some kind but not all the wrestlers are famous like Hogan. It's about having an extra-large personality. That's what makes a guy famous. Hulk Hogan had it. Shermie has it."

"People do like me," I said.

"Sometimes," Lucy muttered.

Gardo put his hand on my shoulder and gave it a manly shake. "Most of the time. And that's his ticket. People remember him. We just have to figure out how to bottle that. Turn his personality into an official image and build his rep. You know, market him."

I nodded vigorously. "Building is good. I like to build."

"You like your ego stroked," Lucy mumbled.

"Among other things." I threw my crumpled napkin at her, but she batted it away easily.

16

"Don't be crude."

"This isn't about Shermie's ego," Gardo said. "It's about his image. Trust me on this one, Shermie, I'm a guy, I know these things."

"And I'm his *coach*." Lucy tapped her colorful binder. "You can't build a house without a foundation. To be a champion, the first things Shermie has to work on are his eating skills. He has to develop a bite technique, learn to control his throat muscles, build his jaw strength . . ." She opened the binder and pointed to one of her graphs: ♥ *The Carr☺t Ch☺mp—Jaw Strengthening Exercises* ♥ "*This* is his ticket."

Gardo glanced at the graph with all its girly hearts and curlicues, then reached out and flipped back a page, where he read the label on the graph Lucy just spent so much time computing.

"Graph one, hot dogs?" He closed the binder with a flip of his wrist. "We need to think bigger than that. We need something that screams Sherman T. Thuff. You want people screaming your name, don't you, Shermie?"

I imagined crowds of people chanting my name. *Thuff! Thuff! Thuff!* My heart started racing. *Thuff! Thuff! Thuff!* Yeah, I could handle that; I was ready to be famous. Del Heiny Junior 13 was peanuts. I wanted the whole world to know who Sherman T. Thuff was. *Thuff! Thuff! Thuff!*

"Thuff! Thuff! Thuff!" I shouted.

"Now *that's* what I'm talking about." Gardo punched me in the shoulder again, even harder this time. "I'm sorry, Lucy, but 'graph one, hot dogs' is just not Thuff enough. Hey!" He pounded the table solidly with his palm, making me and Lucy both jump. "That's it! That's our hook. 'Are *You* Thuff Enuff?' E-N-U-F-F. It's perfect!"

17

I imagined people shouting at me, "Are YOU Thuff Enuff?" and me shouting back, "I AM!"

"Perfect!" I pounded the table, too. "I can already see it, I'll jog up to the hot dog table with ten thousand fans chanting 'Thuff! Thuff! Thuff!,' all of them wearing T-shirts with my name on them. Me, Sherman 'Thuff Enuff' Thuff. Awesome!"

"Oh, we're not stopping at crummy T-shirts, my friend." Gardo picked up another pizza slice and eyed it from different angles. "We'll do hats and sweatshirts and mugs. The memorabilia shop on level four will be begging for Thuff Enuff stuff. Begging! And the endorsement deals, they'll pour in by the boatload." He bit into the slice and talked while he chewed. None of his food spit out, though. "Thuff Enuff, my good man, I am going to make you rich and famous."

I thumped him solidly on the back. "And when I'm rich and famous, Gardo Esperaldo, you can call my play-by-play at the Glutton Bowl."

"Oh, I'll call it, all right." He tossed his slice back into the box and jumped to his feet with his arms spread wide, right in the middle of the food court. "Ladies and gentlemen, boys and girls, sports fans of all ages! I give you the one, the only . . . Sherman 'Thuff Enuff' Thuff!"

He yanked my hand straight up into the air like I was Rocky Balboa himself. I went with it, standing up and throwing my other arm into the air.

"*Sit down!*" Lucy whipped up her binder to hide her blushing face.

Some kids in yellowy-red GO, ROMA TOMATOES! T-shirts pointed at our table from the Nature's Nectar smoothie counter. Seventh graders, probably. Their matching yellowy-red ball caps were tilted back on their heads as they slurped

18

at their fruit shakes. The geeks. One of them dropped his smoothie, splashing pink goo up the front of his jeans.

Please tell me I wasn't that pathetic last year. "So they're looking at us," I told Lucy. "Who cares? We're higher up in the food chain than a bunch of pea-greeners." A seventh grader's opinion was as useful as an empty can of Coke, especially seventh graders from Del Heiny Junior High #11, home of the Roma Tomatoes. I shouted in their direction: "Thank you! Thank you!"

Gardo jumped up on the bench and pointed their way three times. "Are . . . *YOU* . . . Thuff Enuff?"

The tallest one flipped us the bird.

I waved at him with both arms, real exaggerated, a bird in each hand. "I AM!"

Ha! Unless that kid has three hands, I win this round.

Gardo high-fived me again as most of the pea-greeners scowled and wandered off like good little underclassman. They left the goup-splashed kid to fend for himself with the Nature's Nectar napkin dispenser.

Laughing, we climbed down and attacked the rest of the pizza.

Lucy didn't eat anything more, though. She just fingered the colored tabs on her binder silently. We probably embarrassed her too much. Again. She could get oversensitive about that kind of thing.

Gardo ran his mouth enough for the three of us, though, telling us all about how he'd kick butt at his wrestling scrimmage coming up. With all his big-man-on-the-mat talk, he lost interest in the pizza pretty quickly. Me, I was more than happy to focus my energy on the feast in front of us. Hey, I was hungry. I hadn't had much luck with those hot dogs at lunch.

I polished off the truffles first. Clearly Gardo wasn't

going to eat them, and Lucy would have jabbed out her own eye rather than eat a truffle. Working with chocolate all the time made her lose her taste for the stuff. Aversion therapy, I think she called it. I was just glad it didn't work that way with ice cream. After a quick check of my cell phone's clock, I hurriedly slurped the last dribbles of Cookie Dough out of the cup and grabbed one last slice of pizza for my hustle back to Scoops-a-Million. Just fifty-eight seconds left of break. I rushed off with a hasty good-bye, with one last sad look at the milkshakes. No one had touched them. What a waste.

As I dodged my way back to Scoops, I tuned out the drone of the air conditioners, letting the sounds of my up-coming fame fill my head instead: *Thuff! Thuff! Thuff! Thuff!*

I couldn't wait to be rich and famous.

And Now, a Word from our Sponsor . . .

Wiener Lovers of the World, rejoice! A new frank's in town, and it's no lightweight—it's the big and bold Thuff Enuff Wiener!

♫♫
Oh, I want to be a Thuff Enuff Wiener.™
A Thuffie Wiener's™ *what I really want to be.*
I want to be a Thuff Enuff Wiener.™
Won't you be a Thuffie Wiener™ *with me?*®
♫♫

No one packs away the wieners like America's champion hot dog eater Sherman "Thuff Enuff" Thuff! So when Thuff puts his name on a wiener, you know it's a champ! Available in a wide variety of flavors and sizes, Thuffie Wieners™ have it all Big Beefers,™ Totally Turkeys,™ Corny Dogs,™ Big Footers,™ Kosher Longs,™ Veggie Logs,™ Tofu Tubes,™ and Foot-Long Cheesy Cheesers.™ Thuffie has the wiener for you!® And that's not all: Sherman "Thuff Enuff" Thuff promises that every Thuffie Wiener™ is expertly inspected for the highest in tube meat quality!

So the next time you get a hankerin' for a hot dog, ask yourself this: Are YOU Thuff Enuff?®

21

CHAPTER 2

"Vomit. Puke. Throw-up."

Ms. Maxwell's lecture voice boomed throughout the science lab, vibrating the paper jack-o'-lantern hanging above her head. "You know the smell, now you know the name: butyric acid. Used in the manufacture of plastics, butyric acid naturally occurs in sweat, rancid butter, cod liver oil, and, yes, good old vomit." She pulled a stained lab coat over her fitted yellow T-shirt and signaled Lucy, in the first row, to pass out the Experimentation Documentation worksheets. "You, my inquisitive young scientists, will be working with butyric acid in today's experiment."

Girly groans mixed with macho cheers as my class reacted to the news of another Mad Max Lab Day. What a way to follow up a two-and-a-half-day weekend! Science Concepts in Action was every bit as cool as I'd heard it would be. Last week we did an experiment where we lit potato chips on fire with Bunsen burners and measured how much grease dripped out. I didn't eat chips for a whole day after that. The week before, we'd lobbed balloons filled with mustard off the roof to test Newton's Second Law of Motion. What other teacher on the planet would let thirty-two eighth graders on top of a three-story building with balloon bombs? Max didn't even get mad when the mustard splattered the fresh red paint on the walls of the school's office. In fact, I would have sworn she was laughing behind her hand when it happened, not coughing. No wonder she was the most popular teacher in the whole school. It also didn't hurt that she was totally hot.

Butyric acid, huh? I did know the smell. Too well. The sour memory of Friday's hot dog episode was still fresh in my nose. And Lucy had me scheduled for *eleven* HDBs in twelve minutes tomorrow after school, so I had a feeling I'd be on intimate terms with the raunchy stuff soon enough.

Despite the cool gross-out factor, though, today's Mad Max experiment was falling flatter than a pancake. Max explained the steps for the lab clearly enough, but she was cranky the whole time, snapping at us left and right. When she suddenly ripped into the guys at the table next to mine, I almost ducked under my chair.

"What's her problem today?" I whispered to my lab partner, Linus "Tater" Tate, after she'd stormed off. "Did someone let the rats out of their cages?"

"We should be so lucky." Tater had earned his nickname in fourth grade when he jammed four Tater Tots up his nostrils. That got him such a big laugh, he'd been doing it ever since. I guess everyone needed their claim to fame, but I just couldn't look at Tater without staring at his nostrils. He checked to make sure Max wasn't close, then leaned over, his hand on his office aide key ring to make sure the keys didn't jangle. I tried to focus on his eyes. "Word is, one of the science teachers got suspended at that emergency school board meeting. Supposedly he gave his class a lecture on tomatoes, saying they're more acidic ounce for ounce than

23

a car battery. He said they'd burn your stomach lining right out of you if you ate enough."

I nearly gasped out loud. "He said *that*?"

"Uh-huh. He also said there are a thousand tomato bug eyes in every squirt of ketchup."

"Really? Dang." What was that teacher thinking? District policy strictly forbids anti-tomato talk on campus, and the school board strictly enforces district policies. Of course they'd nail him. And of course Max would be ticked off about it. That was just the kind of power trip that burned her Bunsen. If we were living in the seventies, she'd be marching around with hippie braids and a DOWN WITH THE MAN sign. "Shoot, she'll probably be cranky all week."

"Probably." He went back to stirring our gel mixture. Some butyric acid splashed the bottom of his yellow shirt. He scrunched up his big nostrils. "I don't see what the big deal is, though. So he got suspended. I wouldn't mind staying at home for a week. It's not like he got transferred to home ec like that teacher at Del Heiny Junior 7 last year. Now that would suck."

"Seriously." But then, that science teacher had refused to apologize to the school board, or to the PTA, or, worst of all, to the school's almighty sponsor.

In our district, every school had the same sponsor: Del Heiny Ketchup Company. It had been that way for years, ever since the district's budgets got slashed. They needed cash from somewhere, so like cities do with sports stadiums, the school board decided to get a sponsor. The soda companies were out of the running, though, since the state's Department of Cafeteria Nutrition started cracking down on campus soda sales. Which sucked, by the way. How did the D.Caf.Nuts expect us to wash down our hamburgers?

24

With *milk,* for crying out loud? Anyway, Del Heiny Ketchup Company stepped in and saved the day by offering to sponsor the entire district. All the school board had to do was agree to name every school after Del Heiny and turn their mascots into tomatoes. That arrangement passed muster with the D.Caf.Nuts, with ketchup being a vegetable and all. So in one swoop, Del Heiny got an image boost, the district got its money, and I got stuck here, in glorious Del Heiny Junior High #13, home of the oh-so-fierce Plum Tomatoes.

"No, no, no. You're doing it all wrong, Linus. Didn't you pay attention to the instructions?" Mad Max didn't like the consistency of our butyric acid gel mixture.

I didn't like the smell of it. For the sake of science, though, I leaned in for a closer examination—holding my breath, of course. The mixture looked fine to me, like cherry Jell-O. Rubbery and red. Which, like an idiot, is what I said to Max.

"Is this experiment about making cherry Jell-O, Sherman?"

"Well, no, but—"

"Is it about Jell-O at all?"

"No, but—"

"Then the point of your comparison is?"

"I don't know, I just—"

"That's what I thought. Now discard this gel and follow the steps written on your handout. Come on class, let's pick up the pace here! We're running out of time." She clapped her hands and zipped away to terrorize another lab group.

Jeez. I'd almost rather be hanging out with Arthur.

Tater flared his big nostrils and exhaled like a rhino. "Thanks, Thuff. For a minute there I thought she'd assign

25

me after-school cleanup again. I hate cleaning up after lab days. Her experiments always reek by sixth period."

It wasn't like I'd really done anything, but hey, he thought I did. "No problem, man. I got your back." I clapped him solidly on the shoulder, then scooped up the gel tray.

"Wait." He stopped me before I could walk away with it. Pulling out his cell phone, he snapped a quick picture of it. "My brother's not gonna believe this one. I just wish this picture was scratch 'n' sniff."

"He'll be glad it isn't." I left him pulling out his lucky green marker to fill out our worksheet.

When I passed Lucy's desk, she caught my hand and whispered, "Hey, Shermie. Big news. I know how you can get down *thirteen* dogs instead of eleven."

We both looked around quickly. Max was browbeating the troops on the other side of the room, and everyone else was working on their experiments. I knelt down next to Lucy. "Spill it."

"Wet buns."

"Excuse me?" I instinctively covered my rear with my hands, spilling my gel blob onto the floor. It oozed under the table behind us. I made a funny face to make the girls at the table giggle. When they went back to their experiment, I quickly shoveled the red gel back onto my tray with my foot.

"Wet buns," Lucy repeated when I knelt down next to her again. "That's what the pros do. They dunk their hot dog buns in water before they eat them, separate from the wieners. Wet buns go down easier and quicker than dry buns."

Wet buns, of course! I swear, taking Lucy on as my coach

was a stroke of genius. I'd just do whatever she told me, and then the fame and money would come rolling in. *Thirteen-Dog Tuesday, here I come! Next stop, the Nathan's Famous Fourth of July International Hot Dog–Eating Contest, the Super Bowl of competitive eating. Fame will be mine!*

Lucy nudged me away suddenly. "She's coming. Go. *Hurry.*" She turned back to her goo, which was bright yellow, and tried to look studious. "Man, this stuff stinks."

Of course it stank. It was butyric acid. Vomit. Puke. Throw-up. Blood of the evil Porcelain God. And, with thirteen wet HDBs staring me down, probably my new best friend.

CHAPTER 3

Aaaagggh!

Bulging eyeballs. Tears like water rockets. Puffy, blood-bloated sockets.

Aaaagggh!

Thirteen dogs plus thirteen cold, waterlogged buns equaled one toilet bowl of butyric acid.

Aaaagggh!

At least I'd fasted since lunch yesterday. I'd learned from my mistake and made it to thirteen HDBs this time.

Aaaa . . .

Nothing.

Wait, Shermie, wait. . . .

Still nothing.

I hung out a few minutes more while the dry heaves subsided, then stood and flushed. Not bad for a second attempt. Lucy didn't need to know how it ended.

Smiling, I lifted up my white T-shirt and patted my empty belly. *Thump, thump.* Next time, *fourteen* HDBs, I just knew it.

CHAPTER 4

According to the clock on my cell phone, it was 7:26 when my bus finally putt-putted up to Del Heiny Junior 13. Eleven minutes behind schedule. Swell. Air brakes popped and hissed as the oxidized orange clunker lurched to a stop, then settled.

I lodged a complaint with the tooth-challenged driver on my way out.

"Calm down, big guy," he said. "I can't control the traffic, you know. Maybe your watch is wrong."

My cell phone was regulated by satellite. Satellites were never wrong. Riding the bus sucked.

Because she had an early dentist appointment, Lucy wasn't with me as I stepped off the bus in front of our three-story circular school building, which was the dark red of a plum tomato from top to bottom. I sighed. It was like walking into a solid blob of ketchup. The only windows were on the bottom floor, where the principal and his staff had their offices. Ringing the top of the red blob was a crown of white flags, each sporting a plump tomato in its center like the red sun on a Japanese flag. Across the middle of the blob, strung like a big Band-Aid over the double-doored entrance, was a long white banner with GO, PLUMS! in blocky red letters. I swear, I could have kissed the very ground in gratefulness that we weren't assigned the extra-plump Burpee tomato as our mascot. Del Heiny High #4 got that one. The huge GO, BIG BURPEES! sign over their door was the stuff of nightmares. Life was hard enough without being a Big Burpee.

With just five minutes left to get to Mad Max's class way up on the third floor, I beelined for the double doors. Even with my shortcut through the waist-high hedge, the other bus-riding Plums left me in the dust fast. They and the few stragglers rushing from the bike racks looked like muted aliens in a low-budget sci-fi flick. The morning sun was painting their faces a mucky Dijon-mustard color, and the dry wind had their hair poking out from their heads like porcupine quills. It was like the opening scene of *Galactic Warriors'* most popular episode, "Captain Quixote's Glory." In that episode, the aliens really did have quills.

I raced through the doors and past the broken elevator, skidding to a stop just steps beyond. I did an about-face. The elevator doors had GO, MUSTARD! scribbled on them in big, loopy letters with thickly squeezed mustard. I couldn't help it, I busted up. *The Mustard Taggers strike again!* That made five times in two weeks. Principal Culwicki was probably having a seizure that very second, the big Del Heiny butt kisser.

That happy thought launched me up the stairs at full gallop. *Go, Mustard!*

By the time I rushed through door 306 to Science Concepts in Action three floors up, I was the one having a seizure. My white Scoops T-shirt was stuck to my back and I was wheezing and coughing and huffing like Ruffers

Thuff, Grampy's fifteen-year-old dog. Then the tardy bell blared from the speaker over my head, vibrating my entire skull. I had to grab the doorjamb to steady myself.

"Sherman, are you all right?"

I nearly screamed like a girl when Mad Max spoke.

Teachers should never stand behind their classroom doors. Ever!

Max leaned in closer and said more quietly, "In this weather, Sherman, you've got to be careful not to overdo it. That goes for everyone, not just you. Now go sit down and catch your breath."

The humiliation.

I did my best not to stumble across the room. Still, I practically fell into my seat next to Tater.

"Hey there, Thuff. Whoa, buddy, are you okay?" He thumped me on the back like I was choking or something. It just knocked more air out of me.

"I'm . . . fine . . . Tater." He kept thumping me, "Tater . . . Stop!"

"Okay, okay."

When I could muster enough power to rip my stare away from his gigantic nostrils, I saw that he'd shaved his head since yesterday.

Now, I was the first to admit that on some people, bald was a cool look. But we were talking Tater here. The guy already had two strikes against him in the looks department—one for each rhino nostril. But that maze of blue veins crisscrossing his albino scalp . . . *yikes*. I'd say this for him, though, at least he didn't have to worry about his hair anymore.

"Hello, Earth to Sherman." Tater waved a hand in front of my eyes, his jangling office aide keys adding to my cranial pain. "Did you hear me? I said did you do the homework last night?"

"Of course I heard you." I hadn't. *Stupid wheezing.* "I hear everything. Homework. Did I do it. I heard you."

"What's wrong with you today?"

"Nothing's wrong. Just leave me alone, okay?" I tried holding my breath to stop the wheeze. But that just made me cough.

Mad Max banged the wall with a tibia bone from the dusty skeleton that hung by the whiteboard. "All right, people, listen up. We're short a science teacher for a while, so we're reassigning students to other classrooms, including this one. It might be a little crowded, but let's make the best of it. Don't make me dole out push-ups." That got our attention more than the banging bone. Last week she'd made a kid do twenty push-ups for missing the trash can with a balled-up Twinkie wrapper.

Satisfied that her threat had sunk in, she whisked open a door that separated our lab from the next one. Ten Plums filed in to fill ten empty single-seater desks lining our walls. I recognized the first guy and the two girls who followed him. They were all Scoops regulars, so they smiled when we made eye contact. Maybe slaving for Grampy had some perks after all. I adjusted my Scoops shirt. Without it I was a *complete* nobody.

The next five Plums were just faces from the halls. Several of them had on yellow T-shirts, which a lot of kids had started wearing last week after the Mustard Taggers called for a "Revolt Against Red." The ninth guy, though, made me groan out loud. A monster in a GO, PLUM WRESTLING! T-shirt, the kid was unmistakable: He was a Finn twin, twenty feet tall, at least, and ugly as sin, with

32

his nose bent to the left like his identical brother. The mark of the Devil.

Science Concepts in Action just took a nosedive.

Traipsing in behind the Devil's spawn was Gardo, also wearing his Plum Tomato wrestling shirt. They were teammates on our junior varsity prep wrestling team. Man, my buddy looked like a dwarf next to the Finn. And since I was two inches shorter than Gardo, I'd probably be face level with the Finn's armpits even if I stood my tallest. Not that I ever planned to stand next to the big oaf and measure. My only Finn contact was last week when their jock jerk captain Shane Hunt had one Finn grab my legs and the other grab my arms for a big swing into the trash can. I had no intention of getting that close again.

So which Finn was this, the one who had my arms or the one who had my legs?

As if hearing my thoughts, the Finn looked my way. I snapped my eyes back to Gardo, who grinned and winked as he slid into a desk seat. A girl sitting between us giggled softly and wiggled her fingers at him. She must have thought he was flirting with her—which he was now that she'd tootle-oo'd at him.

"Chop, chop, people, take your seats!" ordered Max. Then she stopped and watched while the Finn squeezed himself into a desk. She was as mesmerized as we were. The top of the desk was attached to the seat by a curving metal arm, so he couldn't push it out at all, he just had to slip into the seat from the side. It was like watching a bear climb onto a trike at the circus.

When the big dumb bear was finally wedged in, Max stepped onto the box behind her podium and switched on her lecture voice. "As I survey the room today, I see that you are all familiar with the topic of today's lecture—at least follically." She smooshed down the hairs frizzing out of her blond bun and adjusted the chopsticks that held it in place. We all automatically smooshed down our own frizzies. Except baldy Tater, of course. He just sat there with his green marker poised over his notebook.

Max stabbed her tibia bone at a huge picture of the bright yellow sun taped to her whiteboard. "The sun. Solar eclipses. Solar flashes. The reasons for our static-struck coiffures . . ."

* * *

The cafeteria was in the very center of our round school, on the bottom floor, with an open sunroof three stories up. A few hundred Plums milled around, buying food from the shiny metal slop counters up front, carrying food trays up and down the aisles, and sitting at long rectangular tables throwing paper airplanes and shooting straw wrappers. The place was louder than the food court at the mall. It was heavier on the eyes, too. Except for the metal fixtures and the bleached white linoleum that reflected the sunlight above, everything in the cafeteria was dark Plum red. Red walls, red trays, red tables, red-aproned cafeteria ladies. To planes passing above, Del Heiny Junior 13 probably looked like a giant doughnut with ketchup icing and little ants scurrying in the center hole.

I was sitting in the unofficial eighth grader section waiting for Lucy, who surely was back from the dentist by now. There was a Halloween pumpkin centerpiece in front of me, its goofy face drawn on with black marker. Tissue-wrapped lollipop "ghosts" lay around its base. The Associated Student Body's spirit officer probably had to get a special waiver from Del Heiny to bring all that in. Pumpkins and lollipops weren't ketchup-dunkable.

I salted my lukewarm Tater Tots, then popped open the soda I'd smuggled onto campus. The can was tucked on the seat between my legs so that the janitors who patrolled the cafeteria wouldn't see it. If it had been a cold soda, I would've been in a world of hurt with it jammed against the Thuff Family Jewels. But because I'd stashed the can in my backpack hours ago, it was now the same temperature as my Tots. I wasn't a fan of room-temp soda—it didn't have the crisp, carbonated bite of cold pop—but a guy did what he could.

"Hey, Thuff!"

I twisted in the direction of the slop counters, where Gardo was waving to get my attention.

"How many?" he shouted.

"Nine!" I shouted back.

"What?"

"Nine!"

"Nine!" Thumbs up. "No problem!" He disappeared into the food zone.

Gardo was skipping lunch because he had to make weight for his upcoming practice game, or meet, or whatever wrestlers called it, so he was fetching more ketchup packets for me. My six corn dogs would be good capacity training for my stomach, but I hadn't grabbed enough packets to reach the recommended ketchup ratio for that many breaded wieners. And ketchup ratios were important, because Del Heiny was adamant about students getting their proper vegetable allotment each day. The company worked closely with the D.Caf.Nuts to make sure everything sold in the cafeteria was ketchup-dunkable. Laminated cards taped down on each tabletop advised just how many packets to use per corn dog, Tater Tot, etc. To reinforce the

Del Heiny Healthy Eating Initiative, the cafeteria's red walls were stenciled with large slogans like A TOMATO A DAY KEEPS THE DOCTOR AWAY and THE WORLD IS YOUR TOMATO and VEGGIES—THEY'RE NOT ALL GREEN.

Crouched at a nearby wall under the slogans were the school's three janitors, all dressed in dill-green coveralls. I probably didn't need to worry about them patrolling for contraband cola today. They had more interesting things on their minds than my measly soda. Between raspy, cancerous coughing fits, they were bickering about who got to glue the humongous tomato decal over the yellow smudge left by the MUSTARD LOVERS UNITE! tag, which had been squeezed across the Del Heiny company logo.

Two kids in yellow shirts passed by the janitors. "Go, Mustard!" one shouted. His buddy high-fived him. Some kids following him laughed despite the janitors' glares.

The next voice that boomed out wasn't so welcome. It belonged to Shane Hunt, the biggest jerk on the planet. "I feel the need to dunk me a big . . . fat . . . scrub doughnut."

Oh, great. My mouth went dry. Last week Shane had declared it Scrub Dunk Week in the cafeteria and then promptly ordered a different eighth grader chucked into a trash can every day. Starting with me. I still had a bruise on my lower back where the edge of the can had dug in. And now here he was, looking for another victim. Apparently the idiot didn't know how long a week was.

Except for a few snickers from the huddled janitors and a "Make it a slam dunk, Shane!" from Shane's table in the ninth grade section, the cafeteria was silent. Like Moses parting water, Shane swaggered down the center aisle with the Finns, both looking like they had a medical condition as they tried to make their bulky bodies swagger like his too-short one. All of them had their yellow baseball caps on backward. Plums unlucky enough to be in the aisle scuttled out of their way. One poor slob spilled his tray, sending Tater Tots every which way. Shane grinned and stomped the Tots.

"You missed one!" a janitor called out.

Shane darted his eyes around the floor, then pointed near Wayne's—or was it Blayne's?—left Nike. Whichever, the sneaker raised, then came down hard. A piece of Tot squilched sideways and splatted against Shane's jeans.

"Sorry, Captain, sir."

Slowly, dramatically, Shane wiped off the splooge, then cleaned his hand on the Finn's red wrestling shirt.

"Let's see," Shane said, gazing around him. "There's an empty trash can. Now which of these jiggly doughboys will it be today?"

At every table except Shane's, Plums cast their eyes downward and held as still as possible, hoping not to call attention to themselves. Me included. It was useless to do anything else. The janitors loved Shane's shows, so they weren't going to stop him. And no one was going to run and tattle like some kindergartner. Jasper Finch stupidly tried to rat them out to Principal Culwicki last Wednesday, but Culwicki was a college wrestling buddy of Shane's dad, so nothing came of it except Jasper getting a lecture on the character-building merits of good-natured pranks. And now Plums call him Jasper *Fink*.

With my eyes locked downward on my white shirt, I couldn't see Shane's roving eyes, but they must have landed on someone because suddenly he sounded almost chipper.

"I've got a better idea," he said. "Grab that for me, Blayne."

The Finn tried to whisper, but I'm sure most of us heard it: "Captain, sir, I'm Wayne."

37

"That's what I said. Now grab the stupid extinguisher."
Louder, Shane announced, "Dunking doughnuts is so last
week. It's time to move on to *sundaes*!"

Next to me, the janitors rose to their feet and rubbed
their sandpapery palms together.

"Duck . . . duck . . . duck . . ."

I peeked up to see Shane thunking random scrub heads.
Head by head, he was moving toward my table.

"Duck . . . duck . . ."

He was now two tables away.

"Duck . . . duck . . ."

One table.

"GOOSE!"

Lunging forward, Shane grabbed Willie Dean's collar and
yanked him backward out of his seat. He pushed him into
the waiting arms of Wayne. Or was it Blayne? Whichever, the other Finn snatched the nearest garbage can and
whisked off the lid like a waiter revealing fine cuisine.

Willie dropped to his knees and pleaded for his life.

I cringed. My mind flashed back to the embarrassing
piggy squeals I'd cut loose with last week when I was
Shane's doughnut dunkee . . . and to the tears I'd cried as he
ordered his Finns to drop me into the can. The memory
made my stomach lurch.

"I said no dunking." Shane sounded annoyed. "Hold
still."

Shane lifted the extinguisher and aimed. *Szhhhhhh!* Fire
retardant exploded out of an extinguisher, decorating the
metal trash can lid with a pile of fluffy white that looked
like whipped cream on a sundae.

"Perfect!" Shane shouted. "Test complete. C'mere, *scrub*."

The Finn held Willie on his knees while Shane lined up

the extinguisher over his head. Willie started to cry. It was awful. Totally completely awful.

I'm so glad it's not me being whipped.

That thought made me cringe even harder. I was a terrible person, absolutely horrible. Last week it *was* me, only I was getting my big butt jammed into a can of half-chewed food, empty milk containers, and goopy ketchup packets. I'd tried so hard not to cry, but my throat went all tight and the stupid tears spilled down my cheeks anyway. I'd been totally powerless to stop it. And as I was dropped into the can, I saw the backs of dozens of kids' heads as they looked away, trying not to witness my shame—just like I wanted to do now. But I knew they saw it. And the whole time, they were probably thinking, *I'm so glad it's not me.*

My face got hotter as I relived the humiliation, which made my eyes tear up again, which made me more upset, which made me even happier it wasn't me being whipped, which made me feel like a total jerk, which made me royally pissed off, which made me want to—

"STOP!" My outburst surprised me, as did the fact that I'd bolted to my feet.

Shane's head whipped my way. "What did you say?"

My throat went tight. "I said . . . stop." The last word came out broken, as if puberty had just kicked in.

"That's what I thought you said, Fat Boy." He straightened then shoved Willie aside, dismissing him. The kid scurried away like a crab at the beach. "I think you need a lesson in how to talk to your superiors, *scrub.*"

No one else said anything, not even the janitors. And that was the way it would stay, I knew. Shane and his thugs were outnumbered big time, yet they were in charge. My goose was cooked.

Tears pooled in my eyes. *Please no, not again.* I'd die if I got canned again.

My only hope was to run. I quickly stretched my neck up to see over Shane's shoulder and—*yes!*—I had a clean shot to the emergency exit if I could somehow get by him. I snorted involuntarily at that thought. Dump trucks couldn't outmaneuver hot rods.

As if sensing my impulse to flee, Shane hunched his head down, leaned his shoulders forward, and spread his arms wide with his feet staggered in some psycho-ballistic wrestling stance. He swayed forward like he was about to lunge in my direction, but before he could take a step, a commanding voice echoed down the hallway into the tense cafeteria.

All heads turned right. In strode Principal Culwicki, his wide green tie flapping up over his shoulder. Rushing after him was Mad Max, followed by a short, waddling man in an olive-green uniform and red armband.

Max was clutching a yellow file folder.

". . . already told you Del Heiny won't go for that, Maureen," Culwicki was saying. "Even if they would, I am *not* putting a rotting pig on the football field. What does that have to do with science? Oh, there's another one!" He stabbed his finger at a mustard slogan that the janitors hadn't cleaned off the wall yet. "Good grief, Eckstein, are these delinquents getting in through the pipes? Rekey all the locks again. And have the janitors order more red paint. Oh, there's another!"

Suddenly Culwicki halted. Max and the campus security officer dominoed into his back. Culwicki stayed solid on his feet, though, his eyes locked on Shane.

Shane slowly uncoiled and smiled at the wiry principal. "How's it going, sir?"

40

Culwicki narrowed his eyes. "What in tarnation are you doing?" He stepped closer. So did Max, a puzzled look on her face. The officer furiously scribbled on his board.

Yes! Shane was finally going down. Maybe Dunk Week had been worth it.

Shane must have come to the same conclusion, because his smile disappeared. "I—"

"Stop. I don't want to hear it." Culwicki took a deep breath, then shook his head in utter disgust. "You're the wrestling coach's *son*, boy. You should know better." He pointed to Shane's left foot. "Move that foot an inch to the left. Your balance will be better. Honestly, if you're going to show off your Sugarfoot stance, at least have the decency to do it right. I never want to see a horror like that again. You hear me?"

No!

Shane grinned. "Yes, sir. Wider stance. Got it."

"Good. Now wipe that smile off your face. Wrestling is serious business. I said wipe it off! Drop and give me twenty. All three of you. Now! Have some pride."

Shane's smile disappeared instantly. He dutifully dropped to the ground, only pausing a moment. But in that nanosecond of hesitation, his eyes practically glowed with hatred. Okay, so maybe he didn't get busted, but at least he was suffering some humiliation. *How does it feel, tough guy?*

Culwicki bent down and yanked off Shane's cap. "And take off that disrespectful hat. Where's your loyalty?" He threw it on Shane's back as he cranked out his push-ups. "You know what? This is the third time I've caught you in a bad stance and had to assign push-ups. That's three times too many. Come with me. I've got my old training photos in my office, I'll show you the proper stance. I think your dad's in some of the pictures, too." Then he took off again,

41

his green tie flapping wildly, the Olive Shirt scurrying after him. "Oh, there's another one! This is an outrage, Eckstein, you need to do something about this. Oh! Another!"

Shane hopped to his feet and smacked a Finn in the back of the head. "Do the rest later. C'mon." Together they all rushed off after our great Plum principal, stuffing their yellow hats into their back pockets on the way.

Max trailed them all. "Cyrus. Will you at least listen to me?" She waved her yellow folder. "The process of decay *is* science in action. It's a key part of forensics, and forensics is hot. Just sign the approval and let me worry about the details. I don't *have* to put it on the football field. . . ."

They disappeared down the far hallway.

In their wake of silence, I started breathing again. With everyone's attention on Culwicki, I'd been able to swipe away my tears without anyone noticing.

Anyone but Lucy, that is. After Culwicki and his entourage disappeared, I saw her standing in the cafeteria doorway, her brown polo shirt and hair making her a smudge of chocolate against the ketchup-red wall. Without saying a word, she walked across to me and lightly nudged me to my seat. I almost shoved her hand away. Then I almost hugged her. Then I felt the biggest urge to just blow right past her, dashing down the hall, away from her, away from everybody in the cafeteria, away from this whole lame school. But I couldn't, because these stupid scrub doughnut legs didn't have any dash in them. And guys didn't dash, anyway. So instead I slumped onto my bench and stared at my corn dogs.

Gardo sat down on my other side. He smiled and laid a pile of ketchup packets next to my training corn dogs, trying to act like nothing had happened. That only made me feel even more pathetic. *Are YOU Thuff Enuff, Sherman Thuff?* Not in this lifetime.

Quietly at first, then more loudly, the Plums resumed their interrupted conversations. They looked over at me now and then, whispering to their neighbors. The janitors went back to their bickering and their mustard cleanup, and Gardo launched into some story about being elbowed in the eye when his teammate fainted at practice because he hadn't eaten in a week and how Gardo wasn't that stupid, no, he'd stashed a bunch of ketchup packets in his backpack to snack on in emergencies while he cut weight, *blah, blah, blah . . .*

Me, I just sat there like a loser, staring at my Tots. Lucy silently handed me the ketchup packets, but I just dropped them next to my paper plate. Eventually the bell rang and we all headed off to class, ending one more agonizing, demoralizing lunchtime for the underclassmen of Del Heiny Junior High #13, the school where boys would be boys, losers would be losers, and ninth graders had all the power, forever and ever, amen.

And now, for a special message from the company that cares . . .

Thuffie Tots,™ yummy tots
Craving taters? We got lots!
Classic Thuffs™ . . .
Pepper Thuffs™ . . .
Wedgie Thuffs™ . . .
Frenchie Thuffs™ . . .
Bake them, dip them, eat them hot.™
Bring me more MORE Thuffie Tots!™

Boys and girls, have you had a hard day at school? A morning of degradation and humiliation at the hands of teachers, bullies, and stick-up-the-rear upperclassman? Then Thuffie Tots™ are for you. Thuffie Tots™ are big, bold, and powerful, the perfect staple for school cafeterias everywhere, where no hot food is ever hot, no cold food is ever cold, and all ice cream can be slurped with a straw. Don't be tempted by other taters, because a French fry's just a French fry, but a Thuffie Tot™ is a Meal.® Available in three shapes, including the classic barrel, Thuffie Tots™ offer the optimum in ketchup-dunking dining. Try them all and rejuvenate at lunch. Become a new student, a new kid, become a Thuffie Tot™ eater!

So the next time you're thinking taters, ask yourself this: Are YOU Thuff Enuff? ®

CHAPTER 5

"Everyone was talking about you after lunch today."

Gardo and I were at Scoops-a-Million for my evening shift. Actually, I had taken over Grampy's shift, because he claimed his psoriasis was acting up. No one wanted a guy with scaly, flaky elbows scooping their ice cream, so what could I do but fill in for him. And I'd have to do inventory for him afterward, too. Funny how the guy always managed to develop some gnarly disease on inventory nights. Arthur was working with me, but he was on break and there weren't any customers. Gardo was gnawing a tiny pink taster spoon.

"Great," I responded. "Now I'm the laughingstock of Del Heiny Junior 13 twice in two weeks." At least I hadn't bawled like a baby again, stud that I was. *Pathetic.* "Are you gonna keep sucking on that empty spoon, or do you want some ice cream on it?"

"Will you relax? I have to make weight. Coach will kill me if I don't. Anyways"—Gardo jabbed his bitten-up spoon at me—"I said they were *talking* about you, not *laughing* about you. You're the BMOC now."

"The what?"

"The big man on campus."

"Give me a break, Gardo."

"I'm serious. Anyone who didn't know you before sure knows you now. When Shane dropped into that Sugarfoot stance today, you just stood up straight and stared him dead in the eye." He scowled. "No one's ever stood up to Shane before."

They thought I was standing up to him? I thought I was looking for an escape. "I don't know about *stood up to him.*"

He eyed me for a second, then said, very slowly, very deliberately, "You stood up to him, Shermie. I saw it, everyone saw it." Then he waved his hand dismissively. "The rest is just details, and nobody cares about details. You've got a rep now, and rep is everything, remember that."

In a pig's eye, I have a rep. I was leaning against the display case, trying not to think about how I just almost got my butt kicked. In front of me, a rainbow of bright-colored ice cream circles lined the display case in side-by-side rows. I thought of the paint set my dad gave me when I was in kindergarten and painting was fun. Now it was just one more thing I sucked at. Maybe I was stupid trying to get famous. Maybe my destiny was to serve up ice cream, simple as that.

"Here," I said, "give me the spoon. I'll put some ice cream on it."

"I said I don't want any."

"You did not."

"I did, too."

"Nuh-uh."

"Fine: I—don't—want—any—ice—cream. How's that?"

Boy, this not-eating thing was turning Gardo into a real

crank. With my luck, he'd start hucking maraschino cherries my way.

"Who doesn't want ice cream?" I said. "Ice cream is the best. I'd scarf down every one of these tubs if I could."

"So do it."

"Shut up."

"*You* shut up." Suddenly Gardo pulled up straight and slapped his palm on the counter, the unmistakable sign that he'd just had a Brilliant Gardo Moment. "Hey! You *should* do it, Shermie. Seriously. You don't have to stick to hot dogs, right? You need to cross-train with lots of different food, right? C'mon, let's see how much ice cream you can eat. Is there already a record for that?"

"Of course there's a record for it. Cookie Jarvis, one gallon, nine ounces, twelve minutes flat."

"What is he, a girl? You can beat that."

"That's a lot of ice cream! And twelve minutes goes by faster than you think."

"Which is exactly why you should practice." He leaned in and lowered his voice confidentially. "I don't mean to disrespect Lucy, but by making you specialize in one food, she's limiting your career. I'm telling you, the more foods you eat, the more competitions you can enter and the more marketable you are as a personality. Look at Bo Jackson. He played pro baseball *and* pro football. His coaches gave him a hard time, but he didn't care. And you know what, now *everybody* knows Bo. How many people can name his coaches?"

Who's Bo?

Not that it mattered. I mean, I got Gardo's point. There *were* a lot of eating competitions out there—burritos, waffles, pumpkin pies, baked beans, shrimp, SPAM, even weird

47

stuff like turducken and hutspot. Lucy told me herself. And in a lot of those competitions, the same names were popping up as winners. Even the invincible Japanese guy, Tsunami, with his fifty-three-and-three-quarters HDBs, held records in foods that weren't hot dogs: 69 hamburgers in eight minutes, 20 pounds of rice balls in thirty minutes, 17.7 pounds of—*ugh!*—*cow brains* in fifteen minutes. So really, Gardo was right. The more contests I entered, the more I'd win and the more exposure I'd get. Specializing would only hurt my career.

Still, Lucy had graphed out a pretty tight game plan for me. "Maybe I should check with Lucy first."

"You don't need to check with Lucy. How can you be a big star if you can't even make a simple decision about ice cream? Quit stalling and start eating. Or don't you think you can?"

"I can." I gazed upon my creamy paint set. Cocoa brown, minty green, banana yellow . . . a rainbow of temptation.

Gardo chanted softly: "Thuff, Thuff, Thuff . . ."

I didn't know why I was wimping out. It wasn't like Lucy would know. Who would tell her? It was just me and Gardo.

". . . Thuff, Thuff, Thuff . . ."

I didn't want to reverse in front of him, though.

". . . Thuff, Thuff, Thuff . . ."

But then, he was right that I needed practice.

". . . Thuff, Thuff, Thuff . . ."

And I did love ice cream.

". . . Thuff, Thuff, Thuff . . ."

Who said I'd have a reversal of fortune anyway? Ice cream wasn't hot dogs. I didn't have to chew it; it would just slide down. "Okay, let's do it."

"Atta boy!" He slam-dunked the empty spoon into the

trash can, then rubbed his hands together, making me think of the Del Heiny Junior 13 janitors. "All right, then, here we go."

I took a huge metal spoon from the drawer behind me and set it in the heated water trough that hung along my side of the display case. Wet metal always slid through ice cream easier than dry metal. "Okay. How much do I eat?"

"I don't know. What are you asking me for?"

"Lucy didn't make graphs for ice cream. I need to establish a base number."

"I'm sorry, did I miss something? Are we in *math class*? Just eat the ice cream until you can't eat anymore."

"I need a time goal, at least. Twelve minutes, just like the pros." I scanned the colored rows. "Which flavor?"

"*Whichever* flavor. Will you start already?"

"You won't tell Lucy?"

"Shermie, look who you're talking to."

I crossed my arms. He'd watched *Galactic Warriors* enough. He knew that the most successful missions were the top-secret ones.

He sighed heavily. "Fine: No, I won't tell Lucy." He pretended to lock his mouth and throw away the key. Through squeezed lips he mumbled, "I'll keep my big mouth shut."

"Good."

As my spoons warmed, I studied the open barrels. Should I go with Bing Cherry? Its fruity sweetness was smooth going down, but the frozen cherries could choke a horse. Mint Chocolate Chip? No, the dusty chocolate flakes probably wouldn't clog my throat, but the mintiness always crept up the back of my nose. Fudge Brownie? That was always a good fallback when I couldn't decide what flavor my mood was. Wait, no, not Fudge Brownie. Grampy had started ordering the kind with walnut brownies, and walnuts taste like dirt. Maybe Spazzy Monkey? In the Sherman T. Thuff Book of Good and Tasty Things, that was the King Kong of ice creams: rich banana ice cream, delicate shards of toffee that packed deep into my molars with just the lightest chew. . . . On second thought, if I didn't chew enough during this speed session, those shards could shred my throat. Maybe I should steer clear of chunks altogether. After all, chewing would only slow me down, and I certainly didn't want to choke. I'd stick with straight ice cream, then. . . . Something with a chocolate base was always good. . . . Heck, I'd just do straight chocolate. No mucking around.

My flavor choice made, I put my right hand on my waist and leaned to the right, stretching my left hand to the sky. I could feel the blood coursing faster through my brain. I repeated the stretch on my left side, then did five jumping jacks and two squats.

"For crying out loud, Shermie, you're eating ice cream, not sprinting in the Olympics. Let's do this already."

"Stuff it, crank. If I'm going to be a pro, I need to train like a pro. Athletes always stretch. Lucy said so." Maybe stopping wasn't such a bad idea, though. I was getting short of breath.

"Athlete? What are you talking about? You're eating ice cream, not wrestling."

Just for that, I did an extra squat. The up part was harder that time. "Eating's a sport that takes training and physical stamina, so I'm an athlete. Don't argue with me, I didn't make the rules. That's just the way of it."

"Fine. You're an athlete." He dropped down into a chair to wait, gnawing another empty spoon.

He was looking right at me, so I leaned right then left one more time before I pulled my spoon from the water. I tried not to let him see that I was breathing hard.

The spoon was hot and drippy now, so it would probably slide right into the ice cream. Dropping my arms down by my sides, I shook them to be sure they were totally relaxed. Then I climbed on my footstool, planted my feet a shoulder's width apart, hunched over the display case, and poised my spoon directly above the chocolate tub. "Okay. Go."

"Go where?"

"Funny." I adjusted my feet. "Announce me. Do my play-by-play."

"Oh, jeez . . ."

"We do this right or we don't do it at all. C'mon, my spoon is cooling off."

Gardo stood up and cleared his throat. But just as he opened his mouth to say something, he suddenly leaned around the display case, swiped his finger across the Triple Chocolate Fudge, then smacked a dark line under each of my eyes. *Smack, smack.*

"Ow!"

"*Now* you're an athlete," he said. Then he planted his own feet and unleashed a ring announcer voice that put Vince McMahon to shame. "Ladies and gentlemen . . . sports fans . . . food lovers everywhere. Welcome to the mecca of competitive eating, the Ground Zero of Gluttony, the icing on the top of the ice cream cake . . . the one, the only, Glutton Bowl Two!"

He did a fake crowd cheer and whistled through two fingers.

"We're here in lovely Scoops-a-Million," he continued, smiling now, "where Cinderella underdog Sherman 'Thuff

Enuff' Thuff has reached the final round. Now he'll go spoon to spoon against the reigning champion of ice cream . . ." He looked at me questioningly.

"Cookie," I prompted.

". . . the reigning champion of ice cream, Cookie Jarvis. Our judges will set the clock for twelve minutes." I pointed to him, then to the wall clock behind him. "Aaaaaand GO!"

I jammed my warm, wet spoon into the hard-packed ice cream, then rocketed it to my mouth. I swallowed the instant the cold ice cream hit my tongue, barely even tasting chocolate. *Holy jeez, that's a serious lump of cold!* The image of a snake swallowing a huge frozen mouse crossed my mind, but I pushed it out. I had ice cream to eat.

I jam-and-rocketed again.

And again.

And again.

And again.

My throat was numbing from the freeze. The roof of my mouth, too. *Don't think about that, Thuff. Focus on technique. Jam and rocket . . . jam and rocket . . .*

Sugary spit collected under my tongue. Cold chocolate lumps choo-chooed down my food pipe, trailing a slippery, sugary residue.

Jam and rocket, jam and rocket . . .

My wrist started to burn. My forearm threatened to cramp. That's when I realized that I was a total idiot. I should've let the ice cream get soft and melty first. The pros probably knew that. At least I'd stretched. Maybe I'd tell Lucy to add weight lifting to her graphs.

Jam and rocket, jam and rocket . . .

Every movement became automatic. Tuning out the burn

and the freeze, I concentrated on my form. My shoulder and upper arm were tucked against my ribs, my wrist and hand worked the scoop, and my elbow bent like an automatic hinge, bringing the spoon up to my mouth and back down to the chocolate tub again, over and over. I unhinged my jaw as best I could—*open wide, stick in spoon, clamp down, pull off with lips* . . . *open wide, stick in spoon, clamp down, pull off with lips* . . . *open wide, stick in spoon, clamp down, pull off with lips* . . .

The muscles in front of my ears were burning.

"Two minutes down!" Gardo hollered.

That's all?

"Ten to go."

Autopilot was kicking in, and my mind started to wander. I heard some voices, so customers were probably coming in. But I didn't want to look up, I didn't want to move my head one iota. If customers were coming in, so be it. They could wait. History was being made.

Jam and rocket, jam and rocket . . .

Two of the voices sounded familiar. I think they belonged to my afternoon regulars, Fudge Ripple and Butter Pecan, two ninth graders from my school.

Jam and rocket, jam and rocket . . .

Yeah, that's who it was. Who was with them?

Jam and rocket, jam and rocket . . .

"Four minutes left!" Gardo hollered. "Four minutes!"

Four more minutes? I didn't know if I could keep it up.

Jam and rocket, jam and rocket . . .

More voices. The shop was filling. Someone shouted, "Go, Thuff!"

My lower face muscles burned as I opened, shut, opened, shut, opened, shut. I started to seriously regret this whole thing as my stomach started objecting. It was cold, it was stretched, it was not happy. It felt like I'd just downed a whole gallon of milk—and not the wimpy nonfat kind, either. No way could I keep up this speed for twelve whole minutes. No way. Maybe I was a sprinter, a two-minute speed eater. Twelve minutes was a mistake.

Jam and rocket, jam and rocket . . .

Ugh. So that was what it felt like to swallow a whole Thanksgiving turkey . . . *when it was still frozen.* And there was still a ton of ice cream in the tub. Where would I fit it all? There just wasn't enough room. Maybe if I threw up— *No!* No. Reversals of fortune were for wimps. I wanted to be champion, I could *do* this.

I'll catch a burp. That'll free up space. Without pausing my arm and mouth, I hopped and wiggled and shook like Tsunami did when he was trying to settle the hot dogs to the bottom of his stomach. A burp was in there, I knew it, caught under the ice cream. I just . . . had to . . . dislodge . . . the . . . ice cream. . .

"Go, Thuff!" someone yelled.

"You can do it!"

"Pack it down, big guy!"

BURRRPP!

Total silence in the room, then laughing and more cheering.

Oh man, that does feel better. Way better. I shook my head like I'd just regained consciousness. Three and a half minutes left. I could last three and a half minutes. That burp was the ticket. *C'mon, Thuff!* I redunked the spoon in the water, splashing everywhere, then jammed it into the ice cream once again.

Jam and rocket, jam and rocket . . . Yes! I got me a second wind, baby! Thank the Gods of Gas for burps. . . . Jam and rocket, jam and rocket . . .

I'd excavated a crater in the center of the chocolate ice cream. My whole lower arm disappeared as I stabbed in for another scoop, then another, then another.

Jam and rocket, jam and rocket . . .

My bulging stomach had gone past prickly cold, right into numb. My throat was totally numb, too, and the icy numbness was traveling upward, into my head, into my br—

"Ow-ow-ow!" I screamed, dropping the spoon and clutching at my forehead.

The crowd gasped. In a tone of hushed horror, Butter Pecan named my pain: "Oh no. He's got *brain freeze.*"

I doubled over, trying to duck the ice pick that was spearing my frontal lobe from the inside. *Brain freeze, my rear end. This is brain* death*!* I was two seconds away from pushing up daisies, I just knew it. I should have stuck with HDBs. The worst thing you could do with those was choke. That couldn't be nearly as agonizing as having your brain matter frozen into solid rock.

Then, just when I couldn't take another dig of the pick, the freeze slid away. Easy as that. It was as if a glaze of warm chocolate flowed right over the hardening brain tissue, thawing it instantly.

Slowly, I stood up straight. My legs were wobbly, but no one could see that because the display case hid my lower body. My shaking hands were visible, though, so I hurriedly dunked them in the warm water trough.

Someone clapped. Then more people clapped and Gardo whistled. I wiped my eyes with my sleeve and focused on the crowd. There in front of me were Gardo, Fudge Ripple, Butter Pecan, Leonard from science, and five other guys, all regulars, all in yellow, all grinning and clapping and coming toward the counter to lean over and thump me on the shoulder.

"Way to go, Thuff!"

"I can't believe you ate all that."

"Look at that tub, man. You dug halfway to China!"

"Awesome!"

Gardo's shout drowned them all out: "Gentlemen, I give you the new Ice Cream–Eating Champion of the Universe, Sherman 'Thuff Enuff' Thuff!"

He leaned over the counter and grabbed my hand, lifting my arm up above our heads, my victory smashing and complete. "Are *YOU* Thuff Enuff?"

"I AM!" I thundered.

"Thuff, Thuff, Thuff!" Gardo started the chant, then the other guys kicked in, cheering and laughing and whistling. It was even better than I'd imagined. Way, way better.

I knew it, I'd found my calling. In facing Gardo's ice cream challenge, I'd revealed The Truth: My destiny wasn't in a big metal scoop, after all. It was in my big mouth. And I hadn't suffered a reversal of fortune proving it. *Glory be and hallelujah! Move over Cookie Jarvis, there's a new ice cream eater in town: Sherman "Thuff Enuff" Thuff!*

"Thuff! Thuff! Thuff!"

Next, on SportsWorld—
The Fastest Spoon in the West . . .

"Good evening, sports fans. Tonight, big things afoot in the world of sports—table tennis's Jim Nguyen shatters his long silence about bigger paddles, angler Wayne Juster hauls in a big catch at the World Bassmaster Invitational, and wishful hall-of-famer Pete Rose releases early excerpts from his new book, *Nothing But the Truth: I Lied When I Lied About Lying About Gambling.*

"But first, belly up to the ice cream bar, folks, there's been a biiiiig upset in America's hottest new sport—competitive eating. Today, rookie eater Sherman 'Thuff Enuff' Thuff froze out veteran record-holder Cookie Jarvis, the reigning Big Cheese of Ice Cream. Let's go to Chuck LaChance on the ice cream–eating floor. Chuck?"

Thuff! Thuff! Thuff! Thuff! Thuff! Thuff! Thuff!

"Thanks, Rick! I'm here at Scoops-a-Million, site of an astounding upset in professional eating. Rookie Sherman 'Thuff Enuff' Thuff has just become the new Ice Cream–Eating Champion of the Universe! As you can hear, the crowd is going wild."

Thuff! Thuff! Thuff! Thuff! Thuff! Thuff! Thuff!

"Thanks for talking with us, Thuff Enuff. First, congratulations on your amazing victory."

"Thanks, Chuck. I couldn't have done it without my fans."

Thuff! Thuff! Thuff! Thuff! Thuff! Thuff! Thuff!

"Let me ask you, Thuff Enuff, we know you're only a rookie, but you ate that ice cream like you've been training all your life. What was going through your brain as you powered through those final spoonfuls?"

"Well, Chuck, I knew that if I just gave it my best one hundred and ten percent, I'd go all the way, there'd be no stopping me. So I got in the zone, then gave myself over to the ice cream. All I could do was my best and make the most of my chance to show that I do have what it takes to eat at the big boys' table."

"Well, you certainly proved that today! One last question, Thuff Enuff: You just won the Super Bowl of ice cream eating, what are you going to do now?"

"I'm going to Disneyland!"

Thuff! Thuff! Thuff! Thuff! Thuff! Thuff! Thuff!

"There you have it, Rick. This is Chuck LaChance reporting for ESPN. Back to you in the studio."

CHAPTER 6

Okay, so maybe −20 °F was a bit cold for a nap. It hadn't seemed like a stupid idea when I was *out*side the Scoops walk-in freezer. But lying there on the frigid cement floor turning into a Shermie-sicle, I was definitely rethinking my ice cream headache remedy.

By the middle of my shift, the brain freeze from my ice cream victory had blossomed into a full-grown interskullular glacier, and every little thing made it worse. The *click-click* of Arthur's metal scoop in the water trough. The *tippy-tap* of the customers' shoes on the brittle linoleum. Even the air itself was a torment—the pore-clogging film of sugary ice cream, the choking dust of crumbled chocolate toppings, the heavy fumes of one hundred percent pure vanilla extract dumped into waffle cone batter. Normally that sweet combination drifted through the store like fine cologne, but tonight I could've scratched it off my skin. *Pound, pound, pound.* My head had throbbed in tune to my heartbeats.

Then I remembered that Lucy's dad got rid of his migraines by lying in a dark room. The only thing close to a dark room at Scoops was the walk-in freezer. Voilà, Shermie in the −20 °F icebox, freezing his gonads off.

What a dink. I sat up, which made my stomach lurch sickeningly. My eyes were inches away from a tub of Chocolate Fudge Brownie. I nearly reversed my ice cream-a-thon then and there.

Lining the shelf next to the Chocolate Fudge Brownie were more pale brown, rounded tubs, each with a colorful label identifying the equally colorful ice cream inside: emerald Mint Chocolate Chip, orange Pumpkin Pie, pink Bubble Gum, fuchsia Bing Cherry, purple Berry Bonanza, yellow Banana Colada, scarlet Red Raspberry Ripple. . . . All around me, floor to ceiling, were labels and more labels, tubs and more tubs, shelves and more shelves. Everything was dusted with snow-white ice crystals.

Lining the floor under the Chocolate Fudge Brownie shelf was a row of square brown boxes filled with toppings. The labels were just as colorful as those on the tubs of ice cream, and the contents even more scrumptious: chocolate jimmies, crumbled Butterfingers, rainbow jimmies, brownie chunks, nonpareils, M&M's, Haribo Gold-Bears—

Hey! We weren't out of gummy bears. Arthur was such a liar.

I picked up the box of Haribo Gold-Bears and wedged my fingers under one of the top flaps. Grampy was a certified cheapskate with the customers, but he ordered only the best for the store. He was always telling me how product quality was the key to his success. It certainly couldn't be customer service. Arthur would have driven us out of business long ago.

With an explosive rip, I popped the flap up and hefted out a clear bag of one-inch colored bears. Red, yellow, orange, green, clear . . . Mardi Gras beads couldn't have been more festive. I tugged and pulled at the frozen bag, but it didn't give. I finally just ripped it open with my teeth and helped myself to candy heaven. I swear, on the list of the best candies ever invented, gummy bears had to be in the top ten, if not the top three.

Grampy stored everything in the freezer because he thought food lasted longer that way, but I seriously doubted gummy bears ever spoiled. Not that I would've pointed this out to him, though, because sucking frozen gummy bears was the best. They were like bite-sized pieces of super-sweet, extra-tough Jell-O, and they took a long time to thaw in your mouth, which gave me time to savor them. I couldn't suck on thawed gummy bears. It was impossible and that was just the way of it. As soon as those hit my tongue, I automatically chewed them. It was some kind of reflex, maybe, like kicking the doctor in the shin when he hammered my knee. It had something to do with the gumminess, was my guess. The good thing was, even thawed gummy bears were a real workout. After years of chewing them by the case, my jaw was stronger than most people's, and Lucy said the best competitive eaters had the strongest jaw muscles.

I liked the clear-colored gummy bears the best. Most people thought they were supposed to be vanilla-flavored, but they weren't. They were pineapple. Yellows, though, those were from the Devil himself. On a good day, they tasted like Lemon Pledge. I could've paved the road from my house to Del Heiny Junior 13 with all the yellows I'd trashed in my life.

I picked out half a dozen clear bears and lined them up on the bottom shelf. "Hey, bears," I whispered. "Any of you got a cure for ice cream headaches?"

"Sherman!"

I whipped my head around toward the freezer door. *Ow!* My cranial pounding kicked up another notch.

Arthur hollered again from outside the freezer. "Sherman! You alive in there? I don't hear anything!"

"That's because I'm dead!" I hollered back.

"Don't eat the gummy bears!"

"I'm not eating the gummy bears! I do have self-control, you know!" Not that anyone thought I did.

I turned back to my gummy friends, slowly this time. I didn't want to jostle my aching brain. Like loyal little puppies, the gummies waited patiently for my attention, no judgment in their eyes, all unconditional love. That was nice for a change. I wasn't stupid, I knew what people thought the first time they looked at me: *big fat doughnut.* Shane said it, others thought it. It was all over their faces. But so what, who wasn't lugging around a little something extra? Movie stars, maybe, but I mean real life. Whenever I looked around at the mall and at school, mostly all I saw were people I'd never call skinny, not even accidentally. I swear, there were way more of us—us *big guys*—than them skinnies. Yet it was the skinnies we were supposed to bow to. Who put them in charge?

I picked up a second gummy bear and put it in my mouth.

Well, I've got news for you, Skinnies, this Big Guy has lots of friends. I'm no social outcast. And it would only get better when I stuffed Tsunami in the Nathan's Famous hot dog–eating contest. Then I'd be more than "that big guy who works in the ice cream parlor." I'd be Thuff Enuff, hot dog–eating champion.

I fished the first gummy bear out of my mouth—it was now warm and soft—and threw it hard at the icy wall. It stuck.

My stomach lurched again. I burped chocolate and pineapple and butyric acid. *Nasty.* To kill the taste, I dug a red gummy bear out of the bag and popped it into my mouth with the clear one. *There.* Cherry-pineapple, like a tropical drink. Just stick an umbrella toothpick in my mouth and I had my own piece of Hawaii in the Scoops-a-Million freezer.

Not that I planned to swallow my tropical delight. My stomach felt full up to my tonsils. I had to get used to the sensation, though, because with all the HDB training Lucy had scheduled for me, I'd probably be feeling this way a lot. Hey, every dream had its sacrifices. I just hoped I wouldn't suffer any more reversals of fortune. They could ruin an eater's career. Do it during a competition, get disqualified; do it after a competition, get laughed at. I had to conquer them. Besides, I hated feeling like my face was exploding.

I gave my hands a big shake. My fingers were going numb. While that was better than the finger cramping and forearm burning I'd suffered in the hours since becoming Ice Cream–Eating Champion of the Universe, it wasn't good for doing the inventory quickly. *Man, why does Grampy always schedule his supplier visits for when Mom and Dad are out of town?*

Because with Mom and Dad out of town, you're at his mercy to make his shopping list, you doofus. Sighing, I dug out the old parka and gloves that Grampy kept in the freezer and grabbed the clipboard. Might as well start the inventorying, it was going to be a long, cold night.

I put another clear bear in my mouth and started counting the Mint Chocolate Chip tubs. *One, two, three . . .*

CHAPTER 7

If there was a competitive sleeping circuit, they wouldn't let me in for a million bucks. Not after last night. Grampy's stupid inventorying took way longer than I'd expected thanks to my headache, so I didn't get home from Scoops until almost a quarter to two, which put me in bed sometime around two-fifteen. Mom would've had a cow if she'd been home. And just to reach home at that hideous hour, I'd had to ride through the park, right up that gnarly hill in the middle. Stupid Grampy refused to drive our truck, claiming the stick shift made his bum knee swell, so I couldn't call him to pick up me and my bike. Twice I almost laid my bike down and died in the grass. What genius puts a mountain in the middle of a park?

At least I had the satisfaction of knowing that I hadn't reversed my fortune in the freezer. Maybe sucking gummies kept my stomach in check. Or maybe the ice cream had frozen in my gut. Whatever the reason, I missed out on another Butyric Acid Event.

What really torpedoed my sleep, though, was the post-park segment of my night: I was up several times each hour sprinting to the bathroom. It turns out that putting that much dairy into the human stomach causes some gross and painful side effects. I ached everywhere . . . in my stomach, my shoulders, my head, and, big surprise, my intestines. Then my guts rumbled like a bulldozer for a while, eventually leading to a smellfest worse than any Butyric Acid Event. Then the bathroom trips started. How humiliating. Was that what professional eaters went through after they competed? They looked so cool and collected, it was hard to believe they got reduced to *that* when they left the competition table.

By sunup, my bloated belly had mostly settled. Even so, I'd tried to tell my mom on the phone that I was too sick to go to school. But she laid into me with all her motivational la-di-da and I caved. You would've thought she was blood-related to Grampy, the way she worked me. So that's how I found myself sitting on the school bus this morning, totally exhausted, with the rickety rocking motion working on me like a baby in a cradle. All around me, Plums in Halloween costumes were hollering and laughing and throwing an empty plastic pumpkin back and forth like a bunch of first graders. Next to me, Lucy was trying to show me a bunch of training graphs she'd worked up last night. Reading in a jostling bus wasn't kind on the eyes or the stomach. It didn't help that I was half comatose.

"I'm thinking we should start focusing on capacity instead of speed." She took a highlighter out of the front pocket of her dress and marked a row labeled HBD CONSUMPTION TALLY on a yellow, red, and green line graph. "Each box represents half a hot dog. This yellow line may only creep up in the short term, but over the long haul you'll see big improvement."

She put the highlighter back in her pocket. She was

wearing a Cinderella costume. Not the fancy, twirling-at-the-ball Cinderella that I'd expect a girl to want, but the scrungy, slaving-in-the-kitchen Cinderella, all sooty and smudged and ratty-haired. That was Lucy. Even on Halloween, she had to buck the system.

My costume, on the other hand, was a spit-and-polish Captain Quixote dress uniform. I liked the shoulder epaulets best. They stuck out way far and official-like, and the sun insignia on them almost glowed against the black fabric background. Then I had a row of medals on my chest showing all of Quixote's First Contacts with alien species. There were fourteen of them. Quixote was the most famous and daring and powerful of all starship captains ever. Everything that guy did screamed Destiny. I bet *he* never got stuck in the john with the runs.

"Now, Shermie," Lucy said, "I know capacity training isn't as exciting as speed-eating, but the final numbers are more dramatic, so you'll like that. Stomach capacity and stamina are where it's at in the twelve-minute competitions. Those heats aren't for the two-minute sprinters."

"Whatever you say." The Nathan's Famous hot dog–eating contest was a twelve-minute HDB eat-off, so this strategy of working on capacity rather than sprint speed sounded smart to me. Maybe eating fast was why the dogs didn't stay down. Even if I hadn't agreed with Lucy, I was too tired to argue anyway.

The plastic pumpkin whizzed at my face, but a Jedi leaned over our seat from behind and snagged it just before it popped me in the mouth. *Boy, he's lucky his reflexes are quick. If that pumpkin had hit me, I couldn't be responsible for my actions right now.*

"I put together some capacity growth graphs—oh, before

I forget!" She interrupted herself and reached into her backpack, digging out a plastic shopping bag. "Here."

I opened the bag. It was filled with packs of gum. "What's that for?"

"For you to chew. It will build up your jaw strength."

"I don't need to work on jaw strength. I eat gummy bears. I could chew a walnut shell into powder with this jaw."

The bus stuttered to a stop and three kids got on. One was dressed as a California raisin, another as Santa, and the third as a penguin.

"You sure?" She leaned in to inspect my jaw.

I turned away. "Yes, I'm sure. Trust me."

"If you say so." She took back the bag reluctantly and drew a giant X through the graph. As she turned to the next page in the binder, I let my head sag back against the seat. "I don't know if you'll like this next graph. Shermie? Shermie!"

I snapped fully awake.

"Sorry." I shook my head to get the blood moving through my brain. It didn't help much. "Do we need to do this now, Lucy? I'm really tired."

"We need to talk about this new graph sooner or later. I don't know how you're going to take it, though. . . ."

I rested my head on her shoulder. "I'm tired, Lucy. I was up late."

"Does your head still hurt?" Her voice was soft in my ear. She'd come by Scoops during her break last night to see why I hadn't met her in the food court. Gardo stood her up, too. I hadn't told her *why* my head hurt, though.

"No. It went away sometime last night. Or maybe this morning. Depends on if you count two a.m. as morning or

67

night." My eyelids slid closed. I swear, my head was just a big, empty, exhausted melon. And the rest of my body wasn't much better. My legs were stiff as wood and my arms were heavy as bricks. Getting out of bed this morning was one of the hardest things I'd ever done. "The rest of me feels like a train wreck, though. I had to ride my bike through the park last night."

"On that hill?"

"Yeah. At night." Her hair brushed my lips. She didn't smell like chocolate today, she smelled like candy canes. I bet she used peppermint mouthwash.

"You're working out?" she asked. "When did you start that?"

"I wasn't working out, I was working late. Stupid Grampy."

"You rode your bike up *that* hill." She was taking in that information. I could only imagine the visual she got in her head. "How did it go? Can you do it again?"

"What?" I sat up straight. *Ow.* "Are you insane? Why would I do it again?"

"Well, that's what I wanted to talk to you about." The bus shuddered to a stop. A ghoul and a nun got on. Lucy lowered her voice. "See, there's this theory. . . ."

She paused and looked around her to make sure no one was listening. Then, slowly, she reached down and turned the page in her binder. There, at the top of a new black and blue bar graph, was a handwritten label: BODY WEIGHT-TO-HBD RATIOS.

"I'm sorry, Shermie, I didn't make this up. It's common knowledge on the circuit. It explains why the big guys are losing to little guys by so much." She touched her finger to the colored bars. "See, Tsunami was only a hundred and thirty-one pounds when he got his first record of fifty-three and a half HDBs, and just one-sixty when he broke that record with fifty-three and three-quarters. For six years the closest anyone else could get was thirty-eight. And that guy was skinny, too. The big guys couldn't even get that many HDBs down. Even a hundred-and-five-pound lady kicked their butts with thirty-seven. Only a hundred and five pounds, Shermie; we're talking toothpick. They call her the Black Widow, and the big guys are terrified of her. She wins nearly every eat-off she's in. Isn't that cool? Anyway, no matter how you look at it, the tiny eaters are the big winners."

I stared at the graph but didn't say anything. What could I say? My left leg weighed more than the Black Widow.

Lucy went on hesitantly. "People think that the skinny guys are eating so much because their stomachs can expand more. The big guys' stomachs can't expand so far because . . . well, because they have this . . . restriction. . . ." She ran her hands back and forth across her belly. The plastic pumpkin hit her elbow and bounced into the aisle, where a fairy quickly snatched it up and threw it toward the front of the bus.

I focused my eyes on the pumpkin, watching as shrieking Plums batted it around the front bench. I was hoping Lucy wouldn't say what I thought she was going to say.

"They call it the Belt of Fat. And you have one, Shermie." She said it.

"I'm sorry, Shermie. But we have to talk about this."

No we don't. "I'm tired and I'm sore. I don't want to talk about training anymore."

"Shermie—"

"No." I scooted painfully over to the window and leaned my head against the glass. It vibrated against my temple.

What's poking me in my . . . Oh. I leaned forward and pulled my Galactic Warrior photon taser stick out of my back pocket. The stupid costume shop was out of taser holsters. Where was a space warrior supposed to store his taser if he didn't have a holster?

Whap! The pumpkin hit my chest and fell into my lap. The Jedi leaned over the back of my seat and nudged my aching shoulder. "Hey, big guy, give it here."

I picked up the pumpkin and dropped it out the window.

"Hey!" he shouted.

"Shermie!"

Lucy was shocked, but so what? I rose painfully and used every ounce of strength left in my arms to slide the window shut. I faced the Jedi. "It's gone. Deal with it."

"You suck, man." He dropped back into his seat. A chorus of *boos* rang out.

Stupid pumpkin. I sat down and leaned my head against the window again. Man, I felt like death warmed over. Maybe I should've tossed *myself* out the window. Wait, silly me, with this belt of fat, I wouldn't have fit. Silly, stupid, *fat* me.

* * *

Our clunker bus got to school about the same time as Mad Max did. I saw her through my window as we drove by the staff parking lot, which at that late time was full of cars but deserted of people. She was unloading a big crate from her trunk, struggling to slide it onto a wheeled metal cart. She must have had one serious costume if an entire crate was needed to get it to her room. She was draping a giant blanket over the cart when I lost sight of her behind the other buses.

I waited for the rest of the costumed Plums to clear the bus before I slogged off into the busy quad, right next to the tomato-shaped bus stop sign. All of its letters except the *st* in STOP had been scrawled over with mustard. Now it read MUSTARD! with a smiley face in the *D*.

Someone touched my shoulder. "Excuse me, Shermie."

I stumbled to the side as a yellow M&M with red hair pushed past me and stood under the sign. Tater stepped up and snapped a picture of the guy with his cell phone camera. Instead of "Cheese," the M&M shouted, "Go, Mustard!"

"Yeah, Auggie! That one's a keeper," Tater said. He waved his cell phone at me. "How about you, Shermie? You want one? They say a picture's worth a thousand words. Go, Mustard!"

"Nuh-uh," I muttered, turning away. I probably should've cheered, "Go, Mustard!" in solidarity or something, but there were no cheers in me this morning, not even for the Mustard Movement.

"Suit yourself." Tater and his M&M disappeared into the crowd.

My bus revved its engine. Lucy stepped up beside me and groaned. "Oh no. Just when I thought it couldn't get any worse."

She was looking past the MUSTARD! sign at our red blob of a school. Two janitors in green overalls were perched at the top of ladders on either side of the double doors. They were hanging a white banner with large red letters. IN DEL HEINY WE TRUST.

Culwicki was striking back.

"It's official, I am living a nightmare." Lucy gazed back longingly at the departing bus. "I gotta wake up from this. Someone please pinch me."

71

For an evil moment, I considered volunteering. *Fat belt, my foot.*

A sudden movement caught my eye. Across the crowded quad, the Finns had just burst out of a pack of yellow-hatted ninth graders and were now sprinting toward the janitors. They had double-barreled water rifles in their hands and were wearing court jester costumes with yellow bandannas on their faces.

Oh, c'mon. Like no one will recognize you giant idiots behind bandannas. What an embarrassment to the Mustard Taggers. *They* knew how to keep their identities secret.

When the Finns passed the front steps, they paused just long enough to blast each janitor in the back with long squirts of yellow goo and then plunge back into the crowd. Plums all over the quad erupted in cheers and chants of "Go, Mustard!" The startled janitors didn't even have time to figure out the direction of the attack.

"Yet more signs of intelligent life at Del Heiny Junior thirteen," Lucy muttered. "I bet the Finns are Aries. Their poor mom."

The pack of ninth graders that the Finns had launched from was clapping and high-fiving Shane, who was wearing a Henry VIII costume. It was all I could do not to run over and yank that crown down over his smug grin. Clearly he'd ordered the attack. I couldn't believe his nerve, twisting the mustard revolution for his own gain. He couldn't have spelled "mustard" to save his life! Shane was tainting The Cause. And though the janitors were hated by the rest of us Plums, they'd been nothing but nice to Shane and his Finns. No loyalty among jerks, I guess.

"Another day in paradise." Lucy sighed and trudged blobward. "At least this isn't Del Heiny Junior five. I'd kill myself if I was a number five Big Boy."

72

Now *I* gazed longingly after the bus. The stupid thing was long gone.

Lucy noticed I wasn't following. "Are you planning to stand there all day? C'mon, already, I'm not gonna bring you lunch out here. Chop, chop."

"Yes, sir, boss woman, *sir*," I muttered. *I wouldn't want to miss lunch. After all, I've got my fat belt to feed.*

Lucy stopped. "What did you say?"

"Nothing." I plodded past her and into the crowd. *Who does she think she is, anyway, calling me fat? Shane? I expect it from him. Some thanks I get for letting her be my coach. I swear, give someone a little power over you, and they forget what it means to be a friend.*

"Don't give me *nothing*." Lucy pushed through the crowd behind me. "I heard what you said. Come back here."

"Then why'd you ask?" I didn't even pause. I just marched through a pack of pea-greeners and up the mustard-splotched steps.

"I said come back here, Shermie. I want to know what you meant by that. Come back here!"

"You want to know what I meant? Fine, I'll tell you what I meant." I spun to face her, right under Culwicki's new banner. Paint fumes burned my bloodshot eyes. "See, there's this *theory*." I made quotation marks in the air with my fingers. "There are two kinds of people in this world, Lucy. People you can trust, and people you can't."

"What are you talking about?"

"The people you can trust are called friends. I have plenty of those. The people you can't trust are Shanes. They get a little control over you and then, *bam!*, all they want is more. Shanes suck."

She crossed her arms over her chest. "Oh, really? And in this *theory*, which one am I?"

"You"—I crossed my arms right back—"are a Shane."

"What? Who are *you* calling a Shane? You're the one who can't be trusted."

"Me?"

"Yeah, you. You *asked* me to help you, and now you're turning on me. For what? For telling you the truth? That's what a coach is supposed to do. You're such a Leo!"

She was at it again, flinging her fancy names around like they were contagious diseases. I turned to head into the school.

But she wasn't done. She shouted after me from the top step. "Self-centered, inconsiderate, flash-tempered, and totally *completely* ungrateful!" *Shut up, Lucy. Everyone in the quad can hear you!* "Saying I'm controlling you. Well, you certainly can't control your*self*. I swear, I should have seen this coming. Your horoscope this morning said—"

I spun on her again. "Who cares about some stupid horoscope?" Good, she looked shocked. *Take that, Coach.* "Unless it said watch out for traitors, I don't want to hear it."

I headed for the main hallway. This time she didn't follow. *Finally!*

The elevators had an OUT OF ORDER sign. Big deal. I wanted to take the stairs, anyway. I'd just imagine that each stair step was Lucy's or Shane's traitor face and stomp my way right to the top.

Tell me I have a fat belt. I'll show you fat belt. . . .

Daily Horoscope: Leo (July 23–August 22)

Today will be a totally rotten, sucky, nightmare of a day for you. If you can stay in bed, do. You'll be better off. If you can't, watch out for friends who want to control you. Business partners will prove untrustworthy, and the strategies you create together will explode in your face. Enemies and friends alike will strike at your weaknesses just to keep you under their thumbs. Do not let them tear you down or hurt your feelings. Hold your head high. Stay confident. You are a social giant and you have a Destiny. Especially avoid self-righteous, controlling Cancers who color code everything. Now is the time to tell people how it really is. Control your own Destiny and you will succeed.

CHAPTER 8

Stomping up three flights of stairs nearly killed me. My lungs were burning, my head was spinning, and my left calf felt like I was strangling it with a belt.

Gee, I just hope it's not a fat *belt.*

In the room, Mad Max was leaning against her podium, marking her roll book with a pencil. Behind her, HAPPY HALLOWEEN! stretched the entire eraser board in orange curlicue letters, with the *o* gussied up like a smiling pumpkin. She didn't have on a costume, and I didn't see her blanketed cart or wooden crate anywhere.

I made my way to my seat next to Tater. He wasn't wearing a costume, either. Just his usual yellow T-shirt. He might've been the first Plum to go yellow, and he had a huge photo collection of all the taggings thanks to his cell phone camera. He'd tried to convert me to yellow several times, but I was staying true to the Scoops white. Captain Quixote always said that a man wasn't a man unless he knew where his loyalties lay. *Hear that, Lucy?*

Besides, the Scoops white reminded people that I was their ice cream connection. It wasn't Hot Dog–Eating Champion of the World, but it got me some notice.

I thunked into my chair.

"Hey, hey, if it isn't Mr. Thuff Enuff himself," Tater said.

I froze in the middle of wiping sweat from my forehead. "What did you say?"

"Sherman, keep your voice down." Max didn't even look up from her roll book.

I lowered my voice so it blended in with the other chatting Plums. "How do you know about Thuff Enuff?"

"I know all about yesterday's cafeteria showdown, man." Tater clapped me on the back. "Everybody does. Way to go. You've got my loyalty forever. Shane is a jerk."

"Well, yeah, he is a jerk, but how do you know about Thuff Enuff—"

Thwank. A tiny wad of paper landed on my desk.

I looked to my right, where the paper was tossed from. Gardo was there, leaning forward over his new table, giving me the thumbs-up. He was wearing a skimpy white dress with humongous stuffed boobs, a huge platinum-blond wig, fake eyelashes, and blood-red lipstick. A drag queen Marilyn Monroe. Why was that not surprising?

I unwadded the paper. Gardo's handwriting was messy but legible:

Ladies and gentlemen, introducing our MAIN EVENT:
Hot on the heels of his first stunning upset comes
the Hulk Hogan of Hot Dogs . . .
the Rocky Balboa of the Buffet Table . . .
the next CHAMPION OF CHOMP . . .
the brave, the tough, the invincible
Sherman "THUFF ENUFF" Thuff!!!
** Are YOU Thuff Enuff? **

P. S. The word is out, Shermie.
P. P. S. You're welcome.

I looked up from the note. Leonard Chumley, sitting at the table with Gardo and dressed as a jack-o'-lantern, was also giving me the thumbs-up. And so was the chef at the table next to them, Truman Banks. And so was the sheeted ghost next to Truman, and the octopus next to the ghost. One by one, Plum by Plum, Gardo's side of the room went quiet and thumbs went up.

Goose bumps rippled up the back of my neck. There were at least a dozen thumbs aimed at the sun, and every single one was for me. *Me.* Shermie Thuff. Amazing! Gardo was doing exactly what he said he'd do, spinning the hype. And Gardo knew *everybody*. By lunch, I could be class president! This Thuff Enuff thing was actually working. I was getting a rep. I knew I could count on Gardo. *Now* that's *a friend.*

With adrenaline rushing through my veins, I made eye contact with my best buddy and give him a solid two thumbs up back. *You're the man, Edgardo Esperaldo.*

I scanned the room in search of more thumbs. Sure enough, they went up all over. Except for the Finn's, though. When he caught my eyes on him, he put up an entirely different finger for me. But who cared? The rest of the class loved me. Fame was an awesome thing.

Lucy came into the room just as the tardy bell rang. Max stopped her as she crossed behind the podium, and the two had a muted back-and-forth. Finally, Lucy took Max's offered keys and rushed out of the room. I bet Max left her lunch in her car again. Lucy loved getting picked to fetch things for teachers.

Now and then during Max's lecture on the industrial uses of recycled eggshells, costumed Plums went to the pencil sharpener to sharpen their number twos. They had to pass me on the way to the sharpener. Every single one clapped me on the back and whispered stuff like, "Atta boy, Thuff" or "You're the man, Thuff." It was better than any sugar rush. No way was I sleepy anymore.

Lucy missed the whole lecture. Boy, was she going to be bummed. That girl hated playing catch-up.

In the hall after class, more Plums clapped my back and cheered me on. "Way to go, Thuff . . . Get him, Thuff . . . Are YOU Thuff Enuff?" With my Captain Quixote uniform on, I felt like a war vet at a ticker-tape parade. *Hail, the conquering hero!* They knew I'd wipe out Tsunami at the hot dog table. *Ladies and gentlemen, Thuff Enuff has entered the building!* The best, though, had to be when Elizabeth Grace batted her eyelashes at me and said she thought I was brave.

At our locker, I found out that Gardo had told my "Are YOU Thuff Enuff?" slogan to some scrub wrestlers at their early morning workout, and it'd spread faster than syrup on a pancake. I guess Plums respected greatness when they saw it.

"I got the ball rolling for you," Gardo said. "Now it's in your court." He adjusted his wig and straightened his boobs before handing me a white plastic shopping bag. "Here, put this on."

"What is it?"

"It's your new costume."

"What's wrong with the costume I'm wearing?" I reached into the bag and pulled out a white satin boxing robe and a pair of American flag swim trunks. Two boxing gloves sat at the bottom of the bag, along with a pair of blue-striped wrestling shoes.

"That Captain Spaceman look is doing nothing for you,"

Gardo said. "You need to take advantage of the Thuff Enuff momentum. Put it on."

"But this is the dress uniform. It's got medals."

"I don't care if it has a jet pack in the pants. You're Thuff Enuff, now. See?" He took the robe and held it up. It unfurled, revealing red stitching on the back:

I am
Thuff Enuff
Are YOU?

"Trust me, Shermie," he continued, "your image is in a fragile stage right now. Don't let it die."

He did have a point. And at least the costume wasn't a giant hot dog suit. "Okay. I'll go change."

"Atta boy."

But as I turned to go to the john, I saw something white on the side of his neck, just under the edge of his wig. "What's that?"

"What? Oh, nothing."

"It's a piece of tape." I reached up to pull it off.

He batted my hand away. "Watch the stitches!"

"Stitches? What happened?"

"Who cares? It's stupid."

"I care. What happened?"

"Nothing." He shoved at the junk in our locker so he could close the door. "I got cut by a fingernail at practice yesterday, that's all."

"What, were you wrestling a girl?"

"Ha. Ha." He pulled on the lock to check it. "It wasn't any big deal. When you're an athlete, stuff happens." He pushed by me, surprisingly nimble on the Marilyn heels. I would've killed myself on those things.

I hustled after him, but my photon taser stick jiggled out of my pocket several times before I caught up at the water fountain. I almost left the stupid thing on the floor the third time it fell because my left calf tightened up so much bending down to pick it up.

"So that's why you were a no-show at the food court last night," I said, "the stitches?"

"Yeah, sorry about that, man. Now like I was saying, you gotta pick up the ball and run with it. From now on, start acting your part. Selling Thuff Enuff is all in the attitude; you have to earn your legend."

"I have attitude."

"What, like, 'Hey, everybody look at me while I run through the hedge because I'm late for class' attitude? Oh, don't give me that innocent face. I saw you do it." He lowered his voice to an intense whisper. "You're on the road to glory now, man. It doesn't matter if you're at school or in an eat-off, you need to *intimidate*. You got what it takes to make people notice you, you always have. But yesterday at lunch you took it to a whole new level. When you stood up to Shane, you actually made people *wish they were you*."

That's what they were excited about? That I stood up to Shane? But . . . I *didn't* stand up to Shane. I nearly got my butt kicked. If Culwicki had come into that cafeteria just a few seconds later, he would've had to step over my dead body to correct Shane's Sugarfoot. But hey, I wasn't about to open my big mouth and point out this technicality to anyone. In junior high, false fame was better than no fame at all. All that integrity stuff adults liked to preach about was for their world, not for underclass Plums at Del Heiny Junior 13. I'd just have to take this tough-guy rep and refocus it on my competitive eating, that was all.

"So you really think Plums wish they were me?" Me was

the last person I'd wanted to be yesterday, and that was the truth.

"Heck, yeah. Lots of them. You didn't have to throw a single punch, man. All you did was stand your ground when Shane got in your face. You commanded that room." He leaned in closer and stabbed his finger into my chest. *Ow.* "*That's* the attitude I'm talking about."

The trouble was, I didn't *have* the attitude he was talking about.

But I could act. "That? That's nothing." I whipped out my taser stick and posed like Captain Don Quixote in a shoot-out. "I'm *all* attitude, muchacho."

Gardo laughed. "You're all crazy, muchacho." He blew an air kiss at me with his big red lips and tottered off toward our Spanish class.

Grunting, I worked my sleep-deprived body back into a normal standing position and holstered my taser stick down the back of my pants. Then I plodded over to the bathroom to change into my new costume. Along the way, I rubbed the sore spot on my chest where Gardo had poked me.

* * *

Gardo said I had to work on my attitude, and I decided to start at my feet. After all, a guy's attitude showed in his walk. I needed one that was worthy of the Thuff Enuff name. So between classes I worked on holding my head up high and tucking my shoulders back, trying to get as much swagger going as my exhausted body would allow. The wrestling shoes Gardo gave me with my costume were pretty comfy for swaggering, actually. Way better than my clunky Galactic Federation boots. Those things must've had moon rocks in the soles.

82

When Gardo saw my cool new walk at lunch, he halted in his tracks. "What's wrong with you? Did you twist your ankle or something?"

"No. This is my new walk. Like it?"

"It looks like you sat on a plunger and can't pull it out."

"Now who's the funny guy?"

"Well, that's what it looks like. Here, watch me."

Even in high heels, Gardo could cop attitude when he wanted. He balanced his tray on his left hand and let his other arm hang by his side and slightly behind him, swinging it very slightly and just a bit stiff-elbowed behind his butt every other step. I'd seen rapper guys do that in videos. Now *that* was a walk with attitude. Even for a guy in drag.

I followed him to our table, working to get the stiff-elbow thing timed just right.

I'd just reached the table when someone came up behind me and clapped me solidly on the back. *Ow!* I arched from the stinging impact. *Jeez!* Why did guys have to hit each other all the time? I turned to find Kenny Goodman dressed as a Del Heiny Junior 13 janitor.

"Hey, Thuff. I'm with you, man," Kenny said. Then he climbed onto the bench right where I was going to sit. "You just lead the way. I'm with you."

Swell. Now there's nowhere for me to sit. "Think you could be with me a few inches to the left? Shove over."

"Oh, right. Sorry, man."

Even after he scooched left, there still wasn't much room for me to sit. When did my table get so crowded? Leonard, Kenny, William, Truman, Tucker, Brit, Jeff, Tommy . . . they were all sitting there giving me thumbs-up signs between bites. They'd never sat at my table before.

Slowly, I grinned. The Thuff Enuff legend was already working its magic. *Dang, I'm gonna listen to Gardo more often!* I kicked my leg up over the bench and squeezed in between Kenny and Gardo. Fans like rubbing elbows with their heroes, so Kenny probably felt privileged.

Most of the guys at my table were in costume, as were most of the Plums in the cafeteria. It was quite a sight. The sun above us was shining down through the sunroof on strange creatures, famous people, and mythical wonders who were dunking corn dogs in ketchup, chugging milk from brown and white cartons, and blowing straw wrappers into neighbors' ears. At one of the pea-greener tables, Babe Ruth was using a baseball bat to test the strength of a knight's armor. Two tables to their left, Jabba the Hutt threw a Tater Tot at Mark Twain, knocking Mark's mustache into the Pillsbury Doughboy's ketchup bowl. At the cash register, a towering Count Dracula gnawed the neck of a squealing French maid. The cafeteria lady didn't even notice the bloodsucking; she just sat there with her eyes glazed and her hand out, waiting for the vampire's money like a human vending machine.

Despite the Halloween festivities and my newfound fame, I was starting to get nervous. The cafeteria was Shane's turf; sooner or later he'd show up. He probably knew I was becoming famous at his expense and wanted to knock me back into place. I couldn't guess how he'd do it, but the smart money was on pain and humiliation.

I started looking around, wondering how I could make a smooth exit if things went bad. Maybe I shouldn't have been in there today. After all, it was one thing to act ballsy off the cuff like I did yesterday—well, like they thought I did yesterday—but today I had time to premeditate. And premeditation was where the big mind game happened. That's when you knew whether you had big enough cojones to actually do the thing you were premeditating. And right then, my cojones felt about the size of M&M's. The kind without nuts.

"Here, I got extra ketchup today." Gardo tossed a handful of packets across the table to me. He had two hamburgers on his tray and a large plate of fries. I had three corn dogs and some Tots. Our ketchup requirements were high.

I picked up a packet that had landed on top of the ASB pumpkin centerpiece, which now sported a yellow mustache. The Mustard Taggers certainly had an eye for detail. *Go, Mustard.*

"I am *so hungry,* man." Gardo jammed a handful of ketchupless fries into his mouth.

"Do tell," I said. Lipstick smeared his upper lip. "You have the table etiquette of a gorilla, Ms. Monroe."

"Wrestlers don't need manners," he said through the fries. "But I need food. This Friday's practice meet against the Del Heiny Junior nine was just canceled."

"The Beefsteaks?"

"None other. Our fine janitors left a hose running outside the wrestling room, and the water leaked in and ruined all the mats. We can't use the Beefsteaks' gym, either. It's being renovated. Which means I get one more week of not worrying about making weight. I swear, I could *eat* a wrestling mat."

I felt another tap on my shoulder and turned to find Tater standing there with Tweedle dee and Tweedle dum behind him. Both Tweedles wore yellow hats and yellow wristbands with their costumes, and all three guys had loaded food trays.

"Mind if we sit here, Thuff?" Tater asked.

"Here? Yeah. I mean, no, I don't mind. If you can make room."

"We can make room." Tater waved up the Tweedles and they all scrunched and scooted and squeezed until they'd worked themselves onto the bench on Gardo's side. Elbows banged as they ripped at their ketchup packets. Tater took his beloved green marker out of his back pocket and stuck it over his ear. Maybe it was poking him in the rear.

My lab partner introduced the Tweedles as his friends Roshon and Runji. They were cousins. I'd seen them in the halls but had never met them.

"Hey, Thuff," Tater said. "Rumor has it you're the next hopeful for speed-eating champion or something like that. Why didn't you tell me? Is it true that you speed-ate five gallons of ice cream in three minutes yesterday?"

"Five gallons in three minutes?" *Is he nuts?* "Are you crazy?"

"That's what I heard."

"Well you heard wrong—"

"It was *twelve* minutes," Gardo interrupted. "That's a regulation heat. And he didn't even bat an eye."

I shot Gardo a look, like, *What are you talking about?*

He shot back a look: *Shut up and let me handle this.* "Shermie's training to take on Tsunami," he announced. "That's the fastest hot dog eater in the world. Seventy hot dogs in twelve minutes."

Seventy?

"Seventy?" Tater exclaimed. "Gimme a break. Nobody can eat that many hot dogs. And not in twelve minutes."

"Tsunami can," Gardo assured him. "He's a medical marvel. The guy's stomach expands like a popcorn bag in a microwave. But Shermie's going to beat him. He's got the Mustard Yellow International Belt of Hot Dog–Eating in the bag."

"Wow."

The guys were impressed. I wasn't. Gardo was lying through his teeth. Tsunami's record was fifty-three and three-quarters HDBs. And that was pretty near inhuman. Seventy wasn't possible, at least not without some kind of alien stomach transplant.

But Gardo was still running at the mouth. "Ice cream is part of Shermie's cross-training. He's already an expert at it. Five gallons in twelve minutes is nothing. He'll beat that before the week's out."

"See, I told you Chad doesn't lie," Tater told Tweedle Dee, AKA Runji.

Who's Chad? Does everyone know about the ice cream? Oh no—Lucy!

Runji was intrigued. "So Thuff—"

"Thuff *Enuff*," Gardo corrected.

"Sorry. So Thuff *Enuff*, even if you can eat that many hot dogs—"

"Oh, he can."

Shut up, Gardo!

"—how can you eat them that fast?"

All eyes were on me, even Gardo's. He could spin the hype, but he didn't have a clue when it came to actual techniques. Luckily, Lucy had explained those to me already.

"Well . . ." I said, trying to remember them all, "there are several techniques. I haven't settled on one yet."

"Like?"

"Well, like the Chunk 'n' Dunk. That's when you dunk the whole HDB—that's the hot dog and the bun to us eaters—you dunk the whole HDB, then eat it, then dunk it, then eat it."

"What do you dunk it in?"

87

"Water." I shrugged. "Nothing fancy. Or you can eat the HDB regular, just like anybody who eats a hot dog. That's the Traditional Style. Then there's the Japanese Method. In that one, you pull the dog out of the bun, then you eat just the hot dog, followed by just the dunked bun."

"Is that how Tsunami does it?" Gardo was just as fascinated as the others. See, there were things I knew better than him.

"No," I answered, warming up to the spotlight. "He uses the Solomon Method. He pulls the dogs out of the buns, then breaks them in half and eats both halves at the same time. It's pretty cool to watch, actually." My mind replayed the online footage Lucy showed me of Tsunami winning one of his six Nathan's Famous contest titles. It was like watching a ballet dancer or something. He had grit and timing and didn't falter a single bite. "He chomps the halves side by side in three real fast bites. That's it, three. Then he breaks the bun in half, dunks it, and chomps it down the same way. I don't think the guy even swallows. The food just disappears."

As I explained this, I monitored the room. No sign of Shane or the Finns.

"Well, Thuff *Enuff*," Tater said, "I take my hat off to you. I had no idea that this whole semester I've been sitting next to a world champion hot dog eater in the making. And a fearless anti-Shaner, too. Walk silently but carry a big stick, eh? I like that in a Plum. Someday that robe of yours will be hanging on Culwicki's Wall of Fame with the other Del Heiny Junior 13 sports greats."

Gardo grinned wide, clearly pleased with himself for making me wear the boxing robe. I had to admit, he was right about that. I grinned back at him. I was lucky to have him as a friend.

"Gardo's singlet will be up there, too," I said. "You'll see, he's going to wrestle right to the top."

"If the janitors don't burn down the wrestling gym first," Gardo muttered.

"That's so messed up," William said. "Can't they move the meet to the main gym?"

"No. That's already reserved for the girls' JV prep badminton team." Gardo stuffed several fries into his mouth at once.

Tater looked like he had an opinion of badminton—and it wouldn't be a flattering one—when Lucy came up, interrupting him. Ignoring me, she set a white plastic grocery bag on the table and motioned to Gardo with her hand. "Do you mind?"

He dutifully scooted over, which made Tucker, William, and Tommy have to scoot over, too. William was hanging so far off the end of his bench that I could only figure he was holding on by a single butt cheek.

"Thank you." Lucy settled in without acknowledging my presence. She caught a glimpse of Tater as she settled onto the bench. "Nice earring," she told him.

He scowled, then took his lucky green marker from behind his ear and stuffed it back in his pocket, elbowing people in the process.

Lucy reached into her plastic bag and pulled out a container of salad with a clear plastic lid, a small cup of brothy soup, and another small cup of lumpy white stuff that better be cottage cheese. *What did she do, steal Max's lunch?*

I tried to work on my own lunch, but it was just too weird to be sitting two feet from Lucy's face and not talking to her. She was making such a production of opening all her containers and unwrapping her spork . . . I bet she *wanted* me to notice. Well, I wasn't going to.

89

I ate a French fry doused in ketchup and watched the ceiling. For a minute. Then I just couldn't help it, my eyes slid back to Lucy. She was prodding her fluffy pile of green, purple, and red leaves with her spork like it was some strange Mad Max experiment. There were some stringy orange things in the salad, and a few black things, too. Definitely not anything I'd want in my mouth. But even more disturbing was that there wasn't a single tomato as far as I could see. What was Lucy thinking?

"You're gonna get suspended," I blurted before I could stop myself. She didn't look up. Leonard and Tater did. *Shoot. Now I'm committed.* I pointed at her lunch. "You can't have that here. None of that is ketchup-dunkable."

She reached into the bag again. "Neither is what's between your legs."

The guys exploded with laughter. I quickly raised my soda can for them to see. Lucy was no dummy; she knew where I stashed my soda every day.

She had a sly smile on her lips as she pulled out napkins and blotted the corners of her mouth. She probably thought that was a good shot.

Well, she could take all the potshots she wanted, but an illegal soda between my legs wasn't a plate of illegal food on the table for all the world to see. She was just asking for trouble. Culwicki had drilled and drilled and drilled us that first week of school: *All cafeteria food must be ketchup-dippable.* He'd lectured everyone about it in the daily bulletin for a week, and we'd received special mailings at home about it. He was probably afraid of losing precious funding if we ticked off Del Heiny. All the mustard graffiti around campus must've had him crapping bricks already. And it was only escalating. Just minutes after lunch started today

90

they'd found the ketchup packet bin filled with mustard packets. I swear, I'd never seen the cafeteria ladies move so fast. They had the bin refilled to the brim with red packets within minutes.

It was no joke. With a lunch of salad, soup, and white gunk, Lucy was definitely walking on thin ice.

"There's not even a tomato in that salad," I warned her. "I'm telling you, if one of those janitors sees you with that, you'll get suspended."

"How can I get suspended for eating healthy?"

"This is healthy." I pointed to each item on my tray. "Protein in the burgers, grains in the buns, veggies in the French fries and the pickles. And it's all dippable in ketchup—yet *another* vegetable." I raised my milk carton in a toast. "Plus, I'm washing it all down with a nice, cold box of milk. It does a body good." Gardo and I bumped our cartons together. "Cheers!"

The other guys bumped their cartons, too, "Hear! Hear!"

Lucy observed this scene quietly for a moment. "What about mustard?"

"What about it?" I wiped off my milk mustache with my sleeve.

"You like your burgers with mustard. Last week at McDonald's, I had to go back and ask for a bunch of mustard packets for you."

"So what?" I said. "They don't have mustard here."

"Oh yes they do." Kenny and William laughed and flashed mustard packets hidden in their fists. They must've swiped them before the cafeteria ladies swooped in. Like Tater, Kenny and William were hard-core Yellow Shirts, sticking with their yellow gear today instead of wearing a Halloween costume.

Lucy poked her salad with her spork. "My point is, they've outlawed mustard."

I shrugged. "Yeah. So?"

"So, you're going to be the hot dog–eating champ, aren't you? Where's the big eat-off held every year?"

"You know where it's held," I answered. To the guys I said, "At Nathan's Famous."

"Precisely," she said.

I shook my head in confusion. "You lost me."

Gardo was just as confused. "What's Nathan's?"

"Nathan's *Famous*. It's only the most famous hot dog place in the world, Mr. Image," Lucy said. "Or should I say *Miss* Image?"

Gardo winked his false lashes and tipped his wig like a true gent.

"Nathan's Famous is a Coney Island landmark," Lucy said. "Every Fourth of July they hold a huge hot dog–eating contest. It's the Super Bowl for competitive eaters. Shermie, what's your cupboard stocked with at home?"

I had the feeling I was being set up, so I didn't answer.

Gardo did. "He's got mustard in his cupboard. I've seen it. Bottles and bottles of it."

"What kind of mustard?" Lucy asked.

Leonard gave it a try: "French's Classic Yellow?"

Lucy shook her head, then stared at me calmly, waiting for my answer.

I didn't want to answer, but the silence was excruciating. "Nathan's Famous mustard," I finally said.

Nathan's Famous mustard was the highest-rated condiment in the Sherman T. Thuff Book of Good and Tasty Things. I slathered it on everything, not just hot dogs. I even tried it on pizza once. Lucy herself had three pieces of that brilliance. She knew I was crazy about the stuff, and she knew that when I first heard that Nathan's Famous wasn't just a mustard brand but an actual restaurant, one where they hold *the* main eating event of the year, that was what convinced me that choosing hot dogs as my trademark food was destiny. But what did that have to do with her soup and salad?

"I still don't get your point," I said. "So they don't serve mustard in the school cafeteria. So what?"

"So you're letting them dictate which condiment you can put on your food. *Condiment,* Shermie. If that isn't Big Brother, I don't know what is. Who are they to tell us what food we can or can't eat, let alone which condiment we top it with? What if I want relish? I'm gonna get kicked out of school for *relish*?" She pulled a big, shiny yellow lemon out of her grocery bag, scored it with her fingernail, then squeezed the pee-colored juice onto her lettuce. "I will not give in to the Man. Del Hemy may own Culwicki, but it doesn't own the universe."

"She's got a point there," Tater said, tapping his Yellow-Shirted heart.

"Of course I do." She stirred the juice and salad with her finger. Then she stabbed her spork into the bed of colorful leaves and raised several pieces daintily to her mouth. It was as mesmerizing as watching Tsunami execute the Solomon Method.

"That's your lunch?" I'd pass out from starvation if all I ate was salad with a squirt of lemon, a few sips of broth, and some goopy cheese.

"It is."

"I swear," Tater said, shaking his head, "I don't get girls. Lettuce and a squirt of lemon juice? Next thing, you'll be pulling rice cakes and tofu out of your backpack. Are you on a diet or something?"

She made a face when he said "tofu." "I'm not *on* a diet. Everything anybody eats is part of their diet. I'm watching what I eat."

"Why?" I asked. She looked fine to me.

Gardo fielded that one. "Because she's a girl, and girls do weird things with food, man. Don't think about it too hard." He chomped into his second burger. Ketchup dribbled down his chin like blood. "*Man!* Whoever invented hamburgers should get the Nobel Prize."

"No way," I protested. "The inventor of pizza should get it."

"Over my dead body," Leonard cried. "Ice cream wins, hands down."

"No," I countered. "It can't—"

"Don't you argue with me, Thuff Enuff." He cut me off. "You know exactly what I'm talking about. The way you trained with that ice cream yesterday . . . I don't know how you didn't puke from it all."

Lucy's eyes snapped up from her salad. "Ice cream training?"

Gardo nearly choked on his burger.

"Yeah," Leonard said. "Didn't he tell you? He totally pigged—*ow!*" The whole table jolted as he grabbed his leg and glared at Gardo.

Nice shot, Gardo.

Lucy drilled me with her eyes. "Shermie? What's he talking about?"

"Leonard is an idiot," Gardo said quickly, returning Leonard's glare. "He's got Shermie confused with someone else."

It was no use. Once Lucy sank her teeth into something, she didn't let go. "Shermie . . ."

Leonard and his big mouth. I wracked my brain for an answer that wouldn't get me killed. What did a guy have to do for a little divine intervention around here?

"Out of the way, *scrub*," a voice boomed across the cafeteria.

My stomach seesawed. *Shane.* His kind of intervention was far from divine.

But at least he got Lucy's eyes off me. She and the rest of the Plums couldn't help but watch as the ninth grade king strode toward his table with Gabriella Marquez, the hottest eighth grader in the whole school. Gabriella was wearing her own crown and cape and hanging on his arm.

"We got a lady coming through," he declared. "Make way." Another scrub was getting a promotion from Shane.

Using his scepter, Shane poked Plums out of the path to his table. Gabriella was smiling and waving at everyone she passed, looking royally happy. Plodding behind them, the Finns looked royally unhappy in their green tights, red tunics, and floppy green-and-red jester hats. It amazed me what traitors would do to stay in the upper class's good graces.

A hush settled on the cafeteria as a roomful of eyes flicked from Shane to me to Shane to me. The Plums seemed to be waiting for something big to happen. Something big . . . like me.

Quick, Shermie, do something. "Stupid shoe," I blurted then ducked below the table.

"Hey, quit pushing." Kenny didn't appreciate being shoved aside, but that's what he got for squeezing himself in there to begin with. It was a table, not a clown car.

Tugging and twisting at my shoelace, I stayed down there for a while, considering my options. I could sit there and act like everything was normal, just go about my business and hope I'd fly under Shane's radar. Or I could hightail it out of there. That second idea sounded like a winner. Too bad the exit was on the other side of Shane's section. I'd have to be sly about reaching it, waiting for just the right moment, some kind of distraction, maybe. . . .

The cafeteria chatter was picking up again. Maybe the Plums had forgotten about me? I peeked under my armpit. King Shane and his jesters were now seated.

Kenny nudged me in the ribs. "You done yet, Thuff Enuff? My back is cramping. I need to sit straight."

Tommy nudged me on my other side. "Me, too, man."

"All right already." I elbowed both of them back, then twisted and shoved my way to sitting again.

Tommy nudged me again. "There's Shane, man. See him?"

"Will you stop with the poking? I see him." Even as I said that, Shane turned his head and saw me right back. *Crap.*

He started to stand, but Queen Gabriella stayed him with a hand on his arm. Maybe she didn't want her royal "coming out" ruined; I didn't know. But whatever her motive, I was thankful for it. Shane looked at me, then at her, then at me again. Eventually he relaxed back onto his bench.

"What are you waiting for, Thuff Enuff?" Kenny asked. Ketchup dripped off of his Tot, right onto his stupid pickle-colored overalls. "Go kick his butt."

"Yeah, man," Tater urged, "go show him who's Thuff Enuff."

Gardo set down what was left of his hamburger. "I don't know, guys . . ."

"Kick whose butt?" Lucy followed Kenny's pointing finger.

The cafeteria was crowded, but it was obvious who he was pointing at. "Shane's?"

"The one and only." Kenny rubbed his hands together, the green vulture. "This'll be great. Shane's had this coming for a long time. We've been betting on who'd do it. My money was on Tater." He laughed as Tater pegged him with a Tot. "I wish I brought my video camera. The great Shane is going *down*."

Lucy stared at me for a second like I was crazy, then she sized up Kenny, then Gardo, and then the rest of the guys at our table. Finally she picked up her mangled lemon again, inspected it, and said, real calmly, "You are not kicking anyone's butt, Shermie." She licked the yellow rind and made a sour face. "You're training tonight. You need those hands for stuffing food into your mouth. They cannot be broken from pounding in someone's face."

Oh man, I love Lucy. "Well, okay . . . if that's the way it has to be." I tried to sound resigned as I shrugged helplessly. "Sorry, guys, an athlete has to do what his coach tells him."

"Aw, man." Runji muttered something about girls and sports, but part of it was in another language, so I didn't quite follow it. And I probably didn't want to.

Eventually the guys started talking about Gardo's canceled meet again. Then Tater shoved a Tot up his nose, and Runji and Roshon laughed at him hysterically. They seemed to forget all about Shane.

Across from me, Lucy worked on her salad, trying to spear the soft leaves with her spork. When she finally gave up and just picked some up with her fingers, her eyes caught mine. I winked to let her know we were friends again. I wasn't in a bad mood anymore, with the Thuff

Enuff rep on the rise and all, and she did have my back when I was in need.

She lowered the leaves. "Something in your eye?"

"No. Nothing's in my eye." *Jeez, can I just do my thing without her always calling me out?*

She picked up her lemon again and dug into it with her fingernail. A blast of lemon juice squirted across the table at me.

"Ow!" I grabbed the left side of my face. Now I *did* have something in my eye—and it stung!

"Sorry." She smiled and licked the lemon again.

"You did that on purpose!"

"I did not. There, go over to that water fountain and wash out your eye. When you come back, we'll talk about refocusing your training. And your attitude."

Refocus? Who needs to refocus? I don't want to refocus . . . I hustled to the fountain, one hand over my stinging eye. Halfway there, my good eye caught sight of Principal Culwicki running into the cafeteria wearing his green college wrestling singlet.

"Surprise!" he shouted. Plums exploded in shrieks and whistles. "Happy Halloween!" He dropped down into some freakish wrestling lunge and growled.

I slapped my hand over my other eye and spun away. *Ah!* There had to be a law against what I'd just seen! At the very least, several hundred Plums were now in need of serious psychological counseling.

I hunched over the fountain and splashed water in both eyes, as desperate to wash away that image as the lemon juice.

It took a while—not that I was completely sad about it with Culwicki's singlet running free—but eventually my eyes stopped burning. By then, lunch was pretty much over. Dracula, Jabba, Doughboy, and all the other creatures and Yellow Shirts were trickling out of the cafeteria and down the halls to class. With no showdown at the OK Corral on today's menu, there was no reason to hang around.

Shoot. In all the lunchtime excitement, I'd eaten only a few Tots. I'd have to eat my corn dogs on the way to class. At least the fizzies would be bubbled out of my soda by then, so I'd be able to chug that quickly.

The bell rang as I headed back to grab the food from my tray, officially ending this round of lunch with my new rep—and my face—intact.

IT'S INTERMISSION TIME, FOLKS!

♫ ♫

Let's all go to the Lunch Room,
let's all go to the Lunch Room,
let's all go to the Lunch Room
to get Ourselves a Treat.

De-li-cious things to eat.
The Corn Dogs can't be beat.
The bubbly drinks are just daaaandy,
the Tater Tots and the caaaandy.
So, let's all go to the Lunch Room
to get Ourselves a Treat.

Let's all go to the Luuuunch Rooooom,
to get Ourselves a Treeeeeeeeat . . .
♫ ♫

CHAPTER 9

Halloween used to be one of my favorite holidays. I'd buy a cool sci-fi costume and be on the sidewalks by sunset, whisking my pillowcase door to door, charming and coaxing my way to the pick of everyone's candy bowls. Then, sometime around ten o'clock, I'd drag my bulging bag home and spend another blissful hour sorting the booty: *Sour Worms, SweeTarts, Milky Way, Sugar Daddy, more SweeTarts, Milk Duds, Snickers, Twizzlers, Twizzlers again, Circus Peanuts—yuck, trash those—more Swee-Tarts, Snickers, Snickers again, Pop Rocks* . . . Just a few hours of work scored me a candy stash that lasted for weeks. What a brilliant holiday.

Then my stupid body went and got too tall for Halloween, ruining everything. The candy-givers cut me off. "You're too old for this, sonny" "Give it up, kid" "No way, dude. Buy your own stinkin' candy." Oh, the agony.

I even tried draping a sheet over my head and slunching down so people wouldn't know my age. Mrs. Mortimer next door was the only one who fell for that. She gave me a box of raisins. What planet did that woman come from? That was a good way to get your house egged.

This year, I'd just resigned myself to doling out candy to other kids. After last night's inventory and post–ice cream agony, I was pretty wiped, anyway. A big candy-collecting mission would have been tough. And really, it wasn't so bad passing out the loot. Kids had to beg and charm *me*.

As far as my parents knew, Grampy was supposed to be there supervising me as I doled, but of course he wasn't. He and I struck a deal on that a long time ago. As long as I promised not to set the house on fire, I could take care of myself when my parents were gone. So when he was home, he mostly just hung out in his room watching TV. Tonight, though, he and Arthur were at Scoops together.

Gardo was with me instead. Lucy probably would have been there, too, only I kind of forgot to invite her. That is, I was going to tell her about it, but then we had that fight before school and then lunch was over before I could say anything about it and then she didn't show up for the bus ride home and then it was just too late to call her. Anyway, she probably would've given me grief about the ice cream thing if she had come, so maybe I was kind of glad she wasn't there.

Gardo hadn't even asked about Lucy. But his memory went south when he started all this no-eating-cutting-weight business last week. Not that the guy was starving right now, though. At lunch he'd wolfed down all that food after hearing about the canceled wrestling meet, and now he was going to town on my candy bars. Not that I could blame him—it was hard to resist my Halloween choice: Three Musketeers.

Sure, Snickers was supposed to be the most popular candy bar, but I only bought the kind of candy I'd want to get as a trick-or-treater, and Three Musketeers was hands down my favorite. It had the perfect balance of densely fluffed chocolate center to delicately thick chocolate shell. There were no nuts or crispies or caramel or anything else to throw off its pure harmony. It was the Yin-Yang Zen King of candy bars. The brilliance of that bar was lost on Gardo, though. He was on the couch in our living room, kicked back in jeans and his red team shirt instead of his Marilyn drag, stuffing his face and hollering at a wrestling marathon on TV. I didn't sweat his bingeing, though, because I'd bought ten bags of the minibars, so there was more than enough for him to chow down and me to still meet trick-or-treater demand. Besides, it was cheap payment for his launching of the Thuff Enuff legend. When I started raking in prize money, Gardo would get his rightful cut.

Gardo was a good guest. He never arrived empty-handed. He'd showed up at my door tonight with a six-pack of Pepsi. Add that to my mini Three Musketeers bars, and we had one finger-lickin' Halloween feast. Without his contribution, we'd have had to chase our Three Musketeers down with milk. Two years ago my mom banned soda from the house after Uncle Therman, Jr., Dad's brother and a total soda freak, got squashed by a soda vending machine. He'd put his change in the coin slot, but when no soda came out, he got ticked off and tried to shake a can lose. Only he shook the machine too hard and it toppled, crushing him like an empty can.

"Woo-hoo!" Gardo shouted at the TV. "Shermie, you gotta watch this, man. The Undertaker just beaned the ref with a tombstone, then tossed him into a coffin. That's what you gotta do, man, be totally over the top."

"I don't know. . . ." I stopped filling the candy bowl in the front entryway and took a few steps toward the living room to see the TV. A guy in a black hat and trench coat was cracking some clown-wigged meathead in the skull with a big rock. "Lucy says I have to perfect my eating skills first. She says an act is nothing without the skill to back it up."

"*Au contraire,* my misguided friend. In the sports world, a skill is nothing without the act to back it up. Bury him, Undertaker!"

The doorbell rang, so I rushed back to the door. No one was there. "I see you, you little punks!" I shouted into the darkness. I hadn't, actually, but word spread fast if you let doorbell ditchers think they had the upper hand on Halloween. I'd DD'd enough times myself to know that.

I fielded some legitimate doorbell dings while Gardo finished watching his match. When it switched to lady wrestlers, he met me at the breakfast bar with two cans of Pepsi. Bellied up to the bar, we toasted Halloween over a silver bag of Three Musketeers minis. My jaw was stiff thanks to last night's ice cream-a-thon, but the minibars were pretty much bite-sized, so it loosened up quickly.

"I wonder why they call these Three Musketeers bars?" Gardo reached into the bag for another bar. "There's nothing 'three' about them. They don't even have three parts, just chocolate and nougat."

"The bar used to come in three different flavors."

"Really? Which ones?"

"Strawberry, vanilla, and chocolate." My mom hid books about candy under her mattress. Thanks to my snooping, I knew the history of every candy made in America for the last one hundred years. Even Necco wafers. *Gross.* "They used to sell them in a box with three soldiers on the label. Those were the musketeers."

"Strawberry nougat? Nasty."

I bit the bottom off a mini and scooped the nougat out with my pinkie. I liked taking my time with those bars. Something about their mininess called for dainty eating. "I don't know, it might be fun to taste it."

"You'd have to pay me a lot to try strawberry nougat."

"I'll try any food once."

"What about strawberry nog?"

"Instead of egg nog?" I had no idea there were other nogs. My mom didn't have any books about that. Not that I'd found yet, anyway.

"It's seriously gross," Gardo said, making a face. "Nana makes it every Christmas."

"I'd try it."

"Not if you saw it, you wouldn't. How about escargot?"

"Already did. They were slimy."

"Gross! How about chocolate-covered termites?"

"Bugs?" I shuddered. "Bugs are not a food."

"They are in some countries."

"True." I tried to imagine a spoonful of tiny termites dipped in milk chocolate. It would probably look like chocolate rice. Only it would be bugs. In my mouth. *Gross!* I felt butyric acid bubble. "Uh-uh, no way. No termites. Here and now, I draw the line at bugs. Raw, cooked, or candy-covered, it doesn't matter." In the Sherman T. Thuff Book of Good and Tasty Things, bugs were now an official no-no.

"You'll have to eat stuff like that when you start competing." He spun his stool back and forth, back and forth, smudging his chocolatey fingers on the white countertop. "They make you eat cow brains and sticks of butter and gross things like that, right?"

"That's just for headlines. Hot dogs aren't gross. Ice cream sure isn't gross. Who knows, maybe there's a Three Musketeers competition?" I bit the end off another mini, then pinkie-scooped the nougat. "That would be cool."

"How many do you think you'd have to eat? A couple dozen?"

I considered the bag of minis we were finishing off. "I don't know. . . ."

Gardo was quiet a moment; then he smiled slowly. "We could try it, you know, to find out."

"Oh no, no. Lucy won't like that."

"Who's going to tell her? Not me. I can keep my big mouth shut. I didn't say a word to her about the ice cream."

"But she's got all those graphs. . . ." He was right, though, she wouldn't find out. It was just me and Gardo this time, no customers or stupid Leonard to rat me out. And anyway, it didn't really matter *what* I ate, eating was eating. Ultimately it was the volume that mattered. Lucy said so herself, I needed to work on my capacity. Besides, I loved Three Musketeers. "Okay. But we can't eat *all* the Halloween candy. I don't want my house egged for running out. We'll make it a speed-eating competition. Two minutes to eat all the Three Musketeers you can."

"What do I get when I win?"

"When *you* win? I don't think so, little man."

He crossed his arms. "Life is ninety-nine percent attitude, Shermie. If I teach you nothing else, remember that. Now let's put up or shut up. Winner gets bragging rights, loser has to . . . oh, what should you do . . ."

"When *you lose,* Mr. Attitude," I said, knowing exactly how to humiliate the guy, "you will properly bow to my excellence. To you, I will soon and forever more be Grand

Master of All Things Edible and Great. And I expect a lot of genuflecting. You know how to bow to your betters, don't you?"

"Yeah, yeah. Fine. How about when *you* lose?"

I scanned the kitchen and then the living room, my gaze running over my Galactic Warriors fan club magazines in the bookcase, the Pepsis on the table, the candy bar wrappers on the couch and coffee table, the TV screen with some long-haired blond woman twisting another long-haired blond woman's leg over her head—

That's it! "If I lose, I'll let you practice your Cripple Crossface takedowns on me for a whole fifteen minutes."

"Done!" He popped off his stool and ran to fetch more candy from the living room.

Gardo did have attitude; I'd give him that. What he didn't have was a clue about what he'd just gotten himself into. Attitude wouldn't beat natural talent. With all he knew about eating, he'd probably take the traditional route, eating bar by bar, one at a time. I planned to apply the Solomon Method. Lucy said that technique had the shortest bite-to-swallow duration. I just hoped my jaw wasn't too sore. I really didn't want Gardo twisting my legs around my head for fifteen minutes.

Gardo brought over two full silver bags from the coffee table. Ripping both open, he set one in front of me and one in front of himself. Then he kicked his stool away so that he could compete from a standing position. "Okay, there are sixty-three candy bars in each bag. Ready, set—"

"Wait! I need to stretch first."

"Aw, Shermie."

I put up my hand in a *stop* gesture to shut him up, then started stretching. I let my head sag back, then forward, then to the side, then to the other side. I dangled my arms straight, then shook them. My First Contact medals jangled on my chest. I'd put my Galactic Warrior uniform back on for the trick-or-treaters. Actually, I could probably wear it every night and be happy. Slowly, I rolled my shoulders backward and forward, backward and forward.

Gardo stood there with his arms crossed, looking like he was picking his teeth with his tongue.

I pointed to the stove. "Make yourself useful. Go set the timer."

"Aye, aye, sir." He saluted. After setting the timer for two minutes, he remained next to the stove with his finger hovering millimeters from the start button. "Are you done?"

"Done." I climbed back onto my barstool and dumped my bag of Three Musketeers onto the counter. Carefully, I spread the pile of minibars flat with my hands so that I could grab the bars quickly. "Okay, on my mark. Ready . . . set . . . GO!"

He pushed start, then dashed back to the counter. We exploded in a frenzy of hands and candy bars and flying wrappers. As fast as we could, we tore open a wrapper, shook out the candy, then grabbed the bar and shoved it into our mouths. Immediately I realized that the wrappers were slowing us down big-time. We should have taken them off before we started. An amateur mistake, but the clock was running and we'd already filled vital belly space, so I wasn't going to stop the race now. At least we were equally handicapped by the goof.

I pulled ahead of Gardo right away thanks to the Solomon Method. Grabbing one bar in each hand, I fed them into my mouth two at a time, side-by-side, and then *bite, bite, chew, swallow,* real quick. Only it was more like *bite, bite, chew, chew, chew, chew, chew, chew, swallow.*

Too much chewing.

To increase my speed, I started inserting each new set of bars even before I'd finished chewing the ones already in my mouth. *Bite, bite, chew, chew, chew, chew, chew, chew, swallow.*

Still too much chewing! How did Tsunami swallow after only two chews? My bite-to-swallow duration sucked.

I tore two more bars free and kept eating.

Next to me, Gardo was just cramming the minis into his mouth as fast as he could unwrap them. There was no technique in his style. He was a starving man who'd just stumbled into a buffet. His whole face was involved in the chew, his eyes huge, his cheeks puffed out like a chipmunk, his mouth opening wide again and again. He was working a wad of light and dark brown that only seemed to get bigger. Brown saliva trickled out the corners of his mouth and down his chin.

I swallowed and paused to warn him, "That's too much at one time. Swallow some first."

He flipped me off and shoved in another bar.

"Suit yourself," I said. *Bite, bite, chew, chew, chew, chew, chew, chew, chew, swallow . . .*

I glanced at the oven timer. One-fifteen to go. Man, that forty-five seconds flew by. *Bite, bite, chew, chew, chew, chew, chew, chew, chew, swallow . . . Bite, bite, chew, chew, chew, chew, chew, chew, chew, swallow . . .*

I had a huge pile of empty wrappers, but Gardo's empty wrapper pile was starting to look bigger. I had to go faster. *Bite, bite, chew, chew, chew, chew, swallow. Oh, ow!* That was too big a lump to swallow. I could feel it squeezing down my food pipe. The Solomon Method sucked.

Feeling the pressure of the ticking timer, I abandoned the Solomon Method and started shoving the bars into my mouth Traditional Style. One after the other after the other, I stuffed the minis in with both hands, fitting up to four in my mouth at one time. All the while, I chewed fast, swallowing what was around my molars to make room for the new candy bars at the front of my mouth. I was practically unhinging my jaw to open and chew at the same time. Soon enough, though, my movements become smooth and rhythmical: *Rip, shake, grab, swallow, stuff, chew, chew, swallow, chew, chew.* Over and over. Turns out it wasn't easy to chew what was in back while still opening up for more at the front. And solid food was a lot harder to deal with than ice cream—minis had to be chewed small enough for a safe swallow. The last thing I wanted to do was to choke to death with four candy bars jammed in my mouth. Imagine the headlines.

Thanks to my Thuff Enuff "Quick Chew/Small Swallow" version of the Traditional technique, my pile of empty wrappers was growing fast again. With forty-eight seconds left, I was clearly ahead. Gardo saw this and stuffed in even more candy. His cheeks were as big as tennis balls. He couldn't get his teeth or lips all the way down with that giant brown glob in his mouth. His eyes squeezed closed from the effort of trying to chew the hunk. He hadn't swallowed in ten seconds, at least.

Thirty-three seconds to go.

A bar flew free of my wrapper and skittered across the counter. I lunged and grabbed it, then shoved it into my mouth. *Boy, did that thing fly!* I turned to see if Gardo had seen it. His eyes were wide open again. Only he wasn't chewing. He was grabbing at his throat with one hand and swatting frantically at the wad in his mouth with his other. He wasn't making a sound.

Choking! I jumped to my feet and spit my wad of chocolate onto the floor. "Choking! You're choking!"

Balling my right hand into a fist, I hammered him on the back as hard as I could, knocking him forward against the counter. The wad in his mouth popped out. But he was still grabbing at his neck and swatting the air without a sound. More must have been stuck in his throat.

Idiot! You're not supposed to HIT a choker! The Heimlich thing, do the Heimlich thing! I yanked Gardo back up into a standing position with his back to me, wrapped my arms around his waist, and lined my fist up against his stomach. *Where does it go? Where does it go?*

"Where does it go!"

There! My fist fell into the soft cavity just under his ribs. *One—Two—THREE!* I squeezed my arms violently toward my belly and slightly up, my fist sinking deep into his gut. My medals dug into my chest as his feet popped off the ground. But he was still grabbing at his neck, now with both hands.

I squeezed and lifted again.

Nothing.

Again.

Nothing.

Please, please . . .

Again—

Phewp! A brown glob smacked into the kitchen window on the other side of the counter. It stuck to the glass a moment, then slid down slowly, a trail of goo snailing behind it.

Gardo sagged in my arms, coughing and sputtering. I lowered him to the floor, onto his hands and knees, then dropped down next to him, panting. My heart was racing.

OhmyGodohmyGodohmyGod . . .

Still on his hands and knees, Gardo arched his back suddenly.

"Aaaagggh!" He puked a huge gush of Pepsi and chewed candy onto the floor.

I lurched sideways to avoid the splatter.

"Aaaa . . . aaaagggh!" More Pepsi hit the floor, but not so much candy this time. The withering smell of butyric acid hit me full force.

"Aaaa . . . Aaaa . . ."

Nothing.

He hovered over his disgusting puddle, trembling.

I rested my hand on his back. "Wait, Gardo, wait. . . ."

Still nothing.

"Good. Your first dry heave. It's all easy going from here." I patted his back. "You're good, man. You'll be fine. The worst is over."

Beep! Beep! Beep! I whipped my head up. The oven timer. Time was up.

Hauling myself to my feet, I trudged to the oven and turned off the timer. I stood there a moment, stretched over the stove, breathing deeply.

I can't believe what almost just happened. Gardo just . . . almost . . .

I shook my head. He didn't, and that was what mattered now. He didn't.

With shaky steps, I crossed the kitchen and got a new roll of paper towels from the cupboard. I rolled it over near Gardo. Then I got my mom's dishwashing gloves, the sponge, and a bucket from beneath the sink.

Turning the water on full blast, I filled the bucket with soapy water.

By this time, Gardo was sitting back on his heels. He'd

112

taken off his T-shirt and was wiping his face with it. "I'm sorry, Shermie. . . ."

"Shut up. You have nothing to be sorry for."

"I shouldn't have—"

"I said shut up."

I carried the bucket and cleaning supplies over next to him and set to work. First I threw a bunch of paper towels over the whole disgusting sight. Then I used more paper towels to push and sop at the edges of the mess, trying to get it all into one nasty pile that I could scoop up with the dustpan. Sometimes at Scoops-a-Million I had to clean up big ice cream messes, so I knew that the dustpan was the tool to get the job done.

Gardo tried to get some paper towels to help, but I pushed his hands away. "I got this. Go get a clean T-shirt from my closet."

"Man, this is so embarrassing. . . ."

"It's not embarrassing. It's just bad luck, that's all." *Scary luck is what it is.* "It could happen to anyone." Another scary thought. I'd been jamming food into my mouth for over a week now with no one around to Heimlich me if I had choked.

I unwound a fresh wad of paper towels from the roll.

Gardo used the counter to pull himself up, then just stood there, watching me sop and push his puke into a pile. "Good thing you know the Heimlich maneuver."

"Good thing." I looked up at him, but his bloodshot eyes wouldn't meet mine. The knuckles on his right hand were white from squeezing the counter, and the hand that held his pukey wrestling shirt was shaking.

I sat up on my heels and said with more conviction than I felt, "Hey, man, don't sweat it. Even the Grand Master of All Things Great and Edible has been known to choke on

113

the occasional Cheeto. You should see those things fly." I whistled and sliced my yellow-gloved hand through the air like a rocket. The gold band around my uniformed forearm sparkled in the light.

Gardo laughed weakly. "I guess. You know, I *could* kind of breathe, so it wasn't like I was *choking* choking. . . ."

"That's right."

"I mean, when you're an athlete, stuff happens, right?" He gestured to the bandage on his neck. "It's all part of the game."

"Totally. Now quit holding up the counter and get me a trash bag from under the sink." I needed something to put those nasty paper towels in. Man, was this gross. And it reeked. I almost felt like puking, too. "No, wait, get me two. I swear, you must be ten pounds lighter than you were two minutes ago." I didn't know which was worse, smelling someone else's puke, or seeing it.

He fetched some trash bags, and when I went to take them from him, he held his end tight for a second. "Hey, Shermie . . ."

"What?"

He hesitated. "Don't tell anyone, okay?"

I sat back on my heels again and locked my eyes on his. "My big mouth stays shut." I pulled an invisible zipper across my lips.

He smiled, a real smile this time. "I knew I could count on you. Thanks, man." He slugged me in the shoulder and headed down the hallway to my room.

As I watched him go, I thought about how I'd been just a Heimlich away from never seeing him walk anywhere again. Ever.

Now my hands shook.

I turned back to the disgusting mess on the floor. Vapors

of chocolate and butyric acid swirled around me. I hated the smell of butyric acid now more than ever.

Now it smelled like death.

* * *

"Hey, Gardo, give me another bag, will you?"

I'd just closed the front door on a tiny Winnie the Pooh and an even tinier Tigger. They'd been so cute, I'd given them four candy bars each. My bowl was getting low. "I can see bottom here. Unacceptable."

My buddy came over wearing my Galactic Warriors National Convention T-shirt, which looked like a giant black poncho on him. I'd bought the shirt last month at the same booth that took my order for a signature edition Captain Quixote telescope. It was nice to see someone getting some use out of the stupid shirt. It shrank the first time I washed it, so I couldn't wear it. I'd been thinking of tacking it to my wall like a poster.

"Here," he said, tossing me a silver package of minis. I had to lunge for it, which hurt thanks to my stomach being so full of Pepsi and Three Musketeers. "That's the last bag."

I jerked my thumb toward the kitchen. "There's more in the cupboard. Can you grab one?" I wanted to keep him busy. It'd been a couple of hours since the Heimlich thing, but we hadn't talked about it since he came back with my shirt on. If that was the way he wanted to handle it, fine with me. It was his deal, almost choking to death, so I'd follow his lead. "The cupboard to the left of the fridge."

"That is from that cupboard. We're out."

"How can we be out? I bought ten bags." Dang, maybe I was too generous with the candy doling. "We'll just have to give out Mom's candy, then. She bought some Mounds, if

115

you can believe it. Jeez, I hope no one eggs us. I think they're in the fridge, next to her tofu."

"Tofu? Gag city."

"Tell me about it."

The doorbell rang. I opened the door to a pink fairy, a lime-green Hulk, and a blond girl with big glasses and a lightning bolt on her forehead. I put several Three Musketeers in each one's plastic pumpkin.

Gardo hollered from the kitchen. "No more Mounds, either. There's nothing left."

"How can the Mounds be gone? I haven't given any out."

I went to the kitchen and looked over Gardo's shoulder into the fridge, trying not to jostle my full stomach. There was a hint of butyric acid on his breath, but mostly he smelled like coconut.

"Aw, man," I said, "you stink like coconut. You ate the Mounds, didn't you? Gross!"

"What? I was hungry. My stomach was empty, remember?"

"But *Mounds*?"

"What's wrong with Mounds?"

"They're *coconut*." I motioned toward the couch. "Yuck. Go back over there."

"You're the one who bought them."

"I didn't buy them, my mom did. Mounds don't tempt her. She hates coconut." I had to agree with her on that one. The stuff was vile.

"I'm not gonna stay in a separate room from you all night," he said. "Stick some cotton up your nose or rub Vicks under it or something."

"You're the one who ate them."

"You're the one who had them in your house."

116

The doorbell rang, so I went to drop a Three Musketeers bar into the pumpkin of a waist-high pirate with a curly red beard. The kid peered down into his pumpkin. "Just one? *Argh!*"

"Hey, you're lucky I have any left at all." *Ungrateful swabby.* "It's almost nine-thirty. The early bird gets the Three Musketeers, Redbeard."

He stuck out his tongue at me as I shut the door.

Back in the kitchen, Gardo leaned against the open refrigerator door. "Where'd all the Three Musketeers come from if your mom bought Mounds?"

"I bought them. I'm the one who has to scrub the dried eggs off the door tomorrow morning if we give out gross stuff. Move over." There had to be something I could give out. Leaning in painfully, I found a bag of yogurt-covered peanuts behind the mayonnaise jar. Only, there was more green fuzz on them than yogurt. *Nasty.* "No kid wants coconut anything on Halloween."

"I like coconut."

"You'd like dirt if I served it to you on a plate. Every other kid on the planet hates coconut. Seriously, how many trick-or-treaters do you know who dump out their pumpkins at the end of the night and go, 'Ooh, yippee, a Mounds bar'?"

Gardo shrugged and went back to the couch to watch his wrestling marathon.

Getting more desperate by the second, I shoved aside condiments and yanked open crisper doors. *Carrots, celery, a box of croutons. . .* It was one pathetic refrigerator. I never really noticed how empty our fridge was before. Dad and Grampy and I usually ate takeout, if we were even home at the same time to eat together, and my mom only ate salads.

"What's this?" A lumpy plastic bag caught my eye, way in the back, on the bottom shelf. It almost blended in with the white wall of the fridge. I pulled off the twist tie and slowly opened the bag, ready to squeeze it shut if the smell was too awful. "Aw, shoot."

"What?" Gardo asked from the couch. "Did you find some candy?"

"Raisins. Tiny boxes of shriveled, disgusting raisins. I can't even guess how old they are."

"Man, your house is as good as egged."

"Shoot." I slammed the fridge closed as the doorbell rang yet again. This time it was some boy in a Chargers uniform with a fake cast on his leg and a little girl in a blue Star Trek medical officer uniform. Where was the good doc when we needed her a couple of hours ago?

I gave the Trekkie two whole handfuls of Three Musketeers out of Sci-Fi Geek solidarity. Even when pickin's were slim, SFGs had to stick together. She flashed me Spock's *Live long and prosper* sign. I countered with Quixote's *May you always walk in the light of the Sun* wave.

The Chargers boy got a single bar. He complained, but, hey, my stock was low and who cared about football?

When I closed the front door, I took inventory of my candy bowl. Only it wasn't much of an inventory: I had two minibars left. That wasn't enough to give out. The next doorbell might've been a whole crowd, and then what would I do? I couldn't break those tiny bars in half.

I studied the two bars. I was full . . . but they were small. . . . *Aw, what the heck.* I peeled the wrapper off one of the bars and nibbled at the chocolate coating while carrying the other bar to Gardo on the couch. "Wah ih?"

"Didn't your mom teach you not to talk with your mouth

118

full?" He waved off the bar. "I already yakked once. Do you want me to explode?"

I shoved my candy bar all the way in my mouth to plug the laugh that almost came out. Gardo had a die-hard sense of humor. I'd hoped he would dust it off for the Heimlich incident sooner or later.

He patted his tummy gently. "Man, I can't believe I have to starve myself again next week."

"You could just throw up before weigh-in." Hey, he'd opened the door on the topic.

"Very funny. I swear, when I tried out for wrestling, I had no idea making weight was such a big deal. It sucks. I hate being dizzy. And tired." He scowled. "And cranky and thirsty . . . Here." He stood up and snatched the bar from my fingers. "Give me the stupid thing. Might as well eat it while I can. Got any more on you?"

"That's the last one."

"The one I'm holding?"

"Yeah."

"Shoot." He tore open the wrapper and bit down. "I hope you turned the porch light out."

"The light!" I hustled back to the door and lunged at the light switch. But I was too late. The doorbell rang before I could flip the light off. *Dang!* Maybe if I didn't answer it, they'd just go away. Not everyone carried eggs for Revenge Eggings. Some trick-or-treaters just went on to the next house if they didn't have luck at one.

I stood on the tiptoes of my good leg to peer through the peephole. We were in luck. "It's just Lucy," I called out to Gardo.

"I heard that," she said through the door. "Open up. I've got wieners."

My relief about not being egged fell away as I remembered that I hadn't invited Lucy to join us. She might flip if she saw Gardo here with me.

When I opened the door, she stumbled past me and into the kitchen with several bulging plastic grocery bags. She'd changed out of her Cinderella scullery costume, so now she was back to looking like Lucy, with her brown polo shirt and jeans and normal, nonratty hair.

"Sorry I'm late." She heaved the bags up onto the counter with one big, double-armed swing. "Dang, water's heavy."

Late? "You're not that late."

"Are you kidding?" She didn't seem surprised when Gardo joined us at the counter. She just started unloading the bags. One jug of water, another jug, a third. "I should have been here half an hour ago. But it took forever to convince my dad to drive me over. He hates driving in the dark. Total Capricorn. Like his daughter should *walk* in the dark, especially with a full moon. Full moons bring out weirdos. And a full moon on Halloween is just asking for nutcases. What a lovely idea to let children roam the streets tonight."

Lucy hated trick-or-treating. She called it forced begging.

"Halloween is such a stupid holiday," she continued while Gardo helped her take the last two water jugs out of their bags. "People dress up their kids then send them to strangers' houses for candy. What are they thinking? Any other day of the year, taking candy from strangers gets you grounded for life."

Gardo pulled a screwdriver and wire cutters out of a bag. "What's all this for?" He held up a funny-looking hammer. "What is this, a mallet?"

She took the tools and put them right back in the bag. "I need them for a science project."

"Which science project? We don't have a science project."

"It's extra credit. Here, Shermie, this is for your training." She handed me a piece of black construction paper covered with letters and numbers in neon ink. "I charted your horoscope so I could tell how tonight's training would go. I know, I know, you don't believe in horoscopes. But I'm your coach, and I do. The problem with this morning's newspaper horoscope was that it focused too much on Leos' tendency to drama queen when they feel vulnerable and . . . well, we'll forget all that for now. Water under the bridge. My chart goes more in depth than that horoscope, and all signs say this'll be your most important night ever."

"Train? Tonight?" I stifled a cocoa-y burp. *Oh, the sweet relief of burps.* "What signs?"

"The stars, the sun . . ." She pointed to the paper. "It's all in your chart. You're a new man today, Sherman T. Thuff, with a new future. It's very exciting." She pulled hot dogs and buns out of the bags. "Your primary training graph says a round of hot dogs tonight and then another this weekend. Where's your copy of the primary graph? I told you to put it on your fridge. I can't wait to see how the wet buns are working for you. Stomach expansion is definitely our next step. Tankage is power. And I know you don't want to talk about it, Shermie, but we really need to do something about your . . . you know . . . your belt."

Gardo climbed onto a stool. "Stomach expansion?"

"That's right." She shoved a gallon of water out of the way to make way for her binder, opening to the graph with *Cancers* ♥ *H₂O* doodled in the margins in girly curlicues.

Gardo leaned in for a closer look and whistled. "Dang. I hope you like water, Shermie."

"I guess. . . ." My stomach gurgled.

"Drinking large amounts of water will increase the

elasticity of his stomach. He'll have to pee a lot, though."
Lucy paused. "What's that smell?"

Coconut-Puke Boy leaned away quickly.

"You don't want to know," I said. The thought of eating
the scheduled fifteen hot dogs and buns right then made my
stomach queasy. I shot Gardo a help-me! look, but he just
shrugged. "Look, Lucy, I don't mean to go against my
coach or anything, but I can't train tonight. I didn't fast
today. I need to fast before I feast."

"Since when?" She pushed a button on some big, black
G.I. Joe wristwatch. "Fasting is not on any of your training
graphs. Carrots are, though. Have you been eating them for
jaw strength like I said? How does this timer thingie work?"

"Here." Gardo took the watch and started playing with
the buttons.

"Since always. Lucy, I can't tonight. I had a big lunch and
I've eaten a few candy bars." A few *bags*. "I'll do it tomorrow. I promise. I'll fast all day and then you can come over
and time me tomorrow night. I'll do whatever you tell me
tomorrow. I promise."

"Can't. Aunt Enith is making me stay late to redo the inventory system tomorrow night. She keeps running out of
truffles before she thinks she should."

"But Lucy—"

"Hey." She nailed me with a stare. "I haven't said a thing
to you about your ice cream training violation, have I?"

That shut me up.

"That's what I thought." She turned to Gardo. "See if
you can set it for twelve minutes. Shermie, where are your
pots? I'll get some water boiling for the wieners—"

The phone rang, interrupting her. *Saved by the bell!* I
rushed across the kitchen and grabbed the cordless phone.

"Hi, Cupcake."

It was my mom. I put my finger to my lips to shush Gardo and Lucy.

"I hope I didn't wake you," Mom said.

"That's okay."

"But this couldn't wait until tomorrow. Dad and I won't be flying home in the morning after all. He's in the hospital, honey. Food poisoning."

"The hospital?"

My friends stopped what they were doing.

"Don't worry," she said. "He just ate some bad kale. He'll be fine in a couple of days. They're pumping his stomach right now."

I heard gagging sounds. "Is that him? He doesn't sound good." My own stomach clenched. I mouthed, *He's fine* to Gardo and Lucy, and they went back to searching the cupboards for pots.

"It's not so bad, Moon Pic. It just looks like strained spinach. What is that, Herman?" She must have been covering the mouthpiece, because her voice was muffled. "Is that a Chiclet? When did you have Chiclets? Oh no, never mind, it's just corn."

"Mom!" I swallowed hard to stave off the reversal of fortune that was brewing in my gut.

"Oh, Sherman, no drama." She was loud and clear again. "What's a little half-digested food? Look, sweetie, I have to run. Don't you worry about your dad. He'll be fine. He's already filled up half the bucket. Herman, honey, take off your tie, you're splattering. I'll call you when I get new flight information. Tell Grampy he's on duty for a few more d—"

I didn't hear the rest. I dropped the phone and bolted

down the hall to the bathroom so my stomach could pump itself out.

When I was done reversing, I knelt there with my forehead on the front edge of the toilet seat, my eyes closed so I couldn't see the lumps of chocolate floating in the watery brown pool. It was bad enough I had to smell that chocolate butyric acid cocktail. I thought I'd suffered enough of that smell earlier with Gardo's reversal. Maybe Vicks under my nose *would* help.

Before I could muster the energy to move, though, I heard Lucy's voice. "Just a few candy bars, is that what you said?" She was behind me, in the open doorway.

I raised my soggy head but didn't turn. I didn't say anything, either. What could I say?

"What else are you and Gardo doing when I'm not watching? More ice cream?"

"No."

"Did you throw that up, too?"

"No!"

"You two are out of control. I plotted your training out for a reason, you know. You have to ease into it. See what happens when you don't? Jeez, Shermie, what were you thinking? I should've known better than to let a Leo alone with a Libra. You two just feed off each other. Gardo's corrupting you—"

"Gardo's not doing anything." The awful brown muck was perfect for a toilet. I closed my eyes again.

"He is. And I don't want you hanging out with him anymore."

My eyes shot back open. "What?" I turned to look up at her, my butt now on the floor with my back against the toilet. "Did you just *forbid* me from hanging out with my friend?"

"He's a distraction. I'm your coach, and I still need to show you how we're going to chip away at your belt of f—"

"You're fired."

She pulled up. "What?"

"I said you're fired. You're not my coach anymore."

"You can't fire me."

"I just did. I don't need a coach. I can do this by myself."

"But . . ." She paused, then squeezed her lips tight. "Fine. You want to do this yourself, you got it. Good luck, *Thuff Enuff*. Without me behind the scenes, you'll need it."

Then she was gone.

I sagged back against the toilet and stared at the empty doorway. I couldn't believe it. I'd just fired my eating coach.

I'd just fired *Lucy*.

CHAPTER 10

I couldn't sleep. Hours had passed since my Halloween reversal, so my stomach was fine, but my mind was all queasy. Thoughts were racing around my mind, spinning and crashing and exploding. Thoughts of Lucy color-coding those training graphs. Of yellow shirts, and red shirts, and green shirts, and boxing robes. Of hot dogs and ice cream and stitched cuts. Of Marilyn Monroe . . . Captain Quixote . . . Tsunami. Of Gardo and Heimlich incidents. I didn't know what I was supposed to make of the mishmash. The images were all my life, but none was about me.

This was supposed to be my night. Lucy said so. My whole future would change, she'd said. It was right there in her chart, and her charts were always perfect. She'd handed me my future, coded in a rainbow of cotton candy colors, and then I'd fired her.

I fired *Lucy*.

I flipped back the bedspread and swung my legs over the side of the bed. Staggering down the stairs, I entered the kitchen and turned on the light. There it was, on the counter: my star chart.

I'd never seen a star chart before. It was round, with a big inner circle and a thin outer one, like the crust on a pizza. Both circles were filled with numbers and symbols, and they were divided into twelve pizza slices. At the top of the paper, above the chart and in Lucy's curly handwriting, it said, *Composite Chart: Shermie & Tsunami.* At the bottom, under the double pizza, she'd written some notes:

Positive Sun/Moon conjunction
Greatest emphasis falls into ninth house of travel and publicity
Analysis: They're two of a kind, but Shermie can take him if he stays committed. Key = Eliminate Fat Belt.

I stared at the chart, mesmerized. It was kind of pretty, actually. Lucy had used black construction paper and neon gel pens. The circles were white lines, but the numbers and symbols that filled those circles were as colorful as the tubs of ice cream in the Scoops display case. She'd used a soft, powdery blue for the numbers, of which there were dozens, mostly in the upper left portion of the inner circle. For the symbols, she'd used a rich, creamy pink in the outer ring and a milky shamrock green in the inner circle, like the green of the St. Patty's Day milkshakes they had every March at McDonald's. Lucy knew I loved those shakes. The symbols were mostly grouped with the numbers in the upper left, leaving a lot of blank space in the rest of the circles.

Making this chart must've taken her a long time. I couldn't even guess where she'd learned how. Astrology wasn't an elective at Del Heiny Junior 13.

I didn't have any clue what the markings meant, of course. Lucy could've written the combination for Fort

Knox in there; I'd never know. What I did know was that the chart was about me—me and Tsunami. And according to Lucy's notes, I could hold my own against him. Or I could in the stars, anyway. On this planet, I had a bit of work ahead of me for that to happen.

But how was I supposed to do that work now? I had a map of the stars in my hands but no idea how to get my feet off the ground.

"Stupid star chart." I crushed the black paper in my hands and flung it at the counter.

Spinning on my heel, I marched my big, sorry fat belt back to bed.

CHAPTER 11

I was late. It was insane to be late for anything at 6:40 a.m. on a Saturday morning, but I was. I should've been coasting my bike down my driveway at least five minutes ago. Still, if I hustled I could probably make it to the gym before wrestling practice started. In the wee hours of the morning, I'd come up with a plan to get by without Lucy, and I didn't want to waste a second putting it into action.

The sun was barely even up. *What genius decided to start practice this early?* I'd laughed when Gardo first told me about it, but I wasn't laughing now.

I pedaled as fast as I could . . . which meant I was panting and gasping like a dying fish. There was a reason I rode the bus to school. A mile and a half and nineteen minutes later, I was threading my chain through the spokes at the gym bike racks, hoping I wouldn't die. I hadn't stopped to walk my bike once, and now I was paying the price. Sweat dripped from my forehead onto the blacktop, and my legs wobbled as I walked from the bike racks. At least I was upright.

I came to a set of double metal doors painted white, with a big red dot in the middle of each one. *Proud Home of the* was stenciled in red across the top of the left door, and *Plum Tomatoes* stretched across the right. Weird that those doors hadn't been mustard tagged. They seemed like great targets. I grasped the handle and, after taking a few calming breaths—*you can do this, Shermie*—I pulled it open.

I'd never been in the gym before. Not being on the wrestling team or the basketball squad or the badminton team, I'd never had reason to be. The very thought of me in a red-and-white *Proud Plum Tomato* uniform was a joke. I couldn't have hit a shuttlecock if it hit me first, and I didn't dribble except at the table. I certainly didn't hug other guys in tights. That was just the way of it.

The gym wasn't what I'd expected at all. It was dark and gloomy. Only the lights in the center were on, way up high over a patch of red mats. From my dark corner tucked in an alcove between the end of the bleachers and the side gym wall, I could see a dozen guys in red sweats and red hoodies spread out on the mats in a large circle, all bent in jackknife stretches. White helmets were scattered at their feet. In the center of the circle, like the bull's-eye in a target, was a guy wearing a white hoodie, bent over like the others, shouting into his kneecaps.

"ONE one hundred, TWO one hundred, THREE one hundred, FOUR one hundred . . ."

Captain Shane was working his troops.

I lingered in the bleacher shadows. Six-fifty-nine and they were already into their warm-ups. Maybe this wasn't the best idea. I didn't see Gardo over there stretching, so maybe there was still a chance of catching him in the locker room before he joined the practice.

But before I could move toward the double red doors marked *Locker Room*, they swung open and the enormous

Finns emerged, with their bent noses and their red sweat-pants and red hoodies. I backpedaled deeper into the bleacher shadows.

". . . the real power position is behind the front man," one was saying, his voice low but intense. "If he goes down, we'll still be standing. So just do like I said and stop arguing. Let the jerk have his precious spotlight." He suddenly cut off and whipped his head my way when his brother's face registered my presence. "What are you doing here?"

They towered over me, eyeing me like a bug that needed stomping. I almost bolted right then and there. But I didn't. I *couldn't*, not if I was going to make this happen. *C'mon, Shermie, earn the Thuff Enuff legend.*

I pointed to the locker room doors. "I'm looking for Gardo. Is he in there?"

"Who do I look like, Sherlock Holmes? Go find him yourself."

But when I stepped toward the doors, the other Finn grabbed me by the arm.

"Hold it. You don't just go waltzing in there. That locker room is for team members only."

"Then how am I supposed to—"

"That's not our problem, now, is it?"

Shane's voice droned in the background. "And to the LEFT one hundred, TWO one hundred, THREE one hundred . . ."

The Finn let go of my arm, but they didn't walk away. I'd just have to leave and wait until after practice to get Gardo's help.

"Excuse me, ladies!" Shane hollered our way. I nearly dove under the bleachers. "If you two don't get over here by the time I finish this count, you're joining Esperaldo on

131

his bleacher tour. *Aaaaand* THREE one hundred, FOUR one hundred . . ."

I followed the Finns' eyes up into the darkened bleachers next to me. A figure in a singlet topped by a hoodie was jogging up a set of steps in the center. His toe snagged on a step and he fell forward, catching himself with his hands on a higher step. He righted himself and kept going. A few steps higher, he shoved his hood back so he could see. It was Gardo.

I almost stepped around the bleachers for a better look. "What's he doing up there?"

One of the Finns snorted. "Laps. Again."

"Why?"

"Talking smack, probably. Idiot's gotta learn who to mouth off to and who not to. Hurry up, Blayne."

They hustled off toward Shane like a set of loyal bulldogs.

I stared at Gardo. He was running down some steps now, not far from me. It was too dark for me to see his face well, but his feet were moving fast and sure. Too fast, in my opinion. Part of me wanted to shout out to him to slow down. If he tripped again at that pace, he'd tumble straight to the bottom and break his neck for sure. At least that would've been my fate if that were me doing a bleacher tour. But Gardo wouldn't have slowed down even if I told him to. He'd call that being a wuss. As if there was some dignity in doing punishment laps well.

As soon as his foot hit the gym floor, he spun and headed in my direction, toward the next set of steps. I ducked back behind the bleachers again. I couldn't let him see me. He didn't need to know that I'd witnessed his humiliation.

Moving to the set of doors I'd come in through, I was just

132

starting to push down on the exit bar when a door on the other side of the gym crashed open against a wall.

"Shane!" It was Coach Hunt. Short like Shane but densely muscled, the man stalked across the gym like a bulldozer in a rose garden. "What are you doing still stretching them out? It's seven-oh-two, you should be into drills by now. If you want to lead, missy, you need to act like a leader. Go join Esperaldo. Move!" He jabbed a finger at the Finn nearest him in the circle. "Blayne, take these girls through bottom man drills."

"Coach Hunt, sir, I'm Wayne."

"That's what I said. Hurry up!"

"Yes, sir! You heard the man. Partner up, ladies! Let's go!"

"Not you, Blayne. C'mere. I need the new warm-ups moved to the equipment room. The keys are in the office. Usual spot. Double time!"

"Yes, sir!" The other Finn took off at a run.

I slipped through the door to the outside world, squinting in the budding sunlight. No way did I want Coach Hunt spotting me and thinking I was spying on his precious practice or something. I wasn't interested in wrestling, and I certainly wasn't interested in being sent up the bleacher stairs to pull a Humpty Dumpty in front of the whole wrestling team.

After all, I had a rep to protect now.

* * *

"Shermie, wake up."

I opened my eyes. Gardo's face was inches from mine.

"Wake up, man. What are you doing here?"

I blinked rapidly, trying to keep out the bright sun. It was high and strong now, reflecting off everything. When I'd ducked out of the gym and sat down against this wall to wait, the sun was climbing fast but the moon still dominated the sky. I must've dozed off. My stomach rumbled, reminding me that I'd rushed out this morning without breakfast. "What time is it? Is practice over?"

"Yeah. It's after nine. Coach cut practice short today. Shane pulled a groin muscle, the poor baby."

He reached out his hand and helped me pull myself up. My legs had stiffened while I dozed.

"I swear," he said, "you'd think Shane is paralyzed or something. I don't know who took it harder, him or Coach. For crying out loud, when you're an athlete, things happen. Get over it or get out."

"What a wuss."

"Seriously." He slung a backpack over his shoulder. He'd changed his clothes to gray sweats and a gray hoodie with a big black T-shirt over it.

"Hey, that's my Galactic Warriors shirt." I'd forgotten he wore it home last night.

"I know. I like it." He swung his arms around like he was flagging down a plane. "It's nice and roomy. I'll get it back to you after I wash it."

"Keep it. I don't like black, anyway." I slapped some blades of grass from my shorts. "I hope you don't mind me stalking you at practice, but I wanted to ask you something and I kind of didn't want to wait."

"No sweat. C'mon, talk and walk. I need to work out a kink."

Together we walked in the direction of the football stadium, which our school shared with the high school on the other side, Del Heiny High #3, home of the Black Cherry Heirlooms. There was a lot of shouting down on the field, and muffled music, like from bad stereo speakers. Every couple of steps, Gardo stuck his right leg out to the side and gave it a quick shake. "What gives?"

"Well, you know how I want to beat Tsunami. . . ."

"Yeah."

"Well, see, to do that I need to . . . well, the thing is, Lucy said . . ." Wow, this was pretty embarrassing, now that I had to say it out loud.

"Spit it out. The best way to remove a Band-Aid is to just yank it."

We were rounding the fence into the stadium. I motioned for him to follow me to the metal railing in front of the home team bleachers. Yellow toilet paper was wrapped around the bar like wilted candy cane stripes. On the field below us, the high school's marching band was drilling on the left, zigzagging like purple-shirted ants, holding instruments but not playing them. On the right, Black Cherry Heirloom cheerleaders were practicing a synchronized dance. Their boombox was blasting muffled, bass-heavy dance music as they jerked and froze, jerked and froze, smiling mechanically while their ponytails cracked like whips with each crisp move. Dark purple pom-poms were flying every which way, and so were purple-shirted somersaulting cheerleaders.

"So what's the big secret?" Gardo asked.

"It's not a secret, I just . . . I just want to know if you can help me lose my . . . this . . ." I took a deep breath. *C'mon, Shermie, you have to do this.* ". . . my belt of fat."

There. I'd done it. I'd ripped off the Band-Aid.

Gardo looked down where my hand was resting, on my gut. How could he *not*? I'd practically told him to. Then he leaned over the railing next to me and rubbed his hand over his face.

"You can answer any time now," I said, feeling more mortified by the second.

135

He moved his hand from his face and met my gaze. "Does Lucy know you're asking me to help?"

"No. That doesn't matter, though, she's not my coach anymore." Gardo hadn't heard us down the hall last night. He thought she'd left so suddenly because my Halloween candy reversal grossed her out.

"I don't know anything about graphing and HDB ratios," he said.

"You don't need to. I have all the graphs I need. But those are for eating. What I need is for someone to tell me how to get rid of this." I pulled up the front edge of my shirt, exposing my belly button—and all the belly around it. *This is Gardo,* I reminded myself, *you can trust him.* "My stomach can't expand with this in the way. That's why the skinny guys win the eating competitions, they don't have a natural belt restricting them. I've seen pictures of them after a contest, and it's like they're about to give birth to quadruplets, their stomachs are so stretched out. If I'm going to beat Tsunami, I have to be able to expand."

"And you think I can help?"

"You have to cut weight for wrestling. You know how to do this." I lowered my shirt. "Will you help me? Please?"

He stared out over the field, studying it intensely. The grass down there was a green too bright to be real. The crisp white yard lines were permanently painted, and the end zones were a deep Black Cherry Heirloom purple. In the center of each end zone was a giant Del Heiny Ketchup Company logo: a tomato outlined in white, with a big happy face grin and two humongous eyes, one winking like it knew some private joke.

"You'd have to do everything I say," Gardo finally said to the field. "And no back talk. I know how you are. You're an athlete now, and athletes do what their coaches say, even if they don't like it. Can you handle that?"

"I'll do whatever you say." I crossed my heart and spit over my left shoulder.

He stared at me hard for a moment. Then he nodded. "Okay, then, I'll do it. I'll be your weight coach."

"Yes!" I slapped him a high five and danced a little jig. The serious look disappeared from his face.

Smiling, he pointed his finger firmly at my nose. "Just remember, anything I say."

"Anything."

I leaned back on the mustard-swirled railing, the flood of relief relaxing my shoulders. I hadn't realized how tense they'd gotten. I looked over again at my buddy and smiled. Yeah, I'd done the right thing, trusting him. No way would I be able to do this if he hadn't agreed to teach me what he knew.

Across the field, the visitor bleachers were dotted with random people running the steps. I almost joked about them, but I caught myself before the words left my big mouth. I had to remember that I *hadn't* seen Gardo running punishment laps in the gym. He could trust me, too. But hey, at least someone had *made* Gardo run the bleachers. Those people on the visitor side were doing it voluntarily. What a bunch of whackos.

A few feet away from us, a guy who was maybe in college showed up and set down a gym bag and a bottle of water. He took off his T-shirt and started rolling his shoulders, forward and back, forward and back. The guy was cut.

Gardo leaned in close to me and whispered, "Someday you're gonna be ripped like that."

If only. "Give me a break."

137

"We'll target your workouts, you'll see. Ab work up the wazoo."

Mr. Olympia stopped rolling his shoulders and stepped over to the railing. He stretched a leg up over the top and then bent so far over it that his forehead touched his knee, like he was warming up for an act of *Swan Lake*.

This time I was the one who leaned in and whispered. "Talk about a groin pull."

Gardo laughed. "C'mon, let's go to my house. We've got some ab research to do."

I practically skipped back toward the stadium gate with him. I'd just recruited a ringer. Maybe Lucy was right; maybe last night was the eve of great new things for me. With Gardo as my coach, I'd be rid of this fat belt in a few weeks, and then there wouldn't be anything between me and the Mustard Yellow Belt of International Hot Dog Eating, not even Tsunami and his fifty-three and three-quarters HDBs. It said so in the stars, didn't it?

* * *

"Where did you get these?" I asked Gardo.

"They're my sisters'."

We were sitting on his bedroom floor, my back against his big oak desk and his back against his bed, looking through a stack of magazines. Man-hater magazines, he called them. I could understand why. Every other article was "How to Train Your Boyfriend to Beg" or "How to Tell If Your Boyfriend Is a Cheater" or something anti-boyfriend like that.

"This is what girls read?"

"All day long." He shook his head and got up off the floor, shoving a stack of folded clothes off his bed so he could lie across it while he rifled the pages of his magazine. "Sick, isn't it?"

"Truly." I picked up another one and flipped through it.

" 'My Prom Date from Hell.' "

" 'Transform Your Boyfriend from a 2 to a 10.' "

" 'How Playing Hard to Get Will Make Getting Him Easy.' "

Jeez. And girls said guys' magazines depict women badly.

The articles that weren't about how to hate your loser boyfriend were about makeup or dieting or exercising. That's what we were looking through the magazines for. Not the makeup part, the dieting and exercise parts. Gardo said his sisters were always trying the workouts they found in these magazines. Their biggest beef was with their abs and their rears, and he said they swore by the exercises they got from these. I didn't give a fig about my rear, it was the ab stuff I wanted to know. Between those tips and the stuff Coach Hunt was teaching Gardo, I would be smaller than Tsunami by Thanksgiving.

"Here's one that sounds good." Gardo held up a picture of a girl with green circles over her eyes.

"She's got cucumbers on her face."

"Not that page. The other one." That one had some hottie in a pink sports bra hanging off the end of a bed with her hands behind her head. He read the caption. " 'Thinking bikini? Quick ab crunches three mornings a week will minimize unsightly belly bulge.' "

"Who's thinking bikini?"

"You are. At least for the purposes of our research, you are. Your belt of . . . you-know-what . . . isn't on your shoulders, is it?" He ripped out that page. "Here, we'll make a stack of the ones we might use."

I took the article and set it on the floor next to my knee, then went back to flipping through my man-hater rag. The issue was a *Special RELATIONSHIP Edition!* "Did you know that four out of five guys have considered cheating on their girlfriends?"

"Get out."

"No, really, it says so right here. And four out of five girls like chocolate ice cream best."

"What's that got to do with cheating boyfriends?"

"I don't know, but they're in the same box. See?" I showed him the page with the colored squares and X's through boys' faces.

"Weird. Hey, here's another good one. 'Trim your torso with this bejeweled Belly Buster from Queen's Fit. With the heat action of a four-star sauna and the smooth curves of the Queen's Fit Lady Slim girdle, the Belly Buster targets the stubbornest tummies with high-sweat, high-comfort dual latex action. For the sportswoman in all of us.' It sounds like a fancy version of Coach Hunt's Gut Wrap."

"What's a Gut Wrap?"

"That's what he calls wrapping your stomach in plastic wrap to make you sweat off the weight."

"You want me to wrap myself in plastic wrap?"

"That, or wear this girdle. I'll let you have a choice on this one."

"Lucky me." I took the magazine from him. The girdle looked comfortable—stretchy yet snug, and definitely smoothly curved. But I couldn't do it; I couldn't risk someone finding out I wore a girdle. That was the kind of thing that turned up in the *National Enquirer* after you were famous and ruined everything. It would kill the Thuff Enuff legend. "Bring on the plastic wrap."

"Good, I've already stocked up for myself. I'll send you home with a box." He went to his closet and pulled out a bulging paper grocery bag. There must have been a dozen boxes of Saran Wrap in there. He tossed me one. "We also need to talk about what you're wearing."

"What's wrong with what I'm wearing?"

"Nothing . . . if you *like* that belt of yours. But if you're serious about losing it, you need to get some sweats and hoodies like these." He gestured to his outfit.

"I'm serious. See?" I picked the ab article off the pile of potential exercises and waved it. "But we're having a dry warm weather thingee. It's eighty degrees out. Aren't you hot?"

"That's the point. You think I'm dressed like this because I'm cold? They're called *sweats* for a reason. Make sure you wear an undershirt under your T-shirt, too."

"And still wear the hoodie?"

"Yes. You need to sweat out the weight. When we go running tomorrow, I want you wearing long johns, too."

"Running . . ." I nodded my head slowly. "Okay, I figured I'd have to do some running."

"Don't worry, I'll start you out slow. Two miles only." He reached into a dresser drawer and held up a pair of flannels. "Get these kind, they're the thickest. And you'll wear your hood over your head then, too. You lose nearly half your body heat through your head. We want to trap that in so you stay as hot as possible. I swear, Shermie, you've never sweat this much in your life. The weight will fall off, I guarantee it."

He lifted up his shirt and patted his sweaty belly with pride. It was way smaller than mine. I could see his ribs. "Then we'll do sit-ups. I'm working on a six-pack, so I do three hundred. You're new to this stuff, though, so we'll keep that light, too. I started at one hundred a day."

One hundred? What had I gotten myself into? Lucy's training had been hard, but at least that involved eating, not turning myself into a walking sauna. But I'd promised Gardo I'd do whatever he said, no question, and I meant it. I was serious about this. I was going to earn my legend. *Stuff that in your horoscope, Lucy.*

After I tore out the picture of the Belly Buster—*hey, you never know*—I settled back into my spot against the desk. We spent the next two hours poring over magazines and ripping out pages with ab exercises. His sisters would probably be mad when they saw the carnage, but Gardo didn't care. He had those girls wrapped around his little finger, just like every other female on the planet.

A couple of times I asked for a snack break—I'd skipped breakfast because of *his* practice, after all—but he only let me have two pickles and some celery. I liked pickles, but they didn't really fill the void for long. Gardo said they were good for me right now because, with them being mostly water, I wouldn't have to worry about working off calories. So I ate them without complaining. Besides, Lucy's graph had me scheduled for fifteen dogs tonight, so I needed to fast anyway. Fifteen HDBs required a lot of stomach space.

When I rode my bike home that afternoon to change for my shift at Scoops, I felt like a new man. I was focused, I was motivated, and I was more excited about my eating career than ever. Gardo was going to help me beat the belt, and then I'd be world champion when I turned eighteen. I could practically hear hot dogs spitting on the Nathan's Famous grill and smell the salty ocean air of Coney Island.

At the intersection of Lakewood and Palm Avenue, I turned right instead of heading straight. I'd take the long way home and enjoy the breeze on my arms and legs for the last time. After that, I'd have to wear thermals and hoodies for a while.

Plus the leisurely ride just felt good on my legs. They were loose now, all the wobble from my ride to Gardo's practice that morning worked out. I could've pedaled forever. My leg muscles were doing their jobs; my lungs were breathing deep and long. Maybe this exercise stuff wasn't so bad. Maybe I'd like running before school with Gardo. I'd be like Rocky, jogging through the streets of South Philly in his sweats and ski hat and taped-up wrists, only stopping long enough to slug slabs of frozen meat and race up a million steps in front of the Museum of Art. He went from Nobody to Champion, just like me. I was the Rocky Balboa of the Buffet Table. I was Sherman "Thuff Enuff" Thuff, the next Hot Dog–Eating Champion of the World. . . .

And the crowd goes wild. Thuff, Thuff, Thuff! The Champion of the World raises his arms up high, pumping his fists in victory. Thuff, Thuff, Thuff!

My bike hit a rock and I dropped my hands back down onto the handlebars to steady it. A loud gurgle rumbled my stomach.

I hear ya, Big Guy, I hear ya. The Hot Dog–Eating Champion of the World wouldn't have minded a little food.

Ladies and Gentlemen, Friends and Fans . . .

Welcome to Nathan's Famous Fourth of July International Hot Dog–Eating Contest, the most anticipated eating event in the world. We've sure got a match-up for you this year!

Dominating this twenty-eater table we have the reigning WORLD CHAMPION of hot dogs. Hailing all the way from Japan and weighing in at a mere 131 pounds, it's the Mini Monsoon of Meat, the Tiny Tidal Wave of Teeth, the One . . . the Only . . . the Devastating . . . TSUNAMI!

And on the far end of the table, anchoring the assault on Tsunami's reign, is this year's come-from-nowhere challenger, a gustatory upstart from deep in the central valley of California. Weighing in at an amazing 130 pounds, this natural-born eater has been gunning for Tsunami for four years. And now, today, at Nathan's, he finally gets his Big Shot to be the Big Cheese of Tube Meat. Please give a warm welcome to the Rocky Balboa of the Buffet Table, Sherman "Thuff Enuff" Thuff! Are YOU Thuff Enuff?

Thuff! Thuff! Thuff! Thuff! Thuff! Thuff! Thuff! Thuff! Thuff! Thuff! Thuff! Thuff! Thuff! Thuff!

CHAPTER 12

Fasting was for the birds. Or did I mean camels? Oh, who cared, whichever stupid animal it was that went without eating and drinking for years at a time. Because except for the pickles, celery, and two-inch tall cups of water that Gardo called "Gardo Glasses," I'd had nothing to eat and little to drink since my Three Musketeers and Pepsi feast the night before . . . and even that didn't count because of my reversal of fortune. I felt crankier than a camel.

Knowing I had a hot dog training session tonight was the only thing that got me through my sucky day. It went downhill right after my ride home from Gardo's house: I opened the front door into my cheek, I tripped getting onto the escalator on my way up to Scoops, I forgot how to spell my name when I filled out my timecard, and I bounced a scoop of Spazzy Monkey off the rim of a waffle cone. I'd never missed a cone before. I was definitely in need of this training session.

How long does it take water to boil, anyway? I drummed my fingers on the counter. *C'mon, c'mon* . . . I bounced on my toes for a minute, then walked around the kitchen island a couple of times. Like that would make it boil faster . . . I stopped at the counter and drummed my fingers again. *I swear, next time I'm nuking the dogs.*

Waiting at the counter with me was a line of fifteen hot dog buns, ready for action. I pinched the end of a bun. It resumed its shape quickly. Not bad. Lucy had picked out good buns for my training. They were fluffy and fresh, not squished and old and pathetic like some hot dog buns could be.

"C'mon! Boil!" I knew screaming wasn't going to help, either, but I just couldn't help it. This was torture. And it wasn't like I was bothering anyone with my yells. Mom and Dad were still in Tallahassee, and Grampy was closing Scoops tonight. It was just me and my HDBs. "Boil!"

I considered getting out the Nathan's Famous mustard and some ketchup, but condiments were probably illegal on the Gardo Esperaldo Diet and Exercise Program.

Water wasn't illegal, though—as long as I kept to my rations. Gardo said I could have eight of his Gardo Glasses each day without being in "hydration violation." Anything less than that risked dehydration; anything more risked adding pounds to the scale. While I didn't care that water equaled weight on a scale, I did care that weight added inches to my belt. So I would stick to my water ration and be glad for it. I was serious about this, after all.

As least Gardo okayed the fill line that I'd scratched into my plastic bun-dunking mug. He gave me the mug himself after our research session that morning. It would have to be enough to dunk fifteen buns in. And Lucy said that wet buns were the key to victory.

I nudged the water mug a few millimeters closer to the first bun. *Man, cooking takes forever.* The timer on the stove said twenty-six more seconds. *Close enough!* I flipped off the burner, carried the steaming pot over to the sink, then dumped the pot upside down into the colander. Once the cloud of steam cleared, I gazed down on a shiny pile of fifteen plump, juicy hot dogs. I could've eaten twice that many.

When the dogs looked dry enough, I slapped one into each bun and was HDB-ready. *At last!* Wait, not quite. I had one final thing to do while the dogs cooled: stretch. I was an athlete now, my body deserved to be properly warmed up. I put my right hand on my waist and leaned to the right, stretching my left hand to the sky. I repeated this stretch on my left side, then did five jumping jacks and two squats.

Then I remembered Mr. Olympia at the football stadium that morning. Someday I was going to be that cut; Gardo said so. *Might as well start now.* I tried to lift my leg up to the counter in the *Swan Lake* stretch, but I couldn't kick up that high. *Dang.* That guy had made it look so easy.

I dropped my leg to the floor. Maybe I'd just give my arms an extra turn so they wouldn't be trouble. *That* I could do. After all, my wrist and forearm had been pretty sore after the ice cream challenge. I couldn't risk damaging them again during HDB training. Dropping my arms down by my side, I shook them good and long until they were totally relaxed.

There. Done stretching, I planted my feet shoulder width apart, hunched over the HDB lineup, and poised my hands directly above the nearest HDB. It was going to be a great training session, I just knew it. If only Lucy could see me now.

I'd set the oven timer for twelve minutes, with three extra seconds for resuming my go position after pushing the start button. I took a deep breath. *Okay, here we go, fifteen dogs in twelve minutes.* "Aaaaaannnnnd ready . . . set . . . GO!"

I hit the timer button, then scrambled back into my ready stance. When I thought three seconds had passed, I grabbed the frank out of the first HDB, then broke the dog in half and shoved the pieces into my mouth side-by-side. *Bite, bite, bite, bite, chew, chew, chew, chew, chew, chew, swallow.* One dog down!

I was using the new and improved Solomon Method. I called it the Thuff Enuff Dog Dunking Method, and it was for eaters who couldn't swallow after just two chews like Tsunami.

Next up, the bun. I grabbed it with two hands, ripped it in half, then dunked both pieces into the water mug deep and hard. Water flew everywhere when I yanked the soggy globs back out. Shoot. All that H_2O, wasted. I jammed the wet mass into my mouth and to my surprise immediately swallowed. It had slipped right over my tongue and down my throat. *Oh . . . ow . . . ow . . .* The unchewed wad was going down hard, like I'd swallowed a big rock. I flashed on an image of Gardo's face as he'd choked and I started to panic. *Ow . . . ow . . .* I could feel the lump sliding slowly down my throat, millimeter by millimeter. When it was somewhere near my lungs, I looked toward the phone. Would the 911 operator hear me if I was choking? Then, suddenly, the lump was gone. It must've dropped into my stomach.

I'd have to be more careful.

I checked the clock. Forty seconds gone and I'd barely finished my first HDB. It was an awful pace, just awful. According to Lucy's graph, I needed a .8 dogs-per-minute pace if I was going to do just my pathetic fifteen HDBs in twelve minutes. And I knew from experience that I was going to slow down as time ran low. Twelve minutes was too long for me to sustain an eating sprint, at least this early in my career. But I'd have to *learn* to sustain it, for crying out loud, or there was no way I'd catch Tsunami's record. Fifty-three and three-quarters was 4.5 HDBs per minute. *4.5!* At my current pace, I'd be toast. The Thuff Enuff Dog Dunking Method's slower bite-to-swallow duration was killing me. I needed to speed it up.

I attacked the rest of the disgustingly soggy bun like a squirrel: *little bite, chew, chew, swallow, little bite, chew, chew, swallow* . . .

Better. The key wasn't quantity in the mouth, it was speed of the swallow. Now *that* was the Thuff Enuff Dog Dunking Method. Plus there was no chance of choking when the pieces were that small. At least I didn't think so. The memory of Gardo grabbing at his throat was so fresh, so real. I'd seen fear in his eyes last night, total fear.

My heart raced and my gut clenched, neither of which was good for eating. *Don't think about Gardo . . . Focus on the food . . . Little bite, chew, chew, swallow, little bite, chew, chew, swallow* . . .

Yet my mind kept replaying my Heimlich rescue. Only, in this version, it didn't work.

Little bite, chew, chew, swallow, little bite, chew, chew, swallow . . .

I saw Gardo in a casket. His sisters were standing around it, crying.

I stopped chewing. I couldn't do this. No one was here to give me the Heimlich if I choked. I didn't *want* to do this, not tonight. Sports was all about mindset, and right then, my mind wasn't so set on speed. Maybe it was a good night for capacity building. Lucy said I needed to do that. Yeah, I'd work on capacity instead. That was just as important.

I swallowed what was in my mouth then turned off the timer. I'd still eat fifteen HDBs, just like Lucy's graph said, but I'd do it in a lot longer than twelve minutes. Maybe thirty minutes. After all, it wasn't the speed that mattered in capacity training, it was the quantity. And just to show I was sincere, I'd whip up the extra five hot dogs from the second package. Make it an even twenty. Screw the timer.

Once the extra dogs were nuked, I stacked everything on a paper plate and headed for the couch. *Galactic Warriors* was probably on. They were always airing reruns on one channel or another, whatever time of day. Even though I didn't need to dunk since I wasn't trying to get those buns down fast, I brought the water mug with me. I was still as thirsty as a fish. This way, I'd get to enjoy my water the way it was meant to be enjoyed—swallowed straight, not absorbed in a soggy wad of bread. Wet buns might go down way faster and easier than dry buns, but they were gnarly.

I plopped onto the couch with the remote and my plate of dogs next to me. I planned to enjoy every stinkin' bite. The Nathan's Famous mustard in my fridge was calling out to me again, but I held strong. *See, Gardo, I'm serious about this.*

The first dog went down just fine. Well, technically, it was the second dog, if I counted the one I'd downed during the timed portion of this training session. I ate number two traditional style. Without the clocking pushing me, I had time to savor the bun-to-meat ratio that was so important to the hot dog experience. Too much dog in one bite could overpower the salt glands on the tongue, causing excess saliva production that washed out the meaty taste. Too much bun was just blah. Speed-eating with all its separate-the-bun-from-the-dog techniques didn't allow enjoyment of the food. Capacity training was way more satisfying.

As I suspected, I found *Galactic Warriors* pretty easily. It was on two stations, actually. On channel 14 was the "Quixote's Nine Lives" episode. I loved that one. There were nine different phaser cannon battles in nine different dimensions, and Captain Quixote died in eight of them. In the ninth, he foiled the ambush, saved the universe, and sealed his legend. Multidimension episodes ruled. The episode on channel 23 was "T'larian Justice." That one wasn't so exciting, but it was important to know well because it provided the core logic for Captain Quixote's beef with the T'larian magistrate in season three. They were plotting to nuke the Earth's sun, which was the symbol of the Galactic Federation and the heart of its mythology, but only Captain Quixote knew why the T'larians cared about any of that. And even he didn't remember the full reason until the season finale because at the end of this episode, his best friend, Commander Panza, got brainwashed, then popped him in the head with a T'larian Pain Stick.

Flipping back and forth between the two episodes, I worked through my HDBs. Numbers three through seven hit the spot nicely. Lucy had bought the good kind of franks, all juicy and plump, the kind that sent you straight to the ballpark no matter where you ate them. Combined with the top-of-the-line buns she'd picked, I had the perfect ballpark frank experience in my very own living room. Well, perfect if I could've heaped mustard and ketchup and onions and relish on them. But I couldn't, so there you had it.

Thanks to Gardo's strict food regimen, I had a lot of

room for the night's HDBs. But I started sensing trouble when I bit into number ten fifteen minutes into the training session. To be honest, I wasn't so interested in eating it. My stomach was nicely satisfied, thank you very much, and more food didn't strike it as necessary. But my brain knew darn well how to count, and ten was way short of my goal of twenty. What was I thinking, throwing in the extra five dogs? But I was committed now, so I ate it. Then I ate all but one bite of number eleven.

I stared at that last bite for a good minute or two. I was starting to feel the beginnings of *full*. This couldn't be good.

Leaning back into the couch, I burped a few small burps, then stuffed in that final piece of number eleven. The salty dogs were making me thirsty, big time, but with how stuffed I already felt, I was afraid to drink and fill up valuable stomach space. The thirst was pretty overpowering, though, so I sipped just enough water to wet my mouth. On to number twelve.

When the twenty-minute mark hit, I was about a quarter of a dog shy of finishing number fourteen. My tongue felt like it was filling my mouth, and when I test-swallowed with no food in there, just to see that everything was working, the swallow was a lot of work, like my tongue was in the way and I didn't have enough spit to get the job done. I could sense the prereversal gaggy feeling, that sensation of the back of my tongue dipping while the front stuck against my top row of clenched teeth.

But I had to keep going, so I bit the tiniest piece of the HDB, leaving an even tinier piece behind.

Chew and chew and chew and chew and chew . . . I finally made myself swallow, but I wasn't happy about it. And I still had six more dogs to go. *Dang.*

A medium-sized burp surprised me. It felt good, so I forced up another. That one made me feel a tiny bit better, but it wasn't as satisfying as the natural burp was.

I stared at my plate of waiting HDBs and sighed. I really didn't want any more hot dogs. Maybe I was hitting some kind of wall or something. That happened to a lot of athletes. I mean, I knew I *could* eat more if I could just *let* myself eat them, but still . . . No. No *buts*. *Climb that wall, Shermie, climb that wall.*

I peeked at the clock. Twenty-two minutes had passed. I needed to forge on. Clearly I was going to miss my half-hour goal, but I still needed to get my groove on. Sitting up straight, I took a deep breath, then bit half of the tiny piece that remained of number fourteen. *Chew, chew, chew, chew, chew, chew, chew, chew, swallow.* My stomach bulged, and I would've sworn it felt taller inside, too, like it was pushing up as well as out.

Stalling, I swallowed without food, then held my dipped tongue still in fear of the gag. Another burp escaped, but it wasn't a big help. *Six more to go.*

Biting into number fifteen was hard. I focused on my chewing, then swallowing but not really wanting to. I fell back into the couch. I had no interest in leaning forward, and I barely noticed the Galactic Warrior firefight in front of me. Number fifteen was cold, so it was even less appetizing. And it seemed saltier than the rest, somehow. At least the bun helped cut the saltiness.

I took a second bite, trying to chew it way over on the side, not letting it touch my tongue because I was now grossed out by the salty meat that half an hour ago was screaming my name through a bullhorn. I swigged water again to wash away the salty. Half of number fifteen was still left.

I paused. I could feel something, a big air bubble maybe, pushing up from the bottom of my stomach . . . *C'mon, c'mon* . . . yes, it was . . . a big—

BUUUUUUURP!

I tried to catch and hold it out for maximum relief, but with medium success. Ultimately the burp was a seven on a scale of one to ten. But it would do. I rubbed my face and took a deep breath, then shoved the rest of number fifteen into my mouth, trying to not let it touch my tongue. I swallowed tiny bits as I chewed the rest, sneaking the food around the back of my tongue and down my throat.

Two sudden, satisfying burps rocked me. *Relief!*

Gaining courage from the burps, I bit into number sixteen. Only I wasn't sensing trouble anymore—I was *feeling* it. Smack-dab in the center of my belly. I pulled up my shirt and patted my gut. It was taut as a rope, hard as a boulder, full as a canteen.

The rest of number sixteen was going to be T-O-U-G-H.

I bit into number sixteen and chewed with my mouth wide open, afraid to stop chewing because then I'd have to swallow—and that did not sound good. But sooner or later I'd have to, so I chose sooner: I swallowed. *Okay, that went down.* I bit again. *Bite, bite, bite, chew, chew, chew, chew, chew, chew, chew, chew, chew, chew, swallow.* I could do this. *Bite, bite, bite, chew, chew, chew, chew, chew, chew, chew, chew, chew, chew, swallow.*

No I couldn't.

My stomach was a balloon about to burst. I tapped my gut again. Jeez, it was harder after just those two bites. I still had three and three-quarters HDBs to go. No, I couldn't do this after all.

But the very moment I thought that, a wonderful thing

happened: I caught the biggest burp of my life. It was a gnarly, whopping burp, and I managed to drag it out good and long. The drop in belly pressure was immediate. *The glory!*

I scooched to the edge of the couch again, my back as straight as possible. Using my arms and legs as leverage, I bounced up and down a few times to pack the dogs into the bottom of my stomach.

I took another small sip of water. One-fourth of number sixteen to go. I seriously didn't want it. I wasn't going to reverse, but putting that last bit of HDB in my mouth sounded about as appetizing as putting in a spoonful of dead ants. Thirty-eight minutes had now passed, which meant my half-hour guess was way off. But I *would* eat twenty dogs, come hell or high water. So I bit and *chew, chew, chew*ed about a million times until number sixteen was dead and gone.

Groaning, I sagged back into the couch and watched a few minutes of phaser battles while I worked up the strength to go back to my dog pile. Captain Quixote dodged the Icarus 2000 into a sunspot region that brewed and rumbled like it was ready to erupt. The Icarus shook and bounced and a few heat shields peeled off, but it held together as Captain Quixote plowed unwaveringly forward. The man knew no fear.

And neither did I! I could be like Captain Quixote! I could stay the course even if a few heat shields peeled off! I hoisted myself up to the edge of the couch. It was a painful maneuver, but I got there.

Number seventeen was a serious belly strainer, but I ate it over the course of two more phaser battles. *In your eye, T'larians!*

Now I was officially hurting. Big time. Number eighteen was downright agony. My belly felt stuffed worse than any Thanksgiving, maybe three times over. I bet if someone had looked down my throat, they would've seen the food right up near the back of my tongue. I was *that* full.

The back of my throat got warm and sickly ticklish for a moment. I rode it out, but a terrible thought invaded my mind as I did so: I wanted a reversal of fortune. *Badly.* The relief of that burp at number fifteen was long gone.

But I couldn't reverse. That was for losers and I was Thuff Enuff. I could do twenty.

As I forced myself to chew number eighteen, I stared at the center of the hot dog in my hand. There were tiny, disgusting whitish specks in the meat. And the so-called white bread bun had a sickly yellow hue. *Ugh. Why did Lucy pick this brand of bun?* It was too fluffy, expanding into every crevice in my stomach. She should've bought cheap, wimpy buns. *Dang it!*

I caught two more burps, getting marginal relief that let me slump a little instead of needing to sit so ramrod straight. My breathing was shallow since there was no longer room for my lungs.

The last bite of number eighteen was in my hand. No way could I do twenty. Eighteen was a good show; I could live with it. Still, as much as I wanted this nightmare to be over, I could only handle half of that piece right then, so I bit into it long-ways. Now the white specs in the meat were exposed in their full glory. Talk about nightmare. I put the piece on my plate and rotated it so that I was looking at bun instead of massacred meat.

I leaned back, sipped, breathed a few moments, then made up my mind. Grabbing the last of number eighteen, I forced it between my lips. I had to chew it for a millennium, but eventually I swallowed it. *There. I did it.*

I fell back onto the couch. Except for my groaning, the house was silent. There were no cheers, no congratulations, no thumbs-up or high fives. It was just me and my two abandoned HDBs. I'd eaten eighteen HDBs in forty-five minutes. *Big whoop.*

I lowered myself sideways onto the couch, trying to breathe as shallowly as possible so that my lungs and diaphragm wouldn't push down on my stomach. Captain Quixote's Galactic Cruiser exploded into a bazillion pieces, the camerawork spinning and twisting along with the wreckage. I covered my mouth and quickly switched the channel to "T'larian Justice." Not that this episode was any more calming than the battle in the eighth dimension had been. In this one, a T'larian shuttlecraft piloted by brainwashed Commander Panza was on a kamikaze mission aimed at the sun. Captain Quixote was chasing his buddy in the Icarus 2000, which had been specially designed for flying close to the flaming star. He'd passed his heat threshold, but he was determined to extract Panza and escape despite the odds.

Watching scene after swooping scene of the sun's flaming surface, I started to feel flushed myself. Or maybe it was the eighteen HDBs in my gut finally sending my body systems into overload. Sweat was beading up on my forehead, it was hard for my brain to focus on the dialogue, and my eyelids felt heavy. As the IcarusCam recorded the shuttle's loopy swoops at the T'larian ship, I fought the dipping-tongue gag reflex. The pressure in my stomach was intense. No, it was beyond intense. It was death itself.

I can't take it anymore. I have to end the pain. I have to.

Slowly, painfully, I worked myself into a standing position. Macho or not, a man had to do what a man had to do.

I hobbled toward the bathroom. But after only a few steps, I burst into a painful gallop with my hand over my mouth.

Ready or not, butyric acid, here I come!

CHAPTER 13

Everything looked better in morning sunlight. Or at least it was supposed to. This morning, I wasn't so sure about that. The sun was only just rising, and Gardo had me on my porch at the butt crack of dawn on a Sunday morning in shorts, thermal long johns, pants, sweats, snow pants, undershirt, T-shirt, sweater, scarf, ski cap, hoodie (with my hood up!), gloves, and plastic wrap around my stomach and thighs. The garden thermometer next to the porch said seventy-nine degrees. I swear, Gardo had flipped.

But he was the coach, and what the coach says goes. Which, in this case, was me: I was going for the very first jog of my life.

Though it was early and I was bundled up like it was the Arctic winter, I was actually feeling okay about the upcoming jog. The relief of last night's reversal was huge, so I wasn't suffering any after effects from my training session. I felt pretty good, truth be told. I'd conquered eighteen HDBs, and now I was going to work off more of my belt so that I could do nineteen HDBs in Tuesday's capacity training. Life was unfolding nicely. Lucy would've been proud of me. I wanted to tell her, but I couldn't. I'd fired her and that was just the way of it.

"Ready?" Gardo asked. He was alternating between jumping jacks and jogging in place.

I was done rolling my shoulders and squatting, so, yeah, I was ready. "Now or never. Let's pound the pavement, Coach."

"All right, then. Giddyup!"

We took off at a gallop. The sun was rising in front of us, and the moon was falling behind. There was a slight crispness in the breeze that brushed my cheeks. My heart was *pump, pump, pumping* the blood through my body, and my leg muscles were stretching and getting juiced by the workout. Already I could picture myself racing up the steps of the library at Palm and Thirteenth, Rocky style. *I got the eye of the tiger, baby.*

I focused on breathing in, out, in, out. Gardo was next to me, playfully pulling forward and dropping back, pulling forward and dropping back. I kind of liked this, the two of us out here bonding, doing athlete stuff, while the rest of the world slept. It was a whole new side of our friendship.

The first block was all downhill. It wasn't steep, just a slight decline, but it was nice to have gravity working in my favor for the opening strides. I was feeling good, loose and lean. This jogging stuff wasn't so bad.

"You want to speed it up there, Seabiscuit? My granny walks faster than that. Move it, move it!"

Jeez, I didn't know I was running with Coach Hunt. I picked up the pace. My breathing picked up the pace, too. And my heart went from *pump, pump, pumping* to *pound, pound, pounding.*

"Much better," Gardo said. "Granny would have to be in her wheelchair now to catch you."

I flipped him the bird. I would've told him to stuff it, but since I couldn't breathe, I couldn't talk.

The plastic wrap around my belly started slip-sliding with sweat, and wet beads dripped down my lower back, under the plastic, feeling like an army of ants. My left calf twitched threateningly.

Gardo consulted the pedometer clipped to his waistband. "Point three miles down, one-point-seven to go. C'mon, Shermie, pick up those knees, find your rhythm."

I'll show you rhythm. . . .

A beat-up truck zoomed by, kicking up a cloud of dust. A beer bottle flew out the passenger window and exploded on the asphalt. Glass bounced off my shin. *Jeez!* If I hadn't had on twenty layers of clothing, that shard might've sliced an artery. What a lovely way to start a Sunday morning. Whose brilliant idea was this jog?

"When we're done," Gardo said, dropping back next to me again, "we'll have some pickles and a refreshing Gardo Glass of *agua*." He wasn't even breathing hard. "How does that sound?"

"Lovely," I got out between breaths.

Did Gardo know I was scheduled for water training today? I wracked my brain, but I couldn't remember telling him. He was so hard-line on the Gardo Glasses, he might nix that part of my training. Well, I just wouldn't tell him, that was all. I couldn't risk it. Anyway, what was a little water in my belly going to hurt him? He'd let me have hot dogs last night because they were part of my training, and water expansion was just as vital. I had a graph from Lucy to prove it.

The miserable army of sweat ants had now spread from my back to my front, and the skin under the plastic wrap around my belly and thighs was stinging and hot, like when a too-tight shoe rubbed my heel. My head might as well have been in an oven instead of that ski hat and hood. No heat was escaping through my head today. Making things even rosier, the downhill slope was leveling out, so I was losing gravity as a running partner. People did this for fun?

Gardo dropped back next to me again. "How you doing, Shermie? You're looking kind of tired."

Then why the heck are you asking? "Fine." I didn't want him thinking I was a puss.

"You sure?"

"Fine."

"Okay. . . ."

We jogged a few more feet.

"You know," he said, "you could *walk*."

You know, I could stop. "I'm . . . fine."

"There's nothing wrong with walking. My mom walks every day."

He might as well have told me to start carrying a purse. "She's a girl."

"True." A few more feet, then, "She says walking is better for you than jogging. Less pounding on the knees and spine, same weight burn. But you have to walk fast enough. It just takes more time, that's all."

"Then *you* walk."

"Can't. Hunt would have a cow." He pulled ahead again, leaving me to my misery.

I wished I *could* walk. Especially if it was just the same or better than jogging. Jogging sucked. But walking was for girls, and that was just the way of it. Rocky didn't walk. Hulk Hogan probably didn't walk. They were champions, and I was going to be a champion, too. So Thuff Enuff wouldn't walk. Period.

We jogged around the corner of Palm onto Thirteenth. That was when I remembered that Thirteenth Street was

162

uphill. *Steep* uphill. What genius put a library at the top of a hill? Didn't they know kids had to ride their bikes to the library? Didn't they know old people walked to the library? Didn't they know crazy wrestlers made their poor friends jog to the library?

I tucked my head down and pumped my arms harder. My heart pounded in my ears and my breath came in gasps.

"C'mon, Shermie, one foot in front of the other, same as on the downhill. You can do it! You just have to think you can."

I think I can, I think I can, I think I can . . .

Who was I fooling? I couldn't jog up this hill. I'd die before I got halfway. I was just sorry Gardo would witness my Walk of Shame.

I slowed down to a walk and—

"Ow!" I collapsed to the sidewalk, clutching my left calf, the plastic digging into my belly flesh.

"What? What happened?" Gardo stooped over me helplessly. "Are you okay?"

"Calf!" I was wincing hard, barely holding back tears. The muscle was locked so tight that my foot flexed backward, my toes trying to curl under, even inside my shoes. It couldn't have hurt worse if I'd squeezed it in a vise.

Then it locked down even harder.

"Owww!" My tears rolled free.

"Rub it, Shermie, rub it." Gardo dropped to his knees and started kneading my calf.

"Ow! Stop!" I shoved his hands away and rubbed it myself—furiously, with both hands. *Stupid Gardo for making me jog. It's my first time ever, we should've walked. Walking's just as good or better than jogging, his own mom said so. Some friend!*

He was right about the rubbing, though. It was helping my cramp loosen up. As lame as I felt doing it, I kept at it, all the while willing my aching, sweaty, wheezing, pathetic body to relax. But it was slow in cooperating. At least I was able to stop crying. My breath was still gaspy, but it was settling down as the cramp faded, and my pounding heart was slowing to a solid *pump, pump* again. The plastic wrap slid as I shifted around.

Gardo still knelt next to me. "Any better?"

"Some."

"Keep rubbing."

"I'm rubbing!"

"Good. That's the best thing." He sat back on his heels. "I had a calf cramp once. It hurt worse than when I broke my arm."

"Thanks for sharing that."

"Cranking at me won't help. It's just bad luck, that's all. Don't sweat it. You're an athlete now, things happen." He patted me on the back as a bike rider coasted down the hill past us. She was sitting straight up, her long blond hair streaming behind her, her hands stretched to the sky like she was on a roller coaster.

"Yee-hawwwww!" she yelled.

Of course you're happy, you're going down*hill. Gravity is your pal on the downhill.*

Gardo shook his head sadly. "And you were doing so great, too. If it wasn't for the cramp, you'd probably be running up those library steps right now."

He must not have seen my Walk of Shame. There was mercy in this universe.

"Stupid leg cramp," I said, gazing longingly uphill and shaking my own head. "It ruined everything."

Gardo stood and consulted his pedometer. "Not every-thing. We covered half a mile."

A lousy half a mile? Talk about shame. Maybe his pedometer was wrong.

He smiled down at me. "Way to go, man."

Way to go?

"You did great for your first jog ever. I bet Lance Arm-strong didn't ride his bike half a mile his first time out. And you know, by the time we get home, we'll have a whole mile under our belts. Our *smaller* belts. Nope, a mile ain't shabby."

A whole mile? No, that wasn't shabby at all, not for my first jog ever. *Wow, so there you have it, Thuff Enuff starts out strong again. Are YOU Thuff Enuff? I am!*

"Here." He held out his hand and helped me stand. I kept my left leg up, like a stork. Plastic-trapped sweat squooged around my lower back. "Test it"

Test it, my butt. If someone pokes you in the eye, you don't poke in your own finger a few minutes later to see if it still hurts. "I don't want to."

"*Athlete* now, remember? Get over it or get out."

"Fine." Hesitantly, I touched my foot to the ground. My full weight wasn't on it, though, not at first. I wiggled my toes. Then I flexed my ankle. Then slowly, gingerly, I put full weight on my leg. It wasn't so bad, actually. My calf muscle was still tight, but the burn was gone. My breathing was better, too. If I hadn't had the disgusting, slippery plas-tic wrapped around me, I would've been tip-top. "It's okay, I guess."

"Good." He slapped some dirt off the seat of my sweats. I knocked his hand away, scowling. He was the guy who was so worried about image. What if someone saw that?

165

I rested my hands wearily on my waist as a beat-up jeep whizzed by, honking its sick-bird horn and dragging a long, black cloud behind it. It smelled like cigarette smoke in a tar factory.

"Don't just stand there." Gardo bent down at the waist, his knees locked, and touched his toes. "Coach Hunt says to stretch when you feel tight." Then he stood up straight again and rubbed his stomach uncomfortably. "Jeez, it's hard to bend like that with this plastic wrap." He paused and looked around, then leaned in close. "What do you think of Hunt's Gut Wrap?"

"It sucks."

"It does, doesn't it?"

"Seriously."

He glanced around once more, like he was worried we were being spied on. "Want to take it off?"

"Heck, yeah."

"Good. Over there."

He pointed to a tall blue mailbox. We took turns standing behind it and stripping off the sweaty plastic wrap. The relief was immediate. The breeze that grazed my belly before I dropped my undershirt, shirt, sweater, and sweatshirt was like heaven, the lack of girdlelike pressure a blessing. *Gut Wrap, my butt. Try Plastic Wrap from Hell. Hunt is an idiot.*

"Where do we put this stuff?" Gardo was holding up a mess of drippy plastic as big as the slippery blob in my own hand. There was no trash can in sight.

I pointed to the mailbox. "In there."

We quickly opened the metal door and threw in our plastic. I let the door slam shut, and then we hustled away as fast as my calf allowed, just two innocent boys headed for choir practice in twenty layers of sweat-soaked clothing. *Who, us? No, Officer, we don't know anything about sweaty plastic wrap in the mailbox. We swear.*

When we were about to turn the corner back onto Palm, Gardo slapped me in the ribs with the back of his hand and pointed behind us. A black and white police car cruised toward our mailbox. We rushed around the corner and busted up.

"Man," Gardo said, "that was close. I bet the mailman's gonna be seriously ticked tomorrow."

I made a face. "Imagine the smell by then. I'm just glad this stupid calf didn't foil our getaway from the cops."

Gardo put his sweaty arm around my sweatier shoulder. I barely felt it with my thick clothing cushion.

"I'm sorry that happened to you, man," he said. "The first week of wrestling season, I thought I'd die at least three times. It'll get easier, I promise. In the meantime, nobody ever has to know. We got coach-athlete confidentiality." He turned an invisible key at his lips.

I was glad I had Gardo on my team.

We walked past a gray utility box. It was about waist-high, just the right height for a nice sit-down. But something told me not to suggest that to Coach Gardo.

A big rig passing by blared his horn at a little blue BMW. Traffic was picking up on four-laned Palm. Next to us, a gardener in khaki overalls sprinkled pellets on the lawn. Another gardener was hedging the strip of grass between the sidewalk and the road with a weed-whacker. A pack of bike riders in fluorescent colors zoomed by. The sun was now solidly in place in the sky above. The rest of the world was finally waking up.

I couldn't believe how hot and parched I was—or how

woozy I felt. I reached up to push my hood off, but Gardo stopped me. "Just a little bit longer, Shermie. Trust me."

I did trust Gardo. He'd known me since second grade, and he'd never let me down. Plus he knew how hard this athlete stuff was.

"Okay." I adjusted the hood so it wasn't so far over my face. I could live with light-headed for a while. Once my belt was gone, life would go back to normal.

Gardo saw me adjusting my hood and adjusted his hood the same way. Then he kicked into the Gardo Strut, his elbow locked straight and swinging back behind his rear. I did the same, working to time the rhythm of my straight-elbow arm swing just like his. It was hard though, with my bum calf and genetic lack of rhythm, so I started swinging my arm up over my head and then back behind me just as high. Then I started goose-stepping, which hurt my calf like a mama. But it was pretty darn funny to watch, I knew.

Gardo laughed and shoved me sideways. "You're such a dork."

"It takes one to know one." I shoved him back, but he tripped on the lip of the sidewalk and crashed facefirst into the grass.

Oh, jeez.

When Gardo rolled over again, his lips were caked with wet grass and grit. But instead of being mad, he was laughing.

"Nice move, Dancing Queen." I leaned over him and held out my hand. "Have a nice trip?"

"See you next *fall!*" He grabbed my hand and yanked me down.

When I rolled over, my face was caked with grass and grit, too. And I was laughing as hard as he was.

The gardener with the weed-whacker shook his head and moved away as we lay there in the grass, two dorks in twenty layers of clothing in broad daylight, wiping grass off our faces and laughing like a couple of second graders. I couldn't remember the last time I'd laughed so hard. It felt good.

Eventually we stopped laughing and just lay there, resting for a spell. *Finally.* My friend was a tough taskmaster. But I knew he was only being tough because he cared. I asked for this. And he deserved only my best efforts in return. And my honesty.

"Gardo, I have something to tell you." The sky above was the powdery blue of freshly spun cotton candy.

"Spill."

He wasn't going to like this. "I'm supposed to do water training today. Lucy's graph says so."

"I know."

"You do?"

He nodded. "Yeah. I saw the water graph, remember?"

"Oh, yeah." I did remember now. He saw it on Halloween night. Right after he almost died.

I sat up—*ooh, head rush!*—and rested my arms on my knees.

Gardo sat up next to me. "Water training is part of your core training. And core training comes first. Same as with your hot dogs yesterday. You said eighteen dogs, right?"

"And buns."

"Dang. I bet you *still* feel full. Man, I could never eat eighteen hot dogs and buns. I'd be praying to the Porcelain God by number twelve. Maybe number thirteen if I was lucky. You're a natural champion, my friend."

"Oh, well, you know. . . ."

"Just be sure you stick with the Gardo Glasses when you're not water training, okay?"

"Okay." It was so cool having someone understand me as well as Gardo did.

We stood up and resumed our slow walk back to my house. My muscles were cooling down and stiffening up. Not just the ones in my legs, but all over my body, too.

"How much water does the graph say for today?" Gardo asked.

"One gallon. It's always one gallon. But she has me scheduled to water train only on certain days. That way, I can rotate it with my hot dog training." It was all very organized and calculated. Lucy was nothing if not organized and calculated.

Gardo whistled. "Man, you'll be peeing for hours." He put both hands over his belly and then moved them away about a foot in front of him. "With a gallon of water in there, your stomach will stretch like a water balloon. That's gotta hurt. But hey, it can't hurt more than eighteen hot dogs, right? No pain, no gain." He laughed evilly and slugged me in the shoulder.

Ow. "I guess not. . . ." I wasn't so sure about that "no pain, no gain" business. I hated pain. Pain hurt.

I resisted the urge to rub my shoulder. Instead I flashed my biggest Thuff family grin and said what a natural champion should say, "Pain lets you know you're alive. Now let's get a move on, bub, my granny could do laps around you. And my granny is dead."

The flat part of Palm was ending, and now we were moving up the slight incline that just a half hour ago I'd powered down with the help of my friend Gravity. That was the problem with going downhill—you always had to go back *up*hill to get home. But that was life for you, too: Sometimes you went up, sometimes you went down, and sometimes you got a face full of grass and grit. And when grit happened, there wasn't much to do about it except spit it out and move on.

Get over it, or get out.

* * *

Thank the Galactic Sun King for water beds and moms who were paranoid about chiropractors. When Mom forced me and Dad to switch from metal springs to water beds, neither one of us sleep lovers was hot on the idea of giving up our cushy, just-right beds. But this afternoon I was ready to nominate Mom for a Nobel Prize for Brilliance. Every inch of me had screamed in pain when I'd dragged myself and my gallon of water upstairs after Gardo left to finish his jug. Now I was floating on my own personal ocean.

Too bad there was no ocean breeze in my room. Instead, it was a sauna. I had my window shut, just like I'd promised Gardo, and I still had on my hoodie and ski cap. Sweat was running down my face and even my fingertips. The garden thermometer outside the front door logged eighty-two degrees when I got home. I could only guess what the temperature was in my tropical room: ninety degrees? one hundred degrees? one million degrees? But Gardo was the coach.

At least he hadn't forced me to do my sit-ups. When he'd dropped to the ground to do his three hundred, I got to sit next to him and massage my calf some more. It was my first workout, after all, no need to kill me on the first day.

I gave myself one more minute on the soothing water

bed, then forced myself to sit up. Thirst was a more powerful motivator than pain. And my tongue was the Sahara.

Groaning, I swung my legs over the edge of the bed and
reached for my thirty-two-ounce Big Gulp Slurpee mug and
the gallon of distilled water. That was what Lucy'd brought
me, distilled water. I guess she didn't want me ingesting all
the chemicals that they put in regular water. Whatever. To
me, water was water. It was weird enough that they sold it
in stores. I mean, wasn't it free if you turned on the tap?
And what was up with there being *brands* of water? It wasn't
like companies had secret formulas for it; they just dropped
big hoses into rocky mountain springs and pumped the
water into their trucks. How could buying the brand with
the red label be any different than buying the one with the
blue label?

I filled up my mug to the brim and chugged it down, all
thirty-two ounces, without stopping to breathe. *Ahhhh.
Now, that hit the spot.* I was tempted to wipe my drippy
lips with the sleeve of my sweatshirt, but I didn't want to
waste a drop. Instead I licked them dry.

I got eye level with the gallon of water, trying to gauge my
rate of consumption. It looked about three-fourths full now,
which didn't seem bad for my first mugful. At this rate, I just
needed to drink three more mugfuls and I'd have the gallon
conquered. That seemed doable. While I wasn't thirsty anymore, I wasn't full, either. And with the water being cool
(not cold, I couldn't chug cold) my body felt mercifully re-
freshed on the inside. Water training wasn't so bad.

I lifted up my sweatshirt, T-shirt, and undershirt and
tapped my belly. *Thump, thump, thump.* Nice and solid,
like a watermelon. *Way to go, Shermster.* I poured another
mugful and grabbed a man-hater magazine off the stack
Gardo had sent home with me. I'd research while I drank.

172

It turned out that I'd grabbed the summer swimsuit issue. *Nice.* This miserable morning was looking up. Maybe researching wasn't so bad, either. No wonder Lucy liked it.

I propped my pillow against my headboard and shifted and twisted—*ow, ow, ow*—until I was leaning almost comfortably against the pillow, the magazine on my lap and the full mug in my hands. My stomach sloshed loudly, which I took as proof that there was still plenty of room left for more. Lucy had allotted me thirty minutes to get the full gallon down. By my estimate, I'd probably start feeling the urge to visit the loo in thirty-five minutes. Water went through a guy fast.

Sipping from my mug, I flipped to the table of contents. I'd do official research in a minute; right now I wanted to find the swimsuit section. *Health and Beauty . . . Fashion Fair . . . Hollywood Eye . . . Dear Editor . . . Features.* It was probably a feature. *"How to Know If Your Boyfriend's a Tramp" . . . "Beach Bangles and Bags" . . . "Beach-Friendly Workouts" . . . come on, summer swimsuits . . . "How to Hide Any Blemish" . . . "Beauty and the Beach" . . . "Beach Blanket Bikinis"—That's it!* Page sixty. Bikinis were the best kind of summer swimsuits.

I spent the next three or four minutes trying to find page sixty. The stupid page numbers kept disappearing and skipping and doing all kinds of weird things thanks to a million lame ads and lotion samples and subscription postcards and stapled inserts. *No, I'm not going to subscribe for four easy payments of just $4.44, not even if you do jam forty different postcards into the magazine "inviting" me to.* I shoved a pile of postcards and makeup samples onto the floor. Boy, there was a lot of crap in girls' magazines.

Realizing I'd just lost valuable water training time, I tipped my mug to my lips and downed as much as I could.

Halfway through, I came up for air, panting like a dog. The second round was harder, that was for sure. I took another deep breath then downed the rest, which made sixty-four ounces of water in my belly, half the gallon gone. And boy, did sixty-four ounces fill up a guy. I lifted my shirt and tapped my stomach again. *Ow.* No more tapping.

I studied the half gallon still sitting on my nightstand. How was that supposed to go down? The half gallon already in me was starting to hurt even without tapping.

I put my mug on the nightstand and wiped off the fresh batch of sweat that had broken out on my forehead. I'd lay off the water for a few minutes. I needed to give my aching stomach a chance to do some stretching.

Man, sitting in this room is like sitting on the sun. I pushed my hood off. That didn't give much relief.

I took another stab at finding page sixty. *Page fifty-six . . . page fifty-seven . . . ad for hair dye . . . ad for eyelash goo . . . ad for ugly pointy sandals . . . insert for mail-order beauty school degree . . . leaky lotion sample . . .* Were there any *articles* in this stupid magazine? Any at all? I didn't even care what it was about anymore; I just wanted a stinking article to read so I wouldn't have to think about the pain in my belly. *Ad for fat-free baked tortilla chips . . . ad for fingernail polish . . . "Beauty and the Beach"—There!* An article. It wasn't the one I was looking for, but it would do for something to read while I worked on my third mugful.

With my belly feeling like a bushel of watermelons was packed in it and my body locking up like a corpse by the second, I filled my mug a third time, sipped—*ugh, I am sooo not thirsty*—and started reading. The article was mostly just a bunch of tips from experts about how girls could get in shape for their bikinis by summer. I probably should've written down useful tips for losing my belt, but to do that I would've had to stretch to the other side of my nightstand to reach a pen and some paper . . . and there was no stretching anywhere with half a gallon of water in your stomach. I'd just have to remember the tips that might work for me.

"For beautiful beach feet, schedule pedicures at one-month intervals.—Monica Staral, NPA, INPA." Yeah, right, *that's* something I'd use. Too bad I didn't get my pencil to write that one down. Next!

"To give your hair 'natural' summer highlights at the *beginning* of beach season, skip the high-priced salons and lather in freshly squeezed lemon juice after each shampoo.—T'wanda Parkay, FE." Please, while I did like the bite of tart lemonade, I wasn't going to rub it into my hair. What was this woman thinking? And what the heck was a summer highlight?

"Eat a balanced diet, don't starve yourself. Being too light-headed to remember your day at the beach defeats the point of a well-cut bikini.—Shelley Stippen, RDN, RMN." You had that right, Shelley Stippen, RDN, RMN, LMNOP. I didn't know about the well-cut bikini business, but I knew firsthand that being light-headed sucks. *No swimsuit is worth that, girls. Trust me.*

"To look your best on the beach, replace high-cal, high-fat breakfasts with lo-cal, healthy energy boosters like this one: 1/2 cup Cheerios, 1/2 cup low-fat milk, 1/2 banana. Lunches can be quick, easy, and tasty, too: 3 oz grilled chicken, 1 whole wheat tortilla, 1 tbsp low-fat sour cream, 1/2 cup salsa, 1/2 cup favorite veggie with 1 tsp olive oil.—Bea Cantwell, CDN, RDN, LLN." What was all the one-half stuff? Hadn't old Bea heard of rounding up fractions? No wonder my mom has so many measuring spoons and measuring cups and food scales in the kitchen. For her, fixing lunch was like doing a Mad Max experiment. Dad and Grampy and I were the smart ones in the family, we bought our food at McDonald's or ordered takeout, so someone else had to do the math. And with me in training, Gardo was handling all my menus and portions, so this tip wouldn't do me much good. Thank goodness. Math was never my strong point.

I took another sip. My stomach felt droopy over my sides, like maybe it had done some good stretching. Lucy would've been proud of me. Slightly less than two mugs to go and I'd be able to mark off the water graph's square for this session. I took a deep breath and tilted the mug again. *I think I can, I think I can, I think I can . . .*

I stopped to breathe after drinking only a third of the water in the mug. I didn't feel so good. There was a nasty, warm, clenching sensation in the back of my throat. *Breathe, Shermie, breathe.* I leaned back a minute while the clenching subsided. Who would've thought water would be so tough to handle?

When I'd staved off the gag reflex, I turned to the magazine for distraction.

"Staying trim for the summer is not about deprivation, it's about moderation. Eat well all week, then eat whatever you want on Saturday—in reasonable portions. The goal is not to make yourself sick, but to enjoy the food.—Samantha Ordin, RDN, LCN, NNN." Now *that* was an interesting idea. I liked to enjoy food, and I hated feeling sick, and I certainly liked to eat whatever I wanted. That tip could work for me. When I lost my belt, I'd try this Whatever-On-Saturday rule. After all, I'd need to stay trim and beltless for my showdown with Tsunami. *Look out, little man, Thuff Enuff is gunning for you!* I flexed my biceps—*ow!* Now why did that hurt? I didn't jog with my arm.

Maybe I'd start the Whatever-On-Saturday thing now. It would be nice to enjoy food again, even if it was only one day a week. The bad thing about training was that eating had become all about increasing speed, or building capacity, or improving jaw strength. Where was the savoring? Where was the lip smacking and the finger licking? Where was the joy of eating? I missed the joy of eating.

Well, maybe I didn't miss the joy of eating right then. Right then, I'd have happily missed the joy of drinking water. The pressure on my stomach was hideous. I couldn't stand it, I'd have to do something about it.

Carefully clenching my tender abs and twisting ever . . . so . . . slightly, I worked out a huge burp. Then I breathed for a moment and assessed the pressure. It had gone down some, though not as much as I'd hoped.

"To make your skin luminescent in the summer sun, give yourself this home facial. Mix together one tablespoon honey, one egg yolk, one-half teaspoon almond oil, and one tablespoon yogurt. Apply to skin and rub gently. Let set overnight. Rinse and pat dry in the morning. Honey stimulates and smoothes, egg and almond oil penetrate and moisturize, and yogurt refines and tightens pores.—Sylvia Bukowski, RB, CF." Yeah, that's what I wanted to do, slather honey and egg yolk on my face . . . and on my pillow, and on my sheets, and in my hair. Girls were crazy.

Finally I came to the end of the list. "As you get in shape for this summer's teeny-weeny, yellow polka-dot bikini, remember this: The key to successful dieting is balance. A slim, healthy figure is not about extremes. Bingeing and purging is extreme. Refusing to eat is extreme. Don't try to do it all at once. One to two pounds a week is healthy weight loss.—Edna Flougherty, MD." One to two pounds a week? At that rate, I'd be ready for a bikini in 2050! I was *so* glad I wasn't a girl. It was ridiculous, the things they had to do to impress people. They should become athletes, like me and Gardo. That was the way to cut weight.

I checked the clock. Twenty minutes had passed, which meant I only had five minutes left to drink the rest of my water. But I still had one and maybe two-thirds mugs left. *One and two-thirds!* How was I supposed to drink that? Just finishing the third mug was going to kill me, a whole mug after that would never happen. Never.

What was I going to do? Lucy would think I was a loser if she found out I hadn't checked off all the squares on the water graph. Good thing I fired her.

I closed the magazine and laid it on the bed next to me. Focusing every ounce of willpower I had, I put the mug to my lips and downed the remaining water—two-thirds of the mug. Then I shoved the pillow out from behind me and lay flat on the bed, bobbing on the sloshing mattress. There was no sloshing inside my stomach, though, because there wasn't a sliver of space for the water to slosh around in. But there was pain. Oh, was there pain!

"No pain, no gain," Gardo had said. Clearly he'd never water trained. This was a nightmare. I hadn't even finished the gallon and I was in agony. Either my stomach was going to stretch a few feet bigger right that second, or it was going to explode.

As if on cue, the back of my throat clenched involuntarily, and the sick taste of acidy saliva rolled up onto the back of my tongue. *No!* I desperately tried to roll to my side and off the bed to dash down the hall, but I barely had time to turn my head before the water sprayed out of my mouth, all over my bed. Then another burst. Then another! The stench of butyric acid overpowered me as the watery reversal ran down the mattress and soaked into my clothes.

No, no, no . . . All I wanted was to get up out of the disgusting soup, but all I could do with my stiff and sore body was lie in the muck like a pathetic loser. I could've been stuck in Shane's trash can all over again.

Tears stung my eyes. I swear, if the training didn't kill me, I would die from humiliation. Nobody, and I mean *nobody*, would ever ever ever hear about this. Ever.

I stared at the ceiling and tried to will the tears to dry up, but they just keep pooling until my whole room was a wet blur. I couldn't believe competitive eaters went through this. Is this how Tsunami lived, in constant pain, with constant reversals, with no enjoyment of food at all? No way, it wasn't possible. No one would live like this all the time.

Maybe after Gardo helped me lose my belt things would be better. Yeah, that had to be it, or why else would the professional eaters keep at this? Lucy said some eaters even went out to dinner together after competitions. That couldn't all be an act; there's no way you could fake feeling good enough to eat when you felt this bad. They must have trained their stomachs, that's all there was to it. Someday my stomach would be able to expand fully so I'd be able to fit in all the water and HDBs I wanted—and go out to dinner afterward! Then I'd be on the road to hot dog–eating victory.

I wiped my sleeve across my eyes, my nose, my mouth, my whole wet face.

I just had to get through this tough phase, that was all. I

could do that. I was a Thuff, and everyone knew that when the going got tough, Thuffs got Thuffer. Just ask Grampy, it was in my genes. I was Sherman "Thuff Enuff" Thuff, athlete and future champion. *Are YOU Thuff Enuff? I am!*

I rubbed my hand through my pukey hair. *Ugh. I gotta get to a shower.* I wouldn't even try to peel off my disgusting sweats, I'd just step into the shower, clothes and all. Might as well be wet on purpose, and in *clean* water.

Man, the lengths an athlete would go for his sport.

CHAPTER 14

"You stood me up, you bum."

Gardo wasn't happy with me. But I wasn't happy with him, either. Even if I hadn't slept through my alarm this morning, I couldn't have gotten up to meet him for a jog around the track. My body felt like I'd gone ten rounds with Rocky himself.

Last night was rough. I woke up at least eight times to pee, and that was after whizzing my way through the afternoon. It didn't make sense. Hadn't I reversed all the water in my bed? And each time I woke up, I was stiffer and sorer than the last. Whoever said exercise makes you feel good was a dirty liar. I'd had to twist and toss myself out of my bed just to get to the john. I was up pretty much the whole stupid night. At one point I almost woke up Grampy to have him call me in sick to school, but I didn't because then I'd miss Max's test this morning, and she didn't do make-ups. How stupid was it to have a test on a Monday?

"I didn't stand you up," I said. "I slept through my alarm. There's a difference."

"Not on the track, there isn't. You're either there or you're not. You're not taking this seriously."

181

"I am, too. *I slept through my alarm.* Gimme a break. It won't happen again."

He studied me a moment.

Please don't make me do punishment laps. Please don't.

Finally he spoke. "Well, I guess I did sleep through my own alarm on Saturday. Cutting weight makes you sleep hard." He pointed a finger in my face. "I want you to buy a second clock tonight as a backup, got it?"

"Got it." *Phew. No punishment laps.* "Can we get to class now? We'll be late for the test."

"Yeah, we can go." He fell in behind me and delivered hurry-up nudges as I waddled toward the stairwell.

I stopped when I caught sight of Shane through the crowd. His bright red GO, PLUM WRESTLING! shirt stood out like a beacon in the sea of yellow hats and shirts. He was being pushed in a wheelchair by an annoyed-looking Finn, the other Finn twin nowhere in sight.

"Shane's in a wheelchair? I thought you said he pulled a groin muscle."

Gardo followed my gaze. "I know. Isn't it sick?"

"Just a little." *Get over it or get out, Shane. Jeez.*

"Just think if he broke a toenail. His whole body would be in traction."

Then Lucy crossed in front of Shane and I nearly choked. Talk about traction. If she saw me this morning, she'd probably go all Rocky on me. She probably hated my guts. She totally skipped the bus this morning just to avoid me.

I tried to hurry up the stairwell before she could reach it. I was already starting to sweat in the undershirt and hoodie that Gardo ordered me to wear with my Scoops shirt. At least I didn't have to wear the long johns unless we were working out.

Gardo started nudging me again. "Hustle it up there, penguin boy. At your pace, we won't get to science until tomorrow."

"Hey, you're the one who sent me up that hill."

"Just wait till you see what I've got planned for you later." He laughed evilly and slapped me on the shoulder. "That belt is going to fall right off you, buddy. I swear, you are one lucky hombre to know me."

Great. He'll probably have me climbing a mountain with a boulder on my back. And long johns on.

We merged into the crowded stairwell and made our way up to the third floor. Thanks to the bottleneck of Plums, even with my waddling pace we easily left Lucy far behind.

* * *

By "later," Gardo meant lunchtime. I figured that out when he plopped my lunch down in front of me at our table. When he'd agreed to be my coach, he'd demanded menu control, and of course I gave it to him. His first special delivery meal came in a white plastic container with a Gardo Glass of water and a spork.

When I lifted the container's lid and revealed a pile of chopped lettuce and four lemon slices, Tater laughed so hard that a Tot from his lunch trick shot out of his nose.

"What is this, a joke?" I shoved the container away like it was a plate of chocolate-covered cowpies.

"It's no joke, my friend." Gardo set a second lettuce-filled container next to mine and sat down. "I have a meet on Friday, and Coach wants me wrestling at one twelve. I need to drop five pounds by Friday afternoon. That's a pound a day. You and me will be eating the same things all week."

"This isn't eating, it's grazing."

183

"This is what *your coach* prepared for you. You will eat it."

It was Leonard's turn to laugh. "You sound like my mom, Gardo."

"He looks like her, too," Tater said.

Leonard slapped him in the back of the head, sending the other Tot flying. "Shut up, man!"

Gardo hadn't taken his eyes off me. "Eat. That's an order."

I stared down at my pale lettuce, which looked like it'd been run through a paper shredder with a dull blade. It was as mouthwatering as a garden of weeds. But what was I going to do, refuse to eat it? Gardo was my coach, and I was serious about my training. And now that I'd been up for a few hours without breakfast, I was freakin' hungry.

I picked up a lemon wedge and squeezed it over the lettuce. "Someone gimme a stupid napkin."

"That's my boy." Gardo tackled his own lemons and lettuce. "The trick is to chew for a long time so it lasts. Your stomach will think you're eating an eight-course meal."

My stomach isn't that dumb.

While I was chewing my lemony cud and trying to push away memories of Lemon Pledging the Scoops floor, I scanned the cafeteria. As always, it was packed and noisy. Girls were screeching and giggling, guys were hollering and whooping, and the janitors were sniping at each other about who had to clean up which section. That is, two of the janitors were sniping about clean up. The third janitor, who was scrubbing a swirly HAIL, MUSTARD! off the wall, wasn't sniping; he was cussing like a sailor.

How did the Mustard Taggers do it? They were striking almost every night now, yet no one ever saw a thing. Maybe

184

they did crawl in through the pipes, like Culwicki said. Or maybe they were like Spider-Man and scaled the side of the school to the roof. There was a door up there. We'd used it for the Newton experiment, when Max had us compare the falling speed of balloons filled with mustard versus whipped cream or just air. Or maybe the Mustard Taggers had keys and just walked in, easy as that. One campus security officer couldn't cover the whole school at the same time, after all. The video cameras they'd installed over the weekend wouldn't be much help; the lenses were found globbed up with mustard this morning, and would probably be that way every day. The Mustard Taggers were pros at keeping their identities secret. The rumor mill had been in high gear since they'd squirted that first yellow mustache on Culwicki's portrait, but no one had a solid lead yet. Not even Tater, and he knew every rumor before it started. He was the one who broke the news about the mustache. Apparently Culwicki had found the doctored portrait before anyone else and tried to hide it in his office. But Tater had eyes like a hawk, and he used them for the Powers of Good during his office aide period. He'd told everybody, and then the Mustard Revolution was on. Funny how Culwicki didn't think a prank was so funny when it was aimed at him. *Go, Mustard.*

A girl walked through my line of sight, blocking my view of the janitor for a moment. She was carrying a tray with a heaping plate of French fries doused in ketchup. *Man, that looks good.* The fries, I meant, not the girl. *Aw, jeez. Stupid belt theory. It has me checking out food over females. Pathetic.*

My table was just as bustling as the cafeteria. Today there were even more guys I didn't know squeezed onto the benches. They kept trying to talk to me, but as sore and hungry and thirsty and cranky as I was, I didn't bother to answer or find out who they were. If anyone else wanted to sit here, we'd have to drag over another table.

I stab, stab, stabbed at my lettuce, trying for another sporkful. Whoever invented the spork was an idiot. I looked longingly at my Gardo Glass. There was practically nothing in it, but practically nothing was better than totally nothing. I'd save it until after I was done with my lettuce so I could wash down the lemon residue. *There!* Finally a leaf stuck to the tines of my spork. It was an especially juicy piece. Good. Just like with wet hot dog buns, the more lubrication on a piece of lettuce, the better. I stuck it in my mouth and chewed it as long as I could, like Gardo said. I felt like a rabbit.

"Is that lettuce hitting the spot, Thuff Enuff?" Tommy asked. "Can I get you some rice cakes for dessert? Or maybe some wheatgrass?"

"Are you kidding? This is the best lettuce I ever ate. Doesn't it look appetizing?" I opened my mouth wide and showed him.

"Gross!" He bounced a balled-up napkin off my face.

That's what you get, Mr. I'm So Funny. Picking up the napkin, I wiped my chin then stab, stab, stabbed another sporkful. Stuck with being Bugs Bunny, I tried to distract myself by making a game of seeing how many mustard-packet handoffs I could spot around the cafeteria. It was like watching drug deals go down. I'd heard of the black market before, but never a yellow one.

When Lucy walked into the cafeteria, I stopped chewing. She was wearing a yellow polo shirt instead of her normal Chocolat du Monde brown. *Yet another Plum goes yellow.*

She stood there for a long minute, at the edge of the circle of tables, looking around like she was lost.

My heart skipped a beat. Without my table, Lucy had nowhere to sit.

She caught me watching her. I instinctively blocked her view of my lettuce. After the grief I gave her about non-ketchup-dunkable soup and salad, I couldn't let her see my pathetic lunch. But my worry was wasted. Straightening up and holding her head up high, she turned and walked out of the cafeteria.

The humiliation.

Tater hit me in the leg. "Hey, was that Lucy I just saw leaving? What's wrong, Thuff Enuff, trouble with the ladies?"

"Shut up."

"Where's she gonna eat? The library?"

Lunch alone in the library. I'd kill myself. "Who cares."

Gardo reached around me and jabbed Tater in the shoulder. "Eat your Tots, man." Then he leaned close to me and said, real quietly, "You okay?"

"Fine." I leaned over for a better angle at the hall Lucy just disappeared into. There was no sign of her.

Gardo nudged my shoulder with his. "Buck up, bud. You're doing fine. You don't need any more graphs. You got me!" When I didn't say anything, he tapped his plastic spork on my lettuce bowl. "Finish up. I've got a surprise. Well, two surprises."

I mechanically stabbed the lettuce with my spork and lifted it to my mouth, stabbed and lifted. There was a slight crunch with each twangy plastic stab, so I knew that the iceberg lettuce was fresh. That wilty stuff Lucy had for lunch last week was downright sad. She was right about the lemon, though. It gave the salad a citrusy, tarty bite that I wouldn't call appetizing, but it helped the bland leaves slide down my throat. Man, I was about as far from the joy of food as I was from eating fifty-four HDBs in twelve minuets.

All the time I chewed, I watched the door where Lucy left. Maybe she'd come back.

A red-aproned cafeteria lady pushed the French Fry Express cart across the doorway. Steam rose from the paper trays of freshly fried potatoes. I wouldn't have minded a piece of that action.

"Done?"

"What?" I focused back on my table.

Gardo had an impish grin on his face. "I said, are you done?"

I swallowed my last scrap of lettuce. "Done."

"Good. Here." He removed a clear sandwich bag from his pocket and opened it to reveal four long, skinny green wedges. "Surprise!"

Are you kidding me? "They're pickles."

"You didn't think I'd only let you eat lettuce and lemons, did you?"

I rubbed my face with my hand and sighed. "I stopped thinking anything after that first spork of lettuce." The room tilted a bit, and the pickles looked blurry around the edges.

Gardo pointed at his treat proudly with his spork. "These are not just pickles, Thuff Enuff, these are *dill.*"

"Oooh, *dillll,*" Kenny sang. The guys busted up.

"Shut your yap, Kenny," Gardo snapped. Kenny didn't know what a crank Gardo could be when he was hungry. But if Gardo hadn't said it, I would've. I was starting to feel like a bigger, crankier crank.

"Have any of *you* ever tried to make weight?" Gardo

188

asked. He focused on Kenny again. "Yeah, I'm talking to you, muscle man. That's right, cram that burger in your mouth and be quiet."

I took two of the pathetic pickles and started eating. Food was food when you were starving.

"Thanks for my surprises," I mumbled. The guy was trying to keep this making-weight thing fun. I appreciated the effort, at least.

"Actually, the pickles only count as one surprise," he said. "The other is outside. Come with me."

"But I haven't finished my pickles."

"Take 'em on the road. We're running out of time."

"Okay, but I gotta hit the john first." It'd been almost twenty-four hours since my water training yesterday, and I was still peeing like a racehorse. I would never understand why reversing the water hadn't gotten it all out.

Getting up and over the crowded bench was pretty tough thanks to my stiff, sore muscles. Tater was cool enough to let me shove and heave against his shoulder, though, so eventually I was free. I must've looked like the Hunchback of Notre Dame, all bent over and limping to the head. *Stupid training*. I was tired of being stiff, tired of being in pain, tired of being stuffed and thirsty and starving and cranky and dizzy and everything else. Training sucked.

A few feet away from the loo, I got cut off by a bunch of ninth grade girls. They didn't even acknowledge me stumbling backward. Apparently that was the girls' bathroom crossing, and I had wandered into their path. Silly me.

I waited impatiently as they strolled along. Finally there was a break in the line, and I dodged through it toward the guys' bathroom—and nearly tripped over Shane in his wheelchair.

189

He glared up at me. "Watch where you're going, Tub Enuff!"

Are you kidding me? You're in a wheelchair. What're you gonna do, bite me in the stomach? I stepped around him.

He grabbed my arm. "Don't ignore me, *scrub.*"

That's it! "Let go!" I yanked my arm up and it slipped out between his thumb and fingers, just like Captain Quixote did with the T'larian emperor in the "Quixote Strikes Back" episode. My muscles screamed in pain, but I was free.

I stormed stiffly into the bathroom, nearly knocking over a surprised Finn.

"Hey!" he protested.

"Don't start with me," I snapped. "What's a guy gotta do around here to take a pee in peace?"

The Finn paused, and I could almost picture his fist flying into my face. But at the sound of Shane's whiny call from outside, he turned and left. Lucky for him.

I stomped to the urinals on the other side of the room. They were empty, and there weren't any feet visible under the stalls. Finally, a moment to myself.

Only that moment stretched into forever. *Stupid water training.*

The urinal's white porcelain was covered with marking pens of every color. There were phone numbers, shout-outs, cuss-outs, even poems. *Jeez, does anyone take a piss around here without a pen?* The stall doors behind me, which I could see in the face-level mirror, were totally scrawled-over with GO, MUSTARD! in yellow highlighter. I guess even the Mustard Taggers had to answer the call of nature.

When I finally got back out in the cafeteria, the ninth grade ladies were filing back out of the girls' room. *Gee, what timing. Maybe later I'll get lucky and step off the curb in front of a truck. No, wait, I already feel like I've been run over.* I waited for the girls to pass, nearly screaming with impatience at all their strolling and giggling and girl-hugging.

Aw, screw it. I turned on my heel—*ow*—and headed out the other exit. I'd just take the long way around to the stadium. Given Gardo's pickle surprise, I wasn't in much of a hurry to see surprise number two.

* * *

"I am *not* jogging at lunchtime."

Gardo and I were standing on the straightaway part of the dirt track that surrounded the football field. He had his sweatshirt on, with his hood up over a wool ski cap that was so low on his forehead, he had to tilt his head back to see me. The sun was high and warm, though the breeze was cool, thank goodness. There was no one else in the entire stadium to witness us here, but that didn't make it any better. No witnesses were necessary because I'd be showing up to algebra class dripping with sweat, wheezing, coughing, and limping from yet another calf cramp. *Exercise feels good, my butt.*

"We don't have time for a jog," I continued. "The bell rings in six minutes."

"Then we'll do six minutes of walking. We wouldn't be here now if you'd been here this morning." Gardo did a quick leg lunge to each side. "Put up your hood."

I put up my white hood but refused to lunge. "We can't do this now. We'll get all sweaty, and I don't want to be all sweaty for the rest of school."

"Jeez, you can be such a girl sometimes. Here." He fished

my black Galactic Warriors T-shirt out of his gym bag and tossed it at me. "Don't worry, it's clean."

I held it away from me like it had maggots on it. I was *not* going to put that on. It shrank the first time my mom washed it, I couldn't even get it down over my gut. That's why I said he could keep it. How much humiliation could a guy take?

"Fine, don't put it on. Let's go." He started walking away from me down the track. "Shermie, remember our coach rule. What I say goes . . . so *go!*"

Stupid coach rule. I followed after him, the Hunchback of Del Heiny Junior 13. *Ow. Ow. Ow . . .*

"Good," he said, falling back to me. "We're not doing anything insane, just getting our legs moving. This will work out the stiffness."

I grumbled out of principle, but I had a feeling he was right about the working-out-the-stiffness thing. When I rode my bike home after racing to Gardo's wrestling practice the other day, my muscles had felt a lot better. Kind of loose and lean. But then, my wobbly legs after that sprint to the gym were nothing compared to this post-jogging agony.

We reached the first curve on the track.

"The best thing for stiffness is stretching the muscles," Gardo said. "Otherwise, day two stiffness is worse than day one."

That made me pick up the pace. "Worse" was not a word I wanted to hear.

I glanced at my watch. "Four minutes till the bell."

"That's fine. We'll just finish this lap. After school, I want you down here doing three more laps. That'll be a mile of walking. I have practice, so you'll have to do it without me. Got it?"

"Yes, Coach," I muttered.

"What's that?"

"Yes, Coach," I said louder.

"Promise?"

"I promise! Jeez, relax."

We walked the far straightaway in silence. I was less hunchback-y on that side of the track, and my calf felt a lot looser than it had when I'd flipped myself out of bed earlier. A bead of sweat trickled down my back. Thank goodness Gardo said we could dump the plastic wrap from our regimen. Even he'd had to admit that Coach Hunt's Gut Wrap sucked.

We rounded the final bend on the track. I was breathing a little harder than normal, but not a lot. It felt kind of good, actually, cleansing even. This was way better than jogging. I could do this again. The empty stadium was kind of peaceful, truth be told.

Another bead of sweat slipped down my temple. A movement on the school's roof caught my eye, a large bird or something. I whipped my head up for a better look and caught the sun hard in my eyes. The world went suddenly hazy and I stumbled.

"Whoa!" Gardo caught me. "What was that?"

I made sure my feet were firmly under me before I answered. "I don't know. I just got a little dizzy, that's all." I shook my head, making the dizziness worse. "Let me just stand here a minute."

"You need water. Here." He pulled a small water bottle out of the pocket of his sweatshirt. "Drink half of it."

I drank half of the water, and it worked wonders. Almost immediately, the dizziness was gone. I gave back the bottle. "Just thirsty, I guess."

193

"You'll get used to it." He put the bottle back in his pocket. Part of me wanted to rip it right back out and run for my life. "I've been rationing my water since tryouts. It's not so bad now, I'm only dizzy in the morning, after laying down all night. Be glad you don't have to wrestle for two hours every morning and afternoon on top of all the other training."

Amen to that.

"I could get used to this walking stuff, though. Look." I did half a squat and stretched to my left and to my right. Not bad. The muscles were sore, but they weren't so stiff.

We walked the last stretch of track, reaching his gym bag just as the first bell rang. When he picked up the bag, a ring of keys fell out into the dirt.

"Shoot," he said. "I forgot to give Coach his keys back this morning."

"What are you doing with his keys?"

He smiled mischievously. "I could tell you, but then I'd have to kill you."

"Funny."

He shrugged. "Trust me, Shermie, you don't want to know."

I pictured him fetching a box full of Gut Wrap supplies and Gardo Glasses and who knew what else from Hunt's desk. "I think you're right."

"I know I'm right."

We headed up the stairs quicker than I would've liked, but we only had two or three minutes before the second bell. In a few hours I had to be back here, finishing up my three laps. And who knew, a walk might be kind of nice after sitting down and stiffening up for the next few hours. Maybe I'd even stretch before my laps; that would probably make me feel even looser. I'd miss my bus, but that was no big deal, I'd just catch the city bus. It was always running between school and the mall. And I'd be sure to go to the electronics store on level two during my Scoops break to buy another alarm clock. I couldn't miss two mornings in a row with Gardo. He'd definitely have me doing the bleachers then.

Or worse, he might quit on me. And I couldn't risk losing Gardo, too.

* * *

When I walked into the football stadium after school, I couldn't believe my eyes. It was packed. Runners were sprinting around the dirt track, the Black Cherry Heirloom flag team was twirling purple flags in the visitors' end zone, cheerleaders were jumping and shaking purple pom-poms and tossing each other around in the middle of the field, and there was even a woman pushing a triple-wide stroller around the track with three matching boys strapped in it. What was up? That place should've been deserted. When the last bell of the day rang, most Plums I knew fled school like it was on fire. This was crazy.

I sat down in the home team bleachers to figure out what to do. Gardo wanted me to go down there and huff and puff my way around the track, but doing that in front of all these people would kill the Thuff Enuff rep in a heartbeat. He wouldn't want me to ruin my rep, now would he? Besides, I had about as much energy for working out as a turnip.

Rapid footsteps came down the stairs to my left, then stopped suddenly. I glanced up to find Mad Max surveying the field and breathing heavily. She was wearing

195

powder-yellow sweatpants and a matching zip-up sweat-shirt and sweatband.

"Ms. Maxwell? What are you doing here?"

"Sherman, hello! *Phew.*" She dropped onto the wooden slat next to me and jerked her thumb back at the stairs. "I do laps every other afternoon. Keeps me sane."

"Sane" was not the word I would have used for someone who ran steps voluntarily. An angry, hungry growl rumbled from my belly. I coughed to cover it up.

She studied the activity on the field below. "Did they drop anyone yet?"

"Who?"

"The cheerleaders. Someone eats turf at least once a practice."

"Ms. Maxwell!"

"Oh, don't worry, Sherman, those girls are like rubber; they bounce back up like nothing happened." She kicked her shoe up on the bench just below ours to tighten her shoelace. "Cheerleaders are amazing athletes. They don't get the credit they deserve."

I shrugged. "Jumping around with short skirts and pom-poms doesn't help them there."

"No, I don't suppose it does."

We watched the cheerleaders for a moment. A short girl with a long blond ponytail did a bunch of somersaults in front of a pyramid of six other cheerleaders. Just as she cleared the pyramid, another small girl flew up like a fire-work from behind the stack, kicking her legs into splits and touching her toes before landing on the ground with her two feet solidly together. Half a second later, the pyramid collapsed, with cheerleaders rolling in every direction, then hopping up and clapping and cheering like their team just won the Super Bowl. Then they stopped on a dime, dropped their clapping hands and smiles, and got to work on another pyramid, stepping on each other's hands and thighs and backs, completely serious and intense as they did it.

"That one who just did the somersaults," I said, pointing, "she's a Scoops-a-Million regular. Rocky Road, two scoops on a triple-dipped waffle cone, hot fudge, whipped cream, no nuts but two cherries. Every other night, at least. You'd never know it."

"Those girls stay active. I couldn't survive without my Friday fudge."

"I guess."

We watched the girls a minute longer; then Max clapped her hands on her knees and stood up. "Enough yakking. I can feel my heart rate dipping." She turned and raised a foot to start climbing again. "I'll leave you to your spectating."

"Oh, I'm not spectating. I'm here to work out."

She lowered her foot. "Really?"

What, is that so hard to believe? "Yeah, I'm gonna do laps. I did some today at lunch. And I'll be here tomorrow morning, too."

I stood up and pulled my hood over my head so she'd know I was serious.

"Well, that's great, Sherman. Just . . . be careful and take things slowly, will you? Speed kills, you know."

"I'm not doing my laps in a race car."

She laughed.

Hey, I made a teacher laugh. Score one for the Thuffster.

Her laugh trailed off, but her soft smile stayed. Was it any wonder every guy in school was in love with her? "I just mean don't do too much too soon, that's all. Be patient."

Just my luck, a lecture after school. I snatched up my

197

backpack and started down the steps toward the field. "Yes, Ms. Maxwell."

"It's the tortoise who wins the race, Sherman," she called out, "not the hare. Remember that."

"Yes, Ms. Maxwell."

"Work smarter, not harder."

"Yes, Ms. Maxwell."

"Where's your water? Drink lots of water!"

"Yes, Ms. Maxwell."

"And above all, have fun!"

"Yes, Ms. Maxwell!"

When I reached field level, I looked back up into the stands. Max was running up the steps again. She was going pretty fast, too, for a girl. She might've even given Gardo a run for his money.

I turned back toward the field as two runners sprinted by. Fudge Ripple and Butter Pecan. They waved.

"Hey, Thuff Enuff. All right!"

"Atta boy, Thuff!"

Swell. Between them and Max, there was no going back now. I was committed to lapping this crowded field. There was no way I was going to walk it, though. I wasn't a girl.

I hung my backpack on the wire fence, took a sip from the fountain at the bottom of the stairs—*shut up, Gardo, it was just a sip!*—turned to the track, and started jogging. I'd stiffened up again since lunch, so it wasn't a pretty beginning. The hunchback was back. Not as awful as before, but still. *Have fun, my rear. Nothing about this training is turning out to be fun.* After a few steps, my calf started to tighten, reminding me that I'd forgotten to stretch. I stopped and moved over to the grass.

As I was leaning left with my hand over my head, Fudge

Ripple came racing at me. All alone this time, he slowed, then stopped in front of me, bending forward with his hands on his knees and panting like a racehorse.

"Hey, Thuff," he said. Sweat splashed in the dust at his feet.

"Hey." I pushed my hood off for one last bit of breeze. "Where's your partner?"

He wagged his thumb over his shoulder. "Josh didn't want to sprint the last lap."

"You weren't sprinting when I saw you before?"

That made him laugh. "Funny one."

What? I was serious.

He stood up straight and then leaned sideways in a stretch that was just like my own. *See, Max, I know what I'm doing.* Then he switched hands and leaned to the other side.

That was what I was just about to do. So I did.

After a moment, he rolled his head forward, back, forward, back, very intense about it. It looked like it felt good, so I gave it a try. Yeah, it felt good. Next he hula-hooped his hips clockwise, then counterclockwise. *I can hula-hoop.* So I did. It kind of felt like we were doing a disco dance on the football field or something. As we hula-hooped our knees, Butter Pecan jogged slowly up to us.

"Hey, Thuff Enuff." He was winded but not the panting dog that Fudge Ripple had been after sprinting.

I smiled at him but didn't answer because I was being intense about my stretching, too. Fudge Ripple and I stopped hula-hooping, straightened our knees, and then bent forward to touch our toes. Or in my case, to touch the tops of my shins. It felt really good on my hamstrings. My calf, though, was ominously tight. I rubbed it.

Butter Pecan stretched his hand over his head and leaned to his side. "Bad calf?"

"Yeah."

"Rubbing is good. Maybe you shouldn't jog on it, though."

"Really?" *Keep talking, buddy.*

"He's right," Fudge Ripple said. "I strained my calf over the summer, so I walked for a few weeks instead of running. You gotta go easy on a bum calf, otherwise it never heals up. You need to be patient, don't push it."

Butter Pecan nodded, then hula-hooped his waist. "Walking's as good for you as running, so it's okay."

"Then why are you guys running?"

They looked at each other and shrugged. "We like running," Butter Pecan said.

Now I know you're crazy. We worked our legs into wide straddles and reached toward the ground. "Well . . ." I tried to sound thoughtful with my head hanging upside down between my legs, "walking would make me late for Scoops. But if it's best . . ."

"It is," Fudge said with finality. "Hey, will you be working on your ice cream training tonight? That was the coolest. I'd like to try it."

I stood up straight, then nearly keeled over from the head rush. "I . . . uh . . . no. No, I'm not doing ice cream anymore, just hot dogs." The throbbing relaxed and I could see straight again. "Brain freeze sucks."

"You can avoid that, you know," Butter Pecan said.

"You can?"

"Yeah. When you eat the ice cream, spoon it into your mouth upside down. That way, the cold ice cream doesn't touch the roof of your mouth, just the spoon does. No more brain freeze."

I doubt that. "I work in an ice cream parlor, so I know everything about ice cream, and I never heard that before."

"Apparently you *don't* know everything about ice cream."

"Whoa! Them's fighting words, buddy!" I put up my dukes. *Ow.* That maneuver was too quick for my head, and for my sore arms, too.

Butter Pecan threw his hands up to shield himself and backed away in mock fear. "Hey, now, go easy on me, Thuff Enuff. I heard what you did to Shane today."

I dropped my dukes. "Huh?"

"Oh, yeah, everyone's talking about it. You didn't know?"

"No."

"You're kidding? I think the scrubs are about ready to elect you class president. Anyone who can punch out Shane *and* a Finn is freakin' royalty."

Punch out Shane and a Finn? I just snapped at them. How did *that* turn into a punch-out? The Del Heiny Junior 13 rumor mill sucked.

"Look, Thuff Enuff, we gotta take off. My dad is probably already waiting in the parking lot. We'll catch you later tonight at Scoops."

They jogged to the stairs and started climbing. I couldn't think of any more stretches to do, so I stepped onto the dirt track and began walking my three laps. Right away I noticed that the stretching helped. I didn't feel so tight everywhere. And walking was definitely easier on the stiffness than those few steps of jogging had been.

Every once in a while, I stopped and rubbed my calf so that people would know I was walking because I was injured. The rest of the time, I just put one foot in front of the other and envisioned myself drinking a *huge* glass of water, eating Meat Lover's Supreme Deep Dish from Slimmy Jim's,

201

putting ice on my head to quell the pounding headache, and then taking a long, deep nap. And while I was at it, I composed a pretty cool eighth-grade class president acceptance speech.

Hey, crazier things have happened.

Friends, Classmates, Countrymen, lend me your ears. . . .

It is with great honor that I stand before you today, your humble servant and newest eighth grade class president.

When I first came to Del Heiny Junior High #13, I was much like you—a kid without a dream, without a goal, without hope . . . a Plum without a future. Then I discovered my calling, my talent, the reason I was put on this earth, and I realized that the key to my destiny had been within me the whole time. It just needed a little nudge, a little training. I did have a future, and that future was hot dogs. With that realization things tumbled my way—fame, riches, reputation, and, now, the presidency.

I am but a humble representative. My success is your success, and in voting for me, you have voted for yourselves. You have put your trust in me, and I am thankful. Rest assured that I feel my responsibility to my fans and fellow eighth graders. To you all, I pledge to be a president of action and change. My eyes are open to the things that need changing, and I am committed to making those changes. To that end, I, Sherman "Thuff Enuff" Thuff, eighth grade class president, hereby make three essential presidential promises:

Henceforth, all vending machines will dispense soda.
Thuff! Thuff! Thuff!
Henceforth, the cafeteria will stock mustard packets. And relish. Everyone's always forgetting relish. Go, Green!
Thuff! Thuff! Thuff!
Henceforth, the school colors will be changed back to orange and blue, and the mascot will be the Galactic Warrior Royal Ranger!
Thuff! Thuff! Thuff!

And, most importantly, henceforth, all those caught dunking scrub doughnuts will be sentenced to wear embarrassing wrestling singletons at school—ALL day, EVERY day!!
Thuff! Thuff! Thuff! Thuff! Thuff! Thuff! Thuff! Thuff! Thuff! Thuff! Thuff! Thuff!

CHAPTER 15

I was late for my shift at Scoops. I didn't care, though. I
wasn't cutting my afternoon workout short. It was Thursday, and I'd been walking the track at the stadium every
morning and every afternoon since Monday. That first
day's whole-body painfest was long gone, and there wasn't
even a hint of stiffness in my legs. And as of this morning, I
could make it around the track four times in one workout,
no breaking it up between the morning and evening workouts. That meant I was up to two miles a day. Not shabby
at all.

Grampy would probably be ticked that I was late, but
tough, that's what he got for starting my Thursday shifts at
four-thirty. Sure, Thursdays were busy ones at the mall, but
he and Arthur could deal without me for a few extra minutes. It wasn't like we did heart surgery there or anything,
it was just ice cream. People would live if they had to wait
thirty seconds longer to get their scoop. I wouldn't skip my
stretches for that. Those were even better than the walking.

I worked through my stretching routine, breathing in
deeply with the tightening of each muscle, then breathing
out slowly with each loose, limber release. I ended with a

relaxing wide straddle, reaching my arms toeward. Not that I could touch my toes, but my stretched fingers were a little closer to reaching them than they were just a few days ago.

What really mattered, though, was that it felt good to stretch. Nothing else felt even remotely good these days of stomach stretching and belt tightening. Seriously, if I wasn't stuffing my belly like a Thanksgiving turkey, I was delirious with hunger and thirst. I should've changed my name from Thuff Enuff to Stuff & Starve Shermie. I couldn't wait to drop this belt and leave the lettuce eating to the ladies. Let them worry about the ultimate summer bikini, I had my sights set on Tsunami and the Mustard Yellow International Hot Dog–Eating belt and then that would be that.

The breeze was warm again today. Thanks to my thermal shirt, my undershirt, my T-shirt, my sweatshirt, and my new designer trash bag, my chest and back were soaking wet. Of all the layering, I hated the trash bag the most. Coach Hunt had found out that Gardo wasn't Gut Wrapping and ordered him to wear a plastic trash bag with holes ripped for his head and arms. Which meant Gardo was making me wear a trash bag, too. It was tucked between my T-shirt and my sweatshirt. I felt like something that crawled out of the dump. When I shoved back my hood, my hair dripped with sweat. I had to squeeze my head under a water fountain spigot to get any relief after the walk. Luckily, I'd found a fountain at the base of the stadium steps that people didn't seem to know about. It was in a secluded corner; everyone else used the one by the entrance.

When it seemed like no one was paying attention to me, I grabbed my backpack from the grass and slipped around to my secret fountain. There I ripped off my soppy sweatshirt and top, then stuck my head under the faucet. *Ahh, cool water!* I splashed some of it on my chest, then rubbed myself dry with the towel I now kept in my backpack. I gave my belly a pat. Last night I'd downed the whole gallon of water before my fortune reversed, and on Tuesday I'd put away eighteen-and-one-bite HDBs before reversal. Maybe my capacity was expanding because my belt was starting to loosen up with the rest of my muscles. My training might actually be working. I just had to stick to Lucy's graphs and Gardo's workout routine and menus.

I still missed real food, though. Gardo stopped bringing pickles as dessert, and he cut back our water allotment by half this morning. He wasn't even showing up for our break feasts at the mall anymore. Lucy wasn't, either, big surprise. With nobody to hang with at break time, I just found a seat in the food court and people-watched while I gnawed the celery that Gardo cut up and bagged for me. Last night I asked him if I could at least put peanut butter on the celery, and he totally wigged out on me. Apparently peanut butter wasn't part of the Gardo Weight-Cutting System.

I reached into my bag for a fresh Scoops T-shirt. That was when I remembered that even though I'd meant to grab a shirt out of the dryer on my way out this morning, in my rush to meet Gardo I'd blown right by the laundry room. Shoot. I'd have to put my soggy shirt back on again. Disgusting.

I jammed the stupid towel back into my backpack. In the process, my hand pressed against something soft at the bottom. I pulled out a wadded piece of black fabric. My Galactic Warriors T-shirt. The shrunken one.

I stared at it a moment. Then I looked at the sweat-drenched T-shirt lying on the cement. I looked back at the black shirt in my hand. It was dry. *Aw, what the heck?* I pulled it over my head and tugged it down. It was snug around the belly, but it fit.

It fit!

"Woo-hoo!" I danced a wild jig, my hands waving every which way. "Thuff Enuff, you kick butt! Woo-hoo!" Man, I was lucky no one knew about this corner.

I grabbed my soggy stuff, jammed it all into my backpack, then raced up the stairs toward the bike racks. The Gardo System was working, my shrunken shirt fit! I punched the air like Rocky Balboa himself. *Jab! Jab! Jab!* Good-bye, jiggly ol' Shermie belt; hello, Mustard Yellow International Hot Dog-Eating belt! *Jab! Jab! Jab!*

* * *

I was a total loser. In the course of two brief hours I'd burned five waffle cones, cracked six triple dips, spilled a thousand-count bag of taster spoons, drizzled chocolate sauce on my shoes, squirted an old woman with whipped cream, and knocked Grampy's prized Halsey Taylor double bubbler drinking fountain with nonremovable anti-squirt technology right off the wall. All I'd been doing was leaning in for a quick sip of *agua. It was just a sip, Gardo, don't get a nosebleed.*

Maybe I should've seen the bad karma lying in wait for me tonight. When I'd raced through the Scoops entrance, my shin was covered with chain grease and I had a headache to beat the band. Definitely not a great way to start a shift. And then, being twenty minutes late, I immediately caught a cherry in the left ear from Arthur and a verbal kick in the pants from Grampy. And that was the good part of the evening. When I snapped at a woman for making me rescoop the ice cream for her spoiled-brat kids because my scoops "weren't round enough, young man," Grampy finally just kicked me out of Scoops altogether. "Take a break, boy."

"But it's not my break time."

"You're a human wrecking ball. Out!"

So there I was, sitting on the planter ledge near the down escalator just behind a potted plant, the side of my face against the cool glass wall, watching Lucy from above like some pathetic stalker. She was just below me, working the Chocolat du Monde cart at the bottom of the escalator with her Great Aunt Enith. It was kind of funny to watch them. They had the same quick, no-nonsense movements, and they moved like synchronized swimmers—when one ducked, the other bobbed; when one spun, the other tucked. You could set them to music. And they certainly had a lot of opportunity to twist and turn. The cart was pretty busy, and rightly so. Chocolat du Monde had the most awesome truffles ever, and their Black 'n' White Chocolate Glory candied apples were the world's tastiest fruits on a stick.

Lucy balled up a ripped bag, then rolled around her aunt, arching the paper ball into a nearby trash can. *Hole in one!* No, wait, in basketball it was a slam dunk. Whatever.

Lucy blew on her fingertip like it was a smoking gun, making me smile. I hadn't talked to her for a whole week. With all my morning and afternoon workouts, I wasn't riding the bus, so there wasn't much chance to talk even if we'd wanted to. And I didn't. Thuff Enuff's life was just dandy without her. I was in control of my own destiny and I liked it.

We didn't do lunch together anymore, either. She never came near the cafeteria. I had no clue where she ate. Not that I spent a lot of time in the cafeteria, either. Gardo and I spent most of our lunchtimes that week on the track. Eating lettuce didn't take long, so we had time to kill. Hanging out at my table wasn't so much fun without Lucy, and, anyway, if I stuck around it too long, inevitably the conversation came around to me kicking Shane's wheelchaired butt and body-slamming the Finn in the doorway of the guys' john. Gardo had spun that story so big that I could barely stand being in the same room when he started in on it. He should consider being a publicity guy, not a sports announcer. Maybe fame had its price, but it was no fun sitting there while he lied through his teeth about me. I was starting to think that "image" was just a nice way of saying "pack of lies."

It didn't help that sitting at the lunch table also meant I had to watch everyone else eat their hamburgers, corn dogs, or whatever amazing food they had piled in front of them. I could scream, I wanted to attack their food so badly. I was almost glad when the bell rang and I had to go to class, because in class, there was no temptation.

Down below, there was a break in the action at the truffle cart. Great Aunt Enith took off her apron and walked away, probably taking a break. Lucy could fly solo just fine. She was a pro under pressure. Maybe I would go down there and talk to her. Just to let her know I was still water and HDB training, and all. She probably wondered about it.

Even as I thought that, though, I knew I didn't have the energy to lift my face off the glass, let alone go down there. My head hurt too much to try to figure out what to say to her. So I just sat there, motionless, watching as she carefully nudged the truffles in the display window, making sure the stacks were just so. Every few nudges, she licked her fingers. I smiled again. Lucy hated it if food handlers didn't wear plastic gloves when touching her food. She said it was disgusting and if she wanted anyone else's cooties, she'd just ask them to lick her face. She could be very graphic when she wanted to be. That was half the fun of being with her; I never knew what she'd come up with next. Gardo rarely surprised me. He was like the twin brother I never had. We pretty much shared a brain, the poor guy.

Suddenly Lucy looked up my way. I tried to duck, but with this stiff body, ducking was impossible. So of course she saw me. *Shoot.* Now she'd think I was spying on her.

I stood slowly and waved. *That's right, Lucy, I meant for you to see me.* She lifted her hand to her waist in a half wave. *Great. Now I'm locked in. C'mon Thuff, you can do this. Captain Quixote had fourteen First Contacts, seven of them with hostile aliens. You can do one.*

Somehow, I mustered the energy to haul myself up and step around to the top of the escalator. I hated getting on those things even when I didn't have a raging headache. The stupid steps popped out of the floor and then sank so fast that I was always afraid of tumbling down. Trying to focus through my dizziness, I spent a minute timing it so that my foot would go down as a step poked out. But I was just too fuzzy to get it right. Finally I just grabbed the moving railing and jumped forward. My feet landed squarely on a step right before it sank. *Take that, headache.*

I leaned against the railing on the way down, rolling my head forward, back, forward, back. I loved the neck roll part of my stretching routine. It was so relaxing. And by relaxing my neck, shoulders, and upper back this way, I got some relief in my aching head.

Too soon, the escalator dumped me at the bottom. The Chocolat du Monde cart was just steps away. And so was Lucy.

"So you *are* alive," she said, studying me. "Barely."

I didn't want to think about my head, so I gestured at her yellow polo shirt. "You went yellow."

"Yeah. Anything to crack The Man's nuts. Like it?"

I shrugged. "Now you look like a banana instead of a Hershey's bar." *Idiot!* "That's a good thing, really, I like bananas, they're my favorite fruit, and yellow's my favorite color. *Love* it."

She stood there rapidly blinking her eyes like she didn't know what to make of the alien babbling gibberish at her.

"Yeah, it looks great," I continued. "Brings out the yellow streaks in your hair." *Oh yeah, that made things a lot better, you dork.*

But apparently it did make things better, because she smiled wider than I'd seen in weeks. Boy, I missed that smile. I could practically feel my bad attitude slipping away, soothing my sore muscles on the way down.

"They're called highlights, you goof," she said. "You'd make a terrible girl."

"Says you. You haven't seen these legs in a dress." I did a prancy two-step, then flashed her the Shermie Smile, all cheeks, completely irresistible. It didn't feel as fake as it normally did. "How come you're not wearing your uniform?"

"I don't have to anymore. Aunt Enith agreed that as long as I wear the apron, I can wear whatever I want underneath it." She wrinkled her nose. "I hate that apron."

"Just be glad it's not puke pink like my Scoops smock."

"I wish it was pink. Brown is the color of crap."

"Lucy!" I laughed. *That's my girl.*

Even she couldn't resist a light giggle at herself. It was nice to hear that sound again. She needed to laugh more often. Heck, what she needed was more Shermie time. I could make her smile, no problem.

"You know what?" I said. "You should come over tomorrow after Gardo's meet and see how my training's coming. My capacity is way up. Look!" I pointed to my Galactic Warriors shirt, then did a 360 with my hands over my head. It was still snug, but it fit. It fit! "This didn't fit before, now it does. My, uh, my *belt* is going away. I'm going for twenty HDBs tomorrow night."

"Twenty? Really?"

I nodded. She seemed impressed. "And I'm speed-training it. So it's twenty in twelve minutes."

"You're serious?"

"Totally." Yep, she was impressed. Good. Gardo wasn't the only one who can spin the glory tale. Now she knew I was my own man.

Someone yelled my name and we both turned. It was Paul from my American History class walking by the cell phone accessories cart. He gave me a thumbs-up and I waved back.

Lucy looked more annoyed than impressed now. "I don't know. You sure you want me over? You're awfully busy these days."

"Busy? What are you talking about?"

"I'm talking about all your beating up people and *Thuff Enuff*ing." She made invisible quotation marks in the air with her fingers. "Everyone's talking about it. It must be exhausting being a superhero."

213

"Who keeps telling everyone that? I didn't beat up anyone. You know I wouldn't." *You know I couldn't.*

She crossed her arms over her chest. "That's what everyone is saying, that the Great Thuff Enuff beat up Shane and a Finn."

"Well, everyone's wrong."

She didn't respond, just pursed her lips and scanned the busy promenade.

"Look, just come over after the meet," I said. "It'll be fun."

"I'm not going to the meet."

"What?" I couldn't believe it. Gardo had dreamed of being on the wrestling team since his mom bought him that first WWE video in third grade. "You have to come, it's his first one."

"He won't care, trust me." A customer walked up to the cart. "Hi, ma'am, what can I get for you tonight? Shermie, I gotta get back to work. I'll just talk to you tomorrow, okay?"

She'll talk to me tomorrow. . . . More crankiness slid away.

Catching the up escalator wasn't nearly as difficult as the down. Though the Chocolat du Monde cart receded below, the scent of cocoa stayed in my nose. I wished it wouldn't, actually. It made my headache worse, if that was possible. Pounding, aching, dizzy . . . I didn't know how I'd get through the rest of my shift. I'd probably crack twenty more cones, at least. Arthur would be throwing fruit at me all night.

You know what, I'm not going to get through it. I'm going to get my bike, go home, and curl up in my water bed with my last Gardo Glass of the day and my "Summer of

Fun" man-hater bikini issue. Arthur and Grampy could get along without me. They were always calling in sick on my shifts, but I'd never called in sick, not once. They owed me, and tonight was the night I'd collect.

I got off the escalator and stomped toward Scoops, determined to hold my ground in the face of any objection they hurled my way. Or, in the case of Arthur, any fruit he hurled my way. I wouldn't give in. I needed a night off and I was taking it. *Ladies and gentlemen, Thuff Enuff is leaving the building.*

CHAPTER 16

"The Elixir of Life. *Agua.* H_2O . . ."

Mad Max sounded hoarse today. She was sucking on a cough drop while she talked, and every few minutes she paused to sip from a tall yellow tumbler.

"You all know the subject of today's science concept in action as that clear fluid you're stuck drinking when the vending machine is out of Gatorade. Scientists, on the other hand, know it as the most essential part of life next to the almighty atom itself: water. Two parts hydrogen, one part oxygen. All around me I see water—each of your bodies is sixty percent water; each of your brilliant brains is seventy percent water; our school mascot, the oh-so-inspirational plum tomato, is ninety-five percent water. Water is so important to the human body that while we can go a couple of weeks without food, we can only go a few days without H_2O. You, my knowledge-thirsty young scientists, will be working with water in today's experiment."

I groaned. Here I was, back on Gardo Glasses again and so incredibly thirsty that I could barely see straight, and Max assigns a water experiment. The universe was cruel.

Max pulled on her lab coat and nodded at Lucy, who

passed out the Experimentation Documentation worksheet. Then Max put up an overhead of a grape and a raisin. The images made me think of the heaping bowl of raisin bran Grampy had eaten for breakfast this morning, right before his buttered cinnamon raisin toast. I'd pretended to be finishing my Spanish homework at the breakfast table just so I could be close to that buttery cinnamon smell. Twice during breakfast I'd had to wipe drool off my *Entradas* textbook.

Thankfully, Gardo's meet was today. After he weighed in, he'd have an hour to eat and build energy for his match. And since we were in this together, I'd get to "build energy" with him. He promised me it'd be the feast of a lifetime. I'd have the good end of the stick, too, because I'd just get to eat, not grab some sweaty guy in a singleton afterward.

Lucy stepped in front of my desk and handed me a worksheet to share with Tater. She started to move away, but I reached over the desk and touched her hand.

"What did you decide?" I whispered. "Gonna make it to the meet?"

She looked over at Gardo. He was leaning back in his chair, his head lolled back with his eyes to the ceiling. "I don't think *Gardo* is gonna make it to the meet," she said.

He did look like roadkill. And judging by the squinty once-over Lucy gave me, I probably didn't look much better.

"I'll come over after." She moved toward Gardo's desk.

Tater nudged me in the ribs. "Hot date?"

I punched him in the shoulder, hard. "Shut up, man, that's Lucy. That'd be like dating my sister."

"Sorry. Sheesh, someone's touchy."

"I'll show you touchy—"

"Sherman, is there a problem?" Max's eagle eyes drilled into me.

"No, ma'am."

"Then close the mouth and open the ears. I'll be testing you on this information."

"Yes, ma'am." I stomped on Tater's toe. He winced but didn't yell out. *Good, take it like a man.*

"Water is a key element," Max said, launching into the pre-experiment lecture, "one of the Big Four—water, fire, air, and earth. The balance of these four is delicate and essential to all life. If we allow this balance to falter, we throw off the balance of nature itself. Remember our static-charged hair last week?" She picked a black comb up from her podium and walked to the instructor's faucet, pulling out the two wooden chopsticks that held up her hair. Long locks cascaded down her back. Quickly she pulled the comb through her hair twice, turned on the faucet, then held the comb next to the stream of water. The stream bent toward the comb.

"I just covered this comb with negative electrical charges much like we experienced last week," she said. "Now those negatives are attracting the positive charges of the water, actually bending the stream. See that? Imagine the give and take that's going on at a cosmic scale. The sunspot activity last week heated the water temperature in the Pacific Ocean, creating an El Niño effect. This, in turn, results in increased storm activity all along our coast. We'll be seeing a lot of water very soon. Life on this planet is merely a series of delicate balances. The role played by two simple molecules—oxygen and hydrogen—is what we'll be exploring today."

Lucy rose up onto her toes and peered at Gardo's face. His eyes were closed now. *Ha! He's sleeping like a baby!* Max was definitely sick if she hadn't spotted that. Shaking her head, Lucy handed the worksheet to Leonard and moved on to the next table.

When I met Gardo at the track this morning, he was already looking like death in a sweatshirt. Coach Hunt had made the wrestlers practice an extra hour last night, and then everyone who was more than four pounds over their weight goal was forced to run several miles with backpacks full of dirt strapped tightly to their backs. On top of that, Gardo had ended the night with a one-hour stint in the sauna at his mom's fitness club. My buddy was superhuman to even be here today. He'd make weight this afternoon, I just knew it. He wanted to be extra doubly sure, though, so he'd been spitting all morning to cut down on water weight. He even had a plastic sandwich bag in his pocket for spitting during class. He'd also buzzed his hair almost as short as Tater's to make himself lighter. Personally, I wouldn't join any sport that made you shave your head. A guy had to have his pride.

"A gallon of water weighs approximately eight and a half pounds," Max said, setting a jug of water on top of the podium.

Wow. That was how much I drank in water training last night? Well, almost drank. No wonder spitting matters for wrestlers on weigh-in day. Water was heavy.

"The average five-minute shower takes between fifteen and twenty-five of these containers. The average indoor toilet uses twenty-eight of them per day—per *person*. Now imagine just one inch of rainfall on the ground. That doesn't seem like much, I know, but it's actually equal to seven

219

thousand of these puppies. We're talking nearly thirty tons of water falling to the earth in one simple spring shower, my young Einsteins. That's a lot of *agua*."

She went to her office on the side of the room and stepped inside the door. There was a lot of banging around and the sound of a chair being shoved across the floor and then a random crash. She stuck her head back out. "Mr. Finn, will you assist me, please?"

The Finn worked himself out of his desk and joined her behind the door. After more banging around, he came out pulling a large, red metal wagon. Four humongous containers of water sat in the wagon, with nozzled hoses running out of the top of each one.

Jeez, Max, drag a thirsty man to water but don't let him drink, why don't you? The torture!

"Today," she said, following the wagon, "we are going to reproduce Newton's water experiment. Each pair of you will measure out two and a half quarts of water, which is the amount of water a person should consume per day. It comes from all sources—food, straight water, etc. Then we'll . . ."

I was having a hard time concentrating on all the numbers she was throwing around. Or on anything she was saying, actually. Tater seemed like he had a bead on it, though, so I just let my mind drift. He'd get us where we needed to be with this experiment. The guy was way smarter than he acted; I'd figured that out over the semester.

Tater went to stand in line at the wagons. The jugs were huge. Maybe that's what was on her cart in the parking lot Halloween morning. When Tater reached the front of the line, he picked up a graduated cylinder, stuck a nozzle into it, then let fly.

I couldn't take my eyes off the beautiful stream shooting out of that nozzle. It looked so cool and wet and satisfying filling up our cylinder. I held my breath as he carried the container back. *Don't slosh it, Tater, don't slosh it. . . .*

Only when he reached our desk safely did I breathe again. The ripples in the water rolled outward from the center like solar orbits from the sun—perfectly round, perfectly spaced, perfectly synchronized. Max said water was the most important building block for life next to the atom itself. I had a few atoms that could use some water about now. *If I just took a sip . . .*

I glanced over at Gardo. He was awake now, sitting up and staring hungrily at his own cylinder of water. Our eyes met. We held the gaze a moment.

He knew what I was thinking.

And I knew what he was thinking.

If we're both thinking the same thing, then maybe it would be okay to both

In a sudden flash, Gardo grabbed his cylinder, flipped it upside down, then let it go. Water splashed everywhere.

"Hey!" Leonard's legs and feet got soaked as he stumbled backward.

Every head snapped in their direction. The empty cylinder rolled in a wide, lazy circle next to a huge puddle of water. Gardo stood next to Leonard, his pant legs wet, too. His eyes were wide and innocent, and his mouth was open in fake shock.

My mouth was open in real shock.

Max stalked over to Gardo's table, grabbing a stack of brown paper towels along the way.

"Stand back, don't slip." She threw half the stack at the water on the table and dropped the other half onto the

221

puddle. "Sop that up," she barked at Leonard, pointing to the floor. Then she turned her attention to Gardo.

Man, he'll be doing push-ups for the rest of class.

"This is not grade school, Edgardo. If you expect to continue in this classroom, you will conduct yourself like a scientist. And scientists do *not* spill their materials. What if that had been an acid? Go get the mop and bucket from my office."

"Yes, ma'am."

Max turned and clapped her hands. "Back to work, people. And let's try to keep our water *in* our containers. Lucy, show him where the mop is. Leonard, stop! Don't keep splashing in it. Is this kindergarten?"

When Gardo passed in front of me, he winked. "So much for temptation," he whispered.

"You're a troublemaker."

"And don't you forget it."

I waved him off, then reached for our Experimentation Documentation worksheet. Tater had already written our names on it in swirly green ink. All around us, the class settled into the low, soothing hum of young scientists at work.

* * *

Once upon a time, lunchtime was fun. I ate corn dogs and hamburgers and potato chips and fries, I drank smuggled Pepsi and root beer, I hung out with Gardo and Lucy and sometimes a few other friends, and we joked and laughed. Except for Shane's so-called pranks, lunch was the best time of the school day. Now there was barely room to squeeze myself in at my table with all my new friends, I didn't get to eat *anything* (that's right, not even lettuce today!), Lucy wouldn't eat in the same room with me, and

222

laughing was the last thing I felt like doing. How did things go south so fast?

Gardo and I were both slumped at our crowded table with our chins resting in our empty palms. No eating, no talking, no energy. Oh wait, silly me, Gardo had enough energy to occasionally pick up a cup and spit in it. What was I thinking to overlook that lovely sight? Tater was turned sideways so he wouldn't have to see it as he ate. Part of me wanted to tell Mr. Tots up His Nostrils that he didn't have much room to criticize someone else's table etiquette, but the rest of me didn't have the energy to care. Leonard was turned away, too, but it was probably more to hide his smuggled Ring Ding from the janitors than from disgust at Gardo's spit cup.

Leonard probably should've been protecting the Ring Ding from me. Man, that thing looked good. He must have babied it well during the smuggling operation, because I didn't see a single crack in the delicate milk chocolate shell. Would he eat it straight, like a sandwich that just happened to be made of moist chocolate cake and sweet, fluffy cream filling, or would he break it gently in half and scoop out the creamy white filling first?

I shook my head hard. *Jeez, I'm coveting people's food. What a loser.*

Next to me, Gardo spit in his cup again. I never realized what a nasty sound spitting makes.

Where did he get all that spit, anyway? He hadn't had anything to drink since last night before his sauna. He had to suck on hard candy just to generate enough saliva to spit. Personally, I thought he was in food violation, but Coach Hunt was the one who gave him the bag of those round, red-and-white Christmas peppermints after his run last

223

night, so who was I to question it? At least they gave him nice breath.

He spit into the cup again. I tried to focus on the paper turkey on the table, ASB's latest holiday decoration. Man, I wished Lucy were here. She was probably glad she wasn't, though. She'd hate sitting at this table now. I did.

"This is stupid," I mumbled.

"What is?" Gardo moved nothing except his lips.

"Us sitting here not eating. Why are we torturing ourselves in the cafeteria?"

"Would you prefer we torture ourselves in the parking lot? Quit whining and wait for the bell."

"I'm not whining. I'm just making an observation."

"And what observation is that, Einstein?"

"That we're idiots."

Gardo sighed, but he didn't argue my point. "Just a few hours more, Shermie, then we feast. I'll supply a meal that'll make your wig spin. C'mon, we got this far, we just have to tread water a little while longer. We're athletes, remember."

It was my turn to sigh. My lips felt like the desert. "Being an athlete sucks."

"Sometimes."

Runji interrupted us from the far end of the table. "Hey, Thuff Enuff, settle a bet. Roshon says you could put away twenty-five of these corn dogs in ten minutes."

He waved a corn dog in front of his face like a tiny flag at a parade. The gently browned breading extended almost an inch down on the stick, the perfect length for tearing free with your teeth as an appetizer before chomping into the corn dog proper. Like the chips before a Mexican dinner, it was enough to get the juices flowing for the main course.

224

The tip was yellow with smuggled mustard. Boy, did I miss corn dogs.

"I say no way," he continued, "*twenty* corn dogs, at best. How many do you think you can do?"

I didn't even hesitate. "Sixty-two."

"Sixty-two? No way, you're pulling my leg."

"Of course I am. Are you retarded?" *Jeez, does he think before he opens his mouth?*

"That is not how to make friends and influence people," Gardo mumbled. He picked up his cup and spit into it.

"Bite me." I slid off the end of the bench and stalked away from the table, my head woozing with each stomp. Where I was stomping to, I didn't know. But I'd had enough of their Ring Dings and golden-breaded corn dogs and peppermint spit.

"No can do, Thuff Enuff," Gardo called out after me. "I'm not eating today, remember?"

I flashed him the bird over my shoulder and headed for the john. This morning he'd ordered me to pee every hour, get out as much of the residual water as possible. He'd wanted me to spit in a cup, too, but I finally drew the line. I would not carry a bag of spit around in my pocket. Period. Since it had been an hour since my last pee attempt, I figured I might as well stomp over that way and see if the well was truly dry.

And who knew, splashing a little cold water on my face might make me feel better. Heck, it certainly couldn't hurt anything at this point. And maybe if I timed things right, a few drops of that water might *accidentally* slip between my lips. Hey, no one was perfect. Water will do what water will do.

* * *

225

Gardo hadn't shown up in the football stands yet. We were supposed to meet here half an hour ago. I was worried that his being late meant he hadn't made weight—

No. No way. Not with how hard he was working. Not possible.

I straddled a front-row bench at the fifty-yard line. Sprinklers doused the field next to me, slowly washing away the yellow chalk mustaches that had appeared this morning on the Del Heiny end zone logos. Tater was convinced that the mustaches were the work of a copycat tagger, insisting that the Mustard Taggers would only use mustard, never chalk. Like he was some kind of Mustard Tagger expert.

On the other side of the field, way up at the top of the visitors' bleachers, Culwicki was gesturing angrily at the janitors, who were lined up like a row of pickle spears in front of a wall of mustard. The campus security guy was there, too, in his olive-green uniform with red armbands. There was also some guy in a suit with a green tie. He could've been Culwicki's clone, so I figured he was Del Heiny High 3's principal. This was half his field, too, after all.

The line-up looked like a firing squad. They were too far away for me to hear what Culwicki was shouting, but it was definitely aimed at the janitors. Why was everyone always turning on them? I almost felt sorry for the big jerks.

I checked out the gate at the top of my stairs again. *There!* Gardo was running down the steps toward me, his red shirt bright against the gray cement. He carried a bulging brown grocery bag. That had to be a good sign. A brown bag feast meant the famine had worked, right?

"Shermie!" he shouted. "Shermie, I did it!"

"Yes!" I knew it! When Gardo wanted to make something happen, he made it happen. *Bring on the energy building!*

226

"Sorry it took so long," he said when he reached me, "the 7-Eleven on North Hill was closed. I'm so hungry, I thought I'd die when I saw the sign on the door about a power outage. I had to run two extra blocks to the 7-Eleven on South Hill."

He'd brought quite a haul. A footlong sub, super-sized Doritos, Chips Ahoy!, a bag of powdered doughnuts, and four cans of Pepsi.

"None of these packages are open," I said. "You didn't eat anything yet?"

"Nope. I meant what I said; we did this together, we celebrate together." Man, the guy had willpower. "I have to be suited up in half an hour, though, so rip off half that sub for me already, will ya?"

Eyeballing the mid-line, I tore the sub in two. Some ham and pepperoni slices slipped to the ground, but there was more than enough still on the bread. We timed it so that we both chomped into our halves at exactly the same moment.

"Oh, *gawd,* this is good." Bits of bun sprayed out of my mouth, but neither of us cared.

I closed my eyes in ecstasy and relief. The bread was soft and fresh, the lettuce barely soggy with its zesty Italian dressing, its tangy yellow mustard, its lightly spread herb mayo, and its thick dill pickle rounds. You never knew what you'd get in a 7-Eleven prewrapped sandwich, but this had to be the best sandwich of my life. *The joy of eating is back!*

I popped open a Pepsi and chugged it. My thick, dry tongue nearly stood up and saluted. The fizzies bit the back of my throat, but the sweet, syrupy liquid quenched my screaming thirst perfectly. Gardo was cramming chocolate chip cookies into his mouth almost as fast as he'd jammed in those mini Three Musketeers on Halloween.

I paused. I hadn't thought of Halloween for a few days now, not since I'd stopped speed training. I'd been focusing on capacity ever since Gardo . . . well, since he choked.

I swallowed my bite. "Slow down, buddy. You're not racing anyone."

He pointed to his watch and spoke through a wad of cookie. "Racing the clock." He swallowed and wiped his crumbly lips with his forearm. "If I'm late, Coach will have my hide. I'm on his good side right now. He liked that I cut that last four pounds so quickly. All I can say is, I'm just glad I spit out all that water weight. A good clean-out is the key." He shoved in another cookie. "Patrick Walter didn't make weight for the 103s, so Coach wants me to cut down to that weight class next week. He said that to do that, I have to wear the plastic bag the entire week before the meet, even when I sleep. He says when I wake up, I should be swimming in my sheets."

"No way."

He shrugged and finished the cookie. "It's more comfortable than that stupid plastic wrap was. So get ready, Plastic Man, we're doing the bag every day next week, even when we sleep."

The thought of another week of this made me wilt. I couldn't wait until I was as small as Tsunami; then I could get back to normal life. At least I didn't have to cut to a weight class. My mission was about how big my belt was, not how much it weighed. And since my Galactic Warriors shirt fit already, I knew that in just a few weeks I wouldn't have to ever think about the Belt of F . . . the Belt Theory anymore. Poor Gardo had to do it this whole season, then next season, then three more seasons at Del Heiny High 3. What an awful life. I swear, I'd quit the team if that were me. A big red "3" on a high school letterman jacket wasn't worth it.

I chomped into the sloppy sandwich, reveling in its flavors. Empty silver benches stretched around us, lying in metallic lines, end to end, row upon row. Except for me and Gardo, the stadium was empty tonight. Even Culwicki and his crew were gone. I almost hollered out, *"Helloooooo!"* just to hear the echo. I stopped myself, though, because the dead quiet was actually pretty nice. Peaceful, relaxing. There was no pressure to be "on," no feeling like everyone was checking me out, waiting for me to punch somebody out, to eat ten thousand gallons of ice cream, or whatever. No pressure from anyone for anything. It was weird, though. I'd always figured myself a full-stadium kind of guy, but there I was, enjoying the solitude.

Another messy bite of my sandwich dribbled Italian dressing down my chin. "This is *so* good. I'm sick of lettuce and hot dogs " I froze mid-chew. "Oh no."

"What?"

"I just remembered, I have to eat twenty HDBs tonight for capacity training. Wait, no, I'm speed-eating this session because Lucy's coming, so make that twenty HDBs *in twelve minutes.*" Twenty in twelve? What had I been thinking, telling Lucy I was speed-eating that many? How was I going to pull *that* off?

I set the last half of my sandwich down on the bench. It was almost too heartbreaking to bear, but I knew I couldn't eat any more. I shouldn't have eaten any at all. I'd just filled precious stomach space.

"Lucy's coming over?" Gardo asked.

"Maybe."

"You think she'll be happy with your training progress?"

229

I shrugged and rewrapped the crumpled plastic around the sandwich. "Dunno. She doesn't understand the athlete stuff. But she should like the HDB progress. I've been serious about it, just like she said."

"You have. I can vouch for you. Not that my opinion matters for much with Lucy."

"What's that supposed to mean?"

"I don't know." He grabbed a powdered doughnut. "It means what it means. Forget I said it." He bit into the doughnut, showering his jeans with white powder.

"No, tell me, what are you talking about?"

"I'm not talking about anything."

"Gardo." I stopped wrapping my sandwich and waited for him to go on.

Finally he couldn't stand the silence any longer. "I'm just saying I'm hardly Lucy's favorite person, that's all. We kind of annoy each other, actually. C'mon, you never noticed that? We only hang out together because we're hanging out with you."

"Please." I resumed wrapping. "I think starvation is shriveling your brain."

"Oh really? Name something she and I have in common."

"Who cares about *in common*? You don't need *in common* to be friends. Lucy and I just like hanging out together. We don't care what we do or when we do it. What do you and I have in common?"

"For one thing, we're training together. Or didn't you notice?"

"Besides that."

He thought a moment. "We like to watch wrestling together. And *Galactic Warriors*."

"Oh really?" I crossed my arms. "And what is Captain Quixote's call sign?"

He stuck a finger in his ear and wiggled it. "Excuse me? I didn't hear that. What?"

"You heard me just fine. Quit stalling."

He toed his sneaker into a drop of mustard below the bench, dragging it into a thin yellow line then swirling it up with a flourish at the end. "Fine. I don't actually *watch* the show when we watch it. It's nothing personal, Shermie, but . . . I don't know, I don't really care that much about it, I guess. I just like hanging out with you and throwing things at the aliens."

"That's all I do with Lucy. It's not some secret thing, we just come up with stuff that makes each other laugh, that's all. You can do that with her, too."

"Yeah, I guess." He consulted his watch. "Whoa, I've only got three minutes."

He started chucking things into the bag. I snatched a Chips Ahoy! before he grabbed the package. One more cookie wouldn't make a difference to my training tonight, not after the damage I'd already done.

"Are you coming over after the meet?" I asked.

"Can't. Coach is ordering pizza for the team. He says if we plan a victory celebration, we'll have a victory to celebrate." Coach Hunt might've been one nasty midget of a guy, but he had a good head for sports training. Me and Gardo were lucky to have him. "After that, all I want to do is sleep. Listen, Shermie, don't stay up late just because it's a Friday. I'll be over at five-thirty tomorrow morning, same as usual. Get yourself psyched up, because we start jogging again, and we'll get your sit-up routine going. You're losing your belt, now we have to tighten it. You think you feel good now, wait until tomorrow night!"

He took off up the stairs with his grocery bag. The sugar

from the Pepsi and cookies must've been kicking in, because he took the steps at a full run.

Me, on the other hand, I just sat there like a deflated lump. *Who says I'm feeling good right now? Hungry and thirsty is what I am.* The thought of not eating or drinking for another three or four hours—and worse, *jogging* again—sucked out whatever wind was left in my sails. Walking was so much better than jogging. I almost looked forward to walking. But *jogging* . . . *ugh.* I would've skipped eating for another *five* hours if it meant I didn't have to jog.

I'd had it right before, being an athlete *does* suck. Big time.

CHAMPION EATER SAYS SECRET TO GUSTATORY SUCCESS IS IN THE FEET

New York Times News Service

CALIFORNIA—Championship-level competitive eating does not stop at fast jaws or strong stomachs . . . it includes active feet, too. That's the message champion eater Sherman "Thuff Enuff" Thuff has for his fans.

"When I'm not training to increase my jaw speed or expand my stomach capacity, I'm walking the track. That's where the real magic happens." A champion who knows firsthand what it takes to turn daydreams into reality, Thuff Enuff says bigger isn't necessarily better when it comes to packing in the hot dogs. As his astounding success proves, a professional eater's stomach must be free to stretch when the pressure is on. "My fans always ask me, What's your secret? How do you eat so many hot dogs? I tell them the key to eating big is an unrestricted stomach, and the key to an unrestricted stomach is a tight belt, and the key to a tight belt is a brisk walk."

Thuff Enuff certainly knows about belt tightening. He'd dropped to an amazing 130 pounds when he stunned the world by eating fifty-four hot dogs at the Nathan's Famous Fourth of July International Hot Dog–Eating Contest, ripping the Mustard Yellow Belt of International Hot Dog–Eating from the reigning champ and record holder, Tsunami. "I credit my feet for that win as much as my mouth. I owe it to my fans to be clear, though: I'm not talking about jogging. Don't ever let the exercise whackos tell you jogging is the only way to go. Have you ever seen a jogger smile? Walking's just as good. Trust me. I'm a champion athlete, I know these things."

And it seems that when Thuff Enuff speaks, his public listens. Judging by the exploding number of aspiring eaters pounding the sidewalks and rounding junior high and high school tracks, legions of Thuff Enuff fans are following their idol's footsteps on the walking path to eating fame.

"It's so awesome to see that I'm making a difference," says Thuff Enuff. "My fans are the best. I just hope they remember, though, that I'm an eater, not a role model."

233

CHAPTER 17

It wasn't easy talking Grampy into letting me have a Friday night off. In the end, I had to resort to blackmail. He knew Mom would kick his can if I ratted him out for making me ride my bike home in the middle of the night. Not that I ever *would* tell her. If I did, Grampy and I would both be on a shorter leash. But I put on my poker face and made the threat, anyway, and Grampy didn't call my bluff. It was a good win for me. I didn't miss Gardo's first meet, and now I was home for my HDB training no matter what time Lucy came by.

"What's cooking, Thuffaroo?" Grampy cut through the kitchen on his way out to cover Arthur's break at Scoops.

"Just dinner. Lucy's coming over."

He peered into the pot on the stove. "You're serving her hot dogs?"

"We have to eat something."

He shook his head sadly. "My boy, that is not the way to impress the ladies. In my day, you wanted to impress a girl, you cooked veal."

"What's veal?"

"Just the finest of the finest, child." He grabbed a V8

from the fridge. I cringed as he swigged it. V8 tasted like someone took whatever they found in the garden dirt and just threw it into a blender, including the rotted stuff.

Grampy wiped his mouth with his sleeve. "I'll be staying to help Arthur close. You keep that girl downstairs tonight, ya hear? I don't want some angry daddy showing me the business end of a Louisville Slugger."

"Grampy!" I ducked as he mussed my hair.

"Ah, to be fourteen again." He grabbed another V8 and headed for the door. "Not a care in the world, and you don't even know it."

No wonder Grammy Esmerelda used to swat him with dish towels.

I finished cooking the hot dogs then loaded them into the buns, stacking them in a tower on a thick paper plate. Twenty HDBs, my goal for tonight's speed-eating session. It would definitely be tough. I could eat eighteen off the clock, but twenty in twelve minutes   well, I had to do it, and that was that. Next time I'd keep my big mouth shut in the first place.

Admiring my stack, I marveled at the fact that Tsunami could eat fifty-three and three-quarters in twelve. Every time I increased my quota, I realized just how far I still had to go. There were years of training ahead of me, at least, before I could compete on his level. And then I'd have a championship to defend for a few years. The joy of eating could be gone from my life forever.

I miss you, my little gummy bear friends.

But I'd made a commitment, and I was serious about it. Tonight twenty HDBs were going down in twelve minutes flat. No excuses.

And no reversals.

I stuck my plate of HDBs in the nuker so that when Lucy came, I'd just have to give them a quickie touch-up. In the meantime, it was *Galactic Warriors* time. Plus I'd bought yellow, pink, green, and light blue highlighters to bring my HDB graphs up to date. Lucy would want to see the graphs. For the water training graph, I'd only use blue. She'd like it that I was being theme-conscious. Color coding was an important part of graphing.

And when I was done with that, I'd open up my Captain Quixote telescope. It came today while I was at school. I was tempted to rip open the box now, but I'd never get to my graph coloring once I took out that telescope.

Three hours, four graphs, eighteen HDBs, and two episodes of *Galactic Warriors* later, I was flat on my back on the couch, my Polaris Model 76AZ-P 300 Power Captain Quixote Signature Edition telescope propped across my body. My eye was glued to the lens as I searched the moon. Lucy had stood me up, but who needed her anyway? I just ate the freakin' HDBs. Almost all of them. Sure, it took forty minutes instead of twelve, but so what? I did it.

And now I wanted to die.

But I wasn't going to reverse. If I couldn't eat them in twelve, the least I could do was hold them down.

I twisted the zoom knob on the telescope. The night was clear of all clouds, which was perfect for telescoping. So much for Max's great balance of the sun and tides and moon and whatever theory. It was like daytime up there, with the sun lighting the moon brighter than a Hollywood spotlight. I read somewhere that you could see Neil Armstrong's footprints if you looked at the right place hard enough, but I couldn't see them or his flag and I'd been searching for fifteen minutes now. *Stupid footprints.*

I dropped the telescope to my side and let out a gnarly burp. It wasn't much help. I rubbed my eyes.

Lucy liked to tell me that her ruling planet was the moon. She said that's why we've been friends so long, because we balanced each other out, me being a sun-ruled Leo and all. Well, we're not such great friends right now. Maybe there was something in Max's balance theory after all.

In the distance, a lightning bolt shot across the sky. I quickly put my eye to the viewfinder, but I wasn't fast enough to see the bolt magnified. It must've been raining hard somewhere.

I was tempted to scan the sun for the exploding sunflares that Max had lectured about, but I was afraid of going blind. The telescope was supposed to have a special patented solar filter just for sun gazing, but it was still scary. Max said 4.5 pounds of sunlight hit the earth each second. That's a lot of poundage. Maybe the Earth needs to watch its belt, too.

I shifted, groaning with the effort. My belt was killing me.

Jupiter. That'll get my mind off the pain. It's a big planet, it'll be easy to find. Following the directions on the telescope box, I twisted and adjusted until I had Jupiter in the center of my 5 x 24 viewfinder. They called it the Giant Planet, and I could see why. It was definitely hard to miss. It was looped by gas belts that made obsessing about my own stupid belt idiotic.

My stomach roiled. I swallowed hard, suppressing an acidy flush that tickled my throat just as the doorbell rang.

"Lucy!" I rolled sideways off the couch, landing on my knees, nearly reversing then and there. *Keep it in, Thuff, keep it in.* Using the couch for leverage, I pushed myself up, then hobbled to the peephole. Yep, it was Lucy. I flung the door wide. "You came!"

She smiled sheepishly. "I'm late again."

"Late, schmate. Who cares? You're here now, that's what matters. Come in." I stepped aside so she could walk by me. She smelled like chocolate.

She saw the evidence of my eating session on the counter. "Oh. You're done."

"Yeah. Sorry, I didn't think you were coming."

"I should've called."

"Forget it. It doesn't matter." I offered her the stool. "Want anything? Milk? Juice? I've got Pepsi under my bed. Or how about water? I've got a ton of that. It's in the cupboard here and I've even got some clean glasses ready and I can put ice in it if you want. . . ." *Jeez, shut up already.* This was Lucy, for crying out loud, why did I feel like I had to impress her? She'd been coming to my house for years. And she was the one who bought all the water. She knew I had it. If she wanted some, she could help herself.

"I'm fine," she said. "I can't stay that long, anyway. I got out of my shift, but I promised I'd reorganize the inventory after closing. Aunt Enith hates it. This time I'll try multi-colored dot stickers and a numbering system."

"Oh. Good. Dots and numbering. Good." I nodded and looked around the kitchen.

She nodded and looked around the kitchen.

We both nodded and looked around the kitchen.

Someone say something. Please.

"Oh! Let me show you something." I fetched my binder from the living room. The eighteen hot dogs in my belly slowed me down, but I tried to look peppy. I set the binder on the counter in front of her. "Look, I've been filling out my graphs."

"Really?" She slid the binder closer and flipped through the graphs, pausing on the water training page. "All blue. Nice."

Bingo! "See, I've been alternating water and HDB days, just like you scheduled. I'm up to twenty HDBs." She didn't need to know I hadn't broken eighteen yet. I patted my belly. *Ugh. Dumb move, Shermie.* "That's what I ate tonight, twenty."

"In twelve minutes?"

"Yep. In twelve minutes." What did it matter at this point?

"Shermie, that's great."

"Yep. Great."

She closed the binder. "So where's Gardo? I thought he was supposed to be here."

"He's having pizza with the wrestling team."

"Oh." A mischievous smile snuck across her lips. "So how'd the big meet go?"

I grimaced, not from stomach pain, but from the memory of the whole scary wrestling thing. What a nightmare. It kicked off with Shane wheeling around the gym, taunting the Del Heiny Junior 7 Early Girl wrestlers through a bullhorn, telling them how lucky they were that he was injured and couldn't squeeze their heads off in some weird kind of chokehold. Then Plums threw themselves on top of Early Girls and rolled around awhile and then whistles blew and then hands were raised in victory. Wrestling had to be the weirdest sport ever.

"It went fine, I guess." I lowered myself painfully onto the stool next to her, careful to keep my back straight to relieve tummy pressure. "Gardo won. But I couldn't tell you why. He flipped some slippery-looking guy onto the mat, then the guy flipped him onto the mat, then someone bled

on the mat, then the referee slapped the mat . . . I really
don't know what happened except that at the end, the referee was holding Gardo's arm up high and the Plum side of
the gym was cheering. So I guess he won."

Lucy laughed. "You definitely need to leave the play-by-
play to Gardo. ESPN won't be knocking on your door any-
time soon."

"For eating, they will."

"That's true. We all have our strengths." She slid her
hand slowly across the binder, then rubbed out a smudge.
"You know, Shermie, with twenty HDBs, you beat the
champ of the very first Nathan's Famous Hot Dog–Eating
Contest ever."

"Really?"

"Uh-huh. I don't know the guy's name, but he ate thirteen in twelve."

"Just thirteen? Thirteen is nothing." I definitely missed
having Lucy around. She knew useful stuff.

"Your progress has been good. Faster than I predicted,
even. Hey." She picked up the binder and skipped over to
the couch, where the highlighters sat on the coffee table.
"Let's plot a line graph showing my predicted progress versus your real progress. It'll be fun."

Ugh. I didn't want to walk over to the couch again. I didn't
think I *could* walk over to the couch again. But I couldn't let
Lucy know that. So, I worked myself to my feet, nearly reversing twice in the process. My belly pressure was agony.

She smiled and held out the yellow highlighter to me.

This is insane; I have to release the pressure. Just a little.
"Hold that thought," I told her. "I gotta hit the john first.
All that water, you know?" I pointed to my water mug on
the counter. *Shoot.* It was still full. She probably couldn't
see that from the couch, though.

Moving as casually—and slowly—as I could, I headed for the hallway, turning on the radio as I passed. The more noise, the better. Lucy's favorite song was on. What luck. She'd sit back and enjoy it, for sure. I'd have a couple of minutes to do this.

I hurried down the hall but didn't stop at the guest bathroom. It was too close to the living room. Grampy's bathroom would be far enough. Going the extra distance was a risky call, and I had to sprint the last few steps, but I made it there before the reversal. Trying to be quick and quiet, I didn't fight it, I just let it happen.

I got to my feet quickly and put my ear to the door. Good, Lucy's song was still on. I rinsed my mouth out in the sink, but the butyric acid taste wouldn't wash out. *Dang.* My breath would give me away. Maybe there were some peppermint candies in the Christmas decorations. Dad stored them just inside the garage. *I'll just step across the hall. . . .* I put my hand on the bathroom doorknob and pulled. Lucy was standing right there, poised to knock on my face.

We both jumped.

"There you are," she said. "I wondered where . . ."

I slapped my hand over my mouth, but not soon enough. I'd already blown puke breath into her face.

"What are you doing?" Her eyes narrowed. "You didn't do it again, did you? You didn't just throw up your hot dogs."

I started to say no, but then I didn't. Why did I have to defend myself? This was my house. She was the one spying on me. She should have been defending herself. "What were you doing? Listening at the door?"

"What? No. I didn't know where you went. I looked up and you were gone."

"I told you where I was going. You *were* listening at the

241

door. Jeez!" I pushed forward, trying to squeeze by her. "Move."

"I was *not* listening." She nearly tripped backing out of my way. "And don't try to twist this on me, Shermie. You were throwing up, weren't you? Is that what you do now, stuff it in then throw it up?"

"No."

"It's Gardo, isn't it? This is what he's teaching you. It's not normal, Shermie. Food is meant to go down, not up."

I flashed back to myself a few weeks ago, after my first HDB training session. It seemed forever ago.

"That's not how I trained you. You can't pig out then throw up. People who do that have serious problems."

"But you're *not* my trainer anymore. I'm an athlete now. I have an *athletic* trainer." *Aw, jeez, I just compared myself to a jockstrap.*

"Some athlete. You pig out, then puke. Real impressive."

"No one's twisting your arm to stay."

"You got that right. I'm out of here." She stalked back through the kitchen, flung open the front door, then charged through. "Leos suck!"

I chased after her and caught the door. "The name's Thuff Enuff, not Leo!"

"Stuff it, Thuff Enuff!" She stormed down the steps and across the front lawn.

Dense clouds were rolling across the moon, deepening the shadows as I rushed out to the porch. "Just remember, I fired *you*!"

Her long hair snapped viciously as she stormed away. She didn't bother looking for cars when she hit the street; she just stalked across to the other side then turned right, heading up the road toward the park and the mall on the other side. She disappeared into the dark shadows of the Martinsons' large hedge without looking back.

A raindrop landed on my cheek, then another. The clouds had swooped in and now blocked the moon completely. Lucy would be pretty dang wet by the time she reached the mall.

I went back inside and leaned against my closed door. *What just happened? How did a harmless night of training between friends turn into a flash fire?* A bolt lit the sky out the back window, then thunder clapped loudly, trailing off in a wall-shaking rumble. Raindrops pelted the roof. My stomach gurgled and launched an acidy burp, reminding me that I'd just reversed eighteen HDBs. With a sigh, I pushed heavily against the door, working myself up to a full standing position, and plodded to the kitchen.

Another flash lit up the windows. Ducking my head under the faucet, I rinsed my mouth to the rumble of thunder.

Who is Lucy to tell me how to lose my belt, anyway? She isn't an athlete. It was stupid to invite her over. I could've had a lovely evening by myself, just me and my telescope and my hot dogs. I could've done some research, even. I have that special summer swimsuit edition to work through, after all.

I cleaned up the kitchen and went to turn off the light in Grampy's bathroom. The room reeked of butyric acid. I almost threw up all over again. Reaching for the light switch, I caught sight of myself in the mirror. Lucy was right. I did look like hell. My cheeks were speckled with red spots, my eyes were bloodshot, and my skin was almost as pale as Tater's. *Great.* What was I supposed to do about that? It wasn't like I was a girl and could put on makeup. If people saw me looking like this, there'd be a whole different Thuff legend.

Wait, maybe there is something I can do about it. . . . I rushed upstairs to my room. Pulling my magazine out from under the mattress, I thumbed through the pages. That summer bikini tips thing had some mixture you put on your face in the privacy of your own home. It couldn't hurt to look at. No one had to know.

Page fifty-one . . . ad for pimple cream . . . page fifty-five . . . contest for year's supply of teeth whitener . . . ad for tampons . . . ad for tampons . . . ad for more tampons . . . ad for those ugly pointy sandals again . . . page fifty-seven . . . ad for home manicure kit—Good grief, who would use those harpoons on a toe?—more tampons . . . page fifty-nine . . . There. The summer bikini tips.

I climbed in bed and pressed the magazine open on my knees. Leaning back into the pillow, I paused to let the roll of the water bed soothe my exhausted body. I could've slept for a year straight. *Tell me I have a problem . . . I don't have a problem, I'm an athlete. Good thing Gardo's on my team, he understands that things happen. Get over it or get out, he said. Well here I am, getting over it. I'm a Thuff, and when the going gets tough, the Thuffs get Thuffer.*

The thunder rolled low and hard across the house.

I sat up and focused on the magazine. Now where was that? *"For beautiful beach feet . . ." "To give your hair 'natural' summer highlights . . ." "Eat a balanced diet, don't starve yourself . . ." "To look your best on the beach, replace high-cal, high-fat breakfasts . . ." "Staying trim for the summer is not about deprivation . . ." "To make your skin luminescent in the summer sun . . ."* There. I'd found it.

I settled in to study the benefits of slathering honey, egg yolk, almond oil, and yogurt on my face. I'd get myself looking normal again. That would show Lucy. I was more than *a Leo*. I was Sherman "Thuff Enuff" Thuff, aka Rocky Balboa of the Buffet Table, aka Captain Quixote, Savior of the Universe.

My stomach gurgled and a tiny burp popped free.

Now, if the Savior of the Universe could just figure out where his mom would store almond oil . . .

CHAPTER 18

"Let's go, girlie, lift those knees. Move, move, move!"

Gardo's wrestling win last night had really energized him. That, or Coach Hunt had given one heck of a motivational speech at the pizza party, because this morning my personal coach and supposed friend was a hyped-up slave driver. He kept jogging ahead, then dropping back to yell at me; jogging ahead, then dropping back to yell. Once he even dove to the leaf-strewn sidewalk and did push-ups on his knuckles until I caught up with him. It took every ounce of self-control I had not to stuff him down the open manhole we'd just passed.

"I swear, woman, you've got lead in your pants. Are YOU Thuff Enuff? I—don't—THINK—so! Let's GO!"

Despite my pleading back at my house, Gardo was making me jog to the library this morning. Which meant we had to run up the Thirteenth Street hill. I hated, hated, *hated* jogging, and I'd told him so, but in the end, he was the coach, so I had to do what he said. "Always respect the coach, Shermie, always respect the coach." Easy for him to say—he was the coach, and he got the respect. I just got heatstroke and a heart attack.

Starting the run was a mixture of easy and hard. I'd stretched out carefully, which always felt good and made the first few steps of exercise easier. And I'd logged some great zzz's last night, despite all the drama. I'd ordered a pizza while I researched my magazine and then took my own sweet time eating it. The reversal had cleared out my stomach, after all, and it was still a post-meet night, so I wasn't in violation of Gardo's rules. Feasting was part of it. Happy tummy meant happy dreams.

Morning—and my return to reality—was less dreamy. At five-thirty on the dot, Gardo had shouted through my open window that it was time to get my Sleeping Beauty butt up and running. Then he'd ever-so-kindly given me a spoonful of peanut butter and a Gardo Glass of water before we started. The saint. Then he informed me that that would be it for the rest of the day—no more food, no more water. I almost shoved him off the porch and went back to bed. My coach had lost his mind. How could I live on a lick of peanut butter and a drop of liquid? Hadn't Max said something about people needing two and a half quarts of water a day? No way was a Gardo Glass even two and a half *ounces*. I couldn't wait for the training part of my eating career to be over and the fame part to kick in already.

Instead I had dutifully sat there in my ninety layers of clothing, sucking my peanut butter spoon and waiting for him to finish the pull-ups he was doing on our rain gutter. I couldn't even see his face, his ski hat was so low over his forehead and his hood cinched so tight around his face. After fifty pull-ups, he'd dropped down and hustled over to me with a box of plastic trash bags, reminding me that I had to wear them all day every day under my clothes. How stupid was that? People would hear it crinkle when I moved. Crazy homeless guys wore plastic bags, not future champions.

Now every step I jogged, I heard the crinkle and felt the gross slip-slide of plastic over wet skin. If anyone but Gardo ever learned about this, I'd die.

I wasn't the only thing that was wet; the ground was soggy and slick, too. Last night's storm had been crazy— angry thunder and lightning and lots of water, just like Max had said there'd be thanks to the solar flares throwing off the cosmic balance. I bet Lucy got drenched. But hey, that was her choice. Now and then water dripped from the trees, plopping into my eyes. I was tempted to open my mouth and catch a drop or two on my tongue, but I was afraid of what Gardo would do if he caught me.

"I swear, Shermie, I'm gonna buy you a tutu. This isn't a dance class. Run!"

Stupid Coach Hunt and his motivational crapola.

My legs were lead weights, my lungs were on fire, and my dry tongue was the size of my shoe and just as tasty. My head felt every bit the sixteen pounds that Max had lectured, bobbing on top of my suffering body like a brick on a whipped cream sundae. Max had said our bodies were sixty percent water, but since I'd had just a few Gardo Glasses in the last few days, my body was probably sixty percent nothing. Just what did that make my brain, which was supposed to be seventy percent water? No wonder I was jogging at six in the morning with a crazed lunatic: I had nothing in my head but empty space.

"Pump those arms, lady! Get that blood moving, get those feet flapping! Rocky Balboa wouldn't walk. Run, run, run!"

An ocean of sweat sloshed between my skin and the

plastic bag. How could I sweat so much when I was barely drinking anything? Even without the sun at full force yet, my twenty layers of clothing felt like an oven.

A kid on a tricycle pedaled by with his dad jogging behind. He rang his bell happily. *Briiiiiing, briiiiiing.*

Jeez, I've just been lapped by a trike. I'm such a loser.

"Okay, Shermie, stop at the bottom of the hill here. Sit in the grass."

Say no more! I collapsed into the dewy grass, facedown. So what if it was wet; I was already drenched with sweat.

"Very funny, Shermie. Roll over and get into sit-up position. I'll do one hundred, but you can stop when I get to fifty. We'll start you out light."

Fifty is not light. Fifty is impossible. "Gardo, I can't do sit-ups."

"Yes, you can. You just have to believe you can. Coach Hunt says this is the hardest point—the day after the first win, the dawn of a new weight-cutting cycle. But we're not going to slack off, are we? We're Thuff Enuff!" He dropped down next to me and got in a sit-up position, lacing his fingers behind his head and closing his eyes in deep concentration. "ONE, two, three, four, five, six, seven, eight, nine, ten. TWO, two, three, four, five, six, seven, eight, nine, ten. THREE, two, three . . ."

I laced my fingers behind my head and lay back in the dewy grass, staring into the cloudy sky. The sun peeked through for a moment, but the clouds swallowed it up again just as fast.

Man, Lucy would've laughed her head off if she'd seen me there. Big bad Thuff Enuff, lying on the side of the road like an old couch tossed from a truck. Well, I'd just have to show her how it's done, that's all.

". . . EIGHT, two, three, four, five, six . . ."

But first I had to survive Gardo's morning torture session.

". . . seven, eight . . . nine . . . and . . . TEN!" Gardo dropped flat on his back, panting. Seeing that, I heaved a sigh of relief. No way would he get up and run up the hill now.

I pushed myself to a sitting position.

Gardo opened his eyes and smiled. "Now *that* was a workout."

I nodded and pushed my hood off my head. My ski cap was soggy.

"No, leave it on," Gardo ordered.

"But I still have my ski cap on."

"You need both. We're not done yet. We still have to go to the top of the hill." He rolled to his side, then popped up. "Let's go!"

He's lost his freakin' mind! I am not running up that hill. I'll die if I try. That's it, this run is over, here and now. Heaving myself to an almost standing position, I made as if to put my weight on my right leg, then doubled over, clutching my calf.

"*Ow!* Leg cramp!" I collapsed onto the grass. "Not again!"

Gardo dropped down next to me. "What happened?"

"Stupid calf!" I rubbed my right calf furiously. "Shoot, now I won't be able to finish the jog. *Ow!*"

He sat back on his heels and tilted his head to the side. "Wasn't it was your left leg that gave you trouble?"

"No, no. *Owwwww!* It's my right. *Owwww!* It's always been my right." I rubbed harder, wincing for emphasis. Gardo was checking me out hard now, but I was up to the scrutiny. I was Thuff Enuff, future champion, I didn't cave

250

under the gaze of a skeptical public. "I'll just rub it out and limp home. Go on, finish your run. No sense both of us missing out."

He frowned and looked up the hill, then back down at me. I couldn't tell if he was torn because he wanted to leave me here to finish his run or because he wanted to ditch the stupid hill himself.

"You can make it home?" he asked.

"Yeah, yeah. I'll be fine. Walking it out will be good."

He still knelt there, undecided, a ring of sweat soaking the neck of his hoodie.

"Go," I urged. "I'll be fine."

"Okay." He stood and kicked a snail across the sidewalk. "I'll go. But Shermie"—he locked his eyes on mine—"next time, I'm not closing my eyes when we do sit-ups." Then he turned and ran up the hill.

I swear, there were times I thought Gardo and I shared the same brain. And this time, he was letting me have my way. I wouldn't have to run anymore—ever—I just knew it. I'd won this round.

Sit-ups, though, that was another story.

* * *

Gardo's note was depressing. I found it taped to our locker door when I stopped there between third and fourth period. It turned out that even though we'd spent the whole week in high training mode, he wouldn't make weight for his second meet unless he cut three more pounds by three o'clock. So he was going to spend fourth period and lunch in the sauna at his mom's gym.

Which left me without my lettuce and lemon feast, since he was the one who brought it for me every day. And the last thing I'd do was sit at that crowded table watching everyone else eat. That was torture, not training.

Training. Please. Training wasn't anything like I'd thought it would be. I'd reversed at the end of every single session. Some future champion I was.

I walked past the rowdy cafeteria and headed for the main doors. As always, Shane's yelling carried over the din, but it wasn't his taunting stuff, he was just doing shout-outs to his friends from his wheelchair. I swear, the guy was just a waste of a red wrestling shirt now. He spent lunchtimes at his table pounding down huge plates of fries, not a care in the world since he didn't have to make weight anymore. If you asked me, without his daily dose of terror to keep everyone on their toes, he'd lost his power position. Even the Finns had stopped hanging around him so much. One of them stopped by now and then, kind of like a dog sniffing his master's body to see if he was actually dead, but otherwise they weren't much interested. And without Finns, Shane was declawed. He was just a big, annoying goof rolling around wrestling meets with a bullhorn. Some team captain. Gardo said he'd probably be replaced.

I was on my way to the stadium to walk around the track a little. It would be empty and peaceful. And I wouldn't have to worry about anyone seeing me walk. Just like I'd predicted, Gardo had agreed to let me do that instead of jog. He hadn't even put up a fight. "I guess it would be good for your calf," he'd said, "*both* of them. Just make sure you walk *fast.*"

When I was almost at the stadium, I heard the fast *thup-thup-thup-thup-thup* of helicopter blades. I squinted against the sun. A helicopter was coming in low, circling around for a pass not far above my head. I looked around me, trying to see what would interest the pilot, but nothing caught my eye. I did see some movement on the roof, something yellow maybe, but I couldn't quite tell from this angle. Then my gaze dropped and I discovered that I was standing on yellow paint. Someone had graffitied a message on the sidewalk.

I moved off the paint, trying to read the words, which were very large and very messy. I bet they could read it just fine from that helicopter, though, which I now saw was a KPUT news chopper.

It took me a few moments, but I finally worked out what the yellow graffiti said: KETCHUP IS FOR WIENERS!

Yikes. I scurried away. I didn't want to be seen anywhere near this. It was in *paint.* That was a whole level above squeezed mustard and even chalk. *Dang.* The Del Heiny company wouldn't be happy to see this on the news. Which meant the school board wouldn't be happy, which meant Principal Culwicki wouldn't be . . . well, suffice it to say, someone was in Big Trouble now.

All is not peachy in the tomato empire. . . .

Good evening, ladies and gentlemen. This is Dan Druthers reporting from the KPUT News Center.

Del Heiny Ketchup Company is losing control of its high school empire. That's what people are saying tonight as janitors sandblast a large anti-ketchup message sprayed in yellow paint on the Del Heiny Junior High School #13 campus.

According to an anonymous Del Heiny Junior 13 employee, this is not the first anti-ketchup statement on campus. Frequent mustard-yellow taggings have desecrated company logos in the cafeteria, the gym, and the halls of Del Heiny Junior 13. Some believe the Mustard Tagger, as he's been dubbed, is a disgruntled Del Heiny employee. Others theorize it's an inside job, committed by someone who has access to the Del Heiny Junior 13 campus after hours. Still others argue that this is a conspiracy masterminded by the National Mustard Vendors Association, intended to discredit the Del Heiny Ketchup Company and prompt school districts to rebid their sponsorship contracts.

Cyrus C. Culwicki, principal of Del Heiny Junior 13, calls such speculation "a bunch of poppycock. We have no reason to suspect that this is anything more than a student acting out his or her teen angst. We will put a stop to it, and soon, or my name isn't Cyrus Culpepper Culwicki."

Authorities, however, are taking no chances. At this very hour they are setting up after-hours video surveillance of the Del Heiny Junior 13 campus.

And that's the local news spotlight for this hour. This has been Dan Druthers from the KPUT News Center with your local news for Friday, November 14. At KPUT, we break breaking news first.

254

CHAPTER 19

I was refilling the gummy bear topping bin when Grampy announced he was done for the night. We'd be closing in a few minutes, but he wasn't going to help me lock up.

"The arthritis in my back is killing me. I need to go home and lay on your mama's ironing board." His face was scrunched up and squinty, making him look all cheeks, so I knew he was feeding me a line of bull.

I played dumb, though. With Grampy gone, I'd have free rein of Scoops for my post-weigh-in feast. Gardo's second meet was long over by now and he was probably up to his eyeballs in pepperoni pizza, grated mozzarella, and Pepsi, but I hadn't been able to feast because this had been one of our busiest Friday nights ever. I didn't even get a break. I was due a few gummy bears, at the very least.

"That's fine, Grampy. We can't have you dying of arthritis. I'll close up."

"That's my boy. You're a real Thuff, Thuff."

I was a Thuff, all right. My face was all cheeks, I could feel it.

At nine o'clock on the dot, I lowered the big metal gate that locked the shop off from the main mall. There were a few diehard shoppers still roaming the promenade, but gates were dropping left and right, so they'd clear out soon enough. The *bang, bang, bang* of gates echoed for a few minutes, then the Muzak cut off and the place got eerie quiet.

I blew off Grampy's huge list of closing duties and headed straight for the waffle cone stacks. Using a stepstool, I grabbed two mondo-sized triple dips right off the top—one for filling up with an ice cream extravaganza, the other for munching on while I built my frozen masterpiece.

The muncher cone cracked as I snatched it from its perch, but that didn't matter. In fact, it was better that way, like eating potato chips. I put a towel on the counter, laid my muncher down on it, then rested a second towel on top and bashed my fist on it several times. When I pulled up the top towel, there was a glorious spread of triple dip waffle chips below. *How did you get so brilliant, Thuff?*

I set about filling up the intact cone, pausing only to shovel triple dip chips into my mouth. *Yummy, yummy, yummy.* Rich chocolate fudge and the crisp snap of a vanilla sugar cookie rolled as thin as it can go. Heaven on earth. Whoever dreamed up this blessed confection was my new hero. Dang, it was great to enjoy food again. Post-weigh-in feast was better than a million Thanksgivings combined.

The appetizer was great, but it was my main course that would set the record for perfection. Moving along the rows of ice cream with a warm, wet metal scoop, I started with a smooth, uncomplicated base, something that would clean the palette when I got to the bottom of my waffle cone: a half miniscoop of True Vanilla. I patted it firmly into the bottom of the cone. *There you go!* I followed that with a thin scrape of Pralines & Cream for a touch of nuttiness in the final bites. "Into the cone with you." Top that with miniscoops of Chocolate Raspberry Fudge Swirl, Strawberry Cheesecake, and Banana Royal for a virtual taste explosion. "Into the cone!" Then half a scoop of Peanut Butter Caramel Chunk, and another half of Apple Pie á la Mode. "Into the cone!" And finally, topping off the cornucopia of ice cream, a mondo scoop of Spazzy Monkey—the perfect opening act to a symphony of frozen, creamed delight!

I paused for a mouthful of triple dip chips and then burst into a humming rendition of Vivaldi's Four Seasons as I chewed. Mom would've been proud to know I didn't totally tune out during my car rides with her and that annoying classical station.

Next up, whipped cream piled tall but just shy of leaning. Then a quick back-and-forth drizzle of chocolate sauce, crisscrossed by a drizzle of butterscotch sauce. *You've got the touch, Sherman Thuff!* Top it all off with a light dose of crushed almonds and two—*count 'em, two!*—maraschino cherries. *Oh, the ecstasy!* In the Sherman T. Thuff Book of Good and Tasty Things, my sundae would be the cover piece, the crème de la crème. Truly, it was my calling; I was the Master of All Things Ice Cream.

Still humming, I wiped my fingers on my pink smock, stuffed the last triple dip chips into my mouth, grabbed a pink plastic spoon, and waltzed through the open counter door to a table in the middle of the room. It was almost funny how easily I passed through that opening. Only a few weeks ago, that cut-out panel had squeezed my stomach every time. *Down with belts!*

I sat down at the table and swung my feet up on the chair

next to me, my eyes looking right at the sun on our wall. I raised my heaping waffle cone toward the smiling logo in a debonair toast. "Cheers, sun. Here's to enjoying food—and life—again."

I love energy building.

Aiming carefully, I harpooned the whipped cream hill with my spoon, scoring a primo helping of nuts and chocolate sauce with my cream. I left the two cherries untouched. It'd be fun to see how long they could stay afloat without toppling down into the cone. A dessert like this had to be approached strategically, with an appreciation for the fine balance of tastes and a patience for dragging out the mouthwatering temptations.

Then I got that first sweet, soft mouthful of whipped cream and threw strategy to the wind. This was just too good to go slow.

Scooping madly, I plowed through the creamy hill, cherries and all. A few flicks of whipped cream spattered my smock. Good thing I'd left it on. After demolishing the topping, I dug into the Spazzy Monkey. *Love, love, love toffee in ice cream!* I had that down in five heaping spoonfuls—all placed in my mouth upside-down to avoid an ice cream headache—then hit the half scoops of Apple Pie à la Mode and Peanut Butter Caramel Chunk, side-by-side in the cone. I swear, peanut butter went with apples better than any snooty wine went with cheese, especially in sweetened ice cream. Those were gone in three spoonfuls each. Then it was on to the Chocolate Raspberry Fudge Swirl and the Strawberry Cheesecake and the Banana Royal—which, as I'd predicted, made for one fabulous fruity explosion in my mouth. Six rocketlike spoonfuls later, I was grounding my taste buds with the soft earthy nuttiness of Pralines & Cream. Then, as a cool-down lap, the anchor to my speedboat, the calming music to my beast, I dug into the deep and solid True Vanilla. And, oh, how truly vanilla it was—gently sweet but smooth on the tongue, it slid down, sweeping all the rich fruitiness away. Sherman Thuff knew how to wind up an ice cream experience.

After the vanilla, I devoured the waffle cone. The divine film of ice cream that coated it was like dressing on a salad, helping the cone slide down better than any water-logged hot dog bun ever had.

I sat back a moment to ponder the brilliance of my first course. Pulling up my shirt, I patted my belly. *Thump, thump, thump.* Yep, it was happy and satisfied. And I wanted to keep it that way. After all, the poor thing would be in agony all week with Gardo's meal planning. So I had to be wise about my second course, choosing just the right thing—maybe a banana split or an ice cream shake?—and the right combination of flavors and textures. But then again, I had just eaten the best dessert anyone had ever created. Why reinvent the wheel?

Happy with that decision, I marched to the ice cream rows, grabbed another waffle cone, and filled 'er up.

The second Thuff Enuff Waffle Cone Extravaganza went down as fast as the first. The next one, though, lasted a little longer as I took time to study the angles before each spoonful, balancing the ratio of ice cream to nuts to whipped cream even more carefully this time around. Like fire and earth and air and water, the ingredients in a sundae had a very delicate balance. Also, I was starting to feel a bit full—just a tiny bit, not enough to slow me down yet. I wanted to make the most of this feast, because I wouldn't get a post weigh-in energy-building session for another week.

Too bad Gardo was stuck with plain old pizza. And he'd

be spending the whole weekend at a tournament, so when he got back, he'd be on the front end of a shortened cutting cycle, trying to get rid of the food he'd be eating this weekend. He wouldn't set foot in Scoops next week. I definitely had to get him in here after next Friday's meet. He was missing out, big time, and as a true friend I needed to make sure he got his proper dues. Ice cream was the finest of the finest.

There was one downside to ice cream, though: It made you thirsty, especially if you were near death from thirst even before you began eating it. So I had to visit the double bubbler after that third cone. I hated to waste the belly space, but it turned out the water just filled up the nooks and crannies, so it wasn't as big a loss as I'd feared. I still had plenty of room on the top for the dessert portion of my feast: toppings!

I rushed to the topping bins, marveling at the good luck that gave me a Grampy who owned an ice cream shop. I scanned the rows, trying to decide where to start. There were the Sweet Lover's rows: crumbled Heath bars and Snickers and Butterfingers and Oreos and M&M's and nonpareils and brownie chunks and animal crackers and Haribo Gold-Bears and jimmies, rainbow and chocolate. There was the Nut Lover's row: peanuts and walnuts and pistachios and almonds and cashews, crushed and whole. And then there was the not-so-appealing Health Nut's row: syrupy strawberries and peaches and banana slices and raisins and granola and even—*oh, I hate to even look at it*—coconut. That was a lot to choose from, but it wasn't even a contest for me: The Sweet Lover's rows were the perfect dessert for my feast.

Not even bothering with an annoying spoon, I grabbed

handfuls of M&M's, half of them spilling to the floor. I spooned in jimmies, half of those spilling to the floor, too. Then I used my hands and dug into the crumbled candy bars, jamming them into my mouth as fast as I could chew. *I swear, these aren't the Sweet Lover's rows, they're the Sweet Lover's* paradise*!*

I slapped the sticky candy bar crumbs from my chin and moved on to the nut row, where I tore through the almonds and peanuts but left the rest, with their gross dirtlike aftertastes. My stomach rumbled as I twisted to the sundae counter behind me. A quick flick of the wrist and I'd up-ended the chocolate sauce bottle, squirting the smooth syrup directly into my mouth. *Love, love, love chocolate!* Next I squirted the caramel sauce and then the butterscotch. *Man! The world should do more with butterscotch.* Slamming the empty plastic butterscotch bottle onto the counter, I worked up a long, deep burp. That freed up some space. Since no sundae was complete without a banana, I stepped over to the banana basket and rifled through it, grabbing and peeling the yellowest one. With two sure hands, I broke it in half and rammed both pieces into my mouth at the same time, Tsunami-style. In six bites, it was all in my mouth, and after only a few chews, I'd swallowed it.

Atta boy, Thuff! I was getting this technique *down.*

Jazzed by my improvement, I snatched a second banana, peeled it, broke it, and stuck both halves into my mouth.

That's when the world came to a grinding halt.

At the mere touch of the banana, my throat caught and my stomach raised the white flag of surrender. I was full. And not just a little. I was packed-to-the-top-of-your-throat, explode-out-your-belly-button, sit-on-the-floor-and-

261

cry full. I spit out the banana and leaned forward against the counter taking deep breaths.

Not a comfortable position.

I hopped a few times rapidly, trying to pack the food down. All that did was churn up a nasty burp, and another one after that. Neither one gave much relief.

My heart raced and I leaned back against the ice cream display case. The spit in my mouth was sugar-coated. Maybe if I ate some Health Nut stuff, the healthy part would cancel out the sugar overload and I'd feel better.

I studied the row of fruits and granola. What was the smallest thing I could eat and still cut the sweet? Deciding a slice of pear might do it, I popped one in my mouth and chewed it slowly. Yep, that helped. I popped a second one. *Bad idea. Bad, bad, bad idea.* My stomach pushed hard against my belt buckle, cutting into the skin. Two pears was two too many.

I undid my belt and ripped it off, throwing it into a corner. Groaning, I stumbled back to my seat at the table. I hadn't just hit a wall this time, I'd obliterated it. I couldn't even *lick my fingers* right now without suffering a reversal.

The saliva collecting at the back of my throat was now bitter on top of sugary. My tongue was thick as a sneaker tongue. I dropped my head into my hands. A pool of spit caught in my throat, gagging me. I clamped my hand on my mouth—*hard*—to keep from reversing. *Breathe, Shermie, breathe.*

The clock said 9:35. I'd feasted for thirty-five minutes. How long would it take to digest?

I burped a gross acidy ice cream burp. *Someone kill me now.* . . . Then a second acidy ice cream burp rocked me. A sugar rush surged through my brain.

This is stupid. I can't sit here like this all night. I have to reverse, there's no other way.

Placing one hand on the table and the other on the arm of my chair, I pushed myself to a standing position with a groan. It was slow going, but I managed to shuffle to the tall trash can by the door. The domed pink lid pulled off easily. Not wanting to touch the trash liner, I rested my hands on my thighs and leaned over the can, my face just inches above the day's garbage. I'd blown off my closing duties, so the trash was still piled high. Pink plastic spoons with clumps of cold fudge and caramel on them, balled-up napkins smeared with colorful ice creams, paper cone wrappers with their pointed bottoms soggy from leaking cones, all laced with the smell of slightly soured milk. If I hadn't wanted to reverse before, I did after seeing this.

I closed my eyes, opened my mouth wide, and squeezed my stomach muscles tight.

Nothing.

I squeezed and strained again.

More nothing.

Maybe I needed some help, like a spoon to tickle the back of my throat. *Ugh.* I couldn't stand the thought of trying to hobble back to my table. I looked around but there wasn't anything useful within arm's reach. Finally, I just stuck my finger in as far as I could.

Aaagggh!

Bulging eyeballs. Tears like water rockets. Puffy, blood-bloated sockets.

Aaaagggh!

Three waffle cones plus several quarts of ice cream plus three Sweet Lover's rows equaled one trash can of butyric acid.

263

Aaaa . . .
Nothing.
Wait, Shermie, wait. . . .
Still nothing. I was done. I was empty.
I was horrified.
I backed away from the can like there was a dead body in it. I couldn't believe what I'd just done. I'd thrown up, and it wasn't a reversal of fortune. It was deliberate. I'd made myself puke.
Totally, completely, absolutely on purpose.

* * *

I hate food. I hate the sight of it, I hate the smell of it, I hate the taste of it. I wish I never had to eat again. Ever. Whoever invented food sucks.

I was lying on my back on the floor of the walk-in freezer. No sweatshirt, no thermal undershirt, no regular undershirt, no ski cap or long johns. Just my jeans, T-shirt, and smock separated my skin from the frozen cement floor. The cold bit through fabric like a pit bull's teeth. Good. I deserved it.

I was afraid to go back into the shop. That was where the ice cream was, and now that I'd reversed—*no, that wasn't a reversal, you loser, that was a deliberate PUKE!* Now that I'd *puked,* I was hungry again. Well, maybe not *hungry,* maybe more like *not full.* Not that it mattered, the effect was the same: If I went out there, I'd eat another sundae, I just knew it. Even holed up in this freezer, I wanted one. Those were the best sundaes I'd ever had, and it had been such a release to finally eat.

I hated this. I never used to worry about eating. It used to be fun. I ate what I wanted when I wanted, and I enjoyed every single freakin' bite of it. The sweet strength of clear gummy bears, the smoky, meaty depth of a pizza with the works, the tender give of a juicy hamburger . . . It was all good. Then I discovered *competitive* eating.

Now food was one big pain in my butt.

What an idiot I was. Thinking I'd be a natural, that I'd walk into my first competition just swallows away from champion status, that I'd make a fortune and become more famous than Hulk Hogan. Life couldn't get more fun, right? *Wrong!* Competition wasn't about having fun. It was about doing whatever it took to beat someone else.

And no one played to lose.

The cold wasn't biting into my back anymore, so I must have gone numb there. Stiffly, I rolled over to my stomach, my smock pinching snugly as I did so. *Swell. In one night of feasting I've erased all my belt loss.* I groaned and laid my cheek right on the freezing cement. The cold stabbed my face sharply.

With my head turned that way, I was staring directly at a dull brown box of gummy bears. Six more boxes lined the floor next to it. Grampy's shipment had come in that afternoon. Most likely, the bears weren't frozen solid yet; they were probably still a bit chewy from their journey on the unrefrigerated delivery truck. If I were to open a box, just to suck on one or two like hard candies, I would've ended up chewing them instead. Then there'd be no stopping me, I'd work through those boxes in minutes, easy.

I rolled my head the other way, away from the gummy bears, fixing my eyes instead on a tub of hard-packed Coconut Cream ice cream. No temptation there. I'd rather lick the bottom of my shoe than eat coconut.

Lying on a freezer floor was pathetic, I knew. It certainly wasn't how I'd envisioned things when I'd told Lucy I was going pro. We'd made graphs, we'd set goals, we'd worked out techniques. I'd wanted to take the eating world by storm; I'd wanted to build an image, get a rep. I'd wanted to become the greatest, richest, most famous eater ever. The Plums at school would bow when I walked by, they'd all want to be my friend, they'd all know who Thuff Enuff was. Then Lucy brought up that awful Belt of Fat Theory and everything went out the window. Gardo had me starving myself, Lucy thought I was a loser for doing things Gardo's way, and now, even though I was terrified of making myself puke again, all I wanted to do was tear into those gummy bear boxes.

My mind flashed back to Gardo choking on that candy bar. I forced the image away.

I'd thought I had it all figured out. But I hadn't. Maybe all those reversals weren't reversals. Maybe I did them all on purpose. Maybe Lucy was right . . . maybe I did have a problem.

The cold wasn't biting into my belly and chest anymore. Maybe I was going numb there, too. *This is so messed up, me lying here like death.* But what was I supposed to do? In the freezer, things were frozen and safe to be around. The ice cream and toppings out in the display case were thawed and ready to eat. And they were screaming my name— *Thuff! Thuff! Thuff!* There was no way I'd be able to walk past the case and out the front door.

Thuff Enuff, you are one colossal loser.

I slapped the floor suddenly, angrily, like it was my own stupid face, then I scrambled up to my knees and grabbed a box of gummy bears. Leaning hard on the box with one knee, I jammed my fingers into the thin slot between the top flaps and ripped upward. The flaps burst apart. Inside lay the clear package of gummy bears. I grabbed it, throwing the box aside. The bears were cold—very cold—but I could feel a little give in them when I squeezed, a little rubberiness that told me *yes,* just as I'd suspected, they weren't completely frozen yet. If I gave them a few more hours, they'd be rock solid.

Well, they won't get a few more hours!

Tearing off my stupid pink smock, I lifted my T-shirt and jammed the cold bag up under it, between my belly and the fabric. Then I lay down heavily on my stomach. The nearly frozen bears dug into me like sharp ice cubes. I laid my cheek back down on the freezing cement and felt its prickling bite into my skin. *Good. It's what I deserve.*

Once again I was staring at the brown, frost-covered tub of Coconut Cream. The thought of coconut touching my tongue made me sick. I squeezed my eyes closed and held my breath.

I hate food. I wish I never had to eat again. Ever. Whoever invented food sucks.

CHAPTER 20

Listening to whales mate wasn't my idea of an ideal way to spend a Sunday. But then, these last few weeks had taught me that ideal was in the eye of the beholder. I mean, how else could one guy's pickle be another guy's treat? Then again, right then I'd happily call Gardo's pickles dessert. Brined cucumbers were way more appetizing than what I had planned for my lunch.

I swung two grocery bags onto the counter next to the sink. In front of me sat Grampy's battered old boombox, on the ledge outside the kitchen window. I raised the window, and the lovesick whales blared. A cool breeze blew in with the fish songs, ruffling my hair even more than my bike ride had. It had been a great ride, feeling the wind in my hair for a change. Wearing that hoodie and ski cap all the time had been a total drag. I was glad I'd trashed them.

"I'm home, Grampy."

"Shermie?" A hand reached up and dialed the volume lower. Grampy was hanging out on the front porch in his favorite lawn chair, probably with the same *New York Times* crossword puzzle he'd been working on since Halloween. "How long you been in there?"

"I just rolled up." There was a red crease in my palm where the heavy grocery bag had dug into it. *No pain, no gain.* "I came in through the garage. Sorry it took so long."

"Mission accomplished?"

"Mission accomplished. I got two, even."

"Score!" The hand balled into a fist and pumped in victory. "Always send a Thuff when you want the job done right. Throw 'em in the fridge, m'boy. Therman V. Thuff loves, loves, *luuuuuvs* cold honeydew! I'll be in right after I get fifteen across."

In other words, never.

I set the smooth white melons in the fridge. When Grampy found out we were out of honeydews this morning, he totally freaked out. Honeydew with maple syrup and powdered sugar had been his Sunday morning tradition since he was a kid. It helped him feel oriented for a new week or something. And when he got obsessed with something, stand back. He had me searching all the cupboards and Mom's three fruit baskets—he even helped!—but we didn't find a single honeydew. In the year that he'd been living here, that had never happened before, us being honeydewless. The man was so bent out of shape, he made me call Mom on her cell phone to ask where one might be, but she was busy with the Sunday Sunshine Breakfast at the conference and couldn't help us. So I'd offered to bike to the grocery store to get him some. I'd needed to do some shopping of my own, anyway.

I reached for the second plastic grocery bag on the counter and pulled out Grampy's new box of Ex-Lax. He'd given me a note asking for that as I walked out the door. *Jeez, getting old must suck.* I put it in the cupboard.

Now for my haul. One by one, I removed a can of cut

coconut in milk, a package of coconut pecan sandies, a coconut cream pie, a bag of mini Mounds bars, a liter-sized bottle of water, and a pack of spearmint gum. I lined them up on the tile counter in eating order, stifling a shudder of revulsion as I did so. It was one nightmare of a lunch.

Yet even as I shuddered, I had to laugh a little, too. Gardo would've keeled over if he knew I was eating all that for lunch. But I didn't care anymore. I wasn't made for his weight-cutting stuff. I was going to do this my way. I was taking control of my own destiny.

Studying the line-up a moment, I switched the pie and the cookies. Then I studied the change a moment more. Yep, the can of cut coconut first, no question. It was the worst part of the feast, so I had to get it over with ASAP.

Mom's electronic can opener was busted, so I dug my pocketknife out and used its tiny opener to work up the lid, just like I'd done yesterday at the bike rack in front of the store. It was hard work, but eventually I gained access. *Ugh.* The repulsive scent of cheap suntan lotion hit me just as hard this time. "Jeez, that's one heck of awful."

"What's that? I didn't quite hear you."

"Nothing, Grampy. Nice whales."

He snorted. "Sound like dying camels to me. But, the doc says it's good for the blood pressure, so I listen. Hmmm . . . C-A-M-E-L. Bah! Too short."

"I'm sure you'll get fifteen across soon, Grampy."

"Or die trying."

And Mom says I'm melodramatic.

Steeling my nerves, I planted my feet firmly and speared a white coconut wedge with my knife. Yesterday I ate two cans of this horror; it had to be easier today.

It's lunchtime, baby. Come to Daddy. I squeezed my nose

closed firmly with one hand and bit into the wedge, careful to keep my tongue as far away from the disgusting clump as possible. It helped to chew with my mouth open. Coconut milk dribbled down my chin into the sink. Holding my nose wasn't enough to totally cut the taste, so I chewed and swallowed quickly.

Nope, not any easier the second day.

Wiping my chin with a paper towel, I tipped the can and peered inside. There was still an entire coconut wedge in there. *Who's brilliant idea was this?*

Actually, it was my brilliant idea. Coconut was part of my new strategy. Everything I ate from that day forward would have coconut on or in it. That way, I could actually eat enough food to keep me from starving to death, but I wouldn't be able to stand the taste long enough to pig out and resort to an intentional reversal. I was not going to reverse again, ever. Even if I had to eat coconut for the rest of my life. See, Lucy, I don't have a problem. I'm Thuff Enuff, and I'm in control.

And, really, it was a brilliant plan. It had come to me while I'd lain on the freezer floor Friday night, staring at the tub of Coconut Cream. I hadn't needed Lucy to tell me what to do, and I wouldn't need Gardo with his lettuce and lemons. I'd thought of this plan all by myself. I was like Captain Quixote that way: a man of action and ideas all rolled into one. *Watch out, Fat Belt, Captain Thuff Enuff is on a mission!* Coming up with my own strategy had given me the strength I needed to finally peel myself up from the frozen floor and walk steadily past the display case to lock up and leave. I didn't so much as stick a finger in the ice cream as I passed the open tubs. A man wasn't a man till he was in charge of his own destiny.

With a mighty torque of my wrist, I twisted the plastic top off the bottled water and swigged, good and long. Pedaling to the store and back had put a big thirst in me, even without a thousand layers of clothing. The water was on the warm side, but it was refreshing anyway. I swigged again, then again, just because I could. My Gardo Glass was somewhere in the bushes below my window. I didn't give the stupid thing a second look after I chucked it out Friday night. I'm going to drink like a normal person. After all, I'm just trying to loosen my belt, not squeeze into some eighty-pound weight class.

At the grocery store I'd considered buying a liter of Pepsi but went with the bottled water instead. I kind of liked water now. As long as I didn't have to force down a whole gallon at a time, the clean, crisp, pureness of it really hit the spot. Sometimes Pepsi left a syrupy film on my tongue. There was nothing pure and crisp about that.

I plugged my nose and went at the coconut still on my knife. It took a couple of agonizing minutes, but I finally finished it and chased it down with more water. The second wedge in the can wasn't any better.

Cussing ripped through the whale calls. "Bah! I hate the *New York Times*."

"Fifteen across is a hard one, huh?"

"Hard one, my ear. Try impossible. A six-letter word for *red hot in the land without shadows*. Give an old man a break. These yahoos are making up words, I just know it." He grumbled some four-letter words.

"Why don't you just start a new crossword?"

"Bite your tongue, Sherman Tiberius Thuff! You should know better. Thuffs do not give up. It's not in our genes. Remember that."

"I do remember that." I washed the stinky coconut milk

down the drain then removed the plastic lid from the coconut cream pie. The aroma had an undercurrent of sugar sweetness. I could handle that. "I just don't see the point, that's all. Crosswords are supposed to be fun. Where's the fun if you're stuck?"

"What are you talking about? The fun is in the pursuit, boy. If it's not, you're pursuing the wrong thing. Struggle keeps the juices flowing." His hand hit the skip button on the boombox. Jungle bongos erupted on the patio. "Hey, speaking of flowing juices, I saw the news the other night. Someone's painting your school yellow."

I'd forgotten about the helicopter Friday. *Jeez, I hope they didn't get me in their footage.* I guessed Grampy would've said something if they had. "They call themselves the Mustard Taggers. They're against ketchup."

"Against ketchup? What's there to be against?"

"Well, they're not really against *ketchup,* I guess. They're against the ketchup company It turned us into Plums and Big Burpees."

"It saved the school, is what it did. Don't you kids know what's good for you? Del Heiny is giving to the community. They should be applauded."

"I guess." He was too old to get it. I grabbed a spoon and turned the coconut cream pie slowly, looking for the least disgusting angle of attack. "All I know is, kids hate being tomatoes, so the Mustard Taggers are heroes. They're fighting for our right to eat mustard."

"Ah, to have a cause. Even a stupid one."

I rotated the pie right, then left.

"I hope they think jail is worth it."

I nearly dropped the pie. "Jail? They just squeeze mustard on things. It washes off."

"It ain't just squeezed mustard now." He had a point there. "Someone must know something."

"If they do, they're not talking."

"Cowards. Yellow is the right color for them." Grampy's lawn chair creaked as he shifted. "It's wasted energy, tagging. Whatever you're working for, the struggle needs to be productive, not destructive. The hippies weren't good for much, but they knew that, at least. The way to tear down The Man is to build up The People. Or some other hippie crap. I don't quite remember. Anyway, it won't go on much longer. Kids can't keep their mouths shut about things like this."

He didn't know Plums. "I guess."

I decided to go at the pie from the shallow left side. It must have been tilted in the bag when I pedaled home.

The bongo music sped up. I poised my spoon above the coconut cream pie. *Let the countdown begin. . . .*

THREE . . . I breathed a deep, anti-coconut-tasting breath.

TWO . . . I suppressed my gag reflex with happy thoughts.

ONE! I dug into the heinous, godawful pie.

And that was no exaggeration, the pie *was* awful. It had the texture of tapioca pudding and the sliminess of jelly.

But I could get through it, I knew I could. I'd lived through a pie yesterday, too. Having food in my stomach instead of starving was worth it. Anyway, the pie's short-bread crust was kind of nice. It undercut the coconut. So the pie would stay on the Sherman T. Thuff Menu of Gnarly But Necessary Coconut Foods. It was something I could eat without fearing the Binge.

See that, Lucy, this Thuff isn't giving up. I'd tried the

Lucy System. I'd tried the Gardo System. Now I had the Thuff Enuff System, and I could smell victory.

I crinkled my nose at the food lined up on the counter. Too bad victory smelled like coconut.

I shoved away the pie.

The next course was supposed to be the coconut pecan sandies. The picture on the green bag showed thick short-bread cookies speckled with dark brown spots—the crushed pecans, I was guessing—topped with piles of crumbly, white blades of grass. My entire lower face puckered in disgust. At the store they'd sounded like a good idea, but now . . . *dang*.

My eyes slid over to the next item in the line-up: the bag of mini Mounds. *Chocolate! Now we're talking.* I ripped it open. Dozens of small, packaged squares flew in every direction. Some even bounced off the top half of the window.

"Careful in there, boy. What are you breaking?"

"Nothing, Grampy." I dug a minibar out of the coconut pie filling and threw it in the trash.

I'd end lunch with the Mounds and then call it a meal. It wasn't Spazzy Monkey, but dessert was dessert when there was something sweet and chocolate-covered involved. And what were mini Mounds but tiny squares of sweet coconut dipped in rich, dark chocolate. At least that's what the bag said. I could stand that. Another key to my coconut food strategy was an open mind. Mounds couldn't be as nasty as Mom and I thought.

I tore the wrapper off one and bit down. Within two chews, I was hanging over the sink, spitting like a madman to get out the residue. Mounds weren't as awful as we thought—they were *worse!* It was like eating dead grass squirted with chocolate. There was no harmony in this thing, no yin-yang, no balance whatsoever. It was one big mound of—

Arrg . . . I stifled the gag before it turned into a reversal. Grabbing my plastic water bottle, I chugged every last drop. Then I dropped the empty bottle into the sink and I leaned against the counter. My head drooped as I panted like a dog.

Okay, that settles it, Mounds are off the Sherman T. Thuff Menu of Gnarly But Necessary Coconut Foods.

"Shermie?"

I jerked up to Grampy's face peering through the window. He must've climbed up out of his chair while I was gagging.

"You okay? What was that? Are you sick?"

Oh, jeez, how humiliating. I waved my finger vaguely at my throat. "Choked. Better now."

"It sounded terrible."

It tasted terrible. "I'm fine, really. It was stupid." *Now, there's an understatement.*

He stayed there, studying me through the screen. I fumbled my hand around the counter, feeling for the pack of spearmint gum. I held it up. "Want some?"

He shook his head. "You're sure you're all right?"

"I'm fine." I broke out my Thuff family smile for him.

He narrowed his eyes. I was trying to fool a fooler.

Finally he shrugged and climbed back into his lawn chair. "It's your throat."

I located the pull tab on the gum and ripped the end off. *Three pieces oughta do it.* I didn't want to wound the coconut taste, I wanted to kill it for good.

After I'd been chewing my gum for a minute or so, Grampy turned down his bongos. "Hey, Shermie? Can you check the clock for an old man?"

I glanced at the digital clock on the stove. "Twelve-thirteen."

"Twelve-thirteen! Jumpin' jee! I gotta get down to Scoops. Arthur needs his break." The lawn chair creaked as Grampy scrambled up and rushed for the steps. "I'll be there awhile. We've got five ice cream cakes to make for a Girl Scout troop meeting. They want Mint Chocolate Chip in the shape of a Girl Scout cookie. Ha! Life's a hoot, ain't it?"

I spit my gum into the sink, shredded coconut sticking out of it every which way. How would I survive this brilliant idea? "Yeah, Grampy, it's a hoot, all right."

Grampy ducked down the hall to change for work as I gargled tap water to flush out any coconut that might have survived the spearmint wad. At least I was brilliant enough to buy gum. The happy cheeps of birds in the Amazon rain forest lilted in the front window as I straightened up the counter and put the leftovers in the fridge. I leaned my head against the cool door and sighed. Coconut was torture, but the relief of not being dizzy and starving was worth it. And this way, no one else was bossing me around. I was in control. I was tightening my belt on my own, thank you very much, and I didn't have to wear a single trash bag to do it.

Now, that was the stuff of champions.

Thuff Enuff Stuff™
Shirts and more
for the champion in you!®

Official merchandise of the Sherman "Thuff Enuff" Thuff Fan Club

Thuff Enuff T-Shirts

Front: "I AM Thuff Enuff!" logo. Back: Three great Thuffisms to choose from. Made of 100% cotton. White. Sizes: M L XL XXL

    A. SAY IT LOUD . . .
       SAY IT PROUD . . .
       I AM THUFF ENUFF!!
    B. "C" IS FOR COOKIES . . . AND CHAMPION!
    C. Say hello to Destiny for me
        Item #TE0311

Thuff Enuff Baseball Cap

"I AM Thuff Enuff!" logo. 100% heavyweight cotton twill. Unstructured. White cap with yellow embroidery, or yellow cap with white embroidery. Dancing Hot Dog logo on back.
        Item #TE1004

Thuff Enuff Boxing Robe

"Are YOU Thuff Enuff? I AM!" logo. White. Red embroidery. Sizes: M L XL XXL
        Item #TE2867

278

Thuff Enuff World Hot Dog–Eating Champ Replica Belt

Mustard yellow leather belt. Die-cast goldtone buckle. Measures 4'8" and weighs approx. 5 lbs. Fits up to 72" waist.
Item #TE645

Thuff Enuff Gut Buster

Peach, tan, or dark brown. 100% plastic. Three 100-ft. rolls per box. Disposable.
Item #TE1273

"Thuff Enuff in the Rough: The Tub That Made Me" - Documentary

This flavorful documentary chronicles the early days of eating legend Sherman "Thuff Enuff" Thuff. Witness the event that catapulted his career, the ice cream challenge that transformed the mild-mannered Plum into the Ice Cream–Eating Champion of the Universe. See the actual tub of chocolate ice cream, hear the chants of the crowd, watch the lightning-quick spoon techniques that would soon rock the eating world. Go behind the scenes to learn Thuff Enuff's secrets to success—the customized training graphs, the strict training regimen, the special Thuff Enuff Hot Dog Dunking Method and his patented Coconut Eating System. Be there as a starry-eyed hot dog hopeful becomes an eating superstar. Run time approx. 11 min. Scratch 'n' sniff food stickers included.
Item #TE1564

**For more official Thuff Enuff merchandise, go to
www.IamThuffEnuff.com**

CHAPTER 21

For the first time in my life, I was glad the weekend was over. Sitting in class, listening to lectures, taking notes . . . it all seemed so *normal*. The rest of my life took a wrong turn from normal weeks ago. But then, my school was a thousand miles left of normal itself.

"Check it out. Ticks feeding off a human head can swell fifty times their normal size. Dang."

"What? Gimme that." I examined the cover of the book Tater had just pulled off the school library shelf. Panicked people were fleeing as a giant tick rampaged their city. *Ticked Off! The History of Ticks in America.* "Why is this here?"

"The same reason someone wrote it. People want to read it."

"Who wants to read a book about ticks?"

Tater shrugged. "People who like ticks?"

I put the book back on the shelf. "Well, it's not what we're here for. Max is only giving us this period to research bloodstains and we're running out of time. I don't want to be here after school. So quit looking at ticks and start looking for blood."

"Ticks suck blood."

"Tater."

"All right, all right. Books about blood. Sheesh." He disappeared down the next aisle, his office aide keys jangling faintly in his pocket. "People need to loosen up around here. It's like sitting on a volcano. Where'd all the fun go, for crying out loud?"

I sighed and walked to the end of the aisle. Tater wasn't kidding about the tension on campus. If this "volcano" didn't get some relief soon, the top would blow right off. All over the library, Yellow Shirts were huddled in tight clusters, and they weren't gossiping about Max's forensics presentations. There were bigger things afoot at Del Heiny Junior 13 than spatter patterns and cellular decay: Culwicki had launched a counterstrike against the Mustard Taggers.

The change was clear the moment I'd stepped off the bus this morning. Culwicki had a booth set up in the quad offering free red IN DEL HEINY WE TRUST T-shirts, and a bunch of off-duty cafeteria ladies were hawking them through bullhorns like carnival barkers. I didn't see any takers except Leonard, but he'd take anything free, so he didn't really count. Culwicki also had the wrestling team distributing flyers announcing a semester's supply of Del Heiny ketchup to anyone with "information leading to the capture of Mustard Movement leaders." Gardo made some great paper airplanes out of those. One accidentally hit Culwicki in the back of the head, but we ducked before he could spot us. Our principal was such a dink.

Inside the school, things were less like a carnival and more like a police state. Culwicki had deputized the janitors, so now they were patrolling the halls instead of cleaning them. Dressed in the same olive-green uniforms and red armbands that the campus security guy wore, they were officially authorized to terrorize. And they loved it. They kept popping up in the weirdest places around campus, scaring Plums and even pinning the littler ones to walls with brooms trying to get them to talk. One janitor was stationed at the cafeteria entrance during breakfast service, where he searched Yellow Shirts for illegal mustard packets. Even if I'd still been buying my morning doughnuts in there, I wouldn't have gone in today. The last thing I wanted was some Olive Shirt patting me down.

But even worse than all that was the rumor. I wasn't sure if I believed it, but it definitely had everyone on edge. Word was, some Yellow Shirts had been hauled off for questioning when they got off their bus this morning and hadn't been seen since. It was nuts. Now we had to worry about being captured and tortured?

The clusters of Yellow Shirts in the library were starting to break apart and filter into the book rows. I guess they didn't want to be here after school, either. But the filtering halted when a loud crash spun all heads toward the library door, where Gardo was next to an upturned book cart, trying not to fall all the way over it. A class set of *The Chocolate War* paperbacks had spilled across the floor.

Gardo the Klutz strikes again. The guy was a mess. This morning during our workout, he tripped on his shoelaces and did a face plant, he walked into a waist-high pole at the top of the bleacher steps and pretty much went soprano, he slipped off the final step at the bottom and landed on his butt, and then he forgot my name. Twice. I swear, dropping to 103 would kill him long before Friday's weigh-in.

After what seemed like forever with Gardo's arms flailing

in slow motion, he finally got his balance over the spilled cart. Then he noticed everyone's eyes on him. Scowling, he reached out and slugged Leonard in the shoulder. "Watch where you're going, man."

"What? I didn't touch you."

"Don't argue. Just help me pick this up."

Poor Leonard. He stood there shocked for a moment, trying to figure out what was what. Then I guess he just gave up, because he bent down and started gathering books without any more complaining.

I went back to my book search. I couldn't watch anymore. Gardo would spontaneously combust before Friday. If he was smart, he'd try the great Thuff Enuff Coconut Eating System. I certainly felt better than I had in weeks. Actually eating something, even coconut, would do that to a guy.

Finally locating the series about crime scene investigation, I grabbed two of the books then headed for the tables. I didn't get far, though. As soon as I stepped free of the book row, an Olive Shirt blocked my path.

"Hold it, big guy," he said. "Let me see those."

"What, the books?"

"Yes, *the books*. Give 'em." He tried to yank them from my hands but I let them go without a fight. If he thought he needed to approve my library books, more power to him. I was just thankful he was unarmed. I didn't need a broom across my throat.

He read the yellow spines. "*Blunt Trauma 101. Blood Spatter Velocity Studies,* volume three." He flung them back at me. "Seem harmless enough."

"They're for a science presentation."

"Al Capone had the same story. Move on. But remember,

we're watching you." Then he hustled after a girl with a yellow paperback in her hand.

"Join the club," I mumbled.

Tater stepped free of the neighboring aisle, a book in his hand.

"Jeez," he said, "can't a guy check out a book in peace? This is getting out of control." He stared after the Olive Shirt for a moment, then suddenly tossed me his book and went back into his aisle. "Hold that for me, will you? I need to look for something. It's about time someone pulled the cork out of this volcano. . . ."

I nearly dropped my books catching Tater's. *Crime Scene Photography.* At least he was on task. Restacking them in my arms, I carried them to the table where Gardo was now sitting. No, make that lying. He had his head down on the table, buried in the crook of his arm.

"I swear, this place is full of psychos." I dropped the books onto the table with a bang. Gardo didn't flinch. "I practically got frisked. Next they'll be doing strip searches."

He grunted into the tabletop.

I shoved aside his backpack for more room. "Where are your books? You're not researching?"

"Screw research."

"You have to do this assignment. There's an oral report. *Tomorrow.*"

He waved his hand without lifting the rest of his arm. "Leonard can do it."

Across the library, Leonard was shoved up against a wall, the Olive Shirt menacing him with the eraser end of a pencil. "Don't count on it. He's got his own problems."

"Huh?" Gardo lifted his head and followed my gaze. "Ah, jeez."

Max had spotted Leonard, too, and was now streaking across the library like a yellow comet. Lucy jogged the first few steps with her, then stopped. Whether the shock on Lucy's face was because of Leonard's imminent death or because Max had left her side was anyone's guess.

"Hold up. Hold up. Stop!" Max grabbed the pencil over the Olive Shirt's shoulder. "I said stop."

He spun in surprise. Leonard used the opening to escape, looking pretty shaken as he scrambled.

Max didn't look shaken. She looked pissed. Clutching the Olive Shirt by the elbow, she spun him back around and escorted him toward the door. The librarian rushed ahead and opened it, clearly happy to be doing so.

"Hey! What are you doing? I been deputized. I'm on duty!"

"Consider this the neutral zone," Max replied.

"There ain't no such thing as neutral zones."

"There are now. Out." Max gave him a solid shove out the door, and the librarian slammed it behind him. The effect was kind of dulled, though, since it was one of those slow-closing doors, but still, Yellow Shirts all around the library cheered and clapped.

Max spun on them. "Enough. This is still a library, or can't you read the sign?"

"Maureen." The librarian rested her hand on Max's shoulder and gave her a silencing look. Then she released Max and started shooing the nearest Plums into the book rows. "You heard her. The show's over. Back to work. C'mon, now."

Though they grumbled about it, the Plums settled into a low buzz again, eventually melting back into the rows. Max didn't move, though. She just stood there staring at the closed door, massaging her forehead like she had a migraine.

Gardo snorted weakly. "That would've almost been funny, if it wasn't so pathetic."

"I know. Culwicki's getting desperate."

"Doesn't matter." He laid his head back down, his face toward me. His lips were dry and cracked. "The Mustard Tagger can lay low for a while. He can afford to. His rep is solid."

"He?"

"Them. Whatever."

"You think there's only one Mustard Tagger?"

"I don't think anything. I have no control over my tongue." He licked his split lips, then winced from the sting.

I licked my own lips. They were fine thanks to coconut milk, the most putrid liquid known to man. "Well, whoever it is, they should quit while they're ahead. They made Culwicki look bad, let that be enough. Del Heiny will never let Plums eat mustard."

He lifted his head. "You think this is about mustard?"

"It isn't?"

"Who cares about mustard except Del Heiny? It's the movement, that's what Plums like. Just look around."

I did, and I immediately saw that Gardo had a point. Every table around us was filled with Yellow Shirts. More stood at the counter checking out books, and still more peppered the book aisles on both sides of the library. Every one of them was whispering or giggling with at least one other Yellow Shirt. Apparently, if you had a yellow shirt, you had a friend.

Gardo laid his head back down on his arm. "They all want to be a part of it. That's why we're getting copycat taggers. The movement is what's fun."

"Well then they're up a creek without a paddle," I said, "because the fun is disappearing fast. Heck, *Plums* are disappearing. And Culwicki's not about to give up till someone breaks. Maybe Tater's right, maybe the volcano needs to be decorked."

"Tater said that? Huh. He might be on to something." Then he waved his hand dismissively again. "He shouldn't sweat it, though. I'm sure the Mustard Tagger is already working on the Culwicki problem. The important thing is, a legend was born. Plums will be talking about that forever. Freakin' brilliant, isn't it?" He smiled, then winced again and put his hand to his lower lip. When he removed it, there was blood on his fingers.

"Jeez, Gardo, how do you wrestle like this?"

"Just do." He wiped his fingers on his red T-shirt. "Get over it or get out, right?" Then he rolled his head so that his lips were pressed against the cool tabletop. His breath fogged the table around his mouth.

Please. There was no way Gardo could do a Sugarfoot without falling over. He couldn't even sit up. *Get over it or get out, my foot. Try get over it or die.* I'd seen dead skunks in the road that looked better than he did. Please tell me this wasn't what Lucy saw when she ran into me in Grampy's bathroom.

I reached up and touched my cheek. The skin was soft from the egg yolks. I'd planned to do the face concoction again tonight, it felt that good. But a facial wasn't what Gardo needed. What Gardo needed was food. Just a little. To get him by. There was no point trying to cut weight if you couldn't even crawl onto the scale at weigh-in.

I went over to my backpack, dug through it, then returned and sat back down with my hands balled into fists, palms down. *The best way to pull off a Band-Aid is to just yank it off.* "Hey, man, check this out."

Gardo peeked up. "What?"

I glanced around to make sure no Olive Shirts were lurking, then flashed him a quick look at what was tucked in each of my hands.

"What was that?" he asked.

I braced myself. *Here goes.* "Coconut macaroons." *Yank!*

"Coconut macaroons? You're not serious?" He stared at me with wide eyes for a moment, then lunged across the table—at the cookies or at my neck, I didn't know. Totally by reflex, I threw myself backward, nearly dumping my chair over in the process.

He didn't get me. Or my cookies.

After he missed me, he stood there clutching his forehead with one hand and leaning on the table with the other. *"Gawww . . ."*

I knew what he was feeling. Been there, done that. "Head rush, huh?"

"Shut up." He dropped back into his seat. "Don't change the subject. What are you doing with food? You are not authorized to eat *coconut macaroons.*"

"Yeah, well, I kind of wanted to talk to you about that." I scooched my chair back a few inches in case he decided to lunge again. When I came up with the coconut plan the other night, I knew it would come to this, sooner or later. "See, I have this theory—"

"No theories, Shermie. You promised, whatever I said. I'm the coach."

"But look at you. You're toast. You need something to get you over the hump. Just two macaroons. They'll get you through."

"No. And you can't eat them, either. Trash 'em."

"Gardo—"

"Now."

Am I talking to a wall? "Just listen to me for a minute—"

"Nothing to listen to. The coach does the talking."

"But I'm telling you how you can make weight without crossing over to the dark side. I know how it is. I kept getting dizzy and dropping things and I kept"—I stopped myself. I couldn't admit to the intentional reversals. Not even to Gardo. "I kept tripping. My new plan is better. You won't have to worry that once you start eating you won't stop. See, you know how I hate coconut, right? Well—"

"Stop. I don't want to hear it. It's just excuses." He rubbed his hands on his face slowly, like he was just too tired to go on.

"No, it's not. It's a better way. Trust me." I pulled over his backpack and unzipped the front pouch to tuck in the cookies. "You can eat them later, when no one's watching."

"Don't!" He launched forward again, throwing himself across his backpack.

The instant before he landed, though, I caught sight of a green and white box with blue letters in the front pouch.

"What was that, a box of Ex-Lax? What are you doing with a box of *Ex-Lax?*"

"I don't have a box of Ex-Lax." He gathered his backpack to his chest and got to his feet.

"Yes, you do. I live with an old man, I know Ex-Lax when I see it."

"You think you could say it any louder?" he whispered harshly. "Keep your face out of my backpack."

"But I don't understand—"

"You don't see me rummaging through your bag, do you? Coconut macaroons . . . Jeez. What else you got in there? A pizza?"

"Gardo—"

"And here I was thinking you had the goods. No wonder Lucy dumped you."

"Hey!"

"You know what, Shermie? You weren't meant to be an athlete." He swung his backpack behind him and tucked his arms through the straps. "Hunt is replacing Shane as captain, everybody says so, and he's probably gonna pick me. I'll be the first eighth grade captain on the JV prep team ever. The last thing I need right now is someone dragging me down. You violated our pact; you're on your own."

"What? Wait a minute. . . ."

But he didn't wait a minute. He didn't even wait a second. He stalked away before the words had even left my mouth. Gardo Esperaldo, the soon-to-be First Eighth Grade JV Prep Wrestling Team Captain Ever, left me sitting there, all alone. He didn't even pause when he almost ran down Lucy near Max and the librarian. He dodged her at full speed, catching his foot on the same book cart, knocking it over again. *The Chocolate War* paperbacks spilled over Max's feet like spreading lava. The women stared at the mess blankly, not even registering the fact that a student had just walked out the door in the middle of class.

Good going, Shermie. First Lucy, now Gardo. You're two-for-two. Are YOU Thuff Enuff? Give me a break.

I sagged down onto my stack of books, then frowned. A tattered Dixie cup sat on the table just inches from my eyes. Lovely. The soon-to-be First Eighth Grade JV Prep

Wrestling Team Captain Ever forgot his sacred spit cup. What a souvenir.

I smacked the cup to the floor, then buried my head in my arms. The coconut in my stomach gurgled threateningly.

* * *

Black birds shrieked and dove at the school's white-flagged roof like kamikazes. You'd think there was a big plate of birdnip or something on top of our red blob of a building, the way those birds kept swooping in. The sky behind them was a deep, ugly gray as another storm threatened to sog the birds, and the wrestling team jogging the stadium track below, and me, tucked between the two under a row of bushy trees near the bleachers.

Swell. Just what I need, a shower. I pulled my hoodie over my head and hunkered deeper into my nook, which offered a great view of the track below. *Ow!* A bush branch speared me in the back. Spying wasn't nearly as glamorous as they made it look in the movies.

Down on the field, Gardo was the frontrunner. Even with his hoodie and all the other layers of clothing on him, I knew him by his running style. I'd been here about twenty minutes, and I was starting to stiffen up. As I reached behind me to break off the pokey branch, Gardo tripped and slid headfirst in the dirt. Three hooded wrestlers passed him. But he scrambled up and raced past them again, regaining the lead. I almost laughed. Gardo was a tough nail.

I was stupid to have worried about him. I'd gotten myself all worked up, stewing about that stupid box of Ex-Lax in his backpack, when clearly the guy could hold his own. Besides, he'd been spitting into nasty Dixie cups for weeks now to get all the moisture out of his mouth; I should have figured he'd be trying to clear out the other end, too. As gross as voluntarily using a laxative was, it seemed to be working for him. After all, he was ahead of everybody down there, and he was almost captain. So what if he tripped now and then? He got right back up again.

I stood to make my way back up the hill. My Scoops shift started in half an hour, and I'd probably be late as it was. But even as I turned, Gardo went down again, this time taking out the guy behind him in an ugly collision. I instinctively lunged toward the track, as if somehow I could help Gardo from my high perch. I couldn't, of course, so I was stuck watching as the two fallen wrestlers struggled to untangle themselves. As they thrashed, their teammates ran right past them . . . all except the hooded guy at the end. That Einstein smashed right into them, full speed, like he was flat-out blind. His body flew up and over them like a black bird, then hit the dirt hard.

Gardo managed to get to his feet first and barely looked at the other two guys before taking off after the pack. The second hooded wrestler got up and did the same thing. The blind guy just lay there.

Jeez. I hope he's not dead or anything. The doofus.

On the far sideline in his wheelchair, Shane put his bullhorn to his mouth. "Oh, Twinkle Toes, darling. This is your captain speaking. You are at wrestling practice, not a slumber party. What are you waiting for, breakfast in bed? C'mon, on your feet. Do you hear me, Esperaldo? On your feet."

I grabbed the bleacher railing for support. Gardo was the doofus blind guy splayed out in the dirt.

"Helloooo. Esperaldooooo. Did you hear me?"

We all heard you, you jerk. It was all I could do not to run down there and pick up Gardo. Or punch out Shane.

"No one's going to come tuck you in, Esperaldo. At least have the dignity to start crawling. C'mon, scrub, move it. Move it!"

Shane *is talking about dignity? Someone shut him up!*

Even as I plotted ways to kill Shane, Gardo got up, slowly, and started running again. He kept his right arm tucked tightly against his ribs.

I let go of the railing and sat heavily in the dirt. No way could Gardo be up for captain. Even I could see that. He was just spinning hype when he said it. Or maybe he believed it; I didn't know. But the fact was, he couldn't even keep up with the rest of the team. Dropping to the 103 weight class really was going to kill him.

The image of him choking flashed in my head again. I ground my fists into my eyes.

When I finally opened them, Gardo was still limping behind his teammates, though much farther back now. I swear, this whole weight-cutting thing was completely pathetic. The guy spit in cups and took laxatives, for crying out loud. For what? To stumble after his so-called teammates? Nice lot they were, running off while he lay in the dust, dead for all they knew.

But so what? What was I supposed to do about it? Gardo didn't even consider me an athlete anymore; he wouldn't listen to anything I said. And when Gardo's mind was set on something, Gardo did it, no matter what.

I punched the dirt. I hated this.

Spinning, I scrambled up the hill, hard and fast. I couldn't watch this anymore. I couldn't stand even knowing this anymore. Something had to give . . . and that something was me. I was going to give Gardo his space for the rest of the wrestling season, that's what I was going to do. Then everything would be normal and right again. He knew what he was doing; he had a coach telling him what to do. I wouldn't let on that I knew his last-place shame. It was none of my business. I'd already lost Lucy; I couldn't risk losing Gardo, too.

I hate this!

Then I thought of Captain Quixote. He'd think I was such a loser. He never just sat still, waiting for things to right themselves. He tackled problems head-on, no matter how big they were, even nudging entire planets out of their orbits when he had to. That was how he defeated the T'larians and earned his starburst battle patch, by nudging the sun out of orbit temporarily. It had fooled the T'larians long enough for him to erase their nuke codes and neutralize Commander Panza's brainwash implant. Just like that, Captain Quixote saved the galaxy and delivered his friend from evil.

I reached the cement of the empty stadium promenade and stood upright. On the cement wall in front of me was one of Culwicki's free IN DEL HEINY WE TRUST red shirts, duct-taped to the wall and covered with a mustard X. Above it was written, in mustard of course, IN MUSTARD WE TRUST.

"I *hate* this!" I screamed at the top of my lungs. The birds circling the roof broke apart and fled.

I balled my fists into my eyes again, then opened up and refocused. The shirt was still there, of course. As if it would be gone just because I closed my eyes! This wasn't an alternate universe where things came and went in a nanosecond. And Gardo and I certainly weren't Galactic Warriors. This was Del Heiny Junior High #13, and we were Plums.

I looked up at the empty, gray, sunless sky and shuddered. Who would deliver *us* from evil?

CHAPTER 22

A bead of sweat trickled down the back of my neck as I stared at the doorknob. I reached out, only to pull my hand back. Gardo would hate my guts for doing this. But what else could I do? When I got home last night and checked Grampy's Ex-Lax box, the label said in bold type, "Continued laxative use can cause bloating, cramping, dehydration, electrolyte disturbances and imbalances, cardiac arrhythmias, irregular heart beat and heart attack, renal problems, and death." I didn't know what the heck electrolytes or arrhythmias or renals were, but I did know what death was.

I inhaled deeply, then twisted the knob. It stuck at first, then wrenched free and swung wide as I forced out the fakest perky greeting of my life. "Hi!"

Two heads jerked my way.

"Oh, I'm sorry," I stuttered. "I should've knocked."

Lucy stood and faced me, a big piece of graph paper pressed facedown against her thigh. Her face was smudged with dirt, and pieces of hair were sticking out of her long braid.

"Hi," she said quietly.

She was the last person I expected to see in Max's office so early in the morning. I had no idea what to say to her. So I went with the first thing that popped into my head. "Why are you so dirty?"

Make that the stupidest thing.

Lucy thrust her paper at Max, then brushed me out of her way. "I gotta go."

Shoved aside, I stood there lamely watching her cross the empty science room toward the hall door.

"Come in, Sherman." Max's chair creaked as she sagged back into it. A small hunk of foam popped out of a hole in the seat cushion and landed on the scarred linoleum under the chair. "What can I do for you?"

She gestured to a metal stool next to her desk.

I took a step toward it, then remembered the open door. I closed it, jiggling the knob to make sure it was latched. Couldn't have some clueless idiot barging in.

Maxwell watched me silently, her eyebrows raised, as I positioned the stool closer to her, farther from the door and the empty classroom beyond. First period didn't begin for another fifteen minutes, but kids would start arriving soon.

The size of Max's office surprised me. It was barely half the size of my bedroom, making me wonder how she'd fit all those wagons and water jugs and experiment supplies inside it. The few metal shelves bolted to her walls were cluttered with beakers and books and stacks of papers and folders. So was the floor and her banged-up desk. On the wall over her desk was a black-and-white poster of a girl covered with tar, the words *What if smoking did to your outsides what it does to your insides?* along the bottom in bold, black letters. A trash can overflowing with papers and folders was next to her chair. It was one of those huge metal cans from the cafeteria—the same kind that Shane had the Finns stuff me into a million days ago.

Since there was no window in the office, it was closed in and dreary. This was how Del Heiny treated its teachers? No wonder the woman left and voluntarily ran the bleachers after school. The rest of the time she was stuck in a classroom with hundreds of punk teenagers or she was rotting in this hole.

"Ms. Maxwell, I—" A box at her feet caught my eye. It was mostly under her desk, but not totally. There was a yellow tarp in it, with a hammer, a chisel, leather gloves, and a crowbar piled on top. She followed my gaze to the box, then suddenly tossed in Lucy's paper and pushed it all the way under her desk with her foot.

"Sorry for the mess," she said. "I was straightening my office. You were saying?"

I couldn't take my eyes off the spot where the box had been. Those tools hadn't looked like any lab equipment I'd ever heard of—

"Sherman, class starts in a few minutes."

"Right." I tried to collect my thoughts. Captain Quixote wouldn't let himself get flustered when he was in a showdown with hostile aliens. "Ms. Maxwell, I need to talk to you."

"I assumed as much."

"See, I have this . . . this problem." I crossed one leg up over the other, then dropped it back down again and smoothed the edge of my shorts against my knees. "Well, I don't have the problem, my friend does."

"Your friend . . ."

"Yeah. See, I have this friend who is doing something stupid but who I know won't stop even if I tell him it's stupid

298

because he's so stubborn even though it's not even working and now he's mad at me and won't listen to me at all. Maybe you can do something." There, I did it. I nudged something in Gardo's orbit. I did what I could. Sighing in relief, I stood and spit my gum into her trash can, then stepped toward the door. "Thanks, Ms. Maxwell."

"That's it? You're done?"

"Well, yeah."

She kicked the metal stool closer to me. "Care to tell me what this stupid thing is?"

"Oh, right." I reached into my backpack and pulled out the plastic wrap, the Queen's Fit Belly Buster page, and the Gardo Glass, which I'd dug out of my bushes last night. I put them all on top of a stack of papers on her desk.

She studied them a moment. "A box of Saran Wrap, a Dixie cup, and an ad for a girdle."

I nodded. "The ad was in a magazine. I was doing research."

"I don't understand. You think your friend is wearing a girdle while he cooks? And this troubles you?"

"No." This was stupid. I was sorry I came. She didn't get it. "Never mind." I reached out to take back my stuff, but she blocked my arm.

"No, wait a second." She studied my stuff again, then pointed to the Dixie cup. "What is this black line for?"

"That's the fill line. He won't drink more water than that. And only eight of these cups a day. Or maybe none now, I don't really know."

"But that's barely an inch of water."

I shrugged.

Now she was really eyeballing the stuff. "What else does your friend do?"

"Well . . ." I pressed my back against the door, my hand still on the knob. The wood was hard against my back, but I liked the feeling of something solid holding me up. There weren't any sounds beyond it, so either no students had arrived yet, or the door was thick enough to be eavesdrop-proof. "There's the weird eating. Lettuce all cut up tiny with lemon juice . . . when he eats at all. And pickles for dessert . . . And then there's his wrapping himself in plastic and wearing thirty different shirts and jogging and five hundred push-ups and post-weigh-in feasting. And the spitting in cups—lots of it, I just know it. And . . ." I paused, barely able to say the next thing. "There's the Ex-Lax."

"Ex-Lax." Max picked up the plastic wrap and held it a moment, like she was weighing it. "Sherman, do you think your friend needs help?"

I shrugged. *Can I just leave now? Please.*

"You came to me, Sherman. I'm asking you, do you think he needs help?"

I twisted my hand back and forth on the knob, my sweaty palm squeaking against the metal. "I guess."

Max set the plastic wrap on the messy desk, then rested her elbows on her knees, clasping her hands together in front of her mouth. "Sherman," she said quietly over her fingers, locking her eyes on to mine, holding them even though I'd rather have looked at anything else in this sad room, even at the poster of the tarred girl. "Do I know this friend?"

My heart sped up and my face flushed. "I have to tell you that, don't I?"

"It would help."

I can't believe I'm gonna do this. I'm gonna open my big mouth. But what else can I do? Coconut macaroons didn't work. "It's Gardo," I mumbled.

300

Her eyes closed as she took that in.

"Aw, man. Please don't tell him I told you, Ms. Maxwell, he'll hate me forever if he knows I ratted him out." It was a stupid thing to say. Of course Gardo would know I was the one who'd told Max. Who else would it be? But I'd had to fink him out; there was no other way. "He only does it so he can make weight. I don't see why, though. Wrestling is the dumbest sport ever. Why would anyone want to be a wrestler?"

She dropped her hands in her lap and sighed. "You'd be surprised what interests people."

"I don't get it, though. I always thought that because he's got a coach he was okay. But he looks like roadkill or something. He's even worse than the other guys. Except Shane, the wimp. He just sits there in his wheelchair being the captain but not doing any of the work."

"He just might be the smartest one."

I snorted. "He's a puss. Get over it or get out."

Max eyed me a moment. Then she rose and picked her way around the trash can and several stacks of papers to reach a packed bookshelf. "Have a seat."

I released the knob and dropped heavily back onto the stool, suddenly tired. A crack in the metal pinched the skin behind my left knee.

She shoved aside some beakers, revealing a row of maybe twenty book spines with small, gold-stamped lettering. The books were slim and tall, and most had blue covers, but some were red. Max ran her finger along them, parting the thick dust on the leftmost books like sand behind a snake. The books on the right, the red ones, were relatively dust-free. How did dust get into rooms with no sunlight?

"Maybe . . . ," she mumbled, pulling down one of the less dusty books. She thumbed through the back pages rapidly.

I could see the blue cover. It was a Del Heiny Junior 13 yearbook from six years ago.

"No, not this one . . ." She put it back and pulled out the one next to it, another blue one, and peeked briefly at the back pages. "Yes, this is it."

She picked her way back to her seat and handed me the book, open to a spread of black-and-white photos. When she sat down, more foam popped out of her split seat cushion.

The yearbook spread was for the marching band. A lot of the photos showed the same bird's-eye view I'd seen with Gardo of the band practicing down on the football field. But there was a large close-up on the right-hand page of a kid with a tall, furry white hat who was blowing into a tuba, his cheeks puffed, his eyes closed, sweat dripping off his eyebrow, his face so tense I thought his furry hat might shoot into the air like a rocket. The stiff hat strap was strained over his chin, digging into the skin. Why did band people have to wear those hats? They always looked so uncomfortable. Not that the guy looked especially comfortable squeezed into the middle of that tuba, regardless of the hat. Did tuba players have a belt theory?

"Sean was a student of mine," Max said, smiling. "He played a mean Dixieland jazz. West Virginia University gave him a full scholarship."

I read the caption under the photo: *Ninth grader Sean Scholfield, tuba/sousaphone.* "Never heard of him. He's not on Culwicki's Wall of Fame."

"Please," Max said with clear disgust. "It was a band scholarship, not a wrestling scholarship; of course he's not there. You mistake our principal for someone who cares about something besides pinning people on the ground until they holler uncle."

302

She pursed her lips a moment, then pointed to the tuba player. "Music was Sean's passion. But being an overweight tuba player isn't good for getting onto a high-performance college marching band. He did some . . . what did you call it, *stupid things*? . . . to fit into his tuba and beat out the competition for that scholarship. At least, that's what I learned later on. He came to visit me when he was a junior at WVU. It was shocking to see him. He was thinner than I am."

I gestured weakly at the picture. "All that marching . . ."

She shook her head. "He wasn't on the team anymore; he'd lost his scholarship. He couldn't march because his heart couldn't handle it."

She took the yearbook from me and rotated it before setting it on her own lap, where she could look at the photo right side up. "He thought he had everything under control, but he didn't. He finally got help after losing the scholarship, but the damage was done. You can't do that to the human body. Eating disorders may make you skinny— notice I said *may*—but they thrash your insides."

"Eating disorder?" *He's wearing a tuba, not a tutu.* "But he's a guy."

"The biggest myth about eating disorders is that they're girl problems." She closed the book gently. "Plenty of guys have eating issues; they just hide it better. Or people who do notice just think they're being good jocks and push them to do more. Boys have just as much pressure about weight as girls; they just don't talk about it. And once they start, it's a hard ride to get off of."

As she spoke, my face heated up again, the memory of the Finns stuffing me into that trash can coming on hard. *Big, fat scrub doughnut.* I looked down at my shorts, pretending to flick off some lint.

That day was so mortifying. The whole school watched them push me deep into the can, my butt jammed in tight and my legs and arms dangling over the edge, just like they watched Shane and the Finns "dunk" other chubby scrubs. The bent metal lip of that can scraped the back of my thighs and bruised my back something awful. Even worse than the dunking, though, was the fact that I couldn't get out. The big, fat doughnut was stuck. Gardo wasn't around when it happened so he couldn't rescue me, and no one else rushed to my aid out of fear of a secondary attack. So I'd had to swing my arms and kick my legs and throw my weight sideways until the can tipped over and I could crawl out. I felt like a beetle trying to flip over. I never told on them about it, though. All I wanted to do was forget about it. None of Shane's other dunkees said anything about the dunkings, either. Well, Jasper Finch did. But he learned the hard way that nothing would happen to Shane. All Culwicki did was blow Jasper off, calling it a prank, and then people were making fun of Jasper for telling. There was no way he'd shed that rep, not at this school. He should've kept his big mouth shut.

"How are your workouts coming along, Sherman?"

I whipped my head up, surprised by the question. I'd forgotten she saw me at the stadium the first day I walked the track after school. "Fine. They're going fine."

"Still jogging?"

"No. No, I'm walking. I walk every day before and after school. I have a hurt calf." I rubbed my leg for emphasis.

"Walking's just as good as running," she said.

"That's what I hear."

"That's all you're doing, walking?"

"I ride my bike. I like that, it's fun."

"Good. Nothing else? Dieting? Anything like that?"

I clamped my lips shut. I knew where she was going with this, I wasn't stupid. The taste of the coconut milk I'd poured over my Lucky Charms this morning was still with me, souring my mouth. Chewing spearmint gum hadn't killed it completely. I probably had coconut breath. But that didn't matter, I didn't need to feel guilty. The coconut was proof that I was eating. I was no Sean. And I was no Gardo. I was losing my belt the smart way. "I'm not dieting. Everything everybody eats is part of their diet. I'm watching what I eat."

Max nodded. "Sounds wise. Moderation is the key. I don't care what anyone else says, the only way to get and stay in shape is to eat healthy foods in reasonable portions and exercise smartly. Period." She flicked her wrist angrily, sending the yearbook into the papers on her desk. "Not starving yourself, or wrapping yourself in *plastic*."

There was a knock on the door. I shot up, knocking over my stool with a loud crash. "I gotta go."

"Sherman—"

"I gotta go." I righted the stool quickly, then yanked the door open. Gardo was standing there, his red wrestling shirt covering his gray sweatshirt and a sheen of sweat glistening on his hoodless, shaved head. His hand was raised, ready to knock again.

"Shermie?" His face clouded for a moment. Then he lifted his other hand and waved a small pink paper over my shoulder. "Ms. Maxwell"—he flashed his Charming Man smile at her—"will you sign this permission slip for me? Coach Hunt is taking the team on a field trip Friday to a special wrestling clinic. There'll be coaches from three colleges there."

"Unless Coach Hunt will be staying behind to take your unit test for you, you'll need to be in class. Since you're here, though, I want to ask you something. Come in for a second."

"I gotta go." I shoved past Gardo.

"Hey, watch it, Shermie!"

I didn't watch it. I just wanted out of there. I hadn't talked to Gardo since our fight yesterday morning, and I didn't trust what I'd say to him now. Especially now. Because as Gardo stumbled out of my way, it wasn't his protest that echoed in my ears. What echoed in my ears was the unmistakable rustle of a plastic bag.

CHAPTER 23

Twenty-four hours after my betrayal, I was hunched over a bowl of Lucky Charms with coconut milk, so hungry I almost wanted a bite of the vile concoction. I'd been too tense yesterday to deal with nasty coconut, so I hadn't eaten anything after my visit to Max's office. But the first spoonful of coconut-bloated marshmallows and soggy cereal gagged me.

I can't do this! I dumped the horror down the garbage disposal. I'd rather starve than eat coconut again.

My stomach was still growling violently when I walked into Science Concepts in Action. Gardo's seat was empty. Lucy was missing, too. *Nice going, Thuff. Your friends are vanishing faster than T'larian heat probes in the galactic sun.*

I dropped into my seat next to Tater.

"Traitor," he spit out.

My heart stopped. How did he know about me and Gardo?

"I can't believe she went red," he said.

My heart started thumping again. Tater wasn't glaring at me, he was glaring at Max, who'd just come out of her office wearing a red shirt. She was whistling as she strolled across the front of the room.

Max had defected. I couldn't believe it, either.

"Stupid Culwicki," Tater said. "I bet he's behind this. He probably threatened to fire her. Or he had the Olive Shirts chase her with brooms or something."

I wasn't so sure about that. Max didn't look like she'd been broomed. She seemed pretty chipper to me, actually, whistling all the way to her podium, only stopping when she stood behind it and faced the class. Row upon row of hostile Yellow Shirts met her gaze.

She smiled lightly. "It has come to my attention that this school is off balance. We've been working against each other instead of together, and we've lost sight of our common goal. I think it's about time someone spelled it out, don't you?" She stepped away from the podium and posed like a supermodel. Her offending red shirt was one of Culwicki's free *In Del Heiny We Trust* deals. Only she'd blacked out his propaganda and written her own: Go, RE^AD! "Like it?"

The Yellow Shirts stayed stony.

The tardy bell rang and Max broke her pose. Turning to the whiteboard, she set a black marker on the ledge, right next to a small stuffed turkey in a pilgrim's costume. "I'll leave this here for anyone who might need it. Mr. Culwicki has thoughtfully left a booth full of shirts unattended in the quad. I suggest you avail yourselves of it. Ah, Mr. Esperaldo, nice of you to join us today. You know the way to your seat, I presume?"

I twisted in my seat. Gardo was in the doorway, half in and half out. I hadn't seen him since yesterday morning in Max's office. He'd disappeared after that, skipping science and Spanish and even going AWOL at lunch. Now he looked like a totally different person with a solid black

T-shirt on instead of his wrestling red, no sweatshirt or hoodie, and deep, angry creases in his forehead. He shot me a wilting glare as he went to his seat next to Leonard.

And wilt I did.

Next to me, Tater was muttering—though whether to me or to the cosmos, I didn't know. "Who needs her anyway?" he said. "She didn't keep the faith. The Mustard Taggers will get Culwicki off our backs. Mark my words, big things are in the works."

Max pounded the tibia bone on the podium. "All right, people. We're in a school, let's act like it already." She pointed the bone at a giant picture of maggots or something else wormy and nasty that she'd just taped to the whiteboard. "Ham beetles. Blow flies. Flesh flies. We've finally secured approval for an exciting new lab that explores the role of insects in forensic entomology. Today we'll work with insects, and tomorrow I've got a surprise lab starring your newest best friend, Porky the *Sus scrofa Linnaeus*. . . ."

Max might as well have been talking Swahili. My attention was on Gardo for the rest of the period. Not that he acknowledged my existence. He never looked my way, not even once. None of his usual winking, no funny faces behind Max's back, nothing. I wasn't stupid; I could read the writing on the wall: Gardo was done with me. Years of friendship down the dumper. We were through.

When the bell rang, I left without waiting for him. There was nothing to say. He hated me.

But so what? Lucy hated me. I hated me. Shane and the Finns hated me. Who *didn't* hate me?

"Thuff Enuff, buddy!" Tater caught up to me in the stairwell. "Have you heard the latest? Shane got replaced

309

yesterday as wrestling captain. Terence Vanderfite got the job. The first scrub captain ever."

I groaned but kept walking. That explained Gardo's black shirt. He was in mourning.

"Isn't that hilarious?" Tater said. "The great Shane, replaced by a scrub. I love it! I bet the Finns were fit to be tied. Shane sure was. He stood right up out of his wheelchair and threw it at his dad, swearing revenge. Kind of suspicious, don't you think, seeing as how we got trashed last night and all?"

I stopped on the second floor landing. "Trashed?"

"Yeah. You didn't hear? All the Yellow Shirts know about it already. You'd know, too, if you went yellow."

"Will you stop already? I told you, Thuffs stay loyal to Scoops white."

"All right, all right. At least you know how to keep the faith. Even if it's the *wrong* faith . . ."

"Tater. What about something getting trashed?"

"Oh yeah." He leaned in like he was revealing some great secret. "What happened is, someone splashed yellow paint all over the guys' locker room, and a bunch of locker doors were ripped right off. And this happens the same night Shane threatens his dad at practice? *Suspicious.*" He practically sang the word.

"How do you even know all this? Wrestling practice is closed."

He jingled his office aide keys. "Tater has his ways."

Tater is creepy.

I spun and headed down the hall toward Spanish class.

He fell in step beside me again, snickering like a B-movie villain. "I told you, buddy. Big things are afoot at Del Heiny Junior thirteen. It's better than TV."

Not quite. You can change the channel with TV.

Kenny and Runji ran up to us halfway down the hallway. Their eyes were as wide as their grins. Tater and I stopped short. Lucy practically bowled us over from behind. *Where'd she come from?*

"This is a hallway, not a bus stop," she snapped. She had a fresh scrape on her forehead and a large Band-Aid on her arm.

Kenny ignored her and slugged me in the shoulder. "Thuff Enuff! Have you heard? Shane is out of his wheelchair."

"I already know. So what?"

"So then you already know he said he's gonna kick your butt at lunch today, once and for all."

"What?"

"Yeah," Runji said. "Shane's telling everyone he's tired of scrubs putting on airs, and he's gonna make an example out of the biggest scrub of all. That's you! 'Puff'n Stuff needs to be taught some respect,' he said. I told you he'd try for a comeback! And the timing couldn't be better. Both the Finns are absent today, so this is your chance to take him down one on one."

"Take him down?" Lucy said. "Shermie, you're not going to fight Shane. He'll murder you."

"Thanks for the vote of confidence." I had no intention of fighting Shane, but I did have my pride. "Kenny, you know the rumor mill at this school sucks. Nothing's gonna happen." Sure, the Finn hadn't been in Max's room this morning, but that didn't prove anything.

"Oh, we'll make sure he doesn't hide like a wimp," Kenny promised. "You can count on us." They high-fived all around.

The vultures.

311

"I gotta go." I left before anyone else could hit me. "Class starts in four and a half minutes."

Lucy caught up with me as I rushed off, her voice urgent now, not snapping. "You're not actually thinking of fighting Shane, are you?"

"I can't wait to see Max's surprise lab tomorrow."

"Shermie, no fighting."

"Something to do with bugs, she said? Should be cool."

"Shermie . . ."

"Here's my stop. Nice talking to you." I ducked into the guys' bathroom. As the door shut, I caught a glimpse of Gardo standing a few feet behind Lucy. He was looking our way, his face blank. Then the red door closed.

I leaned my forehead against it. What was I going to do? The guys expected me to beat up Shane at lunch. I couldn't do that. Even though he'd been in a wheelchair for two weeks, he wouldn't be weak. He was a muscle-bound jock wrestler. A trained fighter. I was just a fat scrub doughnut—and it wasn't jelly that I was full of.

How did I get myself into this?

CHAPTER 24

Lunchtime was on me faster than ants on a picnic. And news of Shane's upcoming "comeback fight" spread even faster. In between every class, Plums egged me on—or "supported" me, as Tater called it. Boy, was that guy getting caught up in the excitement. That, or he was secretly worried I'd be killed. When I ran into him in the hall at lunchtime, he couldn't talk about anything else.

"You know," he said as we entered the cafeteria, "I've been watching Shane at wrestling practice. He puts up a big act, but he's all talk. He was only captain of the wrestling team because his dad's the coach, not because he's any good. He won't wrestle any of the scrubs or pea-greeners because they'd make him look bad. I bet Coach was looking for an excuse to can him. You'll take him down in one punch, maybe two. No sweat."

Easy for him to say. He thought shooting Tots out of his nose was a high talent.

"It won't even be an issue, Tater," I said as carefree as I could. "Shane's going to avoid me." *I hope, I hope, I hope, I hope.*

"You think?" He looked downright sad for a moment.

"Nah. He'll make his move. He has to try for a comeback. Being decaptained is too humiliating. You know what? Just in case he gets in some lucky wrestling stuff in his desperation, let me show you counters to his favorite moves real quick." He grabbed my left wrist and yanked my arm behind my back.

"Ow! Tater, stop!"

"The key is to grab his wrist. Jackie Chan does that all the time." He wrapped his other arm around my neck.

"Stop!"

"See, if you've got a wrist, you've got control. Now all I have to do is squeeze my forearm to my biceps and I'll crush your windpipe."

"Don't! Tater, let me go!"

He released me but then immediately grabbed at my other wrist. "Here's another one."

I saw it coming this time and pulled away in time. Adrenaline must've juiced my reflexes. "I don't need another one. Just stop."

"Okay. But just let me show you what to do if he gets you on the ground. I saw it in a movie once—"

"Tater, stop! He's not going to get me on the ground. Just chill."

I stomped to the food line. What was he thinking? He couldn't make me a wrestler in two minutes. Even Gardo couldn't do that, and Gardo actually knew what he was doing.

Tater was still with me. *Jeez, he's like a rash.*

"You're probably right," he said. "Shane's all talk. The Finns are the ones to worry about. They'll punch your nose out the back of your head. Shane won't do anything without them here. It doesn't really matter, anyway. Shane'll go down one way or another. You're not the only one who wants some changes around here. Oh, there's Runji. I'll meet you at the table."

He hustled away. *Finally.*

Now that I was in line, I was committed to buying lunch. But I didn't know what to buy. I was hungry, *real* hungry, but without coconut to keep me in check, I probably wouldn't be able to stop eating once I started. That would just land me in the bathroom with my face over a toilet like a total loser. Or like Max's tuba player.

The line moved forward. I picked up a red plastic tray with the Del Heiny Ketchup logo on it. Someone patted me on the shoulder and wished me luck, but I didn't look to see who it was. My eyes were glued on paper bowls piled high with cheese-filled raviolis. They came with low, nearly flat dishes of ketchup on the side for dipping. While ketchup wasn't as good as spaghetti sauce, it was red and tomato-y, so it was close enough.

I lifted one of the bowls, hefting it up and down, weighing it with my hand. *This won't help my belt. . . . Aw heck, who cares about some stupid theory?* I dropped the bowl onto my tray defiantly and shoved over to the next station. I wasn't made for Gardo's weight-cutting craziness. It had turned me into some kind of girl, worrying about diet and belt size and gorging then throwing up. I wasn't a girl, I was Thuff Enuff. Worrying about my waist size was a waste of time. There were lots of Big Boys on the eating circuit, and they'd been racking up the records left and right, so me and my fat belt would do just fine, thank you. Cookie Jarvis was four hundred pounds, and he held records for ice cream, mayo, cannoli, chicken-fried steak, corned beef and cabbage, dumplings, pizza, and all kinds of other stuff. If big Cookie could be a winner, so could big Thuff Enuff. *Thuff Enuff eats what he wants, when he wants.*

The only problem was, if I was going to compete, I *couldn't* eat what I wanted, when I wanted. I'd have to eat what people told me to eat during the competitions. And a lot of it. Like cow brains. Like asparagus. Like fifty-four hot dogs and buns.

Jeez.

Maybe I'd made a mistake with this competitive eating. The only time in my whole training that I'd been able to keep down my HDBs without reversing my fortune was when I took more than an hour to do it—and that was just eighteen HDBs. Eighteen. Why the heck was I killing myself over this? For the fame? That wasn't such a dangling carrot anymore. Here I had all these new "friends," but I could barely sit at my own lunch table anymore. And Lucy and Gardo had sworn me off. I missed being plain old nobody Shermie and hanging out with my old buddies.

Behind the lunch counter, a lady in a red paper hat and apron tossed a cardboard plate onto my tray with a vacant flip of her wrist. Tater Tots spilled onto my tray.

As I gathered them back onto the plate, Shane strode into the cafeteria. I could tell because the whole place went quiet. It was weird . . . nobody greeted him, and his fellow ninth graders didn't clear a seat for him at his table. I guess trashing the locker room wasn't the "comeback" he'd thought it would be.

Squaring his shoulders, he pushed past a girl to get in line behind me. I tried to pretend I hadn't seen him. But he was so close, his foul breath warmed my neck.

I slid my tray along the counter to the next section. Egg

316

rolls. Another red-aproned lady tossed a plate onto my tray. Then I slid over again, to the chicken nuggets section. That plate landed hard, too.

Shane matched my movements slide for slide, only he let his empty tray hang down by his leg so he could stand right next to me.

"Thuff," he hissed into my ear as the nugget lady blankly plopped another dipping dish of ketchup onto my tray. "You've gotten too big for your britches, Thuff, if that's even possible."

Again I slid to my right. This time a birdlike woman with glazed eyes tossed a plate of corn dogs onto my tray.

Again Shane moved up close. "I'm gonna put you on a diet, big shot."

I slid to my right once more, taking on a hamburger and a side of fries.

There was venom in Shane's hiss this time: "Know your place, Thuff." He slammed his shoulder into my back, right between my shoulder blades. *Ow!* A bunch of ketchup packets landed on my food. "Don't forget your ketchup. Man, look at that slop. I just lost my appetite."

Spinning on his heel, he stalked off toward his table, shoving his empty tray into Kenny's hands along the way.

My own hands were shaky as I paid the cashier for my food. Not that she noticed my shakes. She was too busy popping her gum and looking bored.

Slowly I turned and faced a cafeteria full of Plums. My back throbbed where Shane had jammed his shoulder into me. Had anyone see him do it?

A bead of sweat trickled down my temple. My tray got heavier by the second. All eyes were on me except for Shane's. He was standing next to his table talking to the seated guys, his back to me like he couldn't be bothered. They still hadn't scooted over for him, though I spotted one slipping him an illegal mustard packet. Another one offered him something to drink. He was making headway even though all he'd done was jam me in the back. Maybe killing me really would put the king back on his throne.

I had a sudden urge to go to the bathroom . . . not to pee, but to hide in a stall until the bell rang.

No! You won't do that, Shermie. You can't. Even getting my butt kicked in public was better than getting caught hiding in the john.

I took a deep breath. And then another. Finally I willed my shaky legs to transport me to my table at the back of the cafeteria. It was so strange, passing the mustard-scribbled walls without any janitors around to clean them up. The Olive Shirts were missing all the fun.

Tater, Roshon, Kenny, and seven or eight other guys had already made themselves at home. My table was solid Yellow Shirts. No Black Shirt. No Gardo. As I approached, the guys all gawked at me like, *Well?* Their expressions made me think of the Olive Shirts back when they were just janitors, rubbing their sandpapery hands together over a Shane terrorization.

Maybe the bathroom wasn't such a bad idea. . . .

"Sit next to me, Thuff Enuff." Tater scooched over to make room for me between him and Roshon. "There's room."

Great. The guy wanted a ringside seat.

"Hey, where're you going?" he said.

"I got business to take care of." *Taking a leak doesn't make me a chicken. And if it happens to be a* long *leak, then so be it.* I handed Leonard my tray. I would *not* take my food in there. "Here, take this. And don't eat it."

He took the tray from me and dumped it into the trash can next to the table.

"Hey!" I shouted. "Why'd you do that?"

"You said, 'Take this. I don't need it.' "

"No, I didn't!"

"Yes, you did. I heard you."

"Aw, man," I moaned. I knew I shouldn't complain; Leonard had just saved me from myself and all, but *still*. "That was perfectly good food, Leonard. What am I supposed to do for lunch now?"

"Oh. I'm sorry, Thuff Enuff. I really thought you said you didn't want it. Here, I'll get you more." Leonard jumped up and swung a leg over the bench. "You need to keep up your strength." He rushed off.

As I stood there torn between sitting down to wait for food or ducking into the guys' room, an angry shriek ripped through the air. It sounded like the Wicked Witch of the West right after Dorothy soaked her with water. But it wasn't a witch screaming, it was Shane.

Halfway across the cafeteria, the situation was obvious. In hustling to get me replacement food, Leonard had plowed smack into Shane, spilling the jerk's chocolate milk shake all over his sacred red wrestling shirt. Shane was a mess of poo-brown goo.

"You idiot!" he yelled. "Look what you did!"

Leonard froze in shock, but only for a moment. Then reflexes kicked in. Snatching a stray napkin from the table next to him, he attacked Shane's chest and tried desperately to blot the goo.

"Stop!" Shane tried to block Leonard's hands. "Stop! You're making it worse!" The milky poo now oozed down the front of Shane's pants. "Look at this! What were you thinking, you tub of lard? Are you as blind as you are fat?"

319

He grabbed Leonard's collar and tried to yank him forward. But Leonard couldn't be budged by mere yanking, so Shane had to step forward to get in his face. "You're gonna pay for this big time, you stupid loser scrub."

Boy, the Olive Shirts would be bummed that they missed this. The zoned-out cafeteria ladies certainly didn't appreciate the entertainment. Poor Leonard. There was no one to stop Shane. And even Leonard knew rescue wasn't in the cards. He simply closed his eyes and cringed, waiting for Shane's punch.

This is so messed up. You shouldn't have to take one in the kisser just for being a nice guy. And this whole school full of people is going to let it happen. Pathetic. We might as well start genuflecting for Shane. The very thought of that roiled the butyric acid in my gut.

A shaft of sunlight broke through the clouds and spotlighted Leonard and Shane. I squinted in the glare off the white linoleum. With my face scrunched like that, I could be Grampy, going all cheeks and trying to talk me into something I didn't want to do. I could almost hear his voice: "Sherman T. Thuff, this crowd looks tough, and you know what that means: When the going gets tough, the Thuffs get Thuffer! All for one and one for all!"

All for one and one for all . . . I hate Grampy sometimes. Especially when he's right.

"Stop!" I hollered before Shane could sock Leonard. Then, faster than I'd yanked my wrist out of Tater's grasp earlier, I stabbed my arms out right and left and yanked Tater and Roshon to their feet. They were both so surprised, they didn't resist. *There, it's three against one now. All for one and one for all. Take that, Shane.* "Leave Leonard alone."

Plums around the room gasped.

Shane sized up the three of us standing there like a wall—Tater on my left and Roshon on my right, me in the middle bracing them up with my hands around their biceps. He smiled and let go of Leonard's shirt.

"Well, well. So here we have it. Puff Enuff finally makes his move. I honestly didn't think you had the stones for this, *scrub.*"

He raised his right arm up over his head like he was going to hail a cab, then bent his index finger in a brief come-hither motion. Immediately, two hulking, white-haired, bent-nosed goons in red wrestling T-shirts marched out of the guys' bathroom. *Finns!* No wonder Shane wasn't avoiding me. It was an ambush.

Tater tried to sit back down, but I squeezed his biceps hard and locked my elbow to hold him up. We were committed now. Preemptively, I locked Roshon into a standing position on my left. Captain Quixote said victory was in the numbers, and as long as we were standing, we were still three. They couldn't take us all down. Not quickly, anyway.

Shane and the Finns started over to us, marching in step. *Right, left, right, left.*

Roshon whimpered. Tater babbled, "We're dead, we're dead, we're *so* dead. . . ."

Right, left, right, left.

What would Captain Quixote do now? He would've seen the ambush coming in the first place, that's what he would've done! And he sure as heck wouldn't have Tater and Roshon rounding out his three.

Right, left, right, left.

We were gonna get creamed.

Right, left, right, left.

At least I'd die knowing that I hadn't hid in the john.

That realization gave me a rush of pride—a small rush, but it was enough. I held my head up higher. When the going got tough, Thuff Enuff could handle it.

"Stay right there," I commanded, struggling to make my voice steady and strong like Captain Quixote's. But Shane and his Finns kept marching. "I said *stop*."

Jeez, I sounded more like a mouse than the captain of the finest space vessel of all time. I wouldn't have stopped, either, if I were them.

Right, left, right, left.

"The man said stop." The voice came from a table in the pea-greener section. A kid in a black shirt stood up at one of the tables.

Gardo! At a pea-greener table?

Gardo headed directly toward the Finns and Shane, throwing down his backpack like a knight tossing the gauntlet. The Finns' eyes opened in surprise, then narrowed in hate. Shane started pulling at their arms and telling them to stay focused, but it was useless. Their focus had shifted completely to Gardo. One of their own was challenging them, and in the wrong color shirt, no less. No one liked a traitor.

Watching the three eighth-grade wrestlers staring each other down, I realized that Gardo might be a foot shorter, but his back was just as straight and sure as theirs. Even bigger than the height difference though, was the attitude difference: The Finns were scowling, Gardo was smiling.

"Get out of here, Esperaldo," Shane warned. "You're out of uniform. There are penalties for disrespecting your captain and teammates."

"Yeah," sneered Wayne. Or was it Blayne? "Maybe you

322

need another bleacher tour. What do you think, Shane, twenty laps, or thirty?"

"Oh, give it a rest, Blayne," Gardo said with disgust. He looked up at the sun trying to peek through the clouds and breathed in deeply. "Shane's not captain anymore. It's time to pick a new leader." Grabbing his backpack, he walked over to our table and casually tossed the bag on top then added himself to my Roshon-Thuff-Tater wall. "I'm with Thuff Enuff."

My knees wobbled as Shane sized us up again, now four against three.

Suddenly Kenny leaped up and locked elbows with Roshon. "I'm with Thuff Enuff, too."

Kenny! My knees stopped wobbling. *Five* against three.

Next to Kenny, Runji stood up and locked on. "*I'm Thuff Enuff.*"

Six!

"*I'm Thuff Enuff!*" another Plum shouted. Then another shout. And another. All around me, Plums were popping up and locking arms.

Shane's body couldn't keep up with his head as he swiveled to see all around him. It was amazing—in seconds, half of the Plums in the cafeteria were standing up to Shane.

Slowly, like a rumbling storm, a low chant started. "*Thuff, Thuff, Thuff, Thuff . . .*"

The Finns had been surveying the room, too. They looked at each other for a moment.

"*Thuff, Thuff, Thuff, Thuff . . .*"

Then the left Finn nodded as the other turned and patted their former captain on the shoulder. "Okay. We're done."

"What?"

"We're done. It's been real."

"You're *done*?" Shane looked puzzled for a second, then the light bulb must've gone on. "You too? I can't believe this. What's with all the scrubs around here? When did you people forget your place? I outrank you. You're all in serious violation."

"I'll tell you who's in serious violation, Mr. Hunt!" Principal Culwicki's bellow echoed off the walls as he marched into the cafeteria waving a bent locker door like a sword on a battlefield. All three slimy Olive Shirts were with him. "Cuff him."

"What?" Shane backpedaled in our direction as the Olive Shirts rushed forward and grabbed him, cuffing his hands behind his back. "What's going on? Stop! I haven't done anything."

"You *wish* you hadn't done anything." Our principal threw the bent door onto the ground. "Defacing school property is a criminal offense."

"But I didn't deface any—"

"Stop. Enough lies. The entire team heard you threaten your father and this school. You finally got sloppy, Mustard Man."

"Mustard Man?"

"Don't bother denying it. I've got all the proof I need right here, mister. One of your own *honorable* classmates realized it was time to put a stop to your shenanigans." He pulled a piece of paper out of his pocket and waved it in Shane's face, just a few feet from me.

I thought I'd fall over. A Plum had finked. On Shane . . . Shane, the *Mustard Tagger*. Holy cow.

Culwicki continued waving the paper. It had a bunch of photos printed on one side, and when he finally stopped flapping it around, I saw that the other side was a mess of curlicue scribbling.

"Green marker," I whispered in amazement. Gardo and I whipped our heads toward Tater. He unhooked his arms from ours and looked up at the sunroof, whistling.

"Your days as a mustard-loving *artiste* are over," Culwicki declared. "No more tagging for you."

"I'm not a Mustard Tagger!" Now that the paper wasn't thrashing, Shane was getting a good look at the pictures. "There! Look. That's not me. I don't have red hair. That's someone else ripping the door off the locker."

Culwicki paused and pulled the paper closer to his squinting eyes. "That's not red hair. . . ."

"It is, too. I'm being set up, can't you see that? That's my captain sweatshirt, I admit that, but that's not me wearing it. Are you blind? Look!"

"Hold your tongue, boy! I know red when I see it, and that hair was not red." He shoved the paper into Shane's face again. "And your face is crystal clear in *that* one. That is clearly you throwing your wheelchair in the gym."

"Well, yeah, but I—"

"Aha! A confession!"

"No! It's not a confession. I'm not confessing to anything. I don't have anything to confess to." Shane turned on his Finns. "You two. You set me up, didn't you?"

"Who, us?" they asked in unison.

Culwicki seemed to notice the Finns for the first time. He gestured their way. "Take them, too."

"What? No, wait. . . ." The Finns looked like they wanted to bolt as the Olive Shirts pounced on them.

Culwicki held the tipster's note in front of their noses now. "And who's that squirting mustard on our poor janitors? Huh? Huh?" They didn't answer. "That's what I thought. How dare you revolt in *my* school? What are you, a bunch of Big Burpees? This is unacceptable. My office. Now. Let's go."

Without further word, Culwicki spun and marched back through the hallway he'd entered, with the Olive Shirts poking and prodding their prisoners behind him with brooms.

The cafeteria they left behind was quiet enough to hear a French fry drop. No one had their arms linked anymore, but still we stood there, watching the empty doorway.

"Dang," Roshon said quietly. "It was Shane. I can't believe it."

"Neither can I," Gardo said with far less awe. He turned and eyed Tater, who was already sitting at the table slathering his hamburger with mustard. "Tater . . ."

"Yes?" My bald lab partner looked up and batted his eyes innocently.

"What did you do?"

"What did I do? I don't know what you're talking about."

Gardo kept eyeing him. Slowly, a smile crept across Tater's face. Reaching under the table, he picked up his backpack, stuck his hand in, and pulled out a book. *Introductory Forgery: How to Write Like Anyone But Yourself . . . And Not Get Caught.* Looking right at us, he dropped the book into the trash can next to him. Then he took his green marker out of his back pocket and tossed that in, too.

He lowered his backpack to the ground, then dusted off his hands.

"Oh, fellas," he sang out. "I hate to trouble you, but has anyone seen my lucky pen? I think someone stole it." Tsk-tsking, he picked up his hamburger and licked a drip of mustard. "People are so dishonest around here. It's a crying shame." He chomped into the burger, then smiled as he chewed. Mustard oozed down his chin like vampire blood.

Wow. Tater did it—he vented the volcano. No more Plum pressure cooker. Culwicki would be off our backs now, and the Olive Shirts would have to go back to using their brooms on dirt. I had a new hero.

Gardo sat down and gave my hero a napkin. He tapped his chin, then pointed to Tater's. "You know what, Tater? I'm starting to think you're not as dumb as you look."

"Why, thank you, Gardo." He gently dabbed the corners of his mouth, missing the chin mess completely. "How kind of you to notice."

I joined them on the bench as the other Plums sat down, too. The place was still eerily quiet. It was almost as if they expected Culwicki to come stamping back in.

"Wait a minute," I said. "I don't get something. What happens when the Mustard Taggers strike again? Culwicki will know he's got the wrong guy."

"Who says he's got the wrong guy?" Gardo said, reaching into his backpack and pulling out a plastic container.

"What do you mean? Of course he's got the wrong guy."

"How do you know? Maybe Shane is the Mustard Tagger. We don't know that he's *not*." He looked at me long and hard. "Do we?"

Tater stopped chewing and waited for my response.

I considered Gardo's point. Everyone knew that Shane had ordered the mustard-filled Super Soaker attack, and everyone knew he'd ordered my dunking and Jasper's dunking and all the other cafeteria terrorizations. So even if the big jerk hadn't *committed* the Mustard Strikes, he could've ordered them. We had no way of knowing.

So Gardo was right. We didn't know that Shane *wasn't* the Mustard Tagger. "No, I guess we don't."

"That's what I thought."

Tater started chewing again.

327

The drone of low voices was kicking back in. Around the room, yellow hats were disappearing, and jackets and sweatshirts were pulled on over yellow shirts. It was like city lights going out at night, one by one.

Boy, was I glad I never went yellow.

Roshon and his cousin didn't have sweatshirts, so they were sitting shirtless.

The sound of squeaky wheels reached my ears. Max's cart rolled up, the big crate on top blocking my view of the person pushing it. It stopped next to me, and Lucy stepped around it. Her eyebrows arched when she saw Runji and Roshon.

"Nice farmer tans," she said. "When did Del Heiny approve stripping as an extracurricular activity?"

Roshon slouched and crossed his arms over his pale chest.

Runji wasn't fazed. "No more yellow. Didn't you see? Shane is the Mustard Tagger. And Thuff Enuff showed him who's boss."

"I saw," she replied, looking my way. "You unleash a Leo, you better be ready for anything. They rarely do what you expect. People should remember that."

My face got hot. Was she talking about me and Shane . . . or me and her?

She turned to the crate and lifted off the top. "Looks like my timing is good. Me and Max just made these. I thought I'd have to do some convincing to get people to ditch their yellow." She pulled out some Max RE‸AD shirts and handed them to Runji and Roshon. "Here. Unless you're planning to stick with the naked mouse look."

After they pulled on their RE‸ADs, she made them hand out shirts to other Plums, too. Former Yellows started crowding around the crate.

Tater scowled when Lucy handed him a RE$\hat{\wedge}$D. "I hate blending with the walls."

"And you like being a Shane disciple?" she asked.

"No." He pouted but took the shirt and went RE$\hat{\wedge}$D, too.

She held one out to Gardo. He waved it off. "Red is nothing but trouble."

"Trouble in the eyes of The Man is power in the hands of the People."

"Yeah, well, when power comes in another color, we'll talk. Right now I'm in mourning." He pretended to brush some lint off his black shirt.

Lucy pushed her way back to the crate. With the crowd growing next to us, Gardo and I sat side by side. He hadn't opened his container of lettuce yet.

"In mourning, huh?" I asked guardedly. "No more wrestling?"

"I dunno." He shrugged and sighed heavily. "It's more running than wrestling. Maybe I'll join the marching band. I hear they need tuba players."

I cringed. "Max talked to you, didn't she?"

"Of course she did. What'd you think would happen? She'd invite me to a buffet?" He lifted the lid and stared at his container of lettuce and lemon wedges. Suddenly he reached across the table and grabbed a handful of Leonard's Tots.

"Hey!" Leonard protested.

"Hey yourself. Share with the conquering hero." He shoved them all into his mouth at once and chewed like a starving cow. He caught me watching and swallowed. "Jeez, Shermie, the woman made me look at pictures of a guy wearing a tuba. I almost let Shane kill you."

I'd almost wanted him to.

"You could've warned me," he said.

"I tried to."

"Tried to? You gave me a cookie!" He stabbed his Tot in ketchup.

Okay, so that was a retarded thing to do. "What do you want me to say?" I watched him jam his Tot into a mushy red mess. "Fine. I'm a rat. You never have to speak to me again. Is that what you want?"

He took Leonard's napkin and covered the red and brown carnage in front of him. "Would you do it again?"

There it is, the million-dollar question. I nodded.

"Then you're not sorry." The napkin soaked up the water from the ketchup beneath. He poked at it a couple of times. "But you're not a rat, either. You opened your big mouth for the same reason you stood up for Leonard. You'd take a punch in the teeth for Ruffers Thuff if you had to."

I didn't say anything. He was right, and we both knew it.

"Not that it matters, anyway." He scooped up the napkin and the mess and tossed it past Tater into the trash. "I just pledged my loyalty to you in public, so I can't very well kill you now. I'm committed." His smile seemed forced, but at least it was there. He took another Tot from Leonard and offered it to me.

I stared at it.

"Oh, for crying out loud, Shermie, take it. We'll be fine. Jeez."

There was a reason we'd been friends forever. I took the Tot and bit into it. And, man, was it good. *I gotta figure out what to eat already.*

A RE^A^D shirt dangled in front of my face.

"What do you say, Shermie?" Lucy was behind me. "Time to retire the Scoops white?"

I looked at the shirt. If I said no, would she wrap it around my neck? "I don't know. . . . I've been loyal to Grampy this long."

"Loyalty isn't your problem." She tossed the shirt on the table in front of me. "But you could dial down your Leo once in a while. It's a bitch sometimes."

I swiveled to face her and she leaned against the crate, which was being pillaged by half-dressed Plums. She looked good in RE_AD. Better than yellow or brown. Her cheeks seemed rosier or something.

"Hard to believe Shane was behind the Mustard Movement," she said. "He's an idiot."

Next to me, Gardo snorted. "We thought Tater was an idiot, too, till we got to know him." He batted away a Tot that Tater'd aimed at his head. "No offense, buddy, but you do stick food up your nose."

"No offense taken," Tater replied. "I've been thinking about ditching the Snot Tot trick anyway. It might be time for a new image, you think?"

Gardo perked up. "Really? If you're serious, I can make you a legend."

I groaned. *Careful what you wish for, Tater.*

"And that's my signal to run." Lucy stood tall again. "I gotta go, anyway. Ms. Maxwell's waiting for me. We have to finish setting up that lab. It's taking forever." She pointed to her Band-Aid. "And it *hurts*." But instead of leaving, she watched the Plums who were bringing in more red shirts from Culwicki's booth and passing them out. Black markers were uncapping left and right. "It's kind of sad, isn't it?"

"What?" I said. "That Plums are back to wearing red?"

"No. Not that, really. More like sad that we're done being yellow, you know? It was kind of fun—in the beginning,

331

I mean. I liked not being a tomato, at least for a few minutes each day."

"We'll find something else stupid to get crazy over." I picked up the T-shirt she'd dropped in front of me and held it against my chest. It was too small even if I had wanted to wear it. I balled it up like a ripe, round Plum and threw it at her. "This is Del Heiny Junior thirteen. Stupid is a way of life."

CHAPTER 25

"Says here Libras are ruled by Venus, the planet of *luuuv*. We're *a delight to be around*. No wonder I'm so irresistible." Gardo glanced at me over the small booklet in his hands. "Hey, what are you doing, picking corn? You gotta bend *all the way* down for cherry pickers."

I shot him an upside-down shut-up look, then stood and leaned to my left in a long, satisfying side stretch. I didn't care how much *luuuv* Mr. Delightful had going, he was in no position to criticize my stretching techniques. The only leaning he was doing was against the cement step behind him.

Gardo was lounging like a lump on the bottom row of the stadium bleachers. His legs were stretched out in front of him, and he was reading me random facts from a ten-cent astrology booklet as he waited for me to finish my post-walk stretch. The lazy bum hadn't walked the track with me in three weeks, not since he quit the wrestling team. He said he was saving himself for badminton next year. *Jeez, I can't believe we talk about badminton.* Life sure got boring when they kicked out Shane and the Finns. Being a Plum all day every day was as dull as it was pathetic.

Something had to happen around here already or we'd all whither way.

"Oh, I like this one: 'Libras appreciate the finer things in life.' I thrive in aesthetically pleasing surroundings." Scowling, he shifted and sat up straighter. "There ain't nothin' pleasing about this bench."

I made a few "isn't that tragic" noises. A good friend would've probably finished stretching so Gardo's delightful tushy didn't go numb, but the suffering boy was stuck with me. Leaning right, I stretched long and slow. "Where'd you get that thing, anyway?"

"7-Eleven. They sell them next to the register. Hey, did you know John Lennon was a Libra? Bruce Springsteen, too." He turned the page. "Maybe I should start a band."

"Please, Ruffers Thuff sings better than you."

"That didn't stop Springsteen. The guy's throat is a gravel pit, but he's still filthy rich."

"I'm sure they call him the Boss for a reason." I straddled my legs wide, then bent down for another set of cherry pickers—*all the way* down.

I did need to finish up. We were meeting Lucy in the parking lot for an early movie. She'd be finished helping break down the month-long pig carcass lab by now. Building that fake crime scene and double-wire cage had taken her and Max a lot of lunch and after-school time, but the breakdown was supposed to go really fast. All their sneaking around and trying not to be noisy or attract attention while they waited for approval really slowed the setup. Frankly, I was more than happy to see that nasty hog go. I usually liked Max's labs, but a rotting pig smelled a million times worse than any butyric acid lab. And I'd seen enough maggots and ham flies to last me a lifetime.

Max's new unit was on nutrition, which was way easier to stomach. She was giving extra credit to anyone who did a report on the documentary *Supersize Me,* so we were headed to the Kensington Art Cinema, where it was replaying back in the theater. We'd write our reports over winter break, which was just a day away. Plus, Max said people should try to do social things that didn't revolve around food. Going to the movies would cover that—once we passed the refreshment counter without caving, we'd be home free.

I finished my stretch and stood up. Gardo was digging through his plastic grocery bag. When he pulled out a snack bag of Lays potato chips, I saw a takeout box of China Town Express still in the Seven-Eleven bag.

"*Ew.* What are you thinking, buying Chinese food from 7-Eleven?" I didn't know China Town had express stations in convenience stores.

"Shut up. It's good."

"It's disgusting. Seven-Elevens are for packaged snacks, not meals. It'll probably give you scabies or something."

"You don't even know what scabies are."

"I know I don't want them. It doesn't matter anyway, because they won't let you take that into the movies. No one's dumb enough to believe a metal-handled paper box with teriyaki dripping from the bottom is your purse."

"No one will even see it; I'll tuck it down my pants. What are they going to say, 'Hold it there, young man, I believe that bulge in your pants is kung pao chicken'?"

I couldn't help but laugh. "You're an idiot."

"It's a gift."

I reached into my backpack for my water bottle and the graham crackers I'd packed that morning. "You still can't take it. Today isn't about eating. Max said we should do nonfood things. Lucy made a graph about it. If she sees those chips, you're dead meat."

"It'll be dark. She won't even know."

"Not that dark. Hurry up, we gotta go."

He sighed, then suddenly ripped open the Lay's bag and started jamming chips into his mouth. "I'm eating my chips, at least," he declared, spraying bits of potato. He held the bag out to me. "Wah suh?"

I waved it off. "It's not Saturday." I was fine with my graham crackers. They'd been in the Sherman T. Thuff Book of Good and Tasty Things forever, so it was no sacrifice. I could wait until Saturday for chips. On second thought, I'd have a scoop of Spazzy Monkey on Saturday instead. Now *that* was worth waiting three more days for.

I had to admit that I was kind of liking man-hater magazine's Whatever-On-Saturday rule. Max said it was smart, even. That was how she ate, so it couldn't be stupid. And it is true that knowing I'd get a treat on the weekend did make it easier to pass up chips and stuff during the week. I just couldn't eat *a lot* of my weekend treat. But hey, some was better than none. All I had to do was make sure that during the week I stuck to the foods in the book Max gave me. I didn't have to starve or gag myself on coconut.

When Max first handed me a book about "healthy foods," I considered lighting it up with a Bunsen burner. But then I discovered that the foods in it weren't all raw carrots and cauliflower stalks and grass seed from the front lawn. Besides graham crackers, it said I could have baked chips, and apples with peanut butter, and cherries, and even this really good stuff called Uncle Pete's Spiced Pork with Ten-Alarm Salsa. Lucy helped me cook it, and *ten-alarm* was no exaggeration. Best of all, the book didn't have the word *coconut* in it anywhere.

It also said I was supposed to drink lots of water. Heaven! I alternated chomping grahams and chugging water.

"Oh, hey, I got your map." Gardo pulled a shiny black poster folded like a square napkin out of his bag. White lines and colored dots covered the black background.

"She remembered!" I snatched the square from his hands.

It was a star map. Gardo's sister was taking astronomy at the community college and agreed to pick up a star map at the campus bookstore in exchange for one car washing. Gardo said I had to do the washing, but I argued that she meant for him to do it. Either way, I got my map. Only, when I unfolded it to full size, I discovered several smeared fingerprints floating in space around Orion's Belt.

"Aw, man. Look what your greasy chip fingers did. Max will think I did my term paper in a chip factory." I tried to rub the smudges off with the edge of my T-shirt, but it didn't help. Maybe I could get a white gel pen and label them as nebulas.

"What do you want me to do? They're potato chips; you have to eat them with your fingers. Unless you've figured out a way to eat chips with a fork."

"Very funny." My eyes settled on the kung pao. A long, skinny paper sheath was taped to the top of the box, with two cream-colored sticks poking out one end. I pointed at them. "Use those."

"My chopsticks?"

"Sure. Here, I'll show you." I picked them up and arranged them in my right hand, taking his bag of Lay's in my left. "You stick them into the bag like so . . . and then you get a soft grip . . . a very soft grip . . ." I fished around a bit, using my triple-dipping wristwork to grip a chip without crushing it. "And then you carefully pull it out . . . slowly . . . slowly . . . Voilà!"

I yanked out my chopsticks with a flourish and held them up, a pristine potato chip nestled gently between them. I was a natural! "See? It's like using long tweezers. And look, my hands are completely greaseless."

"You're a man of talent."

"Ain't that the truth." I started to flip the chip to a pigeon, but then I stopped myself and examined the sticks and chip more closely. "You know, this isn't such a stupid idea. Someone should seriously invent this, long tweezers for gripping chips. Plastic ones. With little grippers at the bottom. I would buy one." I smiled, quite pleased with my clever brain. Maybe I could be an inventor. I was in tune with the needs of the people. "They have the Chip Clip for clipping bags closed. This could be the Chip Grip."

Gardo slapped his palm on the metal bench. "Sherman T. Thuff, you are freakin' brilliant! That's our ticket!"

"What, the Chip Grip?"

"The *Amazing* Chip Grip. You're a genius, I tell ya. We're gonna invent this ourselves and make a fortune. Think about it. Everyone who eats chips gets stuck with greasy fingers. And since *everyone* eats chips, *everyone* will buy an Amazing Chip Grip." He snapped his fingers. "Poof! Good-bye, greasy fingers; hello, fortune. Man, this'll be bigger than the straw!"

Wow, that was big.

"I *am* a freakin' genius!" I slapped the bench, too, as the cheers in my head turned to chants—*Thuff, Thuff, Thuff, Thuff, Thuff!*—and countless rows of imaginary people

338

waved plastic chopsticks like candles at a rock concert, potato chips wedged gently in the middle. "I can already see it, me, Sherman 'Thuff Enuff' Thuff, the world's youngest and richest inventor. Hey, I could even host my own infomercials."

"Oh, we're not stopping at crummy infomercials," Gardo said. "We'll do talk shows and the Home Shopping Network and radio jingles, too. Before you know it, that gadget shop at the mall, Sharper Image, it'll be begging for the Amazing Chip Grip. Begging! And the money, it'll pour in by the boatload. Shermie, my good man, I am going to make you a very wealthy man."

"Wealthy is good. I like wealthy."

"Wealthy is great." He poured the last of the Lay's into his mouth as I refolded the spotted map, careful not to smudge it more.

Talking through the half-chewed glob, Gardo said, "This invention is way more marketable than that other thing you tried. What was that again, *competitive eating?*" He socked me playfully in the thigh.

I covered my face with the folded map in mock shame. Well, mostly mock. "*What* was I thinking?" I peeked out and grinned, then grabbed my backpack and moved toward the steps. I didn't want to keep Lucy waiting. "The Chip Grip, though, now, *that's* a good idea."

"That it is, my friend." He stepped in behind me and we jogged up the stadium steps.

"I'll tell ya, Shermie," he called out halfway up, not the least out of breath. Neither was I, for that matter. Not yet, anyway. "You and me, we're gonna go places with this one. It can't miss. Trust me, I know these things."

EPILOGUE

The Plum Times *Plus*

UNAUTHORIZED, UNCENSORED, UNDERGROUND

Revolution, The Next Generation

"What the [censored]? Aw, no! Not again!" That's what Del Heiny Junior 13 staffers heard outside Principal Culwicki's office this past Monday morning. Sources close to Culwicki report that the Proud Plum principal was reacting to finding his chair full of relish on his first day back from winter break.

In an investigative exclusive, *The Plum Times *Plus** has obtained a photo of a calling card found at the scene of the incident. The message on the green cocktail napkin gives a fresh spin to last semester's squelched Revolt Against Red by suggesting a sort of union between Red and Green. The napkin reads simply: "Because every condiment needs a complement. ♥The Relish Rebellion."

A leaked internal memo from Principal Culwicki to Del Heiny Ketchup Company acknowledges the emergence of a pro-Green movement and even hints at the principal's openness to peace talks. The memo also officially denies "slanderous rumors" that Culwicki sat in relish. *The Plum Times *Plus**, however, has located an eyewitness who places the principal in the hall near the staff restroom shortly before first period with "chunky green stuff on his butt."

In a related development, *The Plum Times *Plus** has learned that a Del Heiny Junior 13 janitor discovered several dozen green T-shirts imprinted with the red-lettered slogan *Relish the Red* on the school roof Monday morning. The shirts were in Christmas-wrapped boxes with green tags marked *Merry Christmas, Plums!* Rumors that the shirts will be made available at the free T-shirt booth in the quad are being confirmed.

No one has stepped forward to claim responsibility for either incident as of press time. So for now, the identity of the Relish Rebellion leader(s) remains a Christmas mystery.

340

A Note from the Author

I was in tenth grade when I met the new guy in school. He was sweet, smart, and cute. Very cute. He was on the wrestling team, and he was cutting weight for an upcoming meet. His goal: Drop from 115 pounds to 105 pounds . . . in just five days.

Being an athlete myself, I was no stranger to working hard off the field in order to perform well in a game. But my new friend's announcement disturbed me. The hot media topic of the time was a frightening "new" disease called anorexia nervosa, which had just claimed the life of singer Karen Carpenter. Yet no one seemed fazed by a boy who was openly, proudly starving himself. In fact, his weight cutting was acceptable to his coach and applauded by his teammates and friends. *No Pain, No Gain* was stenciled across the wrestling gym's walls, and the team lived it to the letter.

My discomfort with wrestling's weight-cutting practice contributed to my lifelong interest in nutrition and exercise. *Big Mouth* is my way of finally confronting the issue head-on. Shermie Thuff's story may revolve around the ups and downs of friendship, but it's also about choosing balance over unhealthy extremes, about seeing the line between real-life body images and TV reality, and, perhaps most importantly, about recognizing the misguided reasonings that can lead to eating disorders in teenage boys. Seventy percent of high school boys are dieting, with peer pressure, media influences, and the weight demands of sports leading the list of reasons why. Yet people rarely mention guys and eating disorders in the same breath. They keep their mouths shut about it even though 10 to 20 percent of people diagnosed with anorexia and bulimia nervosa are male. And just as many guys suffer from binge eating disorder, or compulsive eating, as girls. Actually, these estimates may be low, as guys tend to see eating disorders as "girl" diseases, so they often go undiagnosed or untreated for much longer than female sufferers.

Not that girls are immune to sports-related dieting. In fact, more than one-third of female athletes report attitudes and symptoms that place them at risk for anorexia nervosa. Eating disorders do not discriminate.

Twenty years after high school, I'm still friends with the new boy. He's still sweet, smart, and cute. Very cute. He doesn't wrestle anymore, though. Ironically, he's now an amateur chef. Did his days of deprivation fuel his lifelong passion for food? *I've* certainly never shaken the impression his weight cutting made on me. And now I have the opportunity to spread the word about it. It's my hope that *Big Mouth* gives guys and girls alike an entertaining, funny, and memorable opportunity to explore and talk about the pressures that lead to eating disorders. Isn't it time we opened our big mouths about it?

For more information about eating disorders, please contact the National Eating Disorders Organization or one of its network members:

National Eating Disorders Organization (NEDA)
www.NationalEatingDisorders.org
toll-free helpline: 800-931-2237

About the Author

Before Deborah Halverson wrote books for teens, she edited books for children of all ages and taught writing at the University of California, San Diego. Armed with a master's degree in American literature and a fascination with pop culture, she creates stories about extreme events and places—tattoo parlors, fast-food joints, and, most extreme of all, high schools. She lives with her husband and triplet sons in San Diego. Deborah's first book, *Honk If You Hate Me,* is available from Delacorte Press. You can visit her at www.DeborahHalverson.com.